D0672341

Highlander
IN LOVE

ALSO BY JULIA LONDON

Highlander in Disguise
Highlander Unbound

JULIA LONDON

Highlander
IN LOVE

POCKET **STAR** BOOKS
New York   London   Toronto   Sydney

An *Original* Publication of POCKET BOOKS

 A Pocket Star Book published by
POCKET BOOKS, a division of Simon & Schuster, Inc.
1230 Avenue of the Americas, New York, NY 10020

ISBN: 0-7394-5708-X

POCKET STAR BOOKS and colophon are registered trademarks of Simon & Schuster, Inc.

Cover art by Franco Accornero; hand-lettering by David Gatti

Manufactured in the United States of America

For my very chic friend Barbara, who could never be the inspiration for any of my less-than-chic characters, and certainly none with the last name of Lockhart matching that description.

꧁ ꧂

EILEAN ROS
FRIDAY, MAY 27

My dear Miss Lockhart:
*I thank you for your kind letter of Wednesday past
concerning the alleged curse of any daughter born to a
Lockhart. I assure you that I think it all a lot of
flummery. I hold firmly convinced that a lass with
your considerable fortitude and spirit might marry
whomever she please without a care for even the devil.
Nor do I believe that a man who has bargained for the
hand of a daughter of a Lockhart, and bargained quite
fairly, if I may be so bold, has anything to fear, other
than the usual danger of death by great exasperation
owing to the Lockharts' stubborn nature in general.*

*Thank you again, Miss Lockhart, for your concern
for my well-being. I look forward to setting the date of
our wedding.*

Sincerely,
Douglas

One

❦

EILEAN ROS, THE TROSSACHS OF THE SCOTTISH HIGHLANDS

*P*ayton Douglas was surrounded by the enemy, his back against the wall . . . or hearth, as it were. The Lockharts advanced on him with an anxious look in their eyes, and he wondered how they had managed to gain entry, today in particular, when he was entertaining some very important men from Glasgow. Men who were, at this very moment, rather deep in their cups, having sampled the barley-bree Scotch whiskey distilled here, on his estate, Eilean Ros.

But his enemies were desperate and, by their own confession, in quite a predicament, for they'd been caught completely unawares when their dear friend, Hugh MacAlister, had purloined their priceless family heirloom—a gold statue of a beastie with ruby eyes—right out from under their noses.

Griffin Lockhart, from whom the beastie had been stolen, had just argued passionately that while this outrageous insult would be avenged in due time, at the moment, it seemed that MacAlister's actions had left the entire Lockhart family near to penniless and faced with the forced betrothal of their only daughter, Mared, to the man who had lent them a princely sum to retrieve the beastie: Payton Douglas.

The very same Payton Douglas who stood with his back against the cold hearth, eyeing the only one of the five Lockharts in his study who seemed inordinately relaxed. Seated at his writing desk, she idly twirled a quill pen as Payton stoically listened to the rather windy speech of her laird father. Frankly, one could scarcely do anything but listen when in the company of so many Lockharts.

This speech, obviously prepared in advance, judging by the way Lady Lockhart's lips moved in unison with her husband's, spoke to how Payton, the son of ancestors who had spilled precious Lockhart blood in every war and time of strife, would take their only daughter to wife, having bargained for her in loaning them a substantial sum that was to be repaid within a year's time.

"'Tis the stuff of popular novels!" Lady Lockhart exclaimed.

Behind her, her daughter Mared smiled as she twirled the pen, as if that analogy amused her.

"Frankly, milady, I've never read a novel as befuddling as this," Payton said. "If I am to understand, do ye mean to say ye'll no' honor our agreement regarding the loan I made ye?"

That question was met with a burst of nervous, high-pitched laughter from the four dark-headed Lockharts standing at this little impromptu meeting: Carson, the aging laird of what was left of the Lockhart clan; his lean and graceful lady wife, Aila; their eldest son and massive soldier, Liam; and his younger brother Griffin, who was slightly smaller and quite debonair.

"Of course no'!" Liam boomed reassuringly. "But surely ye understand that we couldna have *dreamed* MacAlister would betray us so."

"As ye've said several times over now. Nevertheless, it would appear that he did indeed betray ye, and ye owe me a tidy sum, aye?"

The four standing Lockharts looked sheepishly at one another while Mared sighed and opened a book on his writing desk, flipping to the first page.

Grif quickly stepped forward and smiled charmingly. "If I may, milord . . . the problem is that without the beastie, we've no means to repay yer very generous loan—"

"Three thousand pounds," Payton quickly reminded him, "was more than generous. It was sheer insanity."

"Aye, *very* generous," Grif agreed, casting an anxious glance at his family. "But we made a wee error, we did," he said, holding thumb and index finger together to show just how wee the error.

"I beg yer pardon, but there was no error. Yer father signed the promissory papers."

"That he did," Grif readily agreed. "And we promised Mared's hand to ye as collateral on yer loan, and . . . well, plainly put, Douglas, 'tis no secret how she feels about ye—ah, that is to say . . . yer *reforms*," he said carefully, and exchanged a look with his mother.

"I know well how she feels, Grif," Payton responded impatiently. Everyone in every glen in the loch region knew of Mared's objection to marrying a Douglas and of her vehement displeasure at his introduction of sheep in and around the lochs. "'Tis no secret she doesna care for a Douglas. Yer sister, ye might have remarked, is no' a shy lass."

Mared chuckled softly and turned another page in the book he'd left on the writing desk, *On the Winter Production of Wool and the Timely Shearing of the* Na Caorridh Mora, *the Big Sheep.*

"No," Grif said with a bit of a frown for Mared's chuckle. "But ye canna fault the lass for being passionate in her beliefs."

Mared looked up from the book then and cocked a brow above a pair of sparkling green eyes, waiting for his answer.

He, in turn, glared at the Lockharts. This was precisely what was wrong with Mared—she had been reared by this lot of blockheads. They all believed—with the exception of Grif, perhaps, and even that was a questionable assumption—that the sheep he had brought into the lochs were invading the land historically grazed by their cattle and thereby pushing the cattle to smaller areas and smaller numbers and therefore pushing them, the most exasperating family in all of bloody Scotland, into poverty.

They were right in some respects. But Payton believed their cattle could not graze properly in the Highlands and were not, and had never been, a profitable venture. Bloody fools, the Lockharts, who believed in the old system of crofting the land and raising lumbering beeves. And when that did not sustain them, they turned to stealing statues or some such nonsense from their English cousins.

He, on the other hand, believed in a system that allowed a fair wage to all the men the land could reasonably support, and sheep herding and, should a man be so inclined (as he was)—whiskey production. Which was why he was eager to be done with this nonsense and return to the four men who might invest a substantial amount of money in his distillery venture.

Grif laughed uneasily again at Payton's stoic silence. "And . . . and perhaps our Mared deserves just a wee bit of pity, aye?" he tried again. "After all, she's got that wretched curse on her"—Mared nodded emphatically that she did—"and really, Douglas, can ye honestly desire her hand in marriage with that curse hanging over her like a dark cloud?"

Payton laughed derisively. "*Ach,* ye donna believe in that old curse! No one but crofters who fear fairies and goblins believe that old tale!"

"But ye canna deny that no daughter of a Lockhart has ever married," Liam quickly put in. "Perhaps it is just as true that a daughter of a Lockhart willna wed until she's looked into the belly of the beast."

"Do ye think to frighten me with tales of *a' diabhal?*" he demanded, ignoring Mared's amused smile as she leaned back in the chair and idly ran her fingers along the edge of the writing desk.

"Frighten ye!" Lady Lockhart exclaimed, stepping in to put her hand soothingly on Payton's arm. "No, no, milord, no' to frighten ye. Just to speak with ye, on Mared's behalf."

He checked his tongue and spoke evenly. "Frankly, milady, I've never known yer Mared no' to speak on her own behalf. And quite articulately at that."

"Oh! How kindly put, sir!" Mared said sweetly, breaking her silence for the first time since appearing in his study.

"Ye willna honor the loan, is that it, lass?" Payton asked her directly.

"The Lockharts honor their debts, sir," Lady Lockhart interjected as she gave Mared a withering look. "But we need more time. Just a wee bit more time to find Mr. MacAlister."

"How much time?"

"Ten months," Lady Lockhart said quickly. "In addition to the two remaining, of course."

Another year? With a sigh of impatience, Payton shoved a hand through his hair. He had no idea what to say to them, really. He had no idea how he felt about all of it—asking for Mared's hand as collateral on the loan had been an impetuous act, spurred by her devilish smile that afternoon in his parlor. Like the Lockharts, he never believed it would all come to this. He wasn't entirely certain he *wanted* a wife. He looked at her now, as she obviously took pleasure in his discomfort, and thought he certainly must be a madman to want *this* one as a wife.

But the truth, as much as he was loath to admit it, was that he adored Mared Lockhart. He always had.

In the four months since Grif's return to Scotland, Payton had not asked about the loan or pressed the issue of marriage. But now that very little more than two months remained in their agreement—the Lockharts had been given a year to repay the money he had loaned them, or give Mared over for marriage—they wanted more time?

"No," he said decisively. "Ye canna ask this of me—I have given ye a significant sum of money that ye've obviously squandered—"

"No' squandered!" Grif objected.

"What ye did with it is no concern of mine, but ye canna repay me as we agreed, and thereby, ye leave me no choice."

"Land," Grif said quickly. "We can repay ye in land."

Payton considered that for a moment. It was a plausible option, but not terribly desirable. The Lockhart land was separated from his estate by the mountain Ben Cluaran. If he were to take land to repay the debt they owed him, it would leave them with precious little to farm. And it would be near to impossible for him to make much use of that land, separated from his estate as it was, for the manpower required to farm it would be far costlier than the yield. The only way it would be of use to him was if he could put sheep on it, and he rather doubted the Lockharts would allow it, what with their stubborn love of cows.

He shook his head and looked at the laird. "Ye agreed to my terms, Lockhart. I'll ask that ye set a date for the betrothal."

Mared's smile suddenly faded. She slapped the book shut and looked at her father, as did everyone else in that stuffy room. Carson thoughtfully rubbed his chin, then sighed wearily. "We shall set the date a year and a day from whence the loan was made, then," he said after a moment.

"Carson!" Lady Lockhart cried.

"*Ach, mo ghraidh*, he's right, ye know he is! We agreed to the terms of the loan, as did Mared—"

"Under considerable duress, Father!" Mared interjected.

"Aye, perhaps," he said, turning to look at her. "But ye agreed all the same. We knew there was a possibility Grif wouldna succeed, and now we must honor our word, daughter. Ye must do so, as well."

Lady Lockhart gasped.

"'Tis too late, Aila," Carson said gruffly. "What else is left to her, then? Douglas is the only man in the parish who puts no stock in fairies and goblins and will have her!"

That did not soothe Lady Lockhart or Mared, whose expression grew quite murderous.

"Ye must no' fear yer welfare, lass," Payton softly assured her. "On my honor, I will always treat ye well."

"*Ach*, how can ye pretend so?" she demanded. "The Douglases and the Lockharts have been sworn enemies for hundreds of years!"

"Ye donna *understand*, Payton Douglas!" Lady Lockhart insisted firmly. "'Tis no' Mared's welfare that we fear—'tis *yer* welfare."

She said it so earnestly that Payton couldn't help but laugh. "I donna fear her," he laughingly assured her. "Ye've nothing to fear, then, for she canna hurt me," he said and laughed again at Mared's glower.

She had come to her feet, was standing behind the desk with her arms folded implacably across her trim middle. "I willna marry ye, Payton Douglas."

"Mared!" Lady Lockhart cried.

But Payton chuckled and thought that it might be fun to tame the fire in her in his bed. "Aye, ye will, Mared. And as there is nothing further to discuss, please excuse me. I've guests," he said, and with a curt nod to the impossible Lockharts, he strode out of the stuffy room, smiling inwardly at the thought of Mared in his bed.

That night, in her room high above the study in the old tower, Mared was busily at work.

Her spirit was far from broken.

Her family could think of nothing to save her, blast the lot of them, but *she'd* not lie idle. Even now, in the stillness of the night, in her drafty chambers of the even draftier old castle, Mared wrote two letters by the light of a single candle while the rest of them slept.

The first was directed to Miss Beitris Crowley, the daughter of the solicitor in Aberfoyle. Mared had befriended her, had taken long, chatty walks with her along the banks of Loch Ard, across from Eilean Ros, assessing her suitability as the future Lady Douglas.

Aye. The future Lady Douglas.

Mared had come to the conclusion that perhaps if the odious and highly objectionable Laird Douglas had another, more charming alternative to her, he might forgive the ridiculous terms of the loan and take to wife a woman more suitable for him in temperament and mien. She had suggested as much to him; he had laughed and responded that any woman, old or young, fat or thin, rich or poor, would be better suited to him in temperament and mien than she was, and seemed to think himself quite the wit for having said it.

Mared was determined to prove it to him, with or without Beitris's help. Beitris, she had discovered, was painfully shy, particularly in the company of Laird Douglas. She'd put Beitris in his path a dozen times at least, and the lass had still not gained as much as a kiss. He terrified her. Of course he did—he was a creature who had obviously climbed out of the loch.

"He's awfully big, is he no'?" Beitris had asked Mared in a fearful tone of voice one afternoon after they had "happened" to encounter him in Aberfoyle. The man seemed to have that effect on all the young women around the lochs, Mared had noticed.

*You **must**, she wrote to Miss Crowley, remember*
that polite conversation will take you only so far. A
man should like to know that he is well thought of,
and that he, above all others, holds your coveted
esteem. Remember too that a man enjoys the chance to
be gallant, but you must create an opportunity for
him to be so, for rarely are men so clever, left to their
own devices, to create such opportunities. Perhaps you
might drop your linen in his company, or fumble with
your parasol and allow him to rescue you. . . .

Mared was fond of Beitris, she truly was, but sometimes Beitris seemed rather dense when it came to
flirting. She had not, Mared surmised, been courted
outright.

Not that Mared had been courted outright, either.
There was not a man around the lochs who wasn't
deathly afraid of her, given the blasted curse that followed her, but she'd witnessed the many colorful and
courtly romances of her brother Griffin, who had,
with varying degrees of success, she heard tell,
attempted to bed almost every lass in the lochs before
he went off to London and brought back a wife. That
made her reasonably well versed in the mechanics of
courting . . . at least more so than Beitris.

She finished her instructions to Beitris and sealed
the letter with a drop of wax. She then gritted her
teeth and picked up her pen.

The Honorable Laird Douglas, Greatest Ruler in
All the Land . . .

Perhaps a bit dramatic, but she hardly cared. She
wrote on, requesting the honor of calling on his cousin,

Sarah Douglas, who, according to gossips in Aberfoyle, had come to Eilean Ros for the summer.

Mared's eyes narrowed as she read her letter one last time. Satisfied that her writing revealed nothing more than proper civility, she sealed it with a drop of wax, put it carefully on her vanity, and blew out the candle. As she slipped into her bed, a smile curved her lips.

She didn't give a damn about their agreement. She'd not marry that man.

How could she? Marrying him would be admitting defeat, and she was not prepared to do that. Besides, her dream of returning to Edinburgh was very much alive within her. It was that dream that had sustained her in the last few years.

She'd spent a fortnight in Edinburgh ten or so years ago, before the family fortune had begun to disappear. It had been a magical place, teeming with people and arts and it seemed there was a soirée or gathering every night. Yet the best part about it was that no one in Edinburgh knew of or believed in old curses. They treated her as a person. Not like here in the lochs, where everyone looked at her as some sort of witch.

She'd even had a pair of potential suitors in her short time there, and was convinced that, in Edinburgh, her whole life would change.

No, she'd not marry Payton Douglas and remain in the lochs all of her days, where her life was so wretchedly confined. Every word she uttered publicly was guarded, every path she took hidden from superstitious eyes. It would be a joy to live in Edinburgh. It would be a joy to simply live!

Mared fell asleep thinking of Edinburgh. But she

dreamed she was walking along the banks of Loch Ard, in the company of a young man with golden hair who smiled at her and stole kisses from her. They walked until they came upon a rowdy crowd. When Mared moved closer to see what they were shouting about, she realized that they were to witness an execution.

She looked up to the gallows and with a start recognized the first Lady of Lockhart, the beauty who had sacrificed all for love. Her hands were tied behind her back, and she was kneeling at a chopping block.

Next to her was her lover, Livingstone, with a noose around his neck.

As Mared watched in horror, the executioner hanged her lady's lover. And as he twisted beside her, they lay the Lady of Lockhart's head on the block. As the executioner lifted his blade, she screamed, *"Fuirich do mi!"*

Wait for me. . . .

The blade came down and Lady Lockhart's head dropped to the ground and rolled to Mared's feet. Mared screamed and looked around for her beau, but she was suddenly alone. Yet her scream had drawn the attention of the crowd, and they turned on her, recognizing her as the daughter of Lady Lockhart. The accursed one, they said. Spawned by the devil and left to live with the devil.

"A daughter born of a Lockhart will no' marry until she's looked into the belly of the beast!" an old woman spat at her, and the crowd began to chant that she must look into the belly of the beast as they advanced on her.

Screaming, Mared ran with the murderous crowd on her heels. She ran until she reached the river, where the crowd kept coming for her, until Mared fell in. The water closed over her head and she sank to the murky bottom, struggling to free herself of her clothing. But she couldn't hold her breath, and she was choking for air.

With a gasp, Mared suddenly rose up in her bed, her hands at her throat, and the bed linens twisted around her body. Her forehead was wet with perspiration.

She caught her breath, took several deep breaths more, then slowly untangled herself from the bed linens. Unsteadily, she stood, walked to the hearth to stoke it as she willed her heart to stop pounding.

The dream had shaken her badly. It always did.

Payton Douglas would not hold her here. She would not be held captive in a land where she was despised. She would escape the lochs for Edinburgh and nothing would stop her.

Two

✦·✦

*N*ow that the betrothal date had been set, Payton thought it prudent to help Mared along to the inevitable end by making her feel less bartered and more admired. So he endeavored to court her . . . just as hard as she endeavored not to be courted.

He'd sent dozens of Scottish roses to her, along with notes of his admiration. He'd also sent along two of the first bottles of barley-bree to be distilled on his land to her brothers and father. And he had dutifully and respectfully answered each and every one of her letters, of which there was quite a small pile mounting on the corner of his desk.

His cousin, Miss Sarah Douglas, educated in France and now residing in Edinburgh, had come to Eilean Ros to help him find a replacement for his longtime housekeeper, Mrs. Craig, who had died recently after years of faithful service. Since arriving, Sarah had witnessed, with much exasperation, his considerable efforts to woo Mared. Even now, she was pouting atop her little sorrel, riding next to him as they had a look about the estate. "I don't know why ye must go through with this," she complained to Payton, who rode his big bay hunter.

"Why? I'm no' a young man, Sarah. I am two and

thirty. If I am to leave an heir to the Douglas fortune, I best be about it."

"Yes, but with someone else, please. Perhaps it would be wiser to consider this one for the position of housekeeper. At the very least, she'd be an improvement over the half-wits and simpletons we've spoken to thus far."

Payton gave his cousin a sharp look. "That is the future Lady Douglas ye speak of, so be kind, Sarah. She's no' had an easy life here in the lochs, and she may no' be as tender as ye are, but she's deserving of yer esteem nonetheless."

Sarah shrugged. "Perhaps she deserves my esteem, but I can't think why she should deserve such respect from ye, then. Really, Payton—*marry* her? She's a Lockhart!"

Payton suppressed a smile at that—Mared Lockhart may not have earned his esteem, but she had earned his respect years ago. "The time has come to put aside those old feuds. They've no bearing on the present or the future."

And besides, there was something about Mared Lockhart that had attracted him long ago, when they were children. He could remember, as a young lad, wanting the sweetmeat she had held, taking it from her little hand. Mared did not cry, nor did she run to her governess. No, Mared had felled him, a boy who was a full four years older than she, by pushing him into the thistle, then falling upon him and pummeling him until her brother Liam pulled her off.

And when he began to become more aware of the fairer sex, it had been Mared's blossoming and the small buds of her breasts that had afflicted his young dreams. He'd longed even then to touch her.

But it wasn't until years later, when he was a young man and Mared had grown into a beautiful yet untouchable woman—thanks to a bloody curse that seemed to have developed a life of its own—that he had fallen in love with her. It had been her indomitable spirit that had done it.

By then, he'd begun to notice how the suspicious crofters closed their doors when she walked by, had heard them warn their children to steer clear of her. He knew that most of the villagers of Aberfoyle whispered behind her back and avoided her at social functions. Though most people around the lochs treated her as a pariah, he'd come to respect her dignity in the face of such ignorance.

He'd first realized he loved her one evening almost seven years past, on the occasion of her first and twentieth birthday, when he had kissed her for the first time. It had been an impetuous act, one of sheer madness . . . but in that moment, he had felt her firm body respond to his, had felt her rise up to meet him. . . .

And then she'd bitten his lip.

Aye, on that momentous occasion, Payton had come to desire her.

Mared Lockhart was, to him at least, the only spot of color in a gray world, the only shimmering sign of life in a bucolic existence. The insistent flame sparked in him that sultry summer night seven years past had not died, but had kept burning bright for the one woman in all of Scotland who did not esteem him, Laird Payton Douglas of Eilean Ros.

Just the thought of it made him chuckle again.

"Why do you laugh?" Sarah demanded.

"I've really no idea," he said cheerfully and turned

his attention to the lane as it widened around a stand of oaks, and Eilean Ros came into view.

His estate was not really what the name, Island of Roses, implied, but it was built out on a piece of land that jutted into Loch Ard. It was a grand home nestled beneath Scots pines, built two hundred years ago by the fifth laird Douglas. When Payton's father, the ninth laird Douglas, had inherited it, he had dreamed of creating a palace at the foot of the Highlands and had started extensive renovations. He'd died before he could see them through.

Upon his death, Payton had become the laird and had completed the renovations. The work had added another wing to the house, and it now boasted fourteen bedchambers, three salons, and more sitting rooms, dining rooms, and studies than Payton could count. It was indeed a Highland palace. No other Scottish abode could boast such grandeur.

Nor, Payton reckoned, was there another Scottish abode that sounded quite as empty as his.

Time and again, he'd walk the long corridors of his home, hearing nothing but the click of his boot heels on the stone and wooden floors. He had an almost desperate desire to fill that empty sound with laughter and voices and warmth. When his brothers had gone out into the world—Lachlan to India, Padraig to America, he had remained behind as the sole Douglas and heir of Eilean Ros, destined by his firstborn status to carry out the family duties and name. It was, he had come to realize, his cross to bear in some respects. His was a rather lonely existence.

Now, as he and Sarah rode around the stand of oaks, they could see the entire length of the house . . .

and the donkey tethered beneath the shade of an oak tree, beside a cart that looked positively ancient.

"Oh *no*," Sarah sighed, scowling at the cart. "I shan't believe they arrived in *that*."

"Be kind, Sarah," Payton warned her and set his horse to a trot.

Mared and her twelve-year-old English niece, Natalie, were standing beneath a towering portrait of the eighth Lady Douglas, Lord Douglas's great-grandmother, as a pair of servants bustled about, preparing the room for tea under the watchful eye of the butler, Beckwith.

"Her husband killed our great-grandfather in a duel," Mared whispered to Natalie as she stole a glimpse of Beckwith over her shoulder.

"A *duel*?" Natalie gasped, her blue eyes lighting up.

"Aye. They're a sorry lot, the Douglases. Never forget it, lass. This one's husband called out our ancestor for merely having fallen in love."

Natalie looked up again, her mouth open.

"I trust ye gave her a fair accounting, Miss Lockhart." Payton Douglas's voice boomed behind her, startling Mared and Natalie both. Neither of them had heard him approach across the Wilton carpet.

Mared slapped a hand over her heart. "*Diah*, sir! Have a care! Ye might have frightened us to death!"

He smiled wickedly and leaned forward, his deep slate gray eyes peering intently at her. "Ye *did* give the lass a fair accounting, did ye no'?"

All right. So her great-grandfather had loved the woman in the portrait. But honestly, the poor woman had been locked in a horrible marriage—who could blame a Lockhart for desiring to give her a spot of happiness in her bleak existence? "Aye, of course," she said, and with a brazen smile, she sank into an uncharacteristic curtsey and glanced up coyly. "Do ye doubt it?"

He cupped her elbow to lift her up, and there his hand remained as his gaze dipped languidly to the décolletage of her gown. "When it comes to ye, lass, I doubt even my sanity."

Then she was doing something quite right. It brought a smile of satisfaction to her lips, and she put her arm around Natalie, pulling her into her side, forcing his hand from her elbow. "Ye recall our Miss Natalie?"

Natalie dropped into a perfect curtsey. "How do you do, my lord," she said in her English accent.

With a charming smile, Douglas took Natalie's hand and bowed low over it. "I do very well indeed," he said, and kissed her small hand. "'Tis a pleasure to have such a beautiful lass at Eilean Ros."

Natalie's face lit up at that. Aye, that was Payton Douglas, was it not, as charming as the day was long? But then he turned his attention to Mared again, his gaze sweeping the length of her in a way he had of making her believe he could see every bare inch of her, and with a smile that Mared half-expected to melt her gown right off her shoulders.

"May I remark," he said low, "that I canna recall when I last saw ye adorned in such a bright color . . . or *ribbons,*" he added, lifting a curious brow.

Honestly, couldn't a woman don a lovely, albeit borrowed, yellow day gown without astounding the entire region? "Neither can I recall, milord," she responded breezily, "for I canna recall the last time I saw ye." She smiled, pleased with her own wit, and before he could speak, Mared gestured to Beitris.

Beitris, who was blond and petite, looked as bonny as a portrait sitting on one of ten Queen Anne chairs that lined the silk-walled room, her hands clenched in her lap. "What good fortune that I was able to coax Miss Crowley from Aberfoyle, aye?" Mared asked grandly. "I know that ye've grown quite attached to her and thought to be kind to ye, sir, and arrange for ye to enjoy her company again."

"Frankly, ye've been *exceedingly* kind with Miss Crowley's company for quite some time now," he said, but instantly broke into a warm smile and was striding across the room, his legs long and powerful in Wellington boots and buckskins that hugged him like a glove.

Mared did not care to look at him . . . but she could hardly help herself. He wore no coat, no waistcoat, but a plain white lawn shirt. His golden brown hair had grown long, past the collar. If she were the sort of female to be interested in this man's appearance, which she was decidedly not, she'd have no choice but to think him quite handsome.

Beitris, the poor darling, must certainly have thought so, for she all but melted in her silk-upholstered chair. She tried not to look at the laird, but of course, she couldn't *help* but look at him, for the Douglas was, if nothing else, a very commanding figure of a man.

Beitris quickly came to her feet as he reached her. "Milord, thank ye for accepting our call."

He grabbed her hand and bent over it. "The pleasure is indeed mine, Miss Crowley." He touched his lips to her knuckles, and Beitris's fair skin turned pink.

"Payton! Oh dear, did ye not change yer clothes to receive our guests?"

It was Miss Douglas, a slender, fair-haired woman who seemed positively dwarfish next to her cousin. She entered the room wearing an expensive riding habit.

"Sarah, allow me to reacquaint ye with our neighbor, Miss Lockhart."

Mared curtsied alongside Natalie and inquired politely, "How do ye do, Miss Douglas?"

"Quite well. Thank ye, Miss Lockhart."

Was it her imagination, or did she detect a hint of disdain in the voice of the fancy woman from Edinburgh?

"And Miss Crowley," Payton added. "And of course, Miss Natalie Lockhart," he said with another warm smile for the blonde-headed girl.

Miss Douglas nodded at the child, then made a show of fanning herself. "Please do sit, ladies. Tea should arrive shortly. I hope ye will forgive our attire," she added, casting a disapproving look at Payton's buckskins and lawn shirt. "We just returned from a ride about the park. I daresay we did not expect ye quite so promptly," she said and took a seat on the divan whose plush velvet upholstery looked very new. Rather, Miss Douglas took *all* of the divan, sitting directly in the middle of it, leaving no room on either side of her.

Beitris sat gingerly on the edge of a matching settee. When Natalie moved to sit beside her, Mared quickly redirected her to a chair, so that the seat next to Beitris was left vacant.

That left only her and Payton standing, staring at one another across the room.

He flashed that devilish, charming smile again, the one that made her skin tingle, and politely motioned to the seat next to Beitris.

A smile curved the corner of Mared's lips, and she sat hard next to Natalie.

Payton's smile deepened, but he obliged her nonetheless by sitting next to Beitris and stretching his arm across the back of the settee, which, naturally, made Beitris blush and drop her gaze to her lap.

"I donna recall if I've mentioned that Miss Crowley has just this spring come from her studies in Edinburra," Mared said smartly, and glanced at Miss Douglas. "Her father is a solicitor in Aberfoyle."

"Is he indeed?" Miss Douglas asked indifferently, studying a fingernail. "I should think there'd be little call for a solicitor in a village as small as Aberfoyle. There are certainly no housekeepers to speak of."

"Yer father must be quite delighted ye've come home, Miss Crowley," Payton said. "I'd wager he's found himself rather suddenly in the company of all the young bachelors in town, aye?"

Beitris flushed so badly that Mared feared she might faint. Aye, but wouldn't that be lovely! If she fainted, Payton would be forced to revive her. . . . *Faint, Beitris!*

Beitris did not faint. She merely squeaked, "I, ah . . . I wouldna know, sir."

"Indeed he has, for Miss Crowley is quite accomplished," Mared cheerfully interjected. "She's perfectly brilliant on the pianoforte, and she speaks French fluently, and she's rather remarked upon for her archery on the left banks of the lochs."

Payton glanced at Mared, his gray eyes blazing with amusement. "*Quite* impressive. Personally, I find education—as well as the ability to use a bow and arrow—to be quite attractive in a woman."

"Ah, here is the tea," Sarah said, and rose gracefully from her seat to attend it as a footman, under the eagle eye of Beckwith, entered with a large and heavy silver service, piled high with fine china tea pots and cups and a plateful of biscuits—what would have been a veritable feast at Talla Dileas.

"I should very much like to hear about yer studies, Miss Crowley," Douglas continued. "I've oft said that educating our women will bring this country forward, for it is only through education that reform and natural progress may be gained. Ye are to be commended."

That was such rubbish that Mared caught a cry of disbelief in her throat that unfortunately sounded like an unladylike snort.

"I beg yer pardon, Miss Lockhart, did ye say something?" Payton asked with a hint of a smile.

Natalie mistook Mared's snort of disbelief as one of pain and quickly and rather loudly said, "Miss Lockhart is educated, too! There are lots and lots of books at Talla Dileas!"

"I had no idea ye are so keen on educating girls, Payton," Miss Douglas remarked as she directed Beckwith to pour tea.

"No? I am very much indeed. I canna abide ignorance in general, for no matter their sex, ignorant people will perpetuate the old ways and impede the natural progress of a nation."

Of all the ridiculous—Mared could not remain silent, for *progress* to this man meant displacing people from their homes. Cottages were left standing empty all over the lochs as people left for Glasgow or points farther south in search of work. "I should think it quite depends upon what one calls progress, milord," she said. "I suppose *ye* believe that progress is to push tenants from the land in favor of raising sheep, while the old ways are to raise cattle and croft the land so that everyone prospers, aye?"

"Prosper!" He laughed gaily, as if a child had uttered an amusing bit of nonsense. "I hardly call it prosperity when a family canna grow enough in the commons to put food on their table. No, Miss Lockhart," he said congenially, "true progress is about the enlightenment of a people. When the old ways no longer provide, then we must find a new way to prosper. *Together.*"

"And she's quite accomplished at the pianoforte, and she speaks French, too, with only a bit of an accent," Natalie desperately avowed.

"Aye, yer auntie is well accomplished, lass," Payton said with a smile.

Oh, how she wanted to box his bloody ears! "Really, milord, will ye bore Miss Crowley with all this empty talk of progress?" Mared asked cheerfully.

"Oh no!" Beitris quietly protested. "It's really quite interesting."

"Miss Crowley has had occasion to be abroad," Mared continued determinedly, ignoring Beitris. "Did ye no', Beitris?"

"Well, I . . . I did have occasion to travel to France."

"France. I adore France," Miss Douglas remarked, perking up. "Did ye enjoy yer visit there?"

"I canna say that I did," Beitris said, putting aside her tea, inexplicably eager, all at once, to speak. "We had rough seas on our crossing, and I wasna fully recovered for the fortnight I was in Paris. And then there was the voyage *home*—I am still rather weak from it."

Now she would make herself seem too weak for a

man as virile as Payton Douglas. "Miss Crowley, ye are too modest," Mared quickly interrupted. "Ye are the very picture of health."

"Miss Lockhart has not taken ill a single day since she was as old as me," Natalie avowed rather loudly.

"Quite remarkable," Douglas said with a wink for Natalie. "But I believe yer auntie differs from us mere mortals in that her constitution is ironclad."

"Oh no!" Mared exclaimed with a sweet laugh. "'Tis naugh' but the Highland air! It is no' befouled with factory smokes as is the air that comes from the sort of *progress* they enjoy in Glasgow."

Payton gave a snort of laughter at that. "Touché," he said, bowing over his teacup. "Well said. Here in the lochs, we can all rest assured that the lack of progress will, if nothing else, lend itself to our good health."

Oooh, but she could feel her temper rising. The man was as stubborn as the Lockharts' blasted mule! She suddenly put her tea aside and stood up. "Might I have yer leave, sir, to show Natalie a portrait of another deceased Douglas?" she asked sweetly, indicating a large portrait of his grandfather on the far end of the wall. "I hadna quite finished reciting our family histories."

"As ye wish, Miss Lockhart," he said pleasantly.

Mared gave the bloody mule a winsome smile and strode forward, her head high, with Natalie walking quickly to keep up.

As they reached the far end of the room, she heard him say, "Ye've no' yet had the pleasure of viewing our gardens, Miss Crowley. Might I show them to ye?"

"*Oh*," Beitris choked out. "Please!"

"Cousin Sarah, will ye join us?"

"No, thank ye, Payton. I've seen the gardens many times."

Mared listened to the sound of his sure footsteps and Beitris's soft gait until they could no longer be heard in the room. Mared put her hand on Natalie's shoulder and silently indicated she should go sit with Miss Douglas.

Natalie, bless her, went immediately to her post. "Have you ever been to England?" she asked, and began to talk of London, while Mared pretended to be viewing the many portraits of what were really far too many Douglases while covertly moving to the window and peeking out at the garden through the thick lead glass.

Aha, there they were. Their figures were somewhat distorted, but Mared could see them, walking side by side, Beitris's hand in the crook of Payton's elbow—or perhaps that was her parasol?—and his head quite close to hers. They strolled languidly, and Beitris would look up to him, and Mared imagined her face glowing with his undivided attention. At the end of the long walk, which was too far away for Mared to see clearly, Payton Douglas dipped his head and kissed Beitris.

At least Mared *thought* that was what he did. They were at a distance so she couldn't be *entirely* certain, but then again . . . no. She was certain. He'd kissed Beitris.

It was cause for celebration! Her plan was working *beautifully*—so why it should make her belly roil she hardly knew or cared. She turned abruptly from the window, her face a wreath of smiles, and went to join Natalie and Miss Douglas.

When at last Payton and Beitris returned—he

wearing a broad smile, and Beitris wearing a furious blush—he and his cousin saw the three of them out.

He helped Beitris onto the narrow bench of the cart while the groom put the donkey to the cart, and Natalie climbed onto the back. Mared was the last to reach the cart—she'd had trouble donning her frilly bonnet, for she rarely wore the blasted thing—and as she walked to the right side of the cart, Payton met her there and gallantly offered her a hand up.

With a slight frown, Mared reluctantly put her hand in his, and he instantly closed his fingers around hers. Firmly. Possessively. A hot flood of warmth shot through her arm and her chest, and it unsettled her so badly that she quickly lifted up and pulled her hand free so that she could take the reins from the grooms-man.

Only then did she dare to glance down at him. He was looking up at her, his gray eyes shimmering with something very deep and very alarming. "Good day, Miss Lockhart. And thank ye for bringing Miss Crowley and Miss Natalie to call. It's been a very pleasurable afternoon."

"Ye are quite welcome," she said merrily while her heart pounded furiously. "And now, we must be on our way. Good day, then!" She cracked the reins against the donkey's back, sending the beast into such a quick trot that Payton Douglas had no time to move. He was knocked down by the sudden movement of the cart; it was only his cousin's shriek that alerted Mared to the accident.

Three

＊

*I*n spite of Sarah's protestations that he might have been killed, Payton wasn't hurt. He'd had the wind and his pride knocked out of him, but he was otherwise quite all right.

He'd rather sternly suggested that perhaps Mared leave the driving of the donkey to someone with a wee bit more finesse of the reins.

But before he'd hobbled off with the aid of his cousin and his groom, he'd seen the glint of fear in Mared's forest green eyes, the fear of that goddamn curse, and he had said sharply, "I know what ye're thinking, lass, and ye're wrong to think it!"

His admonishment earned him a dark frown, and she had climbed back onto the wagon and driven off.

Payton slept badly that night, dreaming of ancient curses and horrible accidents and Mared's green eyes.

But he was set to rights the next morning and resumed his attempts at courting her. Over the course of the next few days, he sent more flowers and laughed when he received her reply that the Highland ling had given her a curious rash. He sent an invitation to ride about Eilean Ros, but she declined, citing a freshly broken leg. And when he finally rode across Ben Cluaran and called at Talla

Dileas, interrupting a family game of lawn bowling, in which Mared was playing on her miraculously healed broken leg, she deigned to obey her father and allow him to play beside her, then swore on her honor that she did not intentionally drop the heavy ball on the toe of his boot.

Aye, Payton did his damnedest to court the unruly lass, but he kept running into Miss Crowley—curiously, just about every time he turned around. And she was always in the company of Mared, who made a habit of leaving them—and quickly, too. He saw the two of them at the kirk, on the road, at a *ceilidh,* a gathering in Aberfoyle where people from the village and surrounding lochs shared music and drink and gossip.

He'd seen Miss Crowley and Mared most recently in the confectioner's shop, where he always stopped when in Aberfoyle, for he had a rather irrepressible sweet tooth. At Mared's urging for all and sundry to hear, he bought Miss Crowley a sweetmeat, but took great satisfaction in not purchasing one for Mared as well, the exasperating little wench.

He saw Miss Crowley the following day, too, when he returned to the smithy to fetch one of his bays. She was walking in the street with Mared, who, he remarked, was spending an awful lot of time in Aberfoyle of late.

"A happy coincidence, I assure ye," Mared had said with a brilliant smile, and then suddenly, "Oh!" as she remembered the important errand that had brought her to Aberfoyle. She scurried away like a rat deserting a sinking ship, leaving Payton alone with Miss Crowley.

Payton liked Miss Crowley, actually. Once she

stopped being afraid of him, he discovered she was really a very nice lass, and he enjoyed her company— but in a friendly sort of way. Not enough to wed her for all eternity, as Mared obviously wanted him to do. He had the sense that Miss Crowley felt much the same way about him. Frankly, she seemed far more interested in the smithy's son than in him.

He thought that rather fortunate, for he'd not want to see Miss Crowley hurt by Mared's silly games.

On a morning that dawned clear and blue after two days of heavy rain, a restless Payton saddled his big bay hunter, Murdoch, then whistled one of his best sheepdogs, Cailean, to his side, and set out to have a look at his sheep.

The ride was slow; Murdoch kicked up thick clumps of mud from a ground turned to bog as they moved slowly along the base of Ben Cluaran. Even Cailean ceased his running ahead and then behind Murdoch, as sheepdogs were wont to do, and walked wearily beside them. High above, on hills that stretched to the sky in shades of green and gold, Payton could see the tiny dots that were his sheep, grazing as high on the face of the hills as any creature could go.

In a week or two, they'd herd them down. The trick with sheep was to keep them moving so they did not graze to roots in any one spot.

When he reached the mouth of Glen Ard, Payton turned upstream, into a narrow split between hills, guiding Murdoch to a place where he could drink from the fast-running stream.

He found a grassy spot and dismounted and knelt beside his horse to drink himself.

As he did so, he heard a mysterious thud and then the ominous sound of something falling down the steep hillside behind him, crashing into trees and rocks. Still on his haunches, Payton looked over his shoulder and saw an enormous rock tumbling down toward him. Instantly he jumped to his feet, grabbed Murdoch's reins and pulled him upstream. The rolling rock hit a tree and hopped a little to the right, then came crashing into the stream exactly where Payton had been drinking.

Cailean trotted over to have a sniff of the rock, but Payton couldn't move, could only stare, his heart racing. The thing was as big as his largest ram. If he hadn't moved so quickly, the bloody thing would have bowled into him and likely killed him.

"*Mi Diah!*"

The voice came from somewhere above him; Payton groaned, and with his hands on his hips, turned around.

"Are ye harmed?" Mared cried as she quickly picked her way down the sheep trail to him, her two dogs darting ahead of her. She had a basket in her hand, her green and blue wrap of plaid, her *arisaidh*, dragging behind her, and her long black hair unbound beneath an old straw hat.

She leapt off the last rock onto the path by the stream and paused for a moment to stare at the rock before turning to him with an awe-filled expression. "Are ye all right?"

"I am quite all right; it didna touch me!" he said gruffly. "What are ye about, pushing rocks that size down the hill? Ye might have killed me!"

"I did no' push it!" she cried indignantly. "I donna know how it came to fall!"

Payton snorted.

"On my honor! The earth is quite wet—it must have come loose. . . ." Her voice trailed off, and she frowned at his expression. "Really, if I'd attempted to slay ye, I'd have done so in such a slow and painful manner that there'd be no question it was me. I didna touch that blasted rock!"

He couldn't help but believe her—Mared was an impertinent, irreverent, and exasperating woman, but she was not, in so far as he knew, a criminal. He sighed, ran a hand through his hair, and stared at the rock as Cailean trotted over to Mared and stuck his head beneath her hand. She instantly stooped down, smiling and cooing to the dog as she stroked him, oblivious to the tongues and tails of her dogs lapping around her.

Frustrated, Payton watched her. She was such a beauty with her long black hair, wandering the hills above the lochs as she so often did, wearing a gown the color of heather cinched tightly below her bosom and embroidered at the neck and hem. And at her breast, she wore a tarnished *luckenbooth*—a brooch. It was a testament to the wealth the Lockharts had once possessed, its tarnish an indication of how much they'd lost.

"Bonny hat," he said wryly.

With a laugh, Mared rose to her feet. "It was Father's." She squinted at the rock once more, then eyed him curiously. "Are ye harmed, then?"

He shook his head.

"'Tis the curse, ye know," she said matter-of-factly. "Ye may think these are mere accidents." She smiled. "But they are a warning to ye, lad—donna go through with this silly betrothal."

He smiled. "There is no curse, Mared." He eyed her basket. "What have ye there?" he asked, tapping his riding crop against his palm as he moved closer to have a look. "It wouldna be the berries from my bramble bushes again, would it?"

Mared put one in her mouth and nodded unabashedly.

"Ye shouldna pick berries on my land without asking, lass," he said, and helped himself to several.

"I shan't do so again, for they're no' as sweet as they've been in years past. Have ye done something to make them sour?" she asked, peering up at him from beneath the brim of her hat. "Cast yer smile upon them, perhaps?"

"If ye donna care for the berries ye pilfer on *this* side of the mountain, then perhaps ye might pick them on Sorley's land," he suggested genially, referring to Old Man Sorley, who ruled his glen with an iron fist and would not brook the theft of *his* berries, no matter how wild they grew or how beautiful the thief who picked them.

"Aye, but everyone knows Sorley's berries are no' as big as yers, laird," she said, and popped another couple of berries into her mouth.

Payton cocked a brow at her boldness, but Mared calmly chewed the berries, her steady gaze challenging him. Impetuously, he lifted his crop, flipped a thick strand of long black hair over her shoulder. "And what has ye about on such a fine day? The unlawful chasing of Douglas sheep? A wee bit of general mayhem?"

"Sheep! And what would I have to do with yer few puny sheep?" she demanded as a winsome smile curved the corners of her mouth and dimpled her cheeks. "If ye must know, I've come from Donalda."

"Donalda!" Payton groaned. Donalda was an old crone who lived deep in the glen. Some claimed she had magical powers. Others said she was the best medicine woman in the Highlands. Still others, Payton among them, held the belief that she was nothing but an old hag. "Why? Have ye an illness that a trained physician canna cure?"

"I do." She laughed as she handed him another handful of bramble berries. "'Tis called a troth."

He couldn't help but smile. "And how will Donalda dispel this terrible disease? Curse me, will she?"

"She gave me a phial," Mared said, holding up the tiny bottle that was hanging around her neck and wriggling it at him. "I am to use it to open yer eyes to the truth when the time is right."

"*My* eyes? Ah, but, lass, I see the truth and I always have. Never doubt it."

With a small shrug, she dropped the phial and picked another berry. "If ye do indeed see the truth, then ye willna hold me to this ridiculous betrothal."

"Ye agreed to the terms of the loan, Mared," he calmly reminded her. "Three thousand pounds is quite a lot of money."

"What choice did I have?" she asked, raising her gaze to his. "I'd no' have agreed to such a thing, but my family needed it so badly."

"So ye've said on more than one occasion. Nevertheless, ye did agree to it. And really, is what I offer so bad?"

She surprised him with a lovely smile. And she put down her basket and folded her arms across her belly, eyeing him closely. "'Tis no' what ye offer, Payton, for it is more than I could ever hope to know," she said, surprising him with the rare but pleasing sound of his given name on her lips. "But can ye change yer name? Or our mutual history?"

"What history?" he scoffed. "Are ye referring to the time ye beat me with yer fists when I was only ten years of age, and ye six? Or the time ye bit me when I tried to kiss ye? Or perhaps ye mean to recount the *ceilidh* when ye openly cut me before all the Highlands and then had the gall to laugh?"

"I mean to recount the many offenses yer family has committed against mine. Douglas has fought against Lockhart since the beginning of time, have ye forgotten?"

"Because yer bloody Lockharts have always been on the side of foolish pride."

"Yer heathen ancestors burned Talla Dileas," she smartly reminded him.

"Because yer traitorous ancestors betrayed the Highlanders, and besides, there was no' much to call Talla Dileas then. And have ye forgotten that yer thieving ancestors slaughtered a herd of Douglas *coos?*"

"Because half were stolen from Lockharts by *yer* thieving ancestors! And lo how the mighty generous and fair Laird Douglas hanged two good Lockhart men on the word of a mere lad!"

"Aye . . . but he didna manage to hang the bloody rotten bounders before they stole a Douglas lass and had their way with her, did he, now?"

Mared clucked and waved a hand at him. "All hearsay. What of the duel between our great-grandfathers?"

"The Lockhart started it by cuckolding the Douglas."

Mared gasped indignantly. "How dare ye impugn my great-grandfather!"

"Impugn him, my rosy red arse! He was the worst scoundrel the lochs have ever seen. And what of the duel between our grandfathers?"

A burst of gay laughter escaped her. "A Douglas started *that* duel over a silly game of cards! Yet ye can hardly call it a duel, for our grandfathers were so far in their cups that yer Douglas shot our Lockhart in the bum!" She laughed roundly at the tale.

Her laughter was infectious and Payton laughed, too. "There, then, Mared, do ye see how ridiculous it all is?"

"Foolish man," she said with a warm smile. "A Douglas and a Lockhart were never meant to marry. Did ye learn nothing from yer forebearers, then? Our blood is like oil and water—we were no' meant to mix." She laughed again as if his foolishness amused her.

But Payton was not so amused and touched her arm with his crop. "So ye'd give me a lass whose blood will mix with mine, is that it? A lass to take yer place? Where is yer shadow, then, Mared? I thought she accompanied ye everywhere . . . or is it only in the kirk and Eilean Ros and the confectioner's and walkabouts of Aberfoyle?"

Mared's smile instantly brightened. "Do ye miss her, then, Douglas? Shall I bring her round to ye again?"

"How happy Miss Crowley must be," he said, impertinently sliding the tip of the crop up her arm, "to have such a champion in ye. Whatever did she do to deserve it?"

She ignored the question and his crop. "Ye find her quite bonny! Go on—admit it!"

With a derisive chuckle, Payton flipped the crop onto her shoulder. *"Diah,* but ye are as bold as a man! Aye, she's bonny, yer shadow . . . but I've no particular regard for her."

"Oh? Do ye *no,'* milord?" she asked, her eyes suddenly flashing. She rose up on her toes, leaned slightly toward him and said, "Ye certainly kissed her well enough for a man who has no particular regard for her," she said softly, and with a triumphant look, settled back on her heels.

"Kissed her?" he asked, far more interested in tracing the tip of the crop along her perfect chin and up, to push her silly hat back from her face.

"Kissed her!" she shot back, slapping his crop away as her shapely dark brows dipped into a vee. "Donna deny it, ye bloody hound! Ye willna treat Miss Crowley as another of yer conquests! She's far too good for that!"

"As usual, ye make no sense whatsoever." He touched the tip of his crop to her nose and leaned forward as she had done, so that he was only inches away from her. "I *didna* kiss her—"

"Ye *did!"* she cried, wide-eyed now, her hands on her hips. "I saw it with my own two eyes when ye escorted her about yer ridiculously overgrown garden!"

"Have a care with yer tongue, lass," he warned her, falling back on his heels. "The garden is no' overgrown! 'Tis the finest example of a manor garden in all of Scotland! And I didna kiss yer Miss Crowley there, but I will admit I was tempted, for she is indeed a bonny lass with a bonny disposition, and *that,* Mared Lockhart, is quite rare in this long glen!"

"So ye will *deny* that ye kissed her?" she demanded, clearly outraged.

"*Ach!*" Payton cried, casting his arms out wide in frustration. "On my honor, ye are the most vexing woman a man might ever hope to know! One moment I believe ye *want* me to find her bonny for all the times ye've put her in my path and extolled her virtues, and in the next moment, ye act as if ye are jealous that I paid her any heed at all!"

"*Jealous?*" she cried, and threw back her head and gave a shout of laughter that echoed in the little glen. "Ye think me *jealous?* Ye've lost yer fool mind!" she said with a grandly dismissive flick of her wrist. "Miss Crowley is a dear friend, and I only thought to inquire for her benefit and no other reason!"

But her cheeks were quite flushed, weren't they? Damn her, she *was* jealous! This impossible woman, who'd given him every indication she'd just as soon see him bound up and shipped off to Australia was jealous!

And Payton could not possibly have been more pleased. He grinned, slapped his crop playfully against her hip. "Ye're jealous, Mared Lockhart. Ye want a kiss for yerself."

"Donna be ridiculous!" she exclaimed. "I am hardly *jealous.*"

"Ye are!" he said, delighted, and touched his crop to her shoulder as his gaze wandered over her lovely body. "Ye thought to bring Miss Crowley round for yer little scheme, but when ye thought I kissed her, ye wanted *that* for yerself. Ye want me to kiss ye now. *Ye want the kiss of a Douglas.*"

She took a quick step back. "Ye've been dipping in that grog ye call whiskey, for ye'd be mad to believe I want *anything* from ye, especially a bloody *kiss.*"

Payton grinned as he stepped forward and slid the

crop down her shoulder and over her bosom. "Ye *do*," he insisted. "Look at how ye blush now. I'd wager a woman of yer years, a woman who has never known the touch of man, has lain awake more than one night thinking about a kiss—"

"*Aaiie!* Ye insult me!" she cried, her face now crimson.

"Ye've *lain* there," he cheerfully continued, "thinking of my mouth on yer sweet lips," he said, and lifted the crop from her breast to touch her lips with the tip of it. Mared slapped his crop away.

"Ye've wondered if my lips are soft or hard," Payton continued, enjoying the high color in her face, the furious glint in her eyes. "If they are warm and wet . . ."

She made a strange sound and punched him in the shoulder. Payton grabbed her wrist and pulled her into him, and with a laugh, he kissed her hard for a long moment, then lifted his head, smiling.

He'd meant it as a jest, only to tease her, but when he saw those green eyes and heard her tiny little gasp through lips pursed in surprise and wonder, male instinct suddenly took hold of him. He dropped his crop and slid his arm around her waist to hold her to him, put his hand against her warm cheek, smoothed her hair back from her temple, then forced her chin up, so that she could see him.

Her eyes were glittering with anger; she put her hands between them and pushed. "Ye flatter yerself, as always. It may come as quite a shock to ye, but I donna lie awake at night thinking of ye at all! I leave that for the poor, unfortunate Miss Crowley."

"*Uist,*" he softly commanded her. "Be still, lass, for I see the bloody truth in yer eyes—ye have indeed wondered about that kiss, and perhaps even more. A beautiful, bonny lass cursed from ever knowing a man. How she must wonder what it is to lie naked with him, to feel him inside—"

"Ye're incredibly vain!" she cried, pushing against him.

"I'll no' deny it," he said with a lazy grin, "but ye're as much a liar if ye say ye've no' wondered." With both hands he cupped her face, holding her still as he lowered his mouth to hers.

She seemed surprised, as if she hadn't believed he would do it, gasping into his mouth, her body stiffening as he gently pressed his lips to hers, shaped them around hers, sucking her plump flesh between his lips.

His arousal was instant and scorching; he felt a tide of burning pleasure rise in him, and he meant to let her go before he did something foolish; but then Mared was suddenly kissing *him*—awkwardly at first, but earnestly. Her hat fell away and Payton touched the corner of her mouth, her cheek, tried to gentle her, to slow her, and as he did so, he could feel the tension slipping out of her body, until she tilted her head back to better receive his kiss.

When the tip of her tongue touched the seam of Payton's lips, every ounce of proper courting decorum melted away as he met her tongue and eagerly delved into the sweet recess of her mouth, his breath mingling with the sweet taste of berries, her scent arousing every masculine inch of him, her body spreading fire through his veins.

He deepened the kiss, slipping his tongue farther inside her mouth, slipping over teeth, around the soft skin of her mouth, tangling with her tongue.

Mared pressed against him, her body arching into his. He tightened his hold around her waist, pushed his thigh between her legs. She made a little mewl in her throat, and she squirmed against him, her hands sliding up his chest to his head, her fingers grasping at his shoulder and his hair while her tongue darted around his, her lips pressed against his, her hips pressing back against his hardness.

A long and wild sliver of her hair caught between their mouths, but Payton didn't care—he cared for nothing but the erotic pleasure of her kiss, the scent of her body, the taste of berries on her breath. He dropped his hand to her waist, then spanned her ribs, and pressed up, to her breast, to the soft mound of flesh that filled his palm and spilled out of it. His fingers dipped into the bodice of her gown, grazing her soft breasts, sliding into the warmth of her cleavage.

He boldly tweaked a nipple with his fingers, then dragged his lips from hers, dipped down, so that he could kiss the swell of her breast. With his hand, he pulled one breast free, took it in his mouth.

"Oh!" she whispered above him. She rose up and arched her back a little, pushing her breast into his mouth. He teased her rigid nipple with his tongue and his teeth, sucking and nipping at her as he let his hands slide down her body, around to her hips, squeezing and pushing her against him.

With each nip of his teeth, Mared would gasp and arch her back again, until she was scarcely breathing at all. Payton rose up, his lips sliding up her bosom, to her neck, and then to her mouth again. He pulled her tightly to him, pressed her hips against him, her bared breast against his chest.

But his desire had grown to an ache to be inside

her, and he felt only moments away from it. His heart forced his body to stop, for as much as he wanted her, he would not take her there on a sheep trail on the south side of Ben Cluaran.

He dragged his lips from hers, carefully pushed her breast inside her bodice as Mared's head lolled helplessly on his shoulder, then buried his face in her neck and begged her. "Come home with me, Mared, come now, and let me give ye pleasure, lass," he whispered thickly as his hand stroked the top her head, the silk of her hair, the curve of her waist into her hip. "Let me give ye the pleasure ye've dreamed of."

His voice must have roused her, because Mared suddenly gasped and wrenched away, stumbling a little as she gaped at him, her hand on her ravaged breast. He could almost see her rise out of the fog of her own desire to stare at him in horror.

He dragged the back of his hand across his mouth as he watched her fumble with her plaid and dip down to retrieve her hat and basket and his crop. "*Diah,*" she muttered as she straightened. Her gaze, swimming with lust and confusion, roamed the length of him, pausing at the sight of the bulge in his buckskins before rising to his face once more.

He held out his hand to her, palm up, silently offering himself to her.

Mared stared at his hand, at his silent offer, and her eyes, the most arrestingly beautiful eyes in all of Scotland, suddenly welled with tears. "*Diah,*" she whispered again.

"No, no, donna cry, lass . . . ye know I've long adored ye," he said softly. "*Carson a tha eagal ort?*"

"I am no' afraid!" she snapped in response, and slapped the crop into his open palm. "But I'll never fall into yer trap!" she said angrily, and turned on her heel and walked away from him down the glen, her dogs eagerly taking up the walk with her.

Payton stood there, watching her march away, her hair floating behind her, her hat firmly on her head, the basket bumping mercilessly against her hip. He stood there until he could no longer see her, long after his body had ceased to ache.

It wasn't until Cailean whimpered at him that he moved.

Four

❧·❧

After that blistering kiss, Mared walked down the sheep trail in a daze, her body and her mind unable or unwilling to move past the sensation of Payton's mouth on her bare breast.

Oh *aye*, he'd kissed her, hadn't he? It was the sort of kiss she'd believed she'd never know, deep and long and . . . and if it hadn't been for his iron grip on her, she would have melted into a warm little puddle and drowned in happy delirium.

It was as extraordinary as it was unexpected, and had sent a stream of hot desire through her, climaxing in a raw longing that scorched her from the inside out. Her heart had thrashed about in her chest and she hadn't been able to breathe, gasping for air like a drowning woman into his mouth, bringing his breath deep into her lungs.

The memory of it made her shudder violently, and impetuously she turned and looked up the trail. He was standing exactly where she'd left him; his legs braced apart, his crop hanging upside down in his hand.

Mared quickly turned around again, lest he see how he still made her skin burn, even from this distance—but her conscience squeaked a faint protest.

She crushed whatever protest her conscience thought to make, for that was Payton Douglas standing on the trail above her, a man who had almost single-handedly ruined her family by introducing sheep to the hills around the lochs. The same man whose ancestors had tormented hers, whose family had betrayed the Lockharts in more ways than could be recalled, and who would force her into a marriage for a mere three thousand pounds, denying her the chance to live her life on her own terms.

To her, that meant away from here and the curse.

It hardly mattered that the sight of him made her heart pound like a bloody drum and her knees tremble with a weakness that infuriated her. Or that when he smiled, when he gave her nothing more than a *smile,* her blood seemed to simmer in her veins.

He was a man who could easily snare a woman in his web, and it angered her to know how quickly and easily she had surrendered to him, and how his provocative words stirred her so deeply that she trembled when she thought of them. *Let me give ye the pleasure ye've dreamed of. . . .*

She thought of those words often in the following days. In her chamber one dreary, rainy afternoon, Mared recalled the entire experience with a delicious shiver as she studied the phial Donalda had given her.

The very same morning of that blistering kiss, she'd climbed up to the tiny little vale deep in the hills to the little thatched hut surrounded by pink moss campion and white butterworts, in a desperate effort to avoid a betrothal that loomed ever closer like a silent, invading army.

The thatched hut had looked the same as it had

when Mared was a child, when she and her brothers would sneak up to spy on the old woman, playing a child's guessing game at where the stool carved from a fallen tree had come from, or what the several wooden buckets stacked outside her door might have held. Liam had told her the smaller ones were for mushrooms, and the larger ones for the newts and toads and fairies that Donalda caught in the woods at night. *"She's the henwife,"* he'd whisper to Mared, attempting to scare her with the lore from a child's tale of horror.

But as Mared had grown up, she'd learned that Donalda was merely an old widow whose husband had died and left her penniless. Donalda was quick witted, and something of a seer, for she always knew when someone had come into her little vale. And indeed, that morning, she'd come out of the tiny cottage before Mared had entered the clearing, wiping her crooked hands on her soiled apron. "Aye, lass, I knew ye'd come," she said, squinting at Mared, and beckoned her inside.

The little one-room cottage was dark; the only light came from a low fire, over which a kettle hung. Two cats lounged amid bottles and bowls scattered atop a long wooden table. The only other furniture in the room was a single wooden chair and a mattress on the floor near the hearth.

Donalda went to the kettle and lifted the lid; the smell of peat filled the room. She replaced the kettle lid, wiped her hands on her apron, then moved to a shelf high on the wall.

The old woman went up on her tiptoes, and with her hand, she felt around the high shelf until her fingers closed around something. She lowered her hand, turned toward Mared, and opened her palm to show her a small phial.

"Keep it close to yer heart," she said, gesturing for Mared to open her hand. She put the phial in it and closed Mared's fingers over it. "And as the eve of yer betrothal draws nigh, drink this by the light of the full moon."

"What is it?" Mared had asked uncertainly.

Donalda's eyes had glittered, and she had leaned close to Mared and said, "It will open the eyes to the truth," she'd said enigmatically.

"The Douglas, ye mean?"

"I mean whoever must see the truth."

Now Mared stared at the little phial and wondered what potion could open anyone's eyes to the truth about her when she could hardly see it herself.

All right, then, there was one small, niggling truth that she'd never admit—*never!*—But he was right. She *had* lain awake many sleepless nights, her body aching. She had not known the touch of a man, as he so indelicately put it, not like his touch. She knew chaste kisses, holding hands. But not a man's hand on her body, not the sort of touch that made her ache and cause her to toss and turn with dreams filled of earthy, bawdy images of Payton Douglas.

And occasionally, the dark-haired son of the smithy in Aberfoyle.

Now a few days had passed since Mared had seen Payton up in the hills. Days in which she had, at times, felt fevered and terribly restless. Nothing would ease her.

A letter from Beitris only made it worse. She dutifully reported that the laird Douglas had paid a gentlemanly call to her, and that her mother found him

quite agreeable, and her father said he was a gentleman and a scholar.

Mared crumpled Beitris's letter and threw it into
the sad little fire in her chamber. It was just like a man,
was it not, to kiss one woman like Payton had kissed
her—a soul-searing, deeply passionate kiss—then
wander off and call on another woman and present
himself to her parents?

She slapped her palm against her vanity and
angrily reminded herself she had *succeeded*. Her plan
had worked. She would not marry Payton Douglas,
for he would offer for Beitris, and her life would be
quite untangled as a result.

And it would untangle right into one long nothing
unless they found the beastie.

Aye, hers was a bleak existence by some measure,
but a far better one than marriage to a Douglas, she
reminded herself. At least she was free to do as she
pleased at Talla Dileas, even if the old castle was
falling down around them. Even if they were in danger of losing their land forever. But when she went to
Edinburgh, she'd be treated with respect and courtesy. She'd meet men who were just as handsome as
Payton but with a last name that did not strike such
resentment in the heart of a Lockhart.

Aye, she'd find her way there, even if she had to
walk.

Mared sighed wearily, tucked the phial down into
her bodice, walked over to the thick glass-paned window and gazed out over the broken tiled roof of the
observatory below her, to the crumbling stone fence,
and the lush green land around Talla Dileas. She
noticed through the heavy mist a dark shape taking
form on the road. She squinted at it. Then frowned. It

was a carriage, pulled by a team of two, and as it drew closer, Mared could make out the lanterns swinging atop the conveyance and the gilded markings on the door.

Him again. She tilted her head back and sighed heavenward, wishing he wouldn't call on Talla Dileas so freely. Nevertheless, she hurried to her vanity to comb her hair and pinch some color into her cheeks before she went down to find out why he was calling today.

By the time she had marched through the maze of corridors and rooms of Talla Dileas, which was the result of centuries of Lockhart lairds putting their mark on an old castle, to the old great room that now served as their salon, she heard laughter within and rolled her eyes.

She pushed open one of the ancient thick oak doors and stepped inside.

The room was bright and cozy, a fire of peat blazing at the hearth. Inside were her sisters-in-law—Ellie, blonde and blue-eyed like her daughter, sitting prettily on the settee, and Anna, the dark-haired, brown-eyed beauty in an armchair, her hands protectively on her belly, which was beginning to show her pregnancy. The two women were laughing, which wasn't unusual— they had become fast friends since Anna had arrived in Scotland. What was unusual was that they were laughing with Payton Douglas and his cousin.

In fact, the haughty Miss Douglas was actually smiling a little as she sipped tea from one of the few china teacups that had not been sold or broken in the last few years. And Payton . . . *Mary, Queen of Scots*, he was holding Liam and Ellie's baby son, Duncan, in one arm.

Mared was marching forward before she realized it.

Ellie, who had traitorously handed her precious bairn to a Douglas, was the first to notice Mared's arrival.

"Mared!" she cried happily, and everyone turned to look at her, including *him,* who smiled broadly, as if it was quite common for him to be in *their* salon, sipping *their* tea, holding *their* children.

"Oh, Mared! Look who's come to call!" Anna said, moving to find her feet. Naturally, Payton was instantly at her side, the baby in one arm, his hand beneath Anna's elbow, helping her up.

Mared halted in the middle of the room and dipped into a rather shabby curtsey and found a smile for Payton's cousin. "How do ye do, Miss Douglas? Welcome to Talla Dileas."

She nodded stiffly.

"Miss Lockhart, what a pleasure," Payton said, bowing low as Duncan grabbed for his lapel. "The very sight of ye warms our hearts, it does," he said, and as he rose up, he winked at her. *Winked.*

"How lovely," Ellie murmured.

"How preposterous," Mared muttered and frowned at her nephew, who was gurgling up at Payton. "What is this, milord? Do we owe ye our firstborn grandson as well?"

Payton chuckled and looked down at the baby and began to bounce him in his arms. "If I had my druthers, Miss Lockhart, I'd fill the whole of Eilean Ros with a dozen bairns just like this wee one."

"Payton, really," Miss Douglas laughed. "Ye are too bold."

Bold, he was indeed, but curiously, it was the first time Mared had ever heard him express such a sentiment. For some reason, as she stood there watching him hold Duncan high above him and coo in Gaelic that Duncan was a wee fat lad, she could very well imagine him in a house full of wee fat lads, and the vision gave her a peculiar and warm little shiver.

"Lord Douglas has brought us tea, Mared," Anna said, pointing to a box of it on a small end table. "Isn't that lovely?"

"Tea?"

"Aye," Payton said, as he handed Duncan back to his mother. "A wee bird told me that ye were in need of it. Sarah and I would share ours."

"How . . . unusually *thoughtful*," Mared said, taking a seat next to Anna. "Mother will be particularly grateful for it, for she's no' had a decent cup of tea in a fortnight."

Payton politely inclined his head. "Ye are more than welcome."

"Won't you please be seated, my lord?" Ellie asked, having handed off Duncan to Lucy, the only ladies' maid they could afford, and the only ladies' maid who would agree to be Duncan's nurse as well. Lucy tickled the baby's belly as she took him from the room.

With a smooth flip of his tails, Payton seated himself directly across from Mared on a long divan that was in desperate need of reupholstering. The old piece of furniture contrasted sharply with the new divan at Eilean Ros.

"Will you be at Eilean Ros for a time yet, Miss Douglas?" Anna asked.

"Only as long as Cousin Payton needs me. We've searched rather hopelessly for a housekeeper since Mrs. Craig passed. Until we can find one with suitable credentials, I'll stay on. I would not leave Eilean Ros without a feminine touch, for I fear he'd turn the house over to a hunting lodge."

The ladies laughed politely. Mared snorted.

"A pity you've had no luck," Anna sighed. "I'm certain there are women about in need of the work."

"Most women in need of work have gone to Glasgow," Mared said.

"And those that remain behind cannot be depended upon to manage a barnyard," Miss Douglas added.

"How fortunate, then, that the laird doesna require more than that," Mared suggested with an innocent little smile.

She had meant it to be witty, but Miss Douglas looked appalled, and Ellie and Anna turned twin looks of horror on her. Only Payton chuckled softly. "Miss Lockhart, I beg ye, donna spare us yer true feelings for Eilean Ros."

Ellie and Anna tittered with polite relief, but glared at her nonetheless, and Mared wondered when they had gone over to the side of the enemy.

His cousin, however, was less forgiving in her demeanor.

"I do beg yer pardon, laird. Miss Douglas," she said grudgingly, and bowed her head. "It was merely a jest, but apparently one quite lacking in wit." And she smiled.

Miss Douglas sniffed, and Anna, the consummate hostess, quickly asked after Payton's new crop of barley, planted just last year. The question obviously pleased him, for he began to talk with great enthusiasm about his crop. How difficult it had been to drain the field above the loch, how the crop had come in much stronger than he'd expected. How he would use barley to stock the whiskey distillery he was intent on building, how barley-bree would be common in his neighbors' homes. And last but not least, how his sheep could graze the fallow fields. It was obvious he thought himself clever—his eyes were quite radiant with it.

Much to Mared's chagrin, Ellie and Anna ooh'd and aah'd along with him. It rankled her to no end, particularly because even *she*, the only true Lockhart within these four walls, could not help but be enthused by him, no matter how badly she tried not to be.

When he and his cousin took their leave, he bowed gallantly over Ellie's and Anna's hands. Her sisters-in-law were practically swooning with delight. That was the danger of having English women in the house, Mared thought as she watched them beaming at Douglas. They had no sense of history, no sense of how he, by virtue of having brought sheep into these hills, had changed the very course of all their lives. And by virtue of having lent them money, how he would change the course of *her* life. All they saw was a handsome, charming man.

"If I may," he said politely as he escorted his cousin to the door of the salon behind the Lockhart butler, Dudley, "I would extend an invitation to all the Lockharts to be my guests at Eilean Ros on the evening of Friday next, for a *ceilidh*."

Mared was instantly suspicious. She could not recall a time he had hosted a *ceilidh*. "Thank ye, but we canna possibly—" she started, but Ellie was quick to stop her by stepping in front of her and all but shouting, "How very kind!" Then she dipped a curtsey worthy of a duke, not a bloody Douglas, and said, beaming, "I'm certain our laird would be delighted by the invitation."

"No, he—" Mared tried, but Anna eagerly chimed in, "Of course he would! He was just saying this very week how he'd like to go forth a bit more than he's been able."

Mared gave Anna a puzzled look. She could not imagine her father saying any such thing. He was usually far too occupied in fretting about the demise of Talla Dileas.

"Splendid," Payton said. "I shall consider it a favorable reply, then. Good day, Mrs. Lockhart. Mrs. Lockhart," he said, nodding to Ellie and Anna. He shifted his gaze to Mared. "*Miss* Lockhart."

The two Lockhart traitors stood on either side of Mared and wished the Douglases a good day in their badly spoken Gaelic.

When Dudley had shut the door behind the departing Douglases, Mared whirled about, glaring at her sisters-in-law. "Have ye forgotten who the enemy is, then?"

Anna laughed, but Ellie sighed wearily. "Darling, *calm* yourself." She linked her arm with Mared's. "We are quite well aware of the enemy."

"Certainly we are," Anna said. "What woman could ignore him? He's really quite appealing, isn't he? There are times I find it very difficult to remember *why* he is the enemy. He's so handsome—not at all like the fops in London."

"Ye donna understand, Anna—"

"Yes, of course I do," she said before Mared could begin cataloguing the Douglas laird's many faults. "I'm being silly, that's all. Payton Douglas is a blackguard and a traitor and something else quite odious that I cannot now recall. Wasn't it lovely the way he fawned over Duncan?"

"*Everyone* fawns over Duncan, Anna. Apparently even ogres. If ye know he is the enemy, why, then, did ye pretend as if the prince regent himself had come to call?"

"Because *we* have heard the news," Ellie said with a bright smile. "And we shan't tip our hand to him."

"What news?"

"*This* news," Ellie said eagerly. "When Liam traveled to Glasgow in search of work, by chance he encountered Sir Malcolm, and Sir Malcolm told him that Hugh MacAlister's sister, Mrs. Reed, has come from Aberdeen to visit her ailing mother. She's supposedly near unto death."

"So what news does Aileen bring?" Mared asked anxiously.

"We don't know as of yet," Ellie said. "Liam and Grif will set out on the morrow for the MacAlister estate to have a bit of a chat. Grif said that Hugh was rather close to his sister Aileen, and if anyone in the family might know of his whereabouts, it would be her. Not to mention his poor mother's ill health, which would bring even the worst of scoundrels home."

Mared caught a breath in her throat. Was it possible? Her nightmare would disappear if Hugh showed himself anywhere in Scotland with the beastie. Yet she was afraid to hope—her spirits had been dashed to pieces by two false sightings of that bloody rotten scoundrel, Hugh. And each time she heard his name, she could not help but think of the little flirtations he'd whispered in her ear before he and Grif had left

for England. *"I'll come back to ye, Mared, for I canna see
the sun but in yer eyes,"* he'd said. And *"A Scottish rose
ye are. I will carry yer image forever in me heart, and it
shall be me guiding light until I've returned."*

That, he'd said to her the night before his departure. On bended knee no less, as he'd attempted to
coax a kiss from her. Mared had laughed at him, but
she'd enjoyed his attention nonetheless, as well as the
chaste little kiss she'd given him that very night. The
bastard! He hadn't an honorable bone in his body!
"No . . . I daresay Hugh will be in America by now,"
she said morosely, sitting beside Anna. "He'll no'
come back to Scotland for fear of hanging, no' even
for his dying mother."

"Perhaps. But where do dogs go when they've no
place else to roam and they are hungry? My guess
would be home, or as close to a home port as one
might find in a storm," Ellie opined.

"And what has any of that to do with Douglas?
Why accept his invitation? The Lockharts have never
sought invitations to Eilean Ros nor been particularly
well received there."

"But that is the beauty of it," Ellie said quickly,
exchanging a look with Anna. "We shall all be in
attendance Friday evening when Liam and Grif
return to give him the good news that he is to receive
his payment in full, with interest. And not *you*. And
we shall celebrate!" she said with a squeak of delight,
and both of them looked at Mared as if they'd already
discovered Hugh's whereabouts and the beastie, too.

Mared smiled, but she could not feel quite so confident. "What if they donna find Hugh?"

Anna and Ellie exchanged another sly look. "Well
then," Ellie said, as she studied the sleeve of her

gown, "it would only be natural, I suppose, that we would all attend a rather . . . well, a rather important event to get better acquainted with our . . . perhaps future . . . family . . . ah, member."

Mared snorted. "He'll *no'* be a member of this family, Ellie! I'll never consent to marry him!"

"But really, Mared, he's quite—" Anna started, but Mared sprang to her feet and strode to the door.

"He's quite any number of things, Anna, but I'll no' lower myself to marry a Douglas!" she said sternly and quit the room before they could extol the knave anymore.

Five

❧·❦

Mared's instincts, as it turned out, were rather keen—just as she'd suspected, Ellie and Anna's optimism was effectively doused when Grif and Liam returned from the MacAlister estate three days later, covered head to foot in the grime from the road, hungry, and empty-handed.

Not only was Hugh's sister, Aileen, quite ignorant of his whereabouts, she was, at least according to Grif, genuinely surprised and distressed to learn of Hugh's theft of the beastie. Liam was less charitable—he suspected a vile conspiracy in everything the MacAlisters did, and cited Mrs. MacAlister's recovery from her deathbed as proof.

Mared suspected that were she privy to all that had gone on, Aileen would be surprised and distressed by many things her brother Hugh had done. And she chafed at the piteous looks from her family, argued that her attendance at the preposterous *ceilidh* was entirely unnecessary. When her father, tired of the battle, laid down the law and said that she *would* attend, she prepared for an interminable evening at Eilean Ros by sporting a very bad humor and donning her best evening gown, such as it was.

Her best gown was a heavy and rich purple brocade, fancifully embroidered along the sleeves and hem and bodice, and repaired in more than one place. It was a winter gown, the color and fabric ill suited to the long summer nights in Scotland, but it was the only gown she had to wear to important social events. When one's family fell upon hard times, pretty gowns and silk slippers were the first necessities to fall by the wayside.

Not that Mared minded too terribly—mostly, she stood to one side at large affairs such as this, as guests generally seemed vaguely fearful of her. And she hardly cared what Payton Douglas might think of her attire—after all, he'd seen this particular gown enough times in the last few years to form a very firm opinion of it. At a Christmas dance just last year, he'd casually fingered the sleeve of it and remarked, "I would that ye had clothing less somber than this."

Mared had smiled as she moved her arm away from his fingers. "I do indeed, sir, but I intend to wear that gown to my audience with the king. It wouldna do to wear it before that occasion, aye?"

He'd smiled tenderly, blast him, and Mared had felt that smile filter down her spine, all the way to her groin. "One day," he'd said, "ye'll have no need to wear a gown more than once." And he had walked on, leaving her to stand self-consciously against the wall, hating her gown and hating him.

She did concede to a bit of primping by allowing Ellie and Anna to put her hair up in a fashion they said was quite popular in London—a pile of dark ringlets pinned in back and a thin ribbon of silk, borrowed from Beitris, wrapped around her head in Grecian style. A pair of amethyst earrings dangled from her earlobes.

"Are ye certain this is the current fashion?" Mared asked, peering closely at herself in the mirror.

"Yes, of course! Ah, but how lovely you are, Mared," Ellie avowed appreciatively, standing back to have a look at her handiwork.

"You'd be an Original were we in London," Anna opined from her supine position on the bed. "Everyone adores a darkly exotic look just now."

Mared didn't know if she had a darkly exotic look, but she was rather intrigued with her fancy appearance. She really rather liked it and secretly wished for a more suitable ensemble.

The family—save Grif and Anna, who thought it best not to attend in her condition, and Natalie, who was too young to attend—climbed into an ancient old coach they had once kept for emergencies, but now served as their primary form of conveyance, pulled by two braying donkeys, and creaked and moaned their way across Ben Cluaran.

When they arrived they were surprised to see so many carriages and carts parked along the tree line. In the drive, a couple had just disembarked—he was wearing a formal black coat, and she was wearing a sparkling gold gown.

"How lovely!" Ellie cried, clearly enthralled. "It's a *ball*, Liam!"

"Bloody hell," he muttered beneath his breath and stuck a finger between his collar and neck once more in a vain attempt to loosen it.

"A *ball!*" Mared cried, feeling quite ill at ease all of a sudden. "He said nothing of a *ball!* He said a *ceilidh!*"

"Have you any idea how long it's been since I've attended a ball?" Ellie gushed excitedly, her gloved hand at her throat as she peered outside. "And oh, look there! See the woman in pink?"

Mared strained to see—it was none other than Beitris, in a pretty pink ball gown, walking carefully behind her mother and father.

"Mary Queen of Scots," Liam muttered. "'Tis a blasted *ball.*"

"You should be pleased, darling," Ellie said gaily. "You're well acquainted with all the dances, and Anna tells us that during your escapade in London, you did quite nicely on a crowded dance floor."

Liam scowled.

"I've no use for balls," Father said irritably. "I donna like the dancing or the noise."

"Ye'll smile and be quite happy to attend," Mother said calmly and looked pointedly at Mared. "I rather suppose he'd have the whole of the lochs see Mared on his arm. 'Tis what a gentleman does when he intends to take a lass to wife."

That was certainly not something Mared had considered, and the suggestion caused her heart to leap to her throat. She instantly clapped her hands over her ears. *"Ach!* I'll no' hear it!" she insisted as the coach rolled to a halt in the drive.

"It is out of yer hands, Mared. Donna tempt fate," her mother warned her as the door flew open. "A Lockhart never breaks his word!" And with that, she gave her hand to Liam, who had already bounced from the coach to hand them all down.

The ball-disguised-as-a-*ceilidh* was in full swing, and it seemed to Mared as if everyone who lived in the glens surrounding the lochs was in attendance, their brightly clad bodies crowding the salons and spilling out onto the terrace that overlooked a serene Loch Ard. A quartet of fiddlers and a bagpipe were at one end of the grand ballroom, playing waltzes and Scottish reels and quadrilles. Dozens of couples danced, both in the ballroom and on the terrace.

Footmen, dressed in the old-style Douglas livery with powdered wigs and short pantaloons, passed through the crowd, trays of little tots filled with Eilean Ros barley-bree held high above their heads.

Mared helped herself to one tot, discreetly tossing it back as she stood against a wall, watching her mother and father dance a Scottish reel. Ellie danced with the parson of Aberfoyle, while Liam laughed with a group of Highland soldiers.

Payton, however, was nowhere to be seen. Miss Douglas had greeted them at the door and invited them to proceed through the marble entry, to the ballroom. Curious about Payton's whereabouts, Mared thought that perhaps he was on the terrace and considered walking outside to have a look about. But she was ill at ease in her old gown among so many people and self-consciously stayed back.

Besides, she couldn't possibly imagine why she might care where Payton was. She should be overjoyed there were so many in attendance this evening, for it would keep him quite well occupied. He could talk of his sheep at length to the various unmarried women here, who would undoubtedly hang on every single word, just as Beitris tended to do. How tiresome.

And then the devil himself appeared at the terrace door with a beaming Beitris on his arm. As they strolled into the crowded ballroom, she looked perfectly happy, perhaps even a wee bit in love.

And *he* looked . . . handsome. *Diah*, he looked *quite* handsome in his formal tails and white silk waistcoat. And content.

Mared ignored the fluttering in her belly and determined that he and Beitris were perfectly suited to one another. A pretty lass. A handsome laird. Mared could congratulate herself now—she'd done quite well in pairing the two of them.

If only he hadn't kissed her, hadn't touched her like that. If only she hadn't kissed him back.

When a footman walked by with a tray of barley-bree, she took another tot.

It helped soothe her uneasiness, left her feeling warm and fluid.

When the quadrille ended, Douglas handed Beitris over to Mr. Abernathy, the smithy's son. Then he turned and looked directly at Mared, startling her.

He moved in her direction. He had spotted her so damnably easily, she thought, as she lifted her chin and smiled at him with serene indifference as he approached.

He was not the least bit deterred. When he reached her—one corner of his mouth upturned in something of a lazy smile—he bowed. In response, Mared sort of slid a bit down the wall and rose up again in her version of a curtsey.

"Miss Lockhart, how good of ye to attend our affair," he said, his gaze taking in her gown and hair.

"Aye, and thank ye for the invitation to yer ball, which ye cleverly concealed under the pretext of a *ceilidh*."

One dark brow rose high above the other; his eyes sparkled with amusement. "Pretext? I beg yer pardon, but ye are mistaken. This," he said, turning slightly and looking at the crowded room behind him, "is indeed a gathering with a wee bit of dancing to enliven the evening. Is that no' the definition of *ceilidh?*"

"I believe a *ceilidh* is more an informal affair than a full-fledged ball, milord."

He grinned. "Semantics. One canna give a Scot a tot of whiskey and no' expect him to kick up his heels, aye?"

She couldn't help chuckling at the truth in that statement. "I think it quite impossible, aye."

"Then having partaken of a tot yerself," he said, nodding at the two empty glasses on the chair beside her, "perhaps ye might like a turn about the dance floor as well?"

"Ye know me better than this, sir. I willna dance for yer amusement."

"Then dance for yer own amusement," he said, holding out his hand to her.

She shook her head and looked away.

"Come and dance with me, Mared," he said softly. "It would be discourteous to refuse yer host, aye?"

A waltz was forming on the strings of the fiddle, the distinctive wail of the accompanying pipes pounding out the rhythm behind Payton, and she glanced at his upturned hand from the corner of her eye. "They'll think ye've lost yer mind, dancing with the accursed."

He leaned closer. "Mared, *leannan*," he said, using a term of endearment as he touched her hand, "surely ye have gathered by now that I donna give a damn what any of them think. Dance with me." And he smiled.

All right, then. There was simply no denying that magnetic smile—she was lost. The whiskey and the lure of the pipes propelled her forward, and against her better judgment, she awkwardly slipped her hand into his and felt quite helpless when he smiled warmly at her, as if they shared some intimate secret. He put her hand on his arm and covered it with his broad palm, then led her onto the crowded dance floor, boldly ignoring the many critical eyes that turned toward them.

True to his word, Payton seemed not to notice or care. He swept a low bow.

She curtsied properly, smiled when he put his hand steadfastly on her waist, took her hand firmly in his other. She might be lost, she reasoned, but she might as well make the most of it, and with a giggle, she put her hand lightly on his shoulder.

The music started up in earnest; Payton grinned, twirled her to the rhythm of the music, pulling her close to his body, his hand going around to span her waist. This close to him, she could smell his cologne, the musky scent reminding her of that kiss in Glen Ard, the feel of his mouth on her skin, and his thigh between her legs. Much to her horror, she blushed.

He smiled knowingly. "What are ye thinking?"

The question took her slightly aback—could he read her thoughts? Could he possibly know how vividly she recalled that day and that kiss? Flustered by his smile and the gleam that went deep in his gray eyes, Mared did what she always did when she felt threatened. She assumed a certain nonchalance.

"Can ye no' guess? I was wondering why ye would have Lockharts to a silly ball. 'Tis no' the Douglas way."

"Aye, 'tis no' the Douglas way, because the Lockharts, particularly when they travel in a pack, can be a wee bit . . . *fiadhaich*."

Mared laughed, for the Lockharts thought the same of the Douglases—that they were a wild, unruly lot.

Her laughter pleased him, and he gave her a knee-weakening smile that somehow had her feeling completely outside of her body. In the glow of that smile, he pulled her closer, so that their bodies were touching.

She did not resist him but demanded, "What are ye doing? Ye'll create quite a scandal dancing so close to the wretched daughter of Lockhart."

"Hush," he said low. "I enjoy the feel of ye in my arms. There'll be no derision of ye tonight, no' even from yer own lips. Let them think what they will, but let them know that ye will be a Douglas soon enough."

A Douglas . . . Mared reacted to that by suddenly rearing back, pushing against the arm that firmly anchored her to him. "Let me go," she said sharply.

"What is it, then?" he asked impatiently. "Do ye still foolishly deny what will be?"

"Stop it," she said, looking away. "Ye willna provoke me into making a scene."

"Bloody wee fool," he muttered, and easily pulled her closer. "I've courted ye, I've tried my damnedest to make it easy for ye—"

"'Tis no' a matter of *trying,*" she said angrily as a feeling of helplessness began to rise in her throat. "'Tis a matter of being forced against my will—"

"Then I suggest ye no' be so free with yer word of honor, Mared."

"Ye think I was *free* to give it?" she insisted incredulously. "Do ye think a woman is ever free? I do as every woman I know must do—I bow to the will of my father and my brothers!"

"For God's sake, will ye stop yer complaining!" he said irritably. "Ye will do as yer father wisely decides because ye are too foolish when left to yer own devices! I offer ye a good life, but ye are too stubborn to see it."

"Ye donna offer, ye command!" she shot back.

His expression grew dark, and he tightened his hold on her hand. "Donna provoke me, Mared. My patience is at an end and I'll no' stand for such impertinence or willful disdain as ye show me now once we are married."

"Indeed? And pray tell, how do ye think to stop it?"

His expression turned even darker; he clenched his jaw tightly shut and yanked her closer. He refused to look at her, just twirled her one way, then the other, until the music thankfully drew to an end, and at last, he stepped away from her and bowed. She inclined her head and turned to walk stiffly beside him.

But he was not through with her—he put an unyielding hand to her elbow and guided her none too gently toward the doors that opened onto the terrace.

Mared opened her mouth to protest, but he quickly cut her off. "*Ach,* no, donna speak! Ye despise me, ye've made it perfectly clear, but ye are to be my wife, whether or no' either of us can abide it," he said tersely. "I've always thought ye a bonny lass, a bird with a bonny countenance, but this evening, I find ye shrill."

She gasped indignantly and tried to wrench her arm free of his grasp, but he held firm. "Then let go of me!"

"Stop acting the child! I've a gift for ye, Mared. In a moment of abominable weakness, I had a gift made for ye."

"Oh *no*," she moaned heavenward.

He made a sound of disgruntlement, but dropped his hand from her elbow when they reached the balustrade where guests at Eilean Ros stood to view the expansive gardens lit by rush lights below. "Ye've made it all so very difficult," he snapped. "Why ye will no' accept what is—were I a Lockhart, I'd no' stand for yer impertinence," he said as he reached into his pocket.

"Were ye a Lockhart, there'd be no need for this discourse at all."

He frowned darkly at her and pulled something from his pocket. "I had this small token of my esteem made so that ye might come to understand that I intend to honor ye, Mared," he said, and holding out his hand, he opened his fingers.

The gift—an expensive, thoughtful gift—knocked her back on her heels. Mared put her hand to her throat as she stared down at the *luckenbooth*. It was shaped like a thistle, cast in gold and studded with emeralds around a diamond, the Lockhart colors. Along the bottom it was inscribed with the Lockhart motto, *True and Loyal*. It was exquisite, intricately carved.

She'd never owned anything like it and was touched by his thoughtfulness, yet angered by his extravagance, too, and wondered how long a valuable piece of jewelry such as this would feed her entire family.

"I'd no' take ye from the Lockharts," Payton said gruffly. "I mean ye to stay close to yer family's hearth. I quite clearly understand that while ye may be Douglas in name, ye'll always be a Lockhart at heart."

"Oh," she murmured and lifted her gaze, saw a

glimmer of affection in his eyes that made her heart tilt a little. She looked at the *luckenbooth* again.

"Take it, lass," he said, his voice noticeably softened.

Mared wanted to take it; she wanted to hold it in her hand, to feel the weight of it and the warmth of his sentiment, but somehow, taking it seemed almost traitorous.

As if he understood her reluctance, Payton clucked and put his hand beneath her elbow as she stepped back. He pulled her closer, so that they were almost touching, so that she could feel the strength of his body all around her. "Donna deny me this," he said quietly. "I've no use for a Lockhart *luckenbooth* if ye willna have it." He reached up and casually slipped two fingers into the bodice of her gown.

His fingers skimmed her breast, instantly warming her flesh—Mared bit her lip to keep the little mewl of titillation from escaping her. She looked up at him as he pulled the cloth of her gown from her skin and smoothly pinned the *luckenbooth* so that it rested just over her heart. His hand lingered there with his gaze for a moment as he admired it before looking into her eyes.

His gaze was smoldering, as if something was burning beneath the surface of him, and it vaguely occurred to her that perhaps he felt what she did—a burning. Flames melting her from the inside out.

But Payton pulled his hand free of her bodice, then slid his other hand down her arm, wrapping his fingers around her wrist. He bowed his head and gently pressed his lips to the corner of her mouth.

Frozen, Mared stood with her gaze locked on his neckcloth, at a loss as to how she might understand such a gentle kiss, alarmed by the fire he left singeing her lips.

He let go of her and stepped back, a gentlemanly distance. Mared touched the *luckenbooth* he had pinned to her breast as she watched him lean against the balustrade, his arms folded . . .

And then he was falling backward as the balustrade abruptly gave way.

Mared shrieked and reached out to him, but Payton had lost his footing and disappeared, along with the stone railing.

Her shriek brought people running. "Get back, get back!" a man shouted; someone grabbed her shoulders, roughly pulling her back. "Go there, to Ellie," Liam said and pushed her toward his wife as he rushed forward to the end of the broken terrace, shouting at the other men to have a care.

Mared was pulled into the ballroom by someone, and her mother and Ellie miraculously appeared by her side.

"What's happened, what's happened?" Mother asked breathlessly as Ellie stood on tiptoes and craned her neck to see outside along with dozens of other ladies.

Mared's hands were shaking so badly she had to grip them together; she imagined Payton lying on the flagstones below, his neck broken. She squeezed her eyes shut and pressed her hands into her abdomen to keep her fear from bubbling up. "I donna know, I swear it," she said through gulps of air. "He . . . he leaned against the balustrade, and it gave way. I tried to reach him, but he—" She couldn't say it. She couldn't say that he fell, that she had killed him with her curse.

Her mother put a comforting arm around her. "There now, *mo ghraidh.* It was an accident."

"There he is—he's quite all right!" Ellie cried, the relief apparent in her voice. I can see him standing just there, on the terrace."

"He's alive?" Mared asked shakily.

"Of course! He's moving . . . his coat seems to be torn, and there is a bit of mud on his trousers, but he's speaking to those around him."

"Lucky he is," one woman said loudly, "to have survived the curse."

Mared's blood ran cold—she recognized the voice as belonging to Mrs. Dahlstrom. Beside her, her mother stiffened and tightened her hold around Mared's shoulders.

"It looks to me as if he's survived a bit of rotted wood and crumbling stone is all," Ellie said haughtily.

But Mrs. Dahlstrom was not put off and glared at Ellie. "Ye be English, Mrs. Lockhart. Ye donna understand the secrets of the Highlands." With that, she cast a cold glare at Mared.

But Ellie was not so easily dismissed and stepped in front of Mared. "That is true, madam. But I understand superstition and ignorance when I hear it, and really, the laird is quite all right," she said. She turned her back on the woman and faced Mared. "Come, darling, why don't we find a place to sit until the commotion is over? Perhaps have a tot of the barley-bree?"

Yes, barley-bree. A keg of it, Mared thought, and dumbly followed her sister-in-law away from the scene of the accident, her mother protectively at her side.

Six

❧·❧

*P*ayton had known of the weakness in that particular section of the balustrade, but no one had been more surprised than he that it had given way so soon. Years of harsh, wet winters had weakened the cement that held the railing to the terrace, and Payton was thankful he'd been standing precisely where he had, for he'd fallen into shrubbery only a few feet below. Ten feet in either direction, and he might have fallen much farther and onto flagstones.

He might have broken his fool neck.

As it was, he was unharmed. Just a wee bit bruised.

He called Sarah to him, instructed her to have the musicians begin playing as soon as possible and to have more of the barley-bree sent around to the guests by the footmen after they had moved potted trees to keep guests from that section of the railing.

With Beckwith at his side, he hastily retreated to his master suite of rooms to change his clothing. When he reemerged a short time later, he could feel the shift in what had been a festive atmosphere—a palpable and disquieting current now ran through his house.

The terrace had been closed off to guests; the dancing had resumed, at least for a few hearty souls, but most stood back, speaking to one another in small groups. In the dining room, talking low amongst themselves, couples feasted on a repast of collops of beef, a meat pastry known as forfar bridies, and poached salmon. Everything seemed to have returned to normal since the accident, yet it all felt much different, as if a dark cloud had descended upon Eilean Ros.

Payton made the rounds, assuring everyone he was quite all right, that it had been nothing but an accident. It was Sarah who told him what had given his *ceilidh* such a morose pall, as if he needed to be told. There were enough who knew of his bartered betrothal to Mared that he was certain theories of goblins and curses had sprung to life and were spreading like fire.

Sarah confirmed it for him. "I think they'll no' dance until they can be assured she's departed," she whispered to him in the ballroom as they calmly observed the few brave souls who were dancing. "They are frightened of her and the curse. I daresay they half expect ye to fall dead at their feet any moment now, and fret they will join ye by virtue of having come into yer house."

"They are ignorant," he said sharply. "Where is she?"

Sarah shrugged lightly. "I canna say. Lady Lockhart spirited her away."

"Keep them dancing, then," he said curtly, and left Sarah to find Mared. It was, to his way of thinking, absurd to be fearful of an ancient, make-believe curse that was no more real than gnomes and fairies. Yet he knew that Highlanders, even educated ones, could hold fast to their bloody superstitions. He'd end their ridiculous fears tonight, he thought angrily. He'd formally announce his intention to marry Mared Lockhart, then let them see that he lived to do just that.

He had only to convince Mared to join him in the announcement, and this time, he'd brook no argument from her.

He found the Lockharts in the foyer—save Mared—donning their wraps. "Are ye leaving, then?" he demanded.

"*Aye,*" Liam said angrily as he helped his wife into a cloak. "We're no' welcome here any longer."

"Of course ye are!"

"We're no' welcome, Douglas, no' after yer fall—ye need only look at the faces here!" Liam snapped. "They whisper Mared's name and look at her as if she were *a' diabhal* himself. The lass has endured a lifetime of censure, and we'll no' put her through a moment more of it. And neither should ye, man."

The slight admonishment made Payton bristle. "I intend to disabuse my guests of their fears promptly, if ye will grant me but a moment. First, I must speak with Mared."

"She's gone out," Lady Lockhart said angrily, "Away from them."

"A moment," Payton said to Liam. "Give me that." He did not wait for an answer but strode to the door, not breaking stride as a footman hurried to open it for him, and strode through, into the night.

He instinctively knew where to find her, and just as he suspected, she was standing on the edge of the loch, just below the drive, staring out at the water made silver by a big Scottish moon. His dog Cailean was by her side, as if he kept watch over her.

"Mared."

In the bright light of the full moon, he could see her smile as she turned and his dog loped toward him. That was one of the things he truly admired about her—she always smiled, no matter what the circumstance, no matter how or where that brutal curse might taunt her.

"Ah," she said, nodding to his dog. "A true Douglas, the feckless hound."

"Mared," Payton said gruffly, ignoring Cailean. "The balustrade had nothing to do with ye. It was old and rotted and I should have seen it repaired long ago. I was foolish to have leaned against it."

She clucked at him. "Of course it had nothing to do with me, sir! I didna push ye." She laughed thinly at the notion but turned away from him, toward the loch again. "Perhaps for a moment ye believed that I had?"

"No." He paused, shoved a hand through his hair, at a loss as to what to say. "Mared, *leannan* . . . I know they fear ye—"

"Honestly, laird, have ye come to speak to me of that silly curse?" she asked breezily, quickly cutting him off. "For if ye have, I've made a vow to myself that I willna waste a moment of my life on superstition and sorcery. There's really no' a lot to be gained from it."

"That's good," he said, nodding thoughtfully as he moved toward her. "But I would put to rest any doubts about that bloody curse this very night."

Mared snorted and glanced at him over her shoulder. "And how do ye think to do that, then? How will ye change what people of the lochs have believed for nigh on three centuries now?"

"By formally announcing our engagement."

She made a cry of alarm and suddenly whirled around. "Ye wouldna do so!"

"I would, indeed! We are to be married, and I see no time like the present to put this absurdity behind us once and for all! All of it. The curse, the loan—"

"*Criosd!*" she suddenly cried to the heavens. "Why do ye persecute me? Why do ye insist on this? I donna *want* to marry ye, Payton Douglas! I canna say it any plainer than that! I donna want anything to do with ye at all!"

He struggled to keep his anger in check, clenching his fists at his side. "Ye are fearful of the curse, Mared," he said low. "I know ye are. I see it in yer eyes and in the tremble of yer hand."

"Ye know *nothing!*" she spat at him. "God in heaven, why will ye no' see how compatible in mien and spirit ye are with Beitris Crowley and offer for *her?*"

"Because I donna care for Beitris Crowley, and well ye know it!" he said sharply. He forced himself to take a breath. "And I believe ye are more fearful of that curse than anyone at Eilean Ros tonight—"

She groaned with exasperation and covered her face with her hands.

Payton caught her by the elbow and made her look at him. "Ye fear that one of us will die before the betrothal date, but it willna happen, aye? I give ye my vow I will no' allow anything to happen to ye, no' now. *Never*, Mared."

With a groan, she shook her head and looked to the loch. "Heaven help me, ye truly donna understand!"

"But I *do*," he said, and slid his hand down her arm to her hand, and brought it to his mouth to kiss her bare knuckles. "Ye have my word I will protect ye with all that I have, lass. I will always keep ye well."

For a moment, the briefest of moments, Payton thought he saw the glisten of tears in her green eyes, but Mared abruptly jerked her hand free of his. "Ye will keep me well, is that it?" she repeated venomously. "Do ye truly believe it is the *curse* that holds me back?"

"Aye," he answered honestly.

"*Ach*, ye are a simpleton!" she cried, dismissively flicking her hand at him. "I donna *want* to be a Douglas! I'd rather die by the bloody curse than be a Douglas! I've told ye that I've no regard for ye *or* yer kin, yet ye keep on!"

His frustration was mounting, he put his hands at his waist and lowered his head, glaring at her. "Old feuds have nothing to do with us now—"

"They have *everything* to do with us now!" she cried, and suddenly held out her fist. "*Take* this. I donna want it!" She opened her fist—the *luckenbooth* was in her palm, blinking up at him.

He hadn't noticed she'd taken it from her breast until this moment and felt angry disappointment roil in his belly. "What do ye mean by this?" he asked sharply. "That is a betrothal gift!"

"But I donna want to be betrothed to ye!" she cried. "Ye force it on me as easily as ye forced the demise of my family!"

"What—"

"Donna pretend to be thickheaded! Ye brought sheep into these lochs, and now we struggle to keep our cattle. Ye *forced* the change in our fortune with yer selfish ways, and now ye would force a change to my future with yer selfish ways! I donna want to marry ye, Douglas!" she cried, flinging the *luckenbooth*. It hit him on the chest and fell to his feet, somewhere in the mud between a litter of rocks.

"I *never* wanted to marry ye!" she said vehemently. "I can scarcely bear yer presence! I donna esteem ye, I donna love ye, and I will *never* love ye, aye! Do ye hear me? *I will never love ye!* And if ye had a decent bone in yer body, ye'd cry off and release me from this damn betrothal I didna seek or want!" she sobbed. With a gasp for air, she clasped her hands together and beseeched him, "Please, I *beg* of ye, milord—donna force this on me!"

She said it with such emotion that she swayed unsteadily, and Payton unthinkingly reached out to catch her, but she jerked out of his reach. "I *beg* ye."

Rage and disappointment exploded in him, nearly blinding him with the force and conviction of it. He suddenly felt battered and raw and clenched his jaw tightly shut. In his fury, he could see her gather her *arisaidh* tightly about her, as if she feared him.

He rather feared himself and clenched and unclenched his fists to keep rein on the wave of rage that was crashing through him. He had adored her, had done everything in his power to show her that he did, had endured her disdain and her silly attempts to match him with Miss Crowley. He had shown her every courtesy, had given her every allowance, had courted her and treated her like a queen . . . but in this moment, he thought he hated her. For the first time in his life, he thought he hated this woman and frankly wanted never to see her again.

He glanced down, his mind racing, then looked up, and abruptly caught her arm in a tight grip, yanking her forward to him, so that they were nose to nose.

"What are ye doing?" she cried, struggling to free herself.

Payton tightened his grip. "And how do ye propose to repay yer debt?" he snapped. "How will ye return three *thousand* pounds to me now?"

Mared blinked. The fire in her green eyes bled out, and confusion rose up. He shoved her away from him in disgust and pointed to the drive. "Go, then. Leave me and mine."

"But—"

"No!" he roared at her. "Ye've spoken, Mared! Ye've been quite plain, ye've made yer choice, and now I shall make mine! *I* shall determine how yer debt will be repaid, and this time, ye will abide by the terms of our agreement or I'll take this matter to a court of proper authority! Now *go!"*

She hesitated briefly, then ran past him as lithely as a cat, up the grassy hill to the drive, to the Lockhart coach, where Payton could see Liam waiting, his legs braced apart. Whatever she said, Liam hurried her into the old carriage, and Payton watched them drive away.

And yet he remained at the edge of the loch a quarter of an hour more, his chest heaving with each furious breath, his heart weighing heavy, until he had managed to calm himself sufficiently to return to the *ceilidh* he had so foolishly held in her honor.

Seven

❦

$\mathcal{M}$ ared knew the moment Dudley informed her that she was wanted in the study that Payton had named his terms.

She'd been waiting for it with dreaded anticipation every moment of every day since that ignoble night she'd left Payton standing next to the loch, looking so furious and wounded all at once. She hadn't wanted to hurt him—she *did* esteem him in her own strange way—but he had forced her with his betrothal gift and his plans to announce it to the entire region that very night. And she'd panicked. . . .

Mared took one look at herself in the tarnished mirror above her dressing table, saw the dark smudges under her eyes, wrapped her *arisaidh* tightly around her, and made her way down to the family study.

On the main floor, as she and Dudley walked the long corridor to the study, Mared could hear the familiar voice of her father, and Grif's raised above his. As she reached the door to the study, she could see the train of her mother's gown, and clasping her *arisaidh* tightly in one hand, she lifted her chin and entered the room.

She could feel the force of his presence before she

actually saw him standing at the hearth, still clad in a cloak, his legs braced apart, and his hands clasped behind his back. He was as tall as Liam, but today, he seemed somehow taller, towering over them all. His gaze was wintry cold.

For a moment, Mared could not find her tongue; she felt herself blush under his intense scrutiny and looked to her mother for help. But her mother could not help her now and stared grimly at the floor.

"Come in, come in, lass," her father said wearily, and Mared forced her feet to move across the room. Father gestured to the chair next to him, and she sat, noticing only then that the entire family was present. Liam stood behind Ellie, who looked at Mared with pity. Grif was standing before the writing desk looking rather grim, and Anna was seated, her head bowed.

Mared glanced at her father and was inwardly startled to see how weary he suddenly looked—much older than his sixty years. The lines around his green eyes were pronounced, and the stubble of beard on his chin a steely gray.

He sighed. "Mared, *leannan*," he said, and leaned across to put his palm to her cheek. "Ye are too stubborn for yer own good."

She blinked in surprise, and Father dropped his hand. "What did ye think we would do, then? Did ye think three thousand pounds and more would miraculously appear to pay Laird Douglas?"

"N-no," she said quickly, and glanced at the others in the room. All of them were glaring at some inanimate object, save her mother, who looked as if she might burst into tears at any moment. She risked a glimpse of Payton, who had not moved, not so much as blinked, but continued to stare at her coldly, all the warmth in him gone. Vanished.

"Ye know we must repay our debts, aye?" Father said again, patting her hand.

"Aye." Of course she knew it. How could she possibly forget it? She'd thought of nothing else in every waking moment, searching for an answer, trying to think what they might sell to raise the money they needed to repay Payton Douglas, cursing the day they had ever borrowed from him.

"What, then, did ye think Hugh would come back to us and present us with the beastie?"

With a frown, Mared shook her head. "Hugh will no' come back to Scotland. No' ever."

"Aye, exactly," Father said, and leaned forward, so that his face was inches from hers. "So why in God's name, then, did ye refuse Douglas?"

She had prepared herself for this. "Ye know why, Father. He's a Douglas," she said calmly.

"Aye, aye, he's a Douglas, a bloody Douglas!" her father suddenly erupted, rearing back and slapping his hands against the arms of his char. "But what choice have ye left to us *now?*"

He suddenly sprang to his feet and began to pace.

"Aye, ye've made quite a fine mess of things, miss! Ye've left us with no options, ye've closed every bloody door! Would ye give over Talla Dileas before ye'd honor yer word?"

"Carson!" her mother cried, but Father waved her off.

"No, Aila, no, I willna hear yer pleas for leniency! Were it only her fancy, aye, I'd agree, she'd marry whomever she pleases. But 'tis no' her fancy! Her actions affect us all! Look what she has done! Look what she forces us to do!"

"I donna understand," Mared said, suddenly alarmed. "What have I forced ye to do?"

"Be strong now, Mared," Liam said sternly. "Ye must do yer duty for yer family."

"What duty?" she cried, coming to her feet as her heart climbed to her throat.

"Ye gave yer sacred word, Mared! And on yer word, I agreed to the terms of the loan! And now that ye've refused to honor yer word, ye leave us no choice!" her father bellowed.

Whatever Payton had done, whatever he'd demanded, Mared could feel the full force of it shake her very foundation. "What do ye mean, Father?" she helplessly insisted. "What choice?"

"What he means is that ye will still be mine," Douglas said, his voice silky and dark.

Her fear faded to fury and Mared whirled around to face him. "What have ye done? What have ye said that—"

"*No,*" he said sharply, pointing a menacing finger at her. "Ye'll no' speak to me thus. Ye will show the proper respect due yer employer."

"*What?*" Mared laughed hysterically. "What rubbish!"

"Mared," Mother said low, clasping her hands together beseechingly. "Please listen. We've no other choice."

Now Mared's heart was pounding so hard in her chest that she struggled to breathe. "Tell me," she demanded of Payton. "Tell me what ye've done."

A single brow rose over his cold gray gaze. "What *I've* done?" He flashed a grin as bleak and cold as the devil's. "I warn ye to hold yer tongue, for I willna abide insolence in my household staff."

It took a moment for his words to sink in, but Mared gasped with outrage at the same moment Grif was at her back, his arm firmly around her waist. "No, Mared," he said in her ear. "*No*. Ye will *listen* now. Ye've said enough already."

"Have ye all gone mad?" she cried, clawing at Grif's arm. "I donna belong to his household staff and I never shall, God in heaven, I never *shall!*"

"But ye do," Grif said softly, and it felt as if her blood began to empty from her veins. She gaped at Douglas and his villainous smile. He was, she understood, triumphant. She'd refused him and now he'd seek his revenge by humiliating her.

Mared abruptly twisted in Grif's arms, away from that cold, hateful smile, and pressed her cheek to her brother's shoulder. "*No*, Grif!" she pleaded on a sob. "No, no, please donna do this—he means to humiliate me."

Grif sighed sadly and put his hand to her head, holding her against him. "Listen to me now, Mared. Ye refused his suit and reneged on our debt, so now it is for Douglas to say what he will have. And he would have our cattle, or . . ." His voice trailed off, and he suddenly moved, grabbed Mared by the shoulders and pushed her back so that he could look in her eye. "He would have our cattle, which we need to survive, or he will have ye as his housekeeper for one year to satisfy the debt."

It was worse than she could have imagined. "*No!*" she shrieked, but Grif's hands held her steady. "Ye canna agree!" she cried out. "It's preposterous! Absurd! Let him whip me in the old bailey, but donna do this, Grif, *please!*"

"We gambled—*ye* gambled—and we lost, Mared!

But we are Lockharts, and Lockharts pay their debts. If ye willna honor yer own agreement, then ye will honor this for us all. Ye *will* do as he demands!"

Mared caught a sob in her throat and dropped her forehead to Grif's shoulder. "I'll walk through the fiery pits of hell before I'd serve him even a moment," she muttered miserably.

"That is no' an option," Beelzebub said at her back. "Ye may have one hour to gather yer things and make yer good-byes."

His stone cold voice infuriated her, and she abruptly pushed away from Grif, twisting about to glare at him. "Donna think ye will order me about as if I were a bloody chambermaid!"

"I will order ye about as I see fit. And when ye address me, lass," he said, walking forward so that she could see the icy glint in his eye and the set of his jaw, "ye will address me as yer laird."

Mared opened her mouth, but Liam caught her by the arm, spun her around, and gave her a healthy push toward Ellie. "Take her from here. Help her pack her things," he said gruffly and turned a murderous look to Payton.

"Ye'll no' silence me! I've scarcely begun to say what I think!" Mared cried as Ellie took firm hand of her, yanking her from the room, with her mother and Anna right behind. But before she could speak, before she could tell him what a bastard he was, she was pulled out of the study and into the corridor, and the door was shut soundly behind them.

That was when she began to sob uncontrollably.

Eight

❧·❧

$\mathcal{M}$ ared sobbed as her mother packed for her and Ellie and Anna desperately urged her to try a different tack with Douglas.

"What tack?" she groaned miserably.

"A softer hand," Anna said. "It's something Grif taught me. It is possible to slay a man with kindness."

That only made Mared wail more loudly, and she continued to sob through her farewell to her family—and particularly when Douglas assured her mother that she'd be free, just as all his servants were free on Sunday afternoons, to leave Eilean Ros and call on whomever she pleased.

Her mother hugged her, whispered in her ear to go, and Mared followed him out onto the drive, where the black coach painted with the crest of Eilean Ros waited.

The footman took her old portmanteau, and Mared hastily wiped the tears from her eyes with the corner of her plaid as she waited for the footman to open the coach door.

But when he opened the coach door, Payton stepped in front of her, and said gruffly over his shoulder, "Ye'll ride atop, with the coachman," and stepped into the luxurious interior of the coach.

The footman shut the door behind him and looked at Mared. When she didn't move, he motioned to the driver's bench and pulled his coat more closely around his throat. "Aye, there's a lass," he said kindly. "'Tis too bloody wet to dally. Come on then, step lively." And he retreated to the back of the coach.

She was mortified and wounded by the sudden and sharp turn in her situation, but Mared was too proud to let the bastard see it. Gritting her teeth, she grabbed onto the iron handles and pulled herself up to the driver's bench and gave the elderly coachman a halfhearted smile. "Looks as if it might rain, aye?"

"That it does. Ho, walk on!" he shouted at the team and sent them out of the drive at a trot.

Mared pulled her *arisaidh* over her head and stared straight ahead, refusing to look back. One day, when she had means, she would hunt Hugh MacAlister down and squeeze the very life from him.

The mist had thickened to soup by the time they drove the windy roads to Eilean Ros, and when they arrived at that grand estate, Mared was soaked through to her drawers. Payton stepped out, dry and neat, and strode purposefully to the house, his cape flapping about his ankles as he jogged up the steps and disappeared inside.

The footman—Charlie, he said his name was—helped her down from the driver's bench and handed her the portmanteau. "Just in there," he said, then jumped on the runner of the coach and slapped the side of it, indicating the coachman should move on.

As the coach rolled out of the drive, Mared looked at the door of the Douglas mansion, swallowed the lump of dread in her throat, and forced herself to walk, struggling with the heavy baggage, resorting to dragging it up the fourteen steps to the oak doors.

Beckwith, the butler, met her in the foyer. He was a small, thin man with a face that seemed permanently pinched with displeasure, and he looked at her stoically as he announced, "Ye are to wait here, Miss Lockhart." With a quick once-over, he turned on his heel and disappeared into the corridor to the right.

"Wait as if I were riffraff," she muttered and dropped her portmanteau with a *thud*, pushed the *arisaidh* from her head, and folded her arms petulantly.

Payton had her as his servant—was there really a need to treat her poorly? She glared at the grand staircase before her, each step made of stone, rising up to the first floor and an enormous candelabra, then up again, to the second. At the top of the second story was a full-length portrait of a long-dead Douglas woman, resplendent in her court dress and jaunty plaid Scots bonnet. She was smiling down at Mared, almost as if she mocked her. *"Foolish lass! Ye might have walked up these stairs a lady, but now ye'll walk up a servant."*

Mared snorted, looked down at her feet. *Diah,* how long would she be made to stand here like some forgotten piece of furniture?

Her answer came shortly thereafter with the sound of his footfall in the right corridor. She would recognize that stride anywhere—long and lean and determined. She lowered her arms, clenched her fists.

He appeared informally, another signal that her status in his eyes had changed. He wore his waistcoat and the tails of his neckcloth dangling down his chest. He hardly spared her a glance as he entered the foyer and walked to the grand staircase and began his ascent. "Just this way, Miss Lockhart," he called over his shoulder.

Mared looked at her portmanteau, then at him, jogging easily up the steps to the first landing, where he paused to turn around and look at her. "Is there a problem?"

"Aye," she said, her hands on her hips. "The luggage is a wee bit heavy."

He glanced at the bag at her feet, then at her. "Ye appear to be a strong lass and quite capable of carrying it. Come then, ye are wasting my time."

Mared gaped at him, but Payton had already turned and continued upward. She muttered her true opinion of him under her breath and leaned down, picked up the heavy bag, and started upward, wincing each time the bag banged against her leg.

When she reached the second landing, she had to pause to catch her breath and drag the back of her hand across her forehead. He made a sound of disapproval above her, and she glanced at him from the corner of her eye. He was standing on the third landing, one leg on the stairs that narrowed and went up to the servants' quarters, his arms folded sternly and impatiently across his chest.

And he was frowning. "Ye keep me waiting."

"Can ye no' have a wee bit of pity, then?" she snapped as she tried to catch her breath.

"No," he said instantly and sharply. "I've no more pity left for ye, no' even a wee bit. If ye will please hurry along, then."

"*Bloody pig,*" she whispered under her breath. She picked up her portmanteau and struggled with it to the top floor.

When she reached the last floor, where the un-
adorned corridor narrowed, Payton was waiting again.
He could wait for an eternity for all she cared, and she
put the portmanteau down and wiped her forehead
once more. He grunted, and suddenly walked back to
where she stood, took the portmanteau from her hands
as if it weighed nothing, and carried it to the last door
on the right, where he disappeared inside. With an irri-
table sigh, Mared followed him.

He had brought her to a small, whitewashed
square room, its only pleasing feature a small dormer
window that she assumed overlooked the loch. A single bed was pushed up against one wall, covered with
a worn cotton coverlet. On the opposite wall stood a
plain, three-drawer bureau in need of paint. The top
of the bureau was graced with a chipped ewer and a
basin for washing. A very small mirror was nailed to
the wall, and Mared could see from where she stood
that it was distorted.

There was no hearth, only a small charcoal brazier
beneath the window. There was one wooden chair, a
small floor mat made of sea grass, and a night table
next to the bed. On that nightstand, there were a half
dozen tapered candles stacked neatly and a single,
tarnished candlestick.

The room was positively Spartan and stifling, and
the notion that she must live within these walls for a
full year made Mared blanch. It was the very opposite
of her chamber at Talla Dileas, with its old sitting
hearth and the thick rugs, and the old, enormous
sleigh bed. The poverty of Talla Dileas was at least
comfortable—the poverty of this room made her ill.
So ill, in fact, that she leaned against the bureau for
support and stared blindly at the floor.

Payton moved her portmanteau aside and pointed to another, small door. "There's a privy in there."

A closet with a chamber pot was hardly a privy, but Mared said nothing.

He walked to the door of the room, put his hand on the old brass door handle, and glanced back at her. "I'll receive ye in the library at promptly half past ten in the morning. I'll outline yer duties then."

She could feel the tears welling in her eyes, the acidity of her frustration and helplessness churning in her belly.

"If ye require anything, ye may call on Beckwith," he said. "Good night."

She didn't look at him—she couldn't, for she felt on the verge of flinging herself at him and clawing his eyes out. She heard him walk through the door and close it, and in a moment of absolute despair and hatred, she snatched up the chipped ewer and hurled it at the door behind him. It shattered in a loud burst as pieces and chips of pottery fell to the floor. "Bloody bastard!" she shrieked.

The door flew open so hard that it banged against the wall as Payton stormed in, striding across the shards of clay, reaching Mared before she could react.

He grabbed her by the arm and pushed her against the wall, then steadied her with his body and a hand to her face.

He was breathing so hard that she could see the flare of his nostrils, feel his hot breath on her skin. His gray eyes glinted with unfathomable wrath. He was a man she'd never known, an angry, fire-breathing man.

"Ye have extended yer debt to a year and a day, aye?" he said hoarsely, his voice trembling with his rage. "And for every outburst such as this, I'll add another day, and another, and another, until ye have no hope of ever going back to yer bloody Lockharts!"

Mared caught a sob in her throat; her eyes filled so quickly with hot tears that she could barely see him. "Unhand me," she said, through gritted teeth, trying to twist out of his grasp.

"*Unhand* ye?" He chuckled wickedly, tipped his head forward, so that his lips were against her temple, his breath warm on her cheek. "I donna think ye understand yet, *leannan*. I'll bloody well take ye in hand whenever and however I please. I *own* ye now, for ye'd no' have it any other way. Ye have no one to thank but yerself for this folly, and ye'll receive no' a wit of sympathy from me. I've lost all regard for ye. I care nothing about ye, other than how ye manage my house. And if ye think to destroy my property, I will exact payment from ye as I do now . . . with yer servitude."

"I. Will. *Never*. Be yer servant!" she hissed.

"No?" He moved his head, so that his lips were just a moment from hers, and Mared was instantly and regrettably reminded of another kiss that had almost dropped her to her knees.

"But ye already *are*, lass. Yer father has kept his bloody cows and given his daughter to me. Aye, ye'll serve me, Mared," he said, and licked the salty tears from her lips. "Ye'll do as I say, when I say it. I'll take ye in hand when I please," he said, and brushed his lips against hers, so lightly, so airily, that her skin tingled savagely. "I'll have ye in my bed if I so desire. Or perhaps," he said, pausing to flick his tongue against her lips, "I'll forget ye even exist." And then he silenced any protest with his mouth.

He kissed her. His tongue swept inside her mouth as if he owned it, his hand found her breast. Mared hated him then, hated him with everything she had. Her heart pounded against her chest and she struggled fiercely beneath his hold on her, finally wrenching her face free. "It will be a cold day in hell before I come near yer bloody bed," she spat.

Payton abruptly let go and pushed away from her, as if he was disgusted by her.

"I hate ye, Payton Douglas," she said shakily, her chest heaving. "I will *always* hate ye."

His eyes darkened. "Aye. Ye've made that perfectly clear," he said, and dragged the back of his hand across his mouth. "But I damn well donna care any longer." He pivoted away from her and strode from the room, slamming the door shut behind him.

Mared stood there a moment, her hand over her mouth to keep herself from screaming, and listened to his footfall move away from her door. When she could hear it no longer, she released her sobbing, and clutching her arms tightly around her body, she slid down the wall onto her haunches and sobbed like a bairn.

How long she sobbed, she really didn't know, for there was no timepiece in her possession, but the coals in the brazier had gone cold when she was finally spent from the sobbing and stopped. She wiped her nose and her eyes and put her hand in her pocket and pulled out the small phial Donalda had given her.

Nine

❦

*P*ayton did not sleep well.

He hated that he'd reacted with such anger, hated even worse that he still could not seem to keep his hands from her . . . especially now that she was under his protection. His emotions, he realized, were so close to the surface that they were bubbling through—anger, desire—it made for a rather toxic combination.

This was, he was realizing well too late, a fatuous, thick-witted plan. It was imperative therefore, he reasoned, that he keep his distance from her.

But Mared startled him when he entered the library the next morning at a quarter past ten, for she was already there, standing at the bookshelves. She was perusing the many books his family had collected over the centuries, her hands clasped behind her back, a long braid of hair reaching almost to her waist, and wearing an old gown the color of a Scottish sunset he'd seen her wear many times.

He instantly suspected chicanery.

She'd have a bloody bad time of enacting her scheme, whatever it was, for this morning his mood was all the more sour, his patience thin, and he prepared to do battle as he strode across the room.

But much to his great astonishment, she turned when she heard him enter and smiled. A full and glorious smile, complete with sunny dimples and the very same sparkling green eyes that came to him in his dreams from time to time. "*Maduinn math,* milord. Good morning."

Payton stopped dead in his tracks and eyed her suspiciously. "Good morning." She nodded; Payton glared at her a moment longer. She smiled again.

No. Whatever the chit was about, he'd not be so easily lured into her trap. He stalked on to the library desk and sat. "Thank ye for being prompt. I hardly expected it. Please be seated," he said, indicating a chair directly across the desk from him.

She did not so much as frown, but crossed the room and sat, her spine straight, her hands in her lap, her smile bright. "Ye've a lot of books," she lightly remarked. "It's quite an extensive library ye have."

He said nothing, just observed her skeptically as she calmly returned his gaze. Quite a change in demeanor from the *banshee* of last evening. Oh, aye, she was up to something, he was certain of it.

"My cousin Sarah shall take her leave of Eilean Ros today. Ye shall attend her," he began, watching Mared closely for any sign of mutiny.

"Very well," she said pleasantly.

Very well his arse. Payton's frown went deeper, and he steepled his fingers, openly studying her. "Miss Douglas will give ye the keys to the stores. I shall expect a competent handling of the household accounts."

One of her brows rose above the other, but Mared smiled and nodded.

"Ye are to wear the black-and-white uniform Mrs.

Craig wore. Miss Douglas will instruct ye as to where they are kept, aye?"

"Aye. A uniform," she said with a resolute nod.

"Now, as to yer duties," he said, and abruptly leaned forward, propping his arms on the desk, his gaze narrowed on hers. "I am a practical laird, Miss Lockhart. I've no need for squads of servants. We've the usual groundsmen and livestock handlers. In addition, I've Beckwith, with whom ye are acquainted, and under him, there are three footmen, a coachman, a groom, and a gamekeeper. We've a cook, and she has the help of a scullery maid. In addition to yerself, there are two chambermaids. Ye will oversee their work in the performance of yer everyday duties."

"All right, then."

She hadn't moved, hadn't even flinched, just kept observing him with that serene countenance, as if she fully accepted her fate. Bloody hell if she did. This was Mared Lockhart before him, not some shy young chambermaid.

Payton leaned forward a little closer and narrowed his eyes again. "I shall expect ye to keep Eilean Ros as clean as if it were Talla Dileas. I shall expect the floors to be polished and scrubbed, the carpets beaten and swept, the furniture and fixtures kept free of dust. Ye shall launder my clothing and attend the master rooms morning and night, aye? And ye will attend the guest rooms. In short, Miss Lockhart, ye will see to it that this house shines like a golden bauble. Do ye quite understand?"

"Quite," she said politely, but he was certain he detected a slight stiffening of her spine.

He leaned back, frowning still. "Forgive me . . . but ye seem remarkably improved from yer rather dramatic arrival, aye? May I trust that we are in complete agreement as to the terms of yer service here?"

He could see her swallow, could see her force herself to smile.

"I couldna rightly say we are in *agreement*, milord, as that would require the suspension of all rational thought. But ye might say that I have accepted where the winds of fate have carried me, and I've determined there is no point in arguing it, for if we do, we shall both remain angry, and that serves neither of us."

Interesting. Was it possible that she had, through some divine intervention, accepted it? No. Impossible. She was far too obstinate and headstrong. Of course he couldn't trust her. He knew Mared, knew how unconquerably proud she could be. . . . It had been one of the many things he'd once admired about her.

Now all he'd admire was her ability to clean his house.

"Ye may take yer meals with the rest of the staff in the servants' dining room," he continued curtly, "and now ye are dismissed to attend Miss Douglas." He stood and turned away from those unreadable green eyes and strode from the room, reminded once again that while he might be enticed by her appearance, he could not abide what was inside her.

When Mared heard the door close, she clenched her fists and banged them on the arms of her chair as she dropped her head back against it, her eyes closed, groaning. She'd never endure this. *Never!*

After drinking the potion Donalda had given her, she'd spent a sleepless night, hoping for a miracle. When one did not come, she considered Anna and

Ellie's advice to slay him with kindness. As she could think of no other practical way to slay him, she had reasoned, in the wee hours of the morning, that it was good advice. Payton expected her defiance—he'd never expect her compliance. He'd not *want* her compliance, as it would bleed all the joy from his degradation of her.

Yet she'd not bargained for her compliance coming at such a high personal cost. Another large piece of her pride had broken off and splintered into dust.

She abruptly vaulted out of her chair and began to pace. *"Ye will see to it that this house shines like a golden bauble,"* she mimicked him. *"And now ye are dismissed.* Bloody rotten tyrant," she muttered. "A repugnant, mean-spirited, slubberdegullion, that one—"

The door swung open; Mared gasped and whirled about, her heart pounding.

It was Beckwith, his face looking even more pinched than usual this morning. "His lordship would have ye attend Miss Douglas forthwith."

"Oh." She glanced around the room, nervously ran her hand along the seam of her gown, wondering how she might endure *this*.

"I believe he intended for ye to go straightaway," Beckwith added coolly.

Mared frowned at him. "I *know*," she said and followed him out of the room, falling in beside him as they strode down the corridor.

She glanced at the butler from the corner of her eye. She judged him to be just a few years older than she. He was a proud man, she could see that in the tilt of his bony jaw and the way his neckcloth was tied to perfection with what seemed the goal of strangulation. "So then, Beckwith . . ." she tried. "We are to be fellow soldiers, aye? Partners of a kind, as it were?"

To her surprise, Beckwith stopped midstride and turned to face her, his lips pursed unpleasantly. "I beg yer pardon but I think *no'*, Miss Lockhart."

"Oh," she said, and thought she should explain to him that contrary to what he might think, she was no longer a member of the Quality.

Before she could say a word, however, Beckwith unabashedly and enthusiastically continued, "I am the chief man in the laird's employ, which means that all the other servants in his employ answer directly to me." He gave her a mean little smile. "That would include *yerself*, Miss Lockhart. Henceforth, ye shall know me as *Mr.* Beckwith."

Mared blinked in surprise.

He turned sharply about and started up the grand stairs. "Do hurry along," he said haughtily. "Ye've kept Miss Douglas waiting long enough, ye have."

Her thoughts and her tongue frozen in astonishment, Mared picked up her hem and hurried after him.

On the second floor, Beckwith stopped before a white door with a painted porcelain knob and rapped lightly. A chambermaid in a white cap answered.

"Stand aside, Rodina," Beckwith said brusquely.

The dark-eyed girl curtsied and stepped aside, eyeing Mared curiously as Beckwith crossed the threshold and bowed. "Miss Douglas, may I present the new housekeeper, Miss Lockhart."

"Oh, is she here, then?" Sarah Douglas chirped from somewhere inside the room.

Beckwith gave Mared a look; she swallowed the last lump of her pride and stepped inside the room.

It was painted sky blue. The walls were made of big square panels and the ceiling cheerfully adorned with papier-mâché ropes and bells painted white. It was a huge room. There were several trunks scattered about, and at the far end, an enormous mahogany vanity, one that, had it been at Talla Dileas, the Lockharts would have easily sold for one hundred pounds.

But Miss Douglas had brought quite a lot of clothing with her, and when Mared joined her she was, apparently, having some trouble deciding which of her many traveling gowns to wear for the drive to Edinburgh. Another plump chambermaid was holding up two gowns. Judging by her pained expression, she'd been holding the gowns for a long time.

"Ah, there ye are, Miss Lockhart," Miss Douglas said with a sigh, glancing over her shoulder. "Ye may leave us, Beckwith."

He gave her a click of the heels and a nod, and quietly quit the room.

"Honestly, I can't decide," she said, turning her attention to the gowns again, and glanced at Mared. "What is yer opinion, Miss Lockhart? Which of them goes well with my coloring?"

"The blue," Mared said without hesitation or thought, but in the interest of leaving this room as quickly as possible.

"The blue? Indeed? I thought perhaps the yellow," Miss Douglas said uncertainly, and stood back to study them critically, seemingly unaware that the poor chambermaid was struggling to keep them aloft for her inspection.

"The yellow is quite nice as well," Mared said. "But I think ye must choose quickly, miss, lest the maid lose the use of her arms."

"What?" Miss Douglas asked, then glanced at the girl. "Oh!" she said, suddenly aware of the poor creature, and nodded firmly. "The blue, then. Ye will dress me," she said, pointing to the plump chambermaid, and returned to her vanity, plopping down on the brocade bench.

"Come in, come in, Miss Lockhart," she said, leaning forward to examine her face closely in the mirror. "We'll not accomplish a blessed thing with ye so far away." She leaned back, turned her head slightly left, then right. "So he's gone and put ye to work as the housekeeper, has he?"

"He has," Mared said brightly so that she might hide the ire she felt as she walked into the middle of the room.

"Very good. It's better this way. Ye can repay yer family's debt and be done with it."

She could be done with it, all right, and refrained from reminding Miss Douglas that her cousin was an ogre of the highest order who had convinced himself of his own self-importance.

"'Tis better this way," Miss Douglas said again with a pert nod. "*Infinitely* better for all parties involved, I should think."

"*All* parties?" Mared asked, unable to hold her tongue. "And what would ye mean by that?"

Miss Douglas looked at her again and blinked innocently. "*Mean?* Isn't it obvious? I meant that ye are really in no position to be the wife of a Douglas laird, are ye? I suppose I mean only that—it would have been a grave mistake on Payton's part to go through with that ridiculous betrothal."

"There was no betrothal, but had there been, the grave mistake would have been mine," Mared said tightly. "The Lockharts are sworn enemies of the Douglases."

"I beg your pardon?" Miss Douglas asked with a laugh. "This has nothing to do with the history of the Lockharts or the Douglases. It is simply a matter of fact that Payton is a laird and a man of property and significant means. It wouldn't do for him to marry a woman of . . ." She paused in her perusal of herself to flick her gaze over Mared. "Of *insufficient* means."

Mared seethed at her insult. "The Lockhart *means* were made insufficient only by the actions of yer cousin."

Miss Douglas laughed lightly and twisted on her bench to have a look at Mared directly. "That's patently ridiculous, Miss Lockhart, and I think ye must know it! Everyone around the lochs knows that yer father has been steadily losing ground with his old ways and his notion of buying out the crofters, particularly when there is nothing to be gained from it but more debt. Had Payton not brought sheep to the lochs, certainly Mr. Sorley would have done so. I've heard he intends to bring some up from the Borders before the autumn." She turned away, picked up something from her vanity, then held up a ring of keys. "Ye'll be needing these," she said.

In a supreme show of strength, Mared forced herself to walk across the room and take the keys, fighting the urge to toss them out the window. But she managed, and instead, she smiled and said, "Ye've come to know quite a lot about the lochs all the way from Edinburra, have ye no', Miss Douglas?"

Miss Douglas bestowed a very dark frown on Mared. "I will forgive ye, Miss Lockhart, for not understanding yer place. But were ye a housekeeper in Edinburra, ye'd be dismissed for such impudence. Now then. Will ye please inspect the trunks and assure me that all is properly done and nothing is misplaced? I've scarcely had a moment to supervise the work."

She said it as if the two young chambermaids were not in the room and missed the look of pure contempt that passed between them.

Mared did not miss it and pressed her lips together to keep herself from chastising Miss Douglas as she was wont to do more often than not—the woman had absolutely no regard for anyone but herself.

She walked to the first trunk. It was open, and from it spilled silk drawers and camisoles, brocade and poplin gowns, embroidered slippers, Spencer jackets, and nightclothes. How could Miss Douglas possibly miss *anything* amid so many articles of clothing? Mared bent over, stuffed everything haphazardly into the trunk, and shut it with a slight kick of her foot.

She straightened, winked slyly at the chambermaids, and announced cheerfully, "All is in order."

"Splendid!" Miss Douglas said airily, and stood, indicating she was ready to be dressed. "By the by, Miss Lockhart, I have left two old gowns in the dressing room. One is gold, the other a pale cream silk. They require some repair, and I should think a letting out of the seams, as ye are thicker than me. If ye are capable of the repair, ye may claim them for yer own use, for I've no need of them."

Fabulous, Mared thought. They'd make bonny beds for her dogs.

"In addition, ye'll find the housekeeping uniforms in the wardrobe of the first room on the third floor.

There should be two in all. Mrs. Craig was buried in the third."

"Thank ye," Mared muttered.

"All right, then. I've only these few things here when I've finished dressing." She discarded her dressing gown and stood with her arms out wide, as the poor chambermaid struggled to fit the blue gown over her head.

Mared rolled her eyes and proceeded to gather up the last of Miss Douglas's things, which the thinner of the two chambermaids took from her with a smile. So Mared stood feeling useless, until there was a rap at the door.

"Answer, Miss Lockhart," Miss Douglas commanded from the bow of her ship.

Mared walked to the door and flung it open, and her false heart leapt to her throat.

Payton was on the other side, leaning against the doorjamb, one leg crossed over the other ankle, arms folded across his chest. At present, she utterly despised him. But the man certainly had a way of looking entirely too masculine. He could, occasionally, make her rather weak in the knees. He could, apparently, do so at this very moment, even as she stood despising him.

He frowned when she did not speak immediately. "Have ye forgotten how to address yer laird, Miss Lockhart?"

Victory through kindness. "Of course no'. How do ye do, milord?" she asked, and sank into a very deep curtsey.

He watched her rise up. "That's a bit too lavish an address, would ye no' agree?"

Mared smiled. "If ye say it is, milord."

Payton frowned.

Mared smiled harder.

"Oh, Payton! Is it ye, then? *Diah!* Just a moment—I am being dressed," Miss Douglas called.

He sighed, shifted his gaze to Mared, who could not help the impertinent smile on her lips—she so enjoyed seeing his displeasure.

"What is it, then?" he growled, obviously succumbing to the pressure of her kindness. "Why do ye stand and gawk? Ye should see to yer mistress."

"Oh, I rather suppose I should!" she chirped and turned away from the door and marched into the room, just as Miss Douglas spoke.

"Payton, do come in. I'm quite decent now," she said.

Payton pushed past Mared.

His cousin was standing in the middle of the room with the chambermaid on her knees, straightening the hem of her traveling gown. "I feared ye'd forgotten that I am to leave today," she said, smiling at Payton.

"I'd no' forget, Sarah." He walked across the room to her, kissed her lightly on the cheek. "I'm sorry to see ye take yer leave—it seems as if ye belong at Eilean Ros."

"Don't be silly, darling. I belong in Edinburra!" she trilled happily. "I do so miss the society there."

He smiled thinly and sprawled lazily across her chaise longue, propping himself on one elbow and letting his boots hang off the end as he watched the maid straighten Miss Douglas's hem. "I owe ye a debt of gratitude for coming to my aid when Mrs. Craig died, Sarah. I canna thank ye enough."

"Why ever thank me?" she asked laughingly. "Ye resolved your problems all on yer own. I rather despaired that ye would, for there is no good help to be had in these parts."

Another look flowed between the two chamber-maids.

"And now, *mo ghraidh,* as we've found a suitable replacement for yer Mrs. Craig, the only thing left is to find ye a suitable match," Miss Douglas blithely continued. "I do wish ye would so that I might rest easy in Edinburra," she added, and satisfied with her hem, she shooed the chambermaid away and went to stand in front of the floor-length mirror.

"I'm really rather fond of Miss Crowley," she continued as she admired herself, turning this way and that. "She'd be a bonny mistress of Eilean Ros."

That comment startled Mared so thoroughly that she dropped the silver hand mirror she was holding, and it landed with a loud *thud* on the floor.

Everyone in the room turned to look at her. With a shrug, she smiled nervously. "How clumsy of me."

"Have a care, Miss Lockhart," Miss Douglas sniffed.

Mared frowned down at the mirror. This was insanity. She *wanted* Payton to offer for Beitris . . . at least she had until he'd imprisoned her and forced her into indentured servitude. Now she wasn't entirely certain what she wanted.

It didn't help that Payton had leaned back on the chaise and propped his hands behind his head to watch her. "Perhaps," he said, his gaze steady on her, "I'll have her and her family to supper."

Mared instantly stooped down to retrieve the blasted mirror. She could feel her face flaming— *Beitris, here?* Her good friend would see her as nothing more than a lowly servant! And to think she'd once sought to put Beitris before this detestable fool! Oh, and how very well he knew it, damn him!

"That would be delightful, Payton!" Miss Douglas cooed. "I do so think Miss Crowley would be a perfect match for ye. She's quite sweet tempered and very well behaved. Do ye think she is? A good match, that is?"

"Aye," he said, still watching Mared when she popped up again, holding the silver mirror. "None better around the lochs. Miss Crowley shall make a fine wife."

Mared gaped at him. He lifted a brow, silently challenging her. But one of the chambermaids walked by and gave Mared a bit of a nudge and a warning look that jarred her back to her senses and her place. She tossed the mirror into one of the open trunks.

"Well I, for one, am quite happy to hear ye say so," Miss Douglas said, oblivious to anything but her reflection in the mirror. "There was a time when I despaired of ye making a poor decision," she said, leaning forward to pinch her cheeks. "And now that ye've set that matter to rights, I shall expect to receive a letter from ye soon, relaying the happiest of news."

"Aye," he said, and suddenly gained his feet. "I shall leave ye to yer dressing. I'll be in the foyer when ye are ready to depart."

"Very well," Miss Douglas said as she busily admired herself in the vanity mirror. Payton kissed her cheek once more. When he turned toward the door, he caught Mared's eye and, holding her gaze without expression, quit the room.

Ten

✥•✥

It seemed like hours later that Miss Douglas's many things were finally packed. The woman had more possessions than most families could possibly own.

When all the trunks were at last carried down, Mared stayed behind to clean the room. By virtue of her family's declining fortune, Mared and her mother had learned to clean and to do so efficiently, for old castles were rather hard to keep tidy. But she had no intention of truly cleaning a blooming thing in this house and tidied Miss Douglas's room by tossing a few things here and there, behind chairs and under the bed. And then, feeling quite emotionally and physically exhausted, she lay down on Miss Douglas's bed and had a bit of a nap.

She awoke a half hour later, quite refreshed, and picked up the two discarded gowns Miss Douglas had left behind, wadded them like dirty linens, stuffed them under her arm, and took them to her room. She'd decide what to do with them later.

In the first room on the third floor, which was bare save one wardrobe, she found the housekeeper's uniform: black gown with long black sleeves, white apron, and a white cap with black trim that Mared, in silent defiance, refused to wear. But once she donned the uniform and peered at herself in the mirror she thought the uniform was not as bad as it might have been, and thought it really went rather well with her walking boots. It did not, however, fit her very well. It was too snug in the bosom and too wide at the hip. But Mared scarcely cared—she'd wear rags if she could.

Dressed in the housekeeper's gown, she determined she should meet the two chambermaids and make a proper introduction. She wandered the entire house, finally finding the two lassies on the basement floor, folding linens. Both curtsied quickly when Mared paused in the doorway.

"Good day. I'm Mared," she said, walking into the linen closet, her hand extended.

The small, dark-haired girl introduced herself as Rodina. Una was the chubby lass with the red hair and apple cheeks. They both looked at her expectantly.

"Well then!" Mared said brightly, clasping her hands together and rocking a bit on her feet. "I'm not entirely certain how this shall unfold, but if ye've any questions of me, please do ask."

Rodina and Una looked at one another. Una blurted, "Is it true, Miss Lockhart? Were ye to marry the laird?"

That was most certainly not what Mared had thought they might ask, and it caught her off guard. "*No,*" she said, blushing furiously, damn it. "The Lockharts and Douglases are mortal enemies—that is why I've been enslaved here as his housekeeper."

"*Enslaved?*" Una echoed incredulously, and looked at Rodina.

"Mortal enemies?" Rodina asked Mared, looking quite confused.

"*Enemies,*" Mared insisted. "And quite firmly enslaved. So then! What are we to do?" she asked brightly in a frantic attempt to change the subject.

The two lassies gaped at her. "Ye donna know?" Una asked.

"I've no' the slightest idea," Mared cheerfully admitted.

More confused than ever, the two girls haltingly told Mared they were to clean the dowager's study after finishing the linens. When Mared confessed to being a wee bit surprised, as there was not now or had there ever been a dowager at Eilean Ros that she was aware of, the girls nodded.

"Aye," Una said, unabashedly rolling her eyes. "'Tis in the north wing that is seldom used. Miss Douglas required the cleaning of that wing every week."

Did she indeed? Mared knew from her experience at Talla Dileas that when one didn't have the required number of servants to maintain a very large house, one shut off as many rooms as possible. If Miss Douglas wanted them open, she could bloody well come back from Edinburgh and clean them.

She smiled genuinely for the first time that day, and asked, "Did Mrs. Craig keep furniture coverings about? I'm no' of a mind to be dusting and cleaning a room that no one will see for a year, aye?"

Rodina and Una blinked at her, then at one another, and then turned twin smiles to Mared. "Aye!" they agreed in unison.

They spent the afternoon inspecting many of the rooms of Eilean Ros, during which time Mared could not help but be awed by the wealth of Douglas. Every room boasted expensive artwork and valuable knick-knacks made of china, porcelain, or gold; fine Oriental rugs and French furniture; and frankly, Mared had never seen so many beeswax candles in her life. There was not a single paraffin candle in the lot of them, and there was a room below that held nothing but beeswax candles.

The magnitude of wealth in this house took her breath away. It was, in a sense, unthinkable. When she'd been a young lass roaming the hills around Talla Dileas, she used to imagine she was someone else entirely—a lass with no curse, obviously. But rich, too. Born of the aristocracy. Worldly and well traveled and beautiful and clothed in silks from Paris. She would have imagined herself in a house just like this, too, surrounded by fawning men.

Instead, she was watching Rodina and Una dust and cover the furniture. Their industrious nature was why she eventually rose from the armchair where she was resting and sat herself at a writing desk to pen a letter to the Dull and Stodgy laird.

She had determined, with Rodina and Una's help, that at least three-quarters of the rooms in the house were so seldom used that it made little sense to keep them open. She'd studiously made a list of those to be closed off—at Una's insistence, for Una in particular seemed to think the laird's permission was required.

Mared was not going to *ask*, precisely. But she did feel it was her duty to inform. And so determined was she in her letter that she was surprised when Una begged her leave to attend supper.

"Supper?" Mared said, looking at a Louis IV mantel clock. "He's no' yet rung for tea."

"He doesna take tea unless he has guests, miss," Rodina said. "It's only the laird, and he prefers an early supper. Early to bed, early to rise, he says."

"Seems perfectly tedious," Mared opined. But Una explained that she set the servants' dining table, and that they all dined together at six.

"As early as that?" Mared exclaimed. "Little wonder there is no tea served in this house. What would be the point of it?"

"Aye, miss," Una said.

Mared shrugged and turned back to her letter. "I suppose, then, I shall join ye promptly at six." And indeed, a half hour later, Mared made her way to the servants' dining room, stopping in the main foyer to lay the note for His Highness on a silver tray where she gathered Beckwith collected the post, and then onward, to the room where several of the other servants were gathered.

The coachman was already seated and nodded politely to Mared. The cook, an elderly woman with gray hair and one good eye, bustled in with a large platter of what looked like lamb chops. She paid Mared little heed at all, except to tell her that they were in need of flour, and that for a couple of shillings and a tart, the gamekeeper's boy would go to Aberfoyle on the morrow to fetch it.

Rodina appeared with a platter of leeks behind a pale scullery maid who curtsied politely. "Ye may sit at the end of the table, miss, across from Mr. Beckwith," Rodina said as she placed the platter of leeks on the table. And as Mared took her seat, Beckwith entered. On his heels were the three footmen. They were a collegial group, obviously, laughing and shoving playfully as they entered the room.

"Is it to be all of us, then?" asked the footman who had introduced himself last night as Charlie.

"Aye, all save Willie. The laird has no' come in," Beckwith said as he took his seat and nodded curtly at Mared.

"Gone off with a lass, has he?" a tall, handsome footman asked and winked at Mared as he laughed with the other men, until a stern look from Beckwith made him move on, around the table, to his chair.

"He's sweet on Miss Crowley," Rodina haughtily informed them as she wiped her hands on her apron. "I heard him say so this very morn."

"In his bed again, Rodina?" another footman asked, and Rodina slapped him on the back of his head, much to the delight of the other footmen.

"Miss Crowley, aye," the tall footman said. "She's a bonny one." He made a crude outline of breasts against his chest, which provoked another round of hearty laughter from most everyone.

Save Beckwith. "Alan!" he snapped. "I'll thank ye to mind yer manners in the presence of the women! And here is our new housekeeper to witness ye behaving so badly!"

Alan glanced at Mared, openly sizing her up as the others took their seats around the large table.

"The new housekeeper is a far sight bonnier than the last," Alan said, smiling at Mared.

"Oh, Alan!" Una exclaimed, frowning. "And Mrs. Craig no' yet cold in her grave!"

"That is quite enough!" Beckwith admonished them. "May I present to ye Miss Lockhart of Talla Dileas. Ye will introduce yerselves according to yer rank," he said and picked up a linen napkin, stuffed it into his collar, and nodded at Una to pass him the lamb.

They went around the table. Charlie and Alan greeted her with big smiles and leering eyes, but Jamie, the third footman, seated on her right, looked at her skeptically and said little as the first course was served.

The coachman, Mr. Haig, nodded politely and informed her that the young groom, William, did not, as a rule, dine with the others, lest there was a visitor. "And then again, the laird, he comes round late many nights," he informed her.

The cook, Mrs. Mackerell, and the scullery maid, Moreen, said little.

It wasn't until the main course of lamb chops and oatmeal bannocks was eaten that Jamie leaned back in his chair and studied Mared with a smirk. "Ye're her, are ye no'? The accursed one?"

That certainly brought the conversation to a grinding halt, and Mared slowly lowered her fork. "I beg yer pardon?"

"Ye're cursed by *a' diabhal*, aye?" he asked, ignoring the gasps of the cook as he eyed her like a curiosity in the Glasgow circus.

"Jamie!" Beckwith said sharply, but the footman was undeterred. "Beggin' yer pardon, Mr. Beckwith, but I heard all of it the night of the *ceilidh*," he said, and leaned forward with a dark grin. "They say ye are a witch," he challenged her.

Mared couldn't help but laugh. "A *witch!* Do they really say so? Then I've come up in the world, sir."

"Then ye confess to being a witch, Miss Lockhart?" he asked, his eyes narrowing.

She laughed again. "If I were a witch, sir, do ye think I'd seek work as a housekeeper?"

Everyone but Jamie laughed at that—but her levity

did nothing to quell the sudden interest in her, and from Mrs. Mackerell, a look of horror and revulsion.

This was the moment she despised, the moment when people around her realized there might be something horribly contemptible or frightening about her, and she could feel a cold, empty space suddenly surrounding her, forcing her apart from the rest of the world. It was a moment like a thousand other moments in her life that had long since settled into a distant hum, for she'd learned long ago, when she was just a child, that there was no point in sulking about it. She did what she always did—she smiled down the table and said with all confidence, "I'm no' a witch."

"A sorceress, then," Jamie insisted.

"No, no' a sorceress," she scoffed playfully. "A *troll.*"

Moreen tittered at that.

"I live beneath the old bridge over the water in Glen Ketrich. Ye know the one, aye? I've a few wee goblins to tend the garden, but mostly, it's just us trolls," she said lightly.

Alan, God bless him, laughed and said, "Aye, I know the bridge. I think the henwife lives there, too, does she no'?"

"Aye!" Mared said brightly. "Why, she's the housekeeper—who do ye think taught me, then?"

Everyone laughed at that; even Mr. Beckwith smiled.

"If ye're no' a witch," Jamie doggedly pressed on, "then why are ye here? Ye are a Lockhart, aye? Quality, ye are. But 'tis the daughter of a Lockhart," he said, turning excitedly to the others, "who is cursed until she looks in the eye of *a' diabhal*—"

"Belly," Mared said with a smile, resigning herself

to the notion that he might as well recite the curse correctly if he was to mention it at all.

"Eh, what?" Jamie asked, startled.

"The daughter of a Lockhart must look in the belly of the beast. No' his eye." At Jamie's look of confusion, she sighed. "If ye are to tell my secrets, Jamie, I'd have ye tell them correctly. 'Tis said that the daughter of a Lockhart will no' marry until she looks into the belly of the beast," she informed them, "which *ye* may take to mean the devil, but for all I know, I should look in the belly of an old *coo!*"

Alan laughed again, but none of the others laughed. They just looked at her curiously, their fascination plainly evident.

"'Tis true, then," Jamie said, his voice lower, his eyes fixed on her. "They say any man who comes round with the intent of offering marriage to her will lose his life . . . or she hers," he said ominously and glanced around at the others. "Ye recall his lordship fell off the terrace the night of the ball? He was no' alone on that terrace—'tis common knowledge. And it's right odd that the balustrade would give way as it did that night."

"Odd, indeed," Mared said and tapped him on the arm. "But ye forget one important fact, sir. The laird was no' intent on offering for me."

"But . . . Miss Douglas said that he was!" Una whispered, wide-eyed.

"That's quite enough!" Beckwith said sharply, slapping his hand down on the table and startling them all. "I willna abide any tales of witches and fairies, and furthermore, the laird was no' set to offer for *any* lass. If there is to be an offer, it will likely be for Miss Crowley, and ye—"

He stopped, quickly raising a hand for everyone to remain silent. They all heard it then—the tingling of the bell. "He's arrived," Beckwith said, and stood abruptly. "Jamie," he said. "Ye are with me."

Jamie did not hesitate to rise and toss his napkin aside and follow Beckwith out.

The rest of them began gathering plates and serving platters. Mared did, too, but as she walked into the kitchen, she noticed Mrs. Mackerell quickly crossing herself.

Eleven

❧❧

$\mathscr{P}$ayton had ridden out with Sarah's coach, then had kept on riding to get as far from Eilean Ros as possible. He could not imagine now what he'd been thinking when he'd conjured up this preposterous scheme. Oh, aye, he wanted some revenge, but he took no pleasure in Mared's anger or her tears as he thought he would. And now she would bedevil him—inexplicably cheerful, entirely inept as a housekeeper, and even worse, those green eyes were now everywhere in his house.

He rode about the vast acreage of his estate looking at sheep and calling on tenants, trying desperately to clear his mind. But as it was obvious those hearty souls had more important work to do than speculate with him about the date of the first frost, he'd gone on to Aberfoyle. After two generous drams of whiskey at the local tavern, he called to Finella, a serving wench he knew intimately, and proceeded upstairs with her.

In the room, he locked the door at his back, turned to a smiling Finella, who was well accustomed to their couplings, and was already massaging her breast in anticipation of what was to come.

"Undress," he commanded her and stood there,

his back to the door, watching her as she disrobed. It was something he enjoyed, watching a woman remove her clothing a piece at a time, but for once, Finella's disrobing did not spark the least bit of interest in him.

And again, when he sank between Finella's fleshy thighs and put his mouth to her large breast, her body did not arouse his usual lusty response. It was, he thought indignantly, Mared he thought of, Mared he saw when he closed his eyes and plunged into Finella.

And it was that abominably angry kiss he thought of, too—the moment he had lost control and taken her lips in anger.

The memory made his tryst laborious—it seemed forever before he found his release, long after Finella had found hers and lost interest. But he wouldn't stop. He *couldn't* stop. It seemed a do-or-die mission, as if completing this single act would prove that Mared hadn't effectively neutered him.

When he at last found his pitiful release, Finella wiggled out from beneath him and began to gather up her clothing. "Beggin' yer pardon, milord, but they'll be looking for me below," she said apologetically and slipped a foot into her stocking, which she rolled up her leg as her breasts swung from her chest.

Lying naked on top of the linens, his head propped up on a stack of pillows, Payton reached for one breast and fingered the nipple absently.

"If ye'll pardon me saying, milord, you donna seem yerself today," Finella observed as she moved to fetch her other stocking.

It was true. He hadn't been himself in more than a fortnight, since the ball. Worse, he'd never, not in his thirty-two years on this earth, not once thought of sex as tedious. He leaned over the bed, picked up his trousers, and fished a five-pound banknote from his pocket and wordlessly handed it to Finella.

Her eyes grew round; she eagerly took it. "Ye're right generous, milord."

"And ye are patient," he said wearily.

"I had a patron much like yerself once," she said as she stuck the banknote in the top of her stockings and picked up her chemise. "A fancy lord, he was. Never gave me more than a few shillings," she said as she wiggled into her chemise and picked up her dress. "But one day, nigh on Easter, he came to the inn and stayed all night, he did."

She paused, pulled her gown over her head, then whirled around, and sat on the edge of the bed so that he might button her. "Aye, and?" Payton asked lazily as he buttoned her gown.

"The very next morn, he gave me three full pounds!" she exclaimed.

"Ye did something quite memorable, I'd wager."

"Oh no," she said, standing once Payton had finished buttoning her. "'Twas naugh' but the usual bit of ruttin'. Yet he gave me the three pounds for it all the same, and I never saw him again." With that, she stuffed the banknote Payton had given her into her bosom. "Will I no' see ye again, milord?"

"Aye, of course ye will."

She frowned a little and shook her head. "I donna think I will. Pity, that—I rather like what we do."

"Donna be silly, Finella," he said dismissively. "A man must have his physical pleasure or he shall fall ill."

"Perhaps," she said thoughtfully. "And perhaps ye will find yer physical pleasure with another, aye?"

She winked at him. "I best be about me work, milord," she said, and opened the door. With a small smile over her shoulder, she slipped out.

Payton frowned. Finella was mistaken—he'd be back. He'd never been able to abstain for very long and where else might he go? He might have had a rough go of it lately, but he'd be his usual randy self before long.

He was certain of it.

So certain, in fact, that he had another dram of whiskey to numb his mind and his heart before he headed back to Eilean Ros.

The sun was sinking behind Ben Cluaran when Payton and Murdoch arrived home. The house was dark, save the flicker of candles in two rooms on the ground floor.

Young Willie met him on the drive, but Payton sent the boy off to have his supper and stabled Murdoch himself. He then walked up the long drive of his house, staring at the dozens of darkened thick-paned windows that were eerily like his mood. They were like windows into his life, he mused—black and empty, devoid of light.

He silently cursed himself again for his singular, crushing weakness—his inability to remove Mared Lockhart from his mind, to keep from brooding about her and the emptiness within him. He'd thought of little else but her since the night she told him she'd never love him. He was a man obsessed with his failure to win her heart and the inexplicable feelings for her that ran as deep as Loch Ard. Aye, and here he was again, a bloody fool, wondering about her, wondering what she'd done today, her first day as a ser-

vant. Did she dine with the others? Had she sulked in
her rooms all afternoon?

His obsession was particularly maddening
because he was not a foolish man—he knew that one
person's desire could not change the desire of
another. That was the way of love—sometimes, two
hearts beat as one. And sometimes, one heart beat for
two.

It annoyed him enormously that while he was
intelligent enough to understand that, he could not,
no matter how hard he'd tried, rid himself of that useless, but tenacious little glimmer of hope. He hated
that wee bit of hope. Abhorred it, loathed it. He
wished for all the world that he could smash it to tiny
pieces and never hope again.

In the foyer, he put his hat and gloves aside and
reached for the three posts in the silver tray Beckwith
had left for him. He felt a grumble of hunger in his
belly, and put the three letters in his coat pocket and
strode down the corridor to the dining room.

It had been formally laid for one. That was Sarah's
doing—she had determined that a man of his stature
must dine in luxury, regardless of how many dined
with him. Payton thought it a tremendous waste of
time and effort, but he had allowed her this custom,
and now it seemed that Beckwith would continue it.

A fire burned at the hearth, undoubtedly refreshed
every half hour until he dined. The table was set with
cloth and a seven-pronged candelabrum in the middle of the table. Two crystal goblets—one for water,
one for wine—accompanied a setting of bone china,
silver flatware, and a small crystal tot for a bit of port
or whiskey after his meal. Payton strode to the sideboard, pulled the bellpull, poured a tot of whiskey,

and tossed it down. He closed his eyes, relishing the burn of it down his throat.

He had scarcely taken his seat before Jamie appeared, carrying a tray laden with three silver-domed platters which he laid on the sideboard. He moved to light the candelabrum, then stepped back and bowed. "Shall I serve ye, milord?"

"Please," Payton said idly, and Jamie removed his plate from the table, took it to the sideboard, and began to fill it with food. Beckwith entered, a crystal decanter of wine in one hand, a pitcher of well water in the other. He filled Payton's glasses as Payton glanced through the post.

One in particular caught his eye. *The Right Honorable Laird Douglas, Master and Despot of Eilean Ros.*

He stared at the missive as Jamie put the plate before him.

"Will ye require ought else, milord?" Beckwith asked.

"Ah . . . no," he said, distracted. Beckwith nodded, stepped back, and quietly quit the room. Jamie stepped back, too, but stood still and silent beside the sideboard, should Payton require anything.

Yet Payton hardly noticed him, for he was far too interested in the letter. He unfolded the paper and read:

> *To the Right Honorable Laird Douglas:*
> *Greetings and salutations from Miss Lockhart,*
> *your indentured housekeeper. I thought you should*
> *know that I have taken the liberty of closing several*
> *rooms in the north wing.*
> *Please know that I have indeed considered the*

*possibility that you believe, for the sake of
appearances, it is important for a powerful and rather
self-impressed laird such as yourself to keep all the
rooms of his enormous house open for Scots far and
wide to admire with awe. Yet I must point out that at
Talla Dileas, where we have no such grand perceptions
of our importance, we find that rooms gone unused for
long periods of time require peat or coal that we can ill
afford, as well as the use of chambermaids who might
be employed in something infinitely more useful than
the tidying of big, empty rooms.*

 *I have, however, noted a few rooms which should be
kept open because they clearly reflect your tastes and
sensibilities; chiefly, the billiard room, for it is very
stark and plain, and the north drawing room, which
appears to have been used for torture during an earlier
period of Douglas history.*

ML

Payton bit back a reluctant smile of surprise at
receiving such a bold missive from his housekeeper
and read it twice more. Aye, he'd long since known
the lass had the grit of the gods. She was not, it
would appear, the least bit disheartened by her situation.

When he had finished his meal, he rang a bell for
Beckwith. "I'll have a port in my chambers." He quit
the dining room, walking purposefully down the corridor and taking the stairs two at a time.

He entered his suite through the dressing room
and stood in the doorway for a moment, peering
closely at his surroundings. His dressing room was,
much to his disappointment, perfectly put together—
his clothing had been put away and his toiletries had

been cleaned and placed neatly on the basin. Even the wardrobe was closed and polished.

His housekeeper, it seemed, was doing more than shutting down half of his house.

Payton continued on to the master bedchamber, shrugging out of his coat and waistcoat, which he carelessly and uncharacteristically tossed onto the floor in his wake.

The master bedroom was also insufferably neat. He sighed as he untied his neckcloth and opened the collar of his lawn shirt and looked around him. There was a fire burning in the hearth and the thick woven rug had the look of being recently swept. The curtains had been drawn and his books stacked in an orderly fashion on the bookshelves. The bed had been neatly made after his thrashing about last night. . . . Ah, but it was the bed that brought a small smile of satisfaction to his face.

When Beckwith arrived with his port, he was sitting in one of two leather wingback chairs before his hearth. Beckwith put the tray on a small table between the chairs, then looked to Payton for further instruction.

"Send Miss Lockhart to me," he said simply.

"The housekeeper, milord?" Beckwith asked uncertainly. "Is there something amiss?"

"Ye must be blind if ye canna see it, Beckwith. Look around ye, then."

Beckwith glanced around the room again and shook his head. "I beg yer pardon, milord, but everything seems in perfect order."

"Then perhaps ye have no' remarked the *bed*," Payton said, sweeping his arm grandly in that direction.

Beckwith looked at it. He seemed to be studying the thick mahogany posters and the canopied top, not the red silk coverlet that Payton's grandmother had embroidered in gold.

"What is the matter with ye, Beckwith?" Payton clucked. "'Tis no' turned down for the night."

"Aye, of course. I shall do so immediately—"

"No, leave it—I would prefer that *she* do it. She is the housekeeper after all, aye? 'Tis the housekeeper's duty to prepare this chamber for the night."

"I shall send her at once," Beckwith said.

As his butler walked out of the room, Payton smiled and helped himself to a glass of fine French port.

He heard her knock a quarter of an hour later and bade her enter. She walked into his room, her enchanting face inscrutable.

"Miss Lockhart," he said and sipped his port, turning his gaze to the hearth and letting her wait.

A mere moment later, she cleared her throat. "Ye sent for me, milord?"

He turned; she was standing in the middle of his bedchamber, her arms folded, the fingers of one hand drumming impatiently against her arm. He casually looked her over, head to toe. She was, he thought, as he let his gaze linger on her body, the most alluring housekeeper he'd ever seen. Except that the gown fit her poorly and did not enhance her lovely curves. But it was deep black and matched the color of the thick braid at her back; her green eyes seemed to leap off her face in a sea of so much black.

He put the port aside and stood. "Come here," he said.

She arched a brow. "Where?"

"Come here," he repeated quietly.

Mared obliged him by taking a small step forward. "*Closer*," he insisted.

Eyeing him warily, she reluctantly moved to stand before him. Payton looked down at her gown, then at her eyes. The dark green irises shimmered with the firelight, but he could see something more there. Apprehension, certainly. Curiosity, too, perhaps.

"The gown does not fit ye well."

She shrugged indifferently.

He studied the gown a moment longer, then grabbed a handful of the black wool at her hip and pulled it taut across her belly. "It should be taken in here," he said.

Mared did not look down, just watched him steadily. Payton let go of the material and slid his hand up her rib cage, to rest beside her breast. "And it should be let out here," he said, looking her in the eye as he brushed his fingers across the mound of her breast. "And here," he added quietly, his fingers skating across the other breast.

Despite the slight blush that rose in her cheeks, Mared lifted her chin. "Is there anything else?"

"Aye," he said, letting his fingers rest on the bodice of her gown, watching her eyes. "It's so tight that ye donna seem to be able to breathe." He moved his hands to the buttons of the gown at her neck and casually undid the first button. "I would prefer that my housekeeper be able to breathe."

Mared's brow knit into a slight frown, but she otherwise did not move, did not blink.

A small smile tipped one corner of his mouth and he unbuttoned the second button, and the third. When he unbuttoned the fourth, his knuckle grazed her bare skin beneath the wool garment. Her lashes fluttered slightly and she quietly drew a long breath.

He shifted closer, just inches from her, taking in her scent as he lazily unbuttoned the fifth button. The fabric opened to show a bit of white chemise. Payton caressed the warm skin just above her cleavage with the back of his hand. His body was responding to the feel of her skin and the scent of her, and for a moment, he forgot his resolve to be free of her. He was aware of only the blood heating in his veins, and he leaned close, so close that his lips grazed her temple, and whispered, *"Can ye breathe?"*

Mared turned slightly, so that her lips were near his neck and responded in a whisper, "I beg yer pardon . . . but was there something ye wanted, then? Or did ye call to complain about the fit of my housekeeper's gown?" And with that, she turned her face away from him and stepped aside, forcing him to drop his hand from her décolletage.

Payton chuckled low in his throat as she casually buttoned her gown. "I sent for ye, Miss Lockhart, because I had hoped that after our brief discussion this morning ye plainly understood yer duties. Did I no' make myself perfectly clear?"

"Of course I understood, milord," she said, fastening the last button. She turned to face him, her arms folded across her middle, her brows forming a vee above her eyes. "Ye could no' have been any clearer, on my word."

"Apparently I could have. Look around ye, Miss Lockhart, and tell me what it is ye have forgotten."

She glanced around the room and suddenly smiled. "I donna believe Una has forgotten a thing," she said with sunny confidence.

"Una?"

"Aye. I asked Una to tend yer chamber," she said

airily, knowing full well, judging by the glint in her eye, that it was not what he'd intended.

But Payton merely narrowed his eyes. "Then *Una* has missed something."

"What?" she asked, glancing about once more.

Payton groaned. "Look at the bed."

She looked at the bed.

"The *bed*, Miss Lockhart. Ye were to turn down the bed, aye?"

She blinked; her smile faded a little and she turned to look at him. "The bed? That's *it?* That is why ye summoned me, to turn down yer bed?" she demanded disbelievingly.

"Would ye suggest I allow a blatant oversight to go unremarked? Come now, what sort of housekeeper will ye be if I ignore yer every failure?"

"*Failure?*" she cried, but quickly checked herself. She forced a smile to her face that belied the clench of her fists at her sides, and with a dismissive cluck of her tongue, she advanced on the bed with determination, grabbed the coverlet, and flung it backward. She lifted the pillows and punched them all. Twice. And rather hard at that. And then she laid them down again and neatly folded the coverlet so that he might slip smoothly into the linens. "There ye are, milord!" she chirped as she moved away from the bed. "Yer bed is *quite* turned down!"

"Aye," he drawled. "Perhaps ye might tend to my chambers yerself so that ye'll no' suffer any other failures."

"Mmm," she said, nodding thoughtfully. "Perhaps."

"Mmm." He was enjoying himself. He resumed his seat, sipped more port, then leaned back, propped

one boot against the seat of the other chair, and gestured lazily to the bed. "Now make it up," he said.
"And turn it down again."

"I beg yer pardon?"

"Make the bed," he said, a little more forcefully,
"and turn it down again."

"Turn it down again! Why should I ever—"

"*Ach*, Miss Lockhart! 'Tis no' yer place to question
me," he interrupted. "I am laird and master of this
house, aye? Ye'll do it again because I *order* ye to do it
again."

Her jaw dropped. A fiery spark filled her eyes. He
could almost see the debate warring within her. Would
she defy him? Bend to his will? Or pummel him as she
had done when they were children? Frankly, it was all
he could do to keep the smile of amusement from his
face. "Do. It. *Again*," he said quietly.

She started uncertainly, then stopped, then started
again, marching forward, making the bed swiftly,
then turning it down again, only this time, with several extra punches to the pillows.

When she had finished, she whirled away from the
bed, sank into a curtsey worthy of a king, and with
her head bowed, said with exaggerated deference, "I
hope it is done to yer exacting satisfaction, *milord*."

Payton shrugged indifferently. "I suppose it will
do," he said, and tossed the last of the port down his
throat as she rose gracefully from her curtsey.

"Very good. Then if ye will excuse me, there is still
work to be done," she said and tried very hard to
smile politely, but failed horribly. It was more along
the lines of a furious glare.

"Ah! It would seem we've a wee problem with
proper dismissal as well, for I've no' given ye leave.

Ye've no' completed yer duties—I've left some clothing for ye in the dressing room. Ye may launder it."

"*May* I!" she exclaimed with false cheer. "And may I launder it now, or on the morrow?"

"On the morrow," he said magnanimously. "No need to overtire yerself."

She whirled about, marched across the room—pausing to stoop and pick up his coat with a bit of a disapproving cluck of her tongue—then disappeared into his dressing room. She emerged a few moments later with his clothing stuffed under her arm like a pile of rags. "Will *that* be all, milord?"

Payton cocked a brow. "No. There is one last item," he said. "A neckcloth."

"I didna see a neckcloth in yer dressing room. Perhaps ye're losing yer sight. It is a common affliction among people of a certain age."

He grinned. "I can assure ye, Miss Lockhart, I havena reached such advanced years. Ye donna see it in the dressing room because it is here," he said, and lifted one of the tails hanging down his chest and wiggled it at her.

"*Mi Diah,*" she muttered, shifted his clothing under her arm, and stalked forward. "And shall ye remove it, or shall I launder it while it still hangs round yer neck?"

"Hold out yer hand."

She held out her free hand.

Payton gazed at the sprinkle of freckles across her nose, the slender taper of her fingers. Mared sighed again and wiggled her fingers indicating he should give her the neckcloth. He abruptly reached up and caught that hand with the wiggling fingers in his larger one. "Patience, lass," he said quietly. "Ye must learn patience." He rose from his seat, her hand still in his.

She looked at her hand in his and smiled impertinently. "I am indeed impatient—impatient for sleep, that is, a very deep slumber—which I am assured I shall have, given the amount of toil I've been forced to endure here, and in spite of the deplorable state of the housekeeper's mattress. But a deep slumber will bring the morrow, and then I shall have only three hundred sixty-five days left in yer employ."

With a wry smile, Payton raised her hand, which he still held, and pressed his palm against hers, lacing his fingers between hers, one by one. "Rest assured ye're no' alone in wanting the three hundred and sixty-five days to be done."

She gasped with surprise and smiled so broadly that it dimpled her cheeks. "'Tis a miracle! At long last we might agree on something, aye?"

But Payton did not respond. He was captivated by her green eyes, the sparkle that he'd wanted to destroy, the eyes that had moved him as he'd lain with Finella.

"'Tis rather odd, sir, how ye go about handing over yer clothing for laundering."

There was something about that brash smile of hers that sent a tiny bolt of desire to his groin, and Payton once again felt like a monumental fool. He'd meant to punish her, to make her feel the indignant pain she'd heaped on him. But it seemed he was the only one to be humiliated, the only one to think of the kiss they'd shared that day high in the hills that had lingered with him for so long afterward.

Aye, he was a bloody fool, for he continued heedlessly to touch her ear and her neck with his free hand.

Her cheeks filled with a blush, and she instantly dipped her head away from his hand.

Payton dropped his hand from her neck, yet he still held the other one tightly in his. "*Ach*, Mared," he said quietly, letting go any pretense. "Ye've tormented me since we were bairns, aye?"

She snorted lightly. "I believe it was ye who tormented *me*, milord."

"'Tis obvious I have tormented ye somehow, in some way, for ye've made it quite clear ye'd no' have me, were I the last man in Scotland."

"I never said so!" she protested with a tiny tilt of her chin. "If ye were the *last* man in Scotland, I'd have cause to reconsider . . . even if ye were a Douglas."

He chuckled softly and shifted his gaze to the ripe lips he desperately wanted to kiss, feeling strongly now the powerful current of desire that had been so blatantly lacking earlier. "Reconsider now, *leannan*," he said softly. "Think of the pleasures we might explore together under this roof."

Her lips parted slightly; he could see the leap of her pulse in the base of her throat.

"Let go the past," he urged her, lifting her hand and tenderly kissing the back of it. "Donna put yerself through this."

Her eyes suddenly flashed with an angry glint. "It wasna *I* who put me here!" she sharply reminded him, yanking her hand free of his. "It is *ye* who put me here, with no more thought than if ye'd penned one of yer sheep!"

Her rebuke annoyed him—he abruptly turned away from Mared, shoved both hands through his hair and roared to the ceiling, "*Diah*, but ye bloody well vex me!"

"The feeling is entirely mutual, so I would suggest that as ye are no' the last man in Scotland, ye give me leave to tend yer blasted clothing!"

"Aye, go, get out," he said sternly, waving a hand at the door. "I'd just as soon no' lay eyes on ye!"

"I'll bloody well go," Mared snapped and grabbed the tail of his neckcloth and yanked it hard from around his neck before whirling around and striding to the door.

"Hold there!" he bellowed. "Ye will take yer leave of me properly! I've warned ye, Miss Lockhart, I willna abide yer insolence in this house!"

She grabbed the door handle and yanked it open. "I will do the best I can to satisfy my family's debt, sir, but if ye donna care for my service, then by all means, as laird and master of this house, ye should dismiss me from yer employ at once!" And with that, she stormed through his door without bothering to close it, so he could hear her marching down the corridor, away from him.

"Bloody rotten hell," Payton muttered and glared at the fire. But when he heard her on the stairs, running down, running away from him, he swiped up his port glass and hurled it with all his might at the hearth and watched it shatter into a thousand little pieces.

It was ironic, he thought, infuriated, that he should feel exactly like that goddam port glass. Somehow, that wretched woman could, with a single word, shatter him into a thousand pieces.

Twelve

❦

$\mathcal{M}$ared wasn't entirely certain why she didn't send Una to his chambers the next morning, but she didn't. She went herself and was, astonishingly, a wee bit disappointed to find he'd already gone.

But he'd made sure to leave behind quite a mess for her—his bed was in furious disarray, as if he'd thrashed about all night, and his toiletries scattered about as if he'd intentionally meant to annoy her. If that was his intention, he had succeeded.

Mared picked up a pillow and held it to her face. There was no smell of perfume there, as she had perhaps feared . . . just the darkly musky scent of Payton that floated down her spine to rest somewhere deep inside her.

His sleep had been as restless as hers, apparently—she'd had trouble ignoring the poignant look in her mind's eye of his handsome face when he'd held her hand last night. It had struck her oddly—his gray eyes had shone dully with fatigue and desire, but there had been something else in them, too, something that warmed her and exhausted her all at once.

Aye, he exhausted her! One moment she was certain what she felt for him—he was her employer, so

firmly in control of her life that she despised him, a
Douglas who was to be endured rather than admired.
But in the next moment, she saw a man, an incongru-
ently vulnerable man with a hard masculine exterior
who wore his heart on his sleeve. And she was not,
she was discovering, above being charmed by it, if
only for a moment. Several moments, perhaps. All
right then, even a lifetime of moments.

The very thought that she might feel anything for
him at all angered her. She tossed the pillow aside and
carelessly made the bed, then turned her attention to
the rest of the room, determined to be done with it.
His clothes were scattered about, his toiletries left all
over the basin. And there were the curious shards of
glass around the hearth.

Just like a Douglas to have no care for expensive
possessions, she thought, and carelessly kicked the
glass into the fire pit. Then she shoved his toiletries
haphazardly into the mahogany box and nudged his
nightshirt under the bed. When she'd finished, she
made her way downstairs to hand his laundry over to
someone who would launder it.

She did not find a washerwoman. But she found
Beckwith, whose pained expression seemed to
brighten considerably when he told her that Eilean
Ros did not employ the services of a washerwoman,
as it was just the laird and a few staff living there, and
that the last housekeeper had done the laundering
every Thursday. Without fail. Or complaint.

"Surely ye jest, Mr. Beckwith," she said, smiling
hopefully. "I've no' laundered as much as a rag before
now."

"Miss Lockhart, why in heaven's name should I
jest?" he asked, and it occurred to Mared that he

couldn't possibly even if he tried. "Follow me, and I will direct ye to the washhouse."

"But . . . but I canna carry all of this!" she protested, gesturing petulantly at the mounds of linens and clothing that had been piled in the linen closet, waiting to be laundered.

"I'll have Charlie bring it round. Rodina will come after ye've finished the laundering and bluing and help with the ironing," he said and proceeded to the kitchen, calling over his shoulder, "Step lively, Miss Lockhart!"

She had a notion to step so lively that he might feel her boot in his backside, and hurried to catch up. Beckwith marched through the kitchen, nodding curtly to Mrs. Mackerell and Moreen as he went by. "I'll no' have her using me good pots, Mr. Beckwith!" Mrs. Mackerell shouted as they passed through.

Beckwith ignored her and continued on, through the kitchen washroom and out the small door onto the lawn. Not once did he look back to see if Mared followed him, but marched like a man on a mad mission.

Down the lawn he went, through a rose garden, through tall, wrought-iron gates, then turning on a small path and finally arriving at a washhouse outside the gate, all alone in a space between the house and the sheep. It was a small, square stone building with a weathered wooden door. Beckwith flung open the door and disappeared inside.

Mared followed him. There was a hearth with a large black kettle hanging over it. Three wooden tubs were along one wall, and leaning up against the wall between them was what looked like a boat's oar. On the opposite wall was a large contraption with rollers of some sort. There were two windows on two walls, the only available light. It looked, she thought, like a dungeon.

"Here ye are," Mr. Beckwith said. "I believe everything is in order. Ye may draw water from the rain barrel on the south side of the washhouse." And then he turned as if he meant to leave.

"Mr. Beckwith!" Mared cried, stepping to block the single door. "I've no notion how to launder! I know only that there's a bit of tallow soap involved, and some boiling of water—"

"There ye have it," he said, and moved to step around her.

"B-but . . . I donna know the order of things or how much tallow is to be used. Am I to blue the clothing? How shall I blue? I've never done such a thing!"

"Miss Lockhart, I trust ye will find yer way," he said irritably. "'Tis no' a mathematical equation. Please step aside. I shall send Charlie with the laundry," he said and stepped around her and stooped to go out the small door.

She gaped at his departing back. She'd never done laundry—Fiona, Dudley's wife, had always done the Lockhart washing, even after all the chambermaids had gone. And while Beckwith was correct in that the wash was not exactly a science, it did require a *bit* of instruction, did it not? *Douglas, damn him!* Why wouldn't he employ the services of a washerwoman as did most lairds in Scotland? It was little wonder he had such wealth, so bloody frugal as he was.

She'd managed to fill the big kettle with water by the time Charlie brought the laundry down. She begged him for help, but Charlie laughed. "I've no' blued a bloody thing in me life," he said good-naturedly. "And I donna intend to start now, lass.

Besides, the laird is receiving guests, and I'm wanted on the drive."

"Aye, thank ye for yer help!" she called after him as he jogged up the path, and received nothing more than a shout of laughter for it.

When the water reached a boil, Mared siphoned some off and poured it in the first tub. She determined she'd start with something rather small to better gauge the amount of tallow soap needed as well as the amount of bluing agent. She dug through the pile of linens and clothing and picked out a handful of neckcloths. She shoved the neckcloths into the first tub, took a cake of tallow soap, and grimacing at the greasy feel of it, she put it in the water and watched it melt. Then she took the paddle, stuck it in the wooden tub, and began to swirl it around.

After a quarter of an hour, she had developed the start of a blister on one hand and determined it was enough swishing around. She put more water in the second tub, then lifted the dozen or so neckcloths from the first and put them in the second to rinse them of the tallow. That took some effort, as the tallow, made from sheep's fat, clung to the neckcloths.

When she'd had enough of the rinsing, she put the neckcloths in the last tub and took the bluing agent from the single shelf in the washhouse and dumped some in. She was standing over the wooden tub, trying to determine if she should stir it or not, when Jamie sauntered in, his hands clasped behind his back.

"Look at ye, then, Miss Lockhart, so very industrious," he observed as he glanced around the washroom. "*Ach*, put down yer paddle and come to the gardens with me. 'Tis a bonny day."

"A bonny day?" Mared laughed. "It is gray and cool, sir, did ye no' remark it when ye came from the house?"

"Aye, but when a lass is in me presence, on me honor the clouds lift and the sun shines."

She laughed. "Rather poetic, sir, but I donna think the clouds will lift today."

"No? Then cast a spell."

Her hackles rose instantly. Jamie was no longer smiling, but watching her carefully. He made her quite anxious, and she instinctively reached for the paddle. "Would that I could," she said, smiling thinly.

He suddenly dropped one hand that he held behind his back and held out a note to her.

"What's this?" she asked.

"The laird has sent ye a note. A love letter by the look of it."

Mared blinked. Her heart, her perfidious, miserable heart, skipped a beat.

"*Aha!*" Jamie exclaimed. "Ye hope that it is, I can see it in yer eyes."

"That's ridiculous!" she said, blushing furiously. "I fear it is more labor that he requires of me." She reached for the note.

But Jamie jerked it out of her reach and waved it above her head. "What favor should I ask for yer love letter, then? Ah—I've a hankering to kiss an accursed lass. Ye'll have yer love letter in exchange for a kiss."

"Jamie!" she cried, trying to laugh. "Have a care! If Beckwith catches ye here, he'd dismiss ye straightaway."

"Beckwith will no' come to the washhouse, no' when there are guests in the salon." He held up the letter. "Come on, then, *leannan*. Give us a kiss."

"Give it over," she quietly demanded.

Jamie laughed nastily and walked closer, the letter held high over his head. "Kiss me now and I'll give it to ye."

She glowered at him, reached above his head for the note, but Jamie chuckled and jerked it out of her reach again and cocked his head to one side. "Well, then?"

Bastard. She felt very vulnerable and frantically thought what to do, her eyes darting to the door behind him, then to him again. Suddenly she smiled. "All right, then, lad. Come here, and I'll give ye a kiss," she said sweetly.

Jamie's eye narrowed, and he grinned lecherously. He stepped forward, but as he reached for her, Mared swung the paddle out of the bluing tub and whacked him soundly in the ribs.

"*Aaiie*," he bellowed and grabbed his side, dropping the letter in his haste. "Ye bloody wench! I was just having a wee bit of sport, 'tis all!"

"Take yer sport from someone else," she said and stepped forward, waving the paddle before him.

"Bloody wench," he muttered again, and still holding his side, he pivoted about and stooped to quit the washroom.

Mared waited until she was quite certain he was gone, and still holding the paddle, she retrieved Payton's note.

M. Lockhart

It was the only mark on the outside of the note. Mared shoved the paddle into the bluing tub and broke the Douglas seal at the bottom of the letter as she moved to the window for light.

*I have received your inquiry and would suggest
that if you have such luxury in your day to pen long
notes informing me what you will and will not do
whilst in my employ, then perhaps you have too much
time on your hands altogether. You might put your
mind to more productive tasks. In that regard, my
cousin Sarah brought it to my attention that the
needlework on some four fire screens in the green
salon and main drawing room are in need of repair. I
suggest you put your hands to the better use of
repairing those screens than the wasting of my ink
and paper.*

*You have my permission to close some rooms in the
north wing, as approved by Mr. Beckwith.*

Douglas

That was it, the sum of his blasted note, and
Mared was enormously disappointed, but moreover,
quite miffed. She balled the note up and tossed it
beneath the kettle at the hearth, and with arms folded
across her midriff, she watched it curl up and turn to
ash.

"That's what I think of yer sodding note," she muttered and turned sharply about . . . and saw the bluing
tub. "Oh no," she said. "Oh *dear*." She had forgotten
all about the bloody neckcloths. Using the paddle, she
lifted the first one out of the tub. Her eyes went round
when she saw it and with a squeal she dropped the
paddle into the water and covered her mouth with
her hand.

The neckcloth wasn't the snowy white it should
have been. It wasn't even tinged blue. It was *purple*.

Mared suddenly burst out laughing. She laughed
so hard that she bent over with it. When she at last

caught her breath and had wiped the tears from beneath her eyes, she fished them all out to dry.

Payton enjoyed a successful meeting with Mr. Bowles from Stirling, a man who was keenly interested in investing in Payton's distillery, and who was, incidentally, already exporting fine Scotch whiskey to England and France. And making a tidy profit from it, apparently.

At the conclusion of their meeting, Payton suggested they walk down to the loch so that Mr. Bowles might see for himself the crystal-clear spring waters that came down from the hills. As they walked outside, Cailean, Payton's dog, came racing around the corner to meet them. He had, Payton noticed, a collar of some sort around his neck. And as they walked on, Cailean trotting ahead of them to the loch, Payton thought he must be seeing things, for he would swear it was a purple neckcloth tied around the dog's neck.

When they reached the edge of the water, Mr. Bowles squatted down and put his hand in the loch, and Cailean put his snout at the man's face. "Ho, there!" Mr. Bowles said, and reached for Cailean's ear, scratching him for a moment before rising to his feet. "Good water is the key to good whiskey," he said.

"Aye," Payton agreed.

"If I may—is that a cravat about yer dog's neck, milord?"

"Ah . . ." Payton paused, leaned down and had a look at the handsomely tied bow. "I believe it is," he said, and mystified, he gave Mr. Bowles a small smile and a shrug.

They talked a little more about the water and walked a little farther around the loch, where one of the highland streams fed into it. When they started back, they passed a pasture where the milk cows grazed. "Idyllic place ye have here, milord," Mr. Bowles said as they walked along the split-rail fence.

"Thank ye."

Mr. Bowles suddenly stopped walking and leaned forward, squinting at the cows.

Payton followed his gaze. And he squinted, too. What in the bloody hell?

"Curious habit, using cravats as collars," Mr. Bowles opined.

"Frankly, I wasn't aware that we'd begun the practice," Payton responded dryly.

Mr. Bowles chuckled. "I'd wager someone is having a bit of fun at yer expense, milord."

"I think ye are right," Payton said with a thin smile and gestured for Mr. Bowles to walk on. He turned the conversation to his distillery, looking back only once at his milk cows with their purple cloths, at the ends of which were tied the bells.

That night, after dressing for supper and dining alone, Payton retired to his study and picked up pen and paper.

Miss Lockhart,

I am compelled to admonish you for the performance, or lack thereof, with regard to the laundering. I am particularly distressed about the purple neckcloths that currently grace my dog and the livestock. I shall not inquire as to whose neckcloths they are, for I fear that I shall take great umbrage with the answer. In addition, I rather inadvertently discovered a nightshirt, belonging to me, shoved carelessly under the bed in my chambers. You must

*have a <u>care</u> with the laundering at Eilean Ros, Miss
Lockhart, or I shall be forced to add more days to your
employ. Enclosed please find a list of chores that you
should complete.*

Douglas

Payton heard nothing from Beckwith about his letter. But he did receive a reply the following day.

*To the Highly Offendable and Endlessly Aggrieved
Laird Douglas:*
*How kind of you to take time from the importance
of being laird and pay such excruciatingly careful
attention to my duties. It is sad that you did not find
the new collars agreeable, but I assure you, the cows
and the dog liked them very much. Nevertheless, I
shall remove them at once. And I fully regret that you
found the nightshirt as you did, for had I known that
you would be on your hands and knees, I certainly
would have swept the carpet.*

Your Indentured Slave,
ML

Miss Lockhart:
*Please do endeavor to sweep the carpets. I have
included a list of additional chores.*

Douglas

Mared crumpled that response and fed it to the fire
as she did all his letters. She hadn't actually *seen* the
tyrant for several days . . . but he never failed to send
a list of tasks and admonishments.

She did what was required of her. She'd made a
halfhearted attempt to repair the small burns in the

intricately embroidered fire screens. And she had cleaned part of the wainscot in the dining room and would have completed it all had she not determined she would be much happier if she indulged herself in a walkabout.

On the day Rodina and Una took the drapes down in the sitting room to shake them clean, Mared was caught up in one of Payton's travel books and had really just lost track of the time. And the afternoon the two lassies spent dusting the millions of tiny little bric-a-brac that cluttered the main salon, Mared had felt unwell and been compelled to lie on the divan, regaling Rodina and Una with tales of the dead Douglases that lined the walls. She was very careful to tell them of the mad Douglas, whose ghost purportedly still roamed the house.

Each time she received a note from his highness, she wondered why he did not deliver his curt little speeches of duty and responsibility in person. And the next time she saw him she only caught a glimpse of him.

She was late to supper one night, having napped too long in the small sitting room of the north wing, and was hurrying down the corridor when she passed the open door of the dining room and saw Payton within, having his supper. Completely and utterly alone.

He sat at the head of a table that could easily seat twenty. It was covered in a damask tablecloth, and candles flamed from silver candelabras all around him. To one side were the discarded silver domes of the meal's courses before him. He ate in silence, the only sound the occasional scrape of his fork against china.

Jamie, next to the sideboard, glared at Mared—he'd not forgiven her the episode of the paddle—but he did not move or otherwise interrupt the lonely meal of his laird.

Slowly, Mared walked on, but the image of his broad back, of him sitting so regally and alone at a massive dining table, stayed with her. It was a dismal picture. She'd never really considered that Payton had no one, and it occurred to her, for the first time, what it must be like for him living alone at Eilean Ros, day in and day out, rambling about such a large house all by himself.

At Talla Dileas, the plaster fell around their ears, but there were Lockharts all around, and they enjoyed one another's company.

It seemed awfully sad to be so alone, she thought, but it served him right. No one could bear to live with such an overbearing, demanding, and disagreeable man.

But that night, when she closed her eyes, she couldn't erase that striking image of him dining alone. And she did not smile, she did not gloat.

She continued to seek him out, but to no avail. Every morning, Mared went to Payton's chamber first, a little earlier than the previous morning—but he was never within. His bed always looked as if forty people had slept in it—the linens were pulled from the corners of the mattress, the beautiful silk coverlet shoved off and onto the floor. Pillows were strewn on the floor around the bed, as if they'd been restlessly kicked and pushed aside.

And every morning, Mared picked up his pillows and held them to her face, breathing in his scent. It was a funny little obsession she had, one she could not explain or begin to understand. But she was exceedingly disquieted that she found such comfort in his scent.

During the day, she went about her business as housekeeper, such that it was. She refused to sweep the foyer and told Beckwith he might take it up with the laird if he did not approve, which stuffy Beckwith assured her he would. She stuffed the silver tea service Payton had bid her to polish away in the china closet and put out a porcelain tea service instead. Any questions she might have for the lord and master of the house she merely dashed off in a letter and left for him in the silver tray. *I should very much like to put up some new drapes in the salon. The red ones are so dreary and outdated.*

Inevitably, a reply would be delivered to her: *No. And do please stop frightening the maids with blatantly false tales of ghosts.* But nothing more than that.

At night, she would go to his chamber to prepare it to meet his exacting standards for sleeping. But no matter how long she lingered there, turning the bed down, stoking the hearth, cleaning his razor strop, or arranging the closed drapes just so, he did not come.

She finally began to understand that he sought to avoid her, and it infuriated her. Not because she wanted to see him, for she didn't in the least. It was just the idea that a man could practically kidnap a woman from her home, put her into servitude, and then go about his business all jolly and carefree as if she had ceased to exist.

Therefore, the more Payton sought to avoid her, the harder Mared tried to gain his attention.

She unexpectedly got her wish late one afternoon when she induced Rodina and Una into walking to

the far side of the loch for a swim. They had suffered through a few days of unusual, brutally hot
weather that had Mared chafing at the bit to be out-
doors. On the far side of the loch, Mared had discovered a small cove where the loch fed into a shallow
pool. It was warmed by the sun and delightfully
cool on a day such as this—she knew this, for she
had dangled her feet in the water on those occasions
she was able to escape the house for a walkabout.

With the laird off to Callander and not expected
back 'til the morrow, they'd waited until Beckwith
had moved to the north end of the house, the footmen
with him, and hurried out from the back terrace with
a picnic basket between them and Cailean trotting
alongside.

Rodina and Una wore bonnets; Mared had donned
her father's old straw hat. They walked along the seldom used trail around the north side of the loch,
laughing and talking about the latest antics of the
footmen and occasionally throwing a stick for Cailean
to fetch.

When they reached the pool, Rodina asked for a bit
of food first, but Mared was quite hot and wanted to
swim. She quickly peeled off the black woolen housekeeper's gown, and while Rodina and Una watched,
she shed her boots and stockings. She paused to let
her hair down. "Eat if ye must," she said lightly, "but I
prefer to swim!"

While they watched—Rodina munching on bread,
Una looking terribly worried—Mared picked her way
around a boulder and down a rocky path, Cailean at
her side, until she reached the water's edge. She
waded in up to her ankles—it was the most wonderful sensation, cool water on her hot feet.

All smiles, she looked back. Cailean sat on his haunches, watching her, as did Rodina, who sat on a rock above the dog, still eating bread. Una stood off to the side and nervously kept looking over her shoulder as if she expected someone to catch them.

"Be easy, Una!" Mared said with a laugh. "No one will find us here! No one uses the path, save Douglas." And to prove her point, Mared impulsively gathered up the edge of her chemise and pulled it up to her waist.

"*Miss Lockhart!*" Una gasped. Even Rodina stopped chewing, her eyes wide, as if she'd never seen a woman before.

Mared laughed and waded in up to her waist, then pulled her chemise over her head and tossed it onto the bank. "Stop gawking like a pair of old maids!" she called out to them. "Come on, then, and join me! The water feels divine!" And down she went, submerging herself completely in the cool loch water.

When she broke the surface again, the two chambermaids were still watching her with awe. Cailean, however, was no longer interested and had wandered back up the trail, barking at a hare or some such creature. Mared waved at Rodina and Una to join her, but it seemed they were speaking to one another, debating it.

With a sigh, Mared shrugged. She could lead them to the pool but she couldn't make them swim—and besides, the water felt too good to fret over a couple of overly modest chambermaids. So she turned away from the bank and swam farther into the pool, alternately diving under, then rising to the top and gliding along the surface. She swam to the far side of the pool, where she turned over on her back and floated for a time.

Until she realized Una and Rodina had not yet joined her in the pool, nor could she hear them. Mared swam back into the middle of the pool to have a look.

Now she couldn't even see them—it looked as if they'd left her. "Pity they canna enjoy a summer day," she muttered to herself and dipped beneath the surface, swimming underwater toward the bank where she'd left them. When she resurfaced, she spied Cailean at the edge of the water, his tail wagging excitedly. Mared laughed, pushed wet strands of hair from her eyes, and looked again at Cailean—

And her heart stopped beating. It literally stopped beating, and for one long moment, she could neither draw a breath nor release one. Her shock was suffocating her, for there, standing just a few feet away from the dog, was Payton, and behind him, Murdoch, stripping foliage from a tree.

It looked as if he had ridden all day—his hair was windblown beneath his hat, and his boots spattered with mud. He was wearing buckskins and a lawn shirt, open to the chest, and she could see the sheen of perspiration glistening on the soft down there. He'd rolled the sleeves up to his elbows and his hands were on his waist, his weight on one hip, his head down, and his expression dark enough to fill her with alarm.

Diah, he'd come home early, then.

But worse than that, far *far* worse than that—she was naked. Thanks to her audacious swaggering for the benefit of Rodina and Una, she had made an enormous mistake. And now she was treading water in the pool, utterly and completely naked, and Payton was glaring at her as if he'd have her head.

Even at this distance, and in spite of being covered

with water from the neck down, she covered herself as best she could with her hands while she continued to tread water.

"Miss Lockhart," he said calmly, his voice cold, "I can only assume that if ye have time for swimming after completing yer daily household chores, then I have no' given ye enough work to occupy yer time, aye?"

Oh, this was not the least bit good, was it? She pondered what to say, having been caught with her hand, as it were, in the plum pudding, and decided that honesty was the best and only course. "I beg yer pardon, sir, but I've no' completed any chores as of yet. It seemed too hot for it."

He cocked his head to one side. "Too hot?"

"Aye. Too hot. *Very* hot."

That caused him to shake his head and look at the ground for a moment. "And do ye think it fair, Miss Lockhart, that the chambermaids in yer charge must toil in the heat while ye enjoy a bit of a swim?"

Well of course she didn't, but she could hardly confess they'd been here, too, not in good conscience, really, since she'd practically forced them here against their will. "No," she said at last.

"Then ye willna mind doing the rest of their chores today so they might seek respite from the heat, too, aye?"

How she hated to be cornered by logic! "No," she muttered at last.

"Very good, then. I told them as much when I sent them back to the house," he said, and damn him if a tiny hint of a smile didn't suddenly appear on his lips. "Come out of there at once."

"I, ah, I . . . I will. At once, I swear it. If ye'd just go on, I'll be along momentarily."

"Oh?" he said, lifting two thick brows. "What is it, Miss Lockhart? Were ye missing this?" he asked, and held out her chemise, which heretofore she had not noticed he was holding. Her *purple* chemise, to be exact, that had once been very white.

Her shame burned all the way to the roots of her hair. "All right then, ye've had a spot of fun," she said. "Just leave it and please go now."

Payton chuckled low. "I think no'," he said, and tossed the chemise to her. "Put it on."

"I canna put it on in the water!"

"The alternative is to put it on here, so I suggest ye try," he said, and with his legs braced apart, his arms folded implacably, he stood watching her.

With a huff, Mared grabbed the undergarment before it sank. She turned her back to him and struggled to put it on. When she turned around again, he had not bothered to hide his pleasure at her embarrassment.

With an icy glare, Mared continued to tread water, her chemise billowing around her. The exertion of donning clothing in the water on top of having swum for so long was taking a toll on her—she was beginning to tire and really needed to come out. "Now will ye go?" she asked him, panting. "I canna swim any longer."

"Then by all means, come out."

"I canna come out with ye standing there!" she protested.

"Ye should have thought of that before ye went in."

"All right, all right, ye've made yer point, sir," she protested with a groan. "I've behaved badly and now I've been humiliated for it. So will ye please turn round? I'm no' decent."

"That," he drawled, "is an understatement." But he turned around, so that his back was to her.

Warily and reluctantly, Mared swam to the edge of the pool. When she found footing, she tried to cover herself with her arms. It was no use—there was nothing she could do to keep the garment from clinging to her or revealing her flesh through the wet fabric. She was, for all intents and purposes, completely exposed to him.

Yet still, she might have salvaged her pride if only he hadn't turned round just then. He was smiling, enjoying her embarrassment . . . but his smile faded when he saw her, and his gaze turned so intent that a strange little shiver jolted her.

Without modesty, he openly looked at her, his gaze leisurely taking her in, skimming down her chest, across which her arms were tightly folded, to her hips and the dark patch of hair between her legs that shone through the wet garment. Then down her legs, all the way down to the very tips of her toes and back.

She could do nothing but stand there and endure his attention, for Payton stood between her and the rest of her clothing. The more he looked, the deeper the shivers ran inside of her.

When at last Payton lifted his gaze to hers, she could see and feel the strength of his desire emanating from him, radiating toward her. And she could also feel her body's response to the look of his desire, rising up in her, flooding her limbs. The sheer intensity of it made her panic—she didn't know what to do with it, how to react. "M-my clothes," she stammered.

"Tie yer chemise," he said quietly. His voice had gone rough; Mared glanced down and realized that her chemise, heavy with water, was hanging so low on her frame that her bosom was all but exposed. She looked up at him; his eyes went to the outline of her breasts and hardened nipples beneath the wet chemise. Mared grabbed the ends of the strings that pulled the fabric together, but her hands were so cold she could not tie it.

She struggled with it until Payton's hand covered hers. "*No!*" she said frantically, knowing instinctively that if he touched her, something would happen. "I can do it."

Payton ignored her; he easily pushed her hands aside and took the strings in his hands. He took a step closer to her and made a lazy loop of one. Mared lost her will to fight and dropped her arms, watching him tie her chemise as if he'd done it a thousand times before. He moved closer again and languidly looped the other string around the first.

When he tied the bow, she risked a look at him and inwardly flinched at the power of his smoldering gaze. It mesmerized her, intimidated her. Payton put his hands on her shoulders, casually pushed wet hair over her shoulder. And then he let his hands slide down her arms, over the thin straps of her chemise, to her hands, his touch light and reverent, his fingers leaving a trail of fire in their wake.

She was feeling things inside her that astounded her, parts of her igniting that she had never felt before. She bit her lip as his hands moved to her waist, then deliberately slid his palms up to her breasts and over them, turning his hands so that his knuckles glided over her collarbone, then turning them again to caress her breasts and nipples. And then moving again, around her back, slowly down to her hips, and around, to the swell of flesh at the apex of her legs.

His hands stopped there; he lifted his gaze and looked her in the eye as he cupped the swell with one hand. With his other hand, he gathered the material of her chemise, pulling it up, giving it slack, and slipping a finger between her legs, lightly touching her in a way that made Mared believe she might actually faint.

She gasped, drawing a ragged breath. The feeling was so exquisite that she turned her head to one side and closed her eyes, her body focused entirely on his hand and finger and the wild burst of sensual pleasure that had suddenly erupted in her. He pressed a hand against the small of her back and pushed her into his body. His mouth skimmed her forehead and her temple while his finger slid deeper and deeper into the folds of flesh between her legs, rubbing gently. He moved his mouth down her cheek, to her lips, gliding over them so lightly that they tingled with the whisper of his kiss, then returning again to kiss her delicately, his mouth as careful and light as his finger.

Mared's pulse was beating so hard that she could not seem to catch her breath; she sighed into his mouth. Payton pressed against her as he cupped her chin with his hand, turning her head slightly and kissing her so delicately that she could feel herself sliding fast down a long slope into something soft and warm and utterly explosive.

He dragged his mouth from her lips to her ear and bit her lobe. "Let me pleasure ye, lass," he whispered, moving his finger faster.

Mared opened her eyes, saw the sun behind the trees. *Diah*, her body wanted it, more than she'd ever wanted anything, and she could feel herself coming perilously close to ecstasy. Yet it seemed wrong somehow, so wrong to want him, so wrong for him to want her. There was little that would make her his more completely than this, and as much as she desired him, she did not want to marry him. But his finger was moving faster and harder, and her skin seemed to be melting away from the bone.

"Let me pleasure ye," he said again, his voice gone coarse with desire. Mared was frantic to feel the eruption that was imminent, and just as frantic to stop this and move away. She gasped at the spiraling sensation and opened her eyes, her gaze landing on the black wool of her housekeeper's gown. It was the gown that broke her from her trance, and she brought her hands up to his chest, pushing as she cried out *"No!"* at the exact moment she erupted with pleasure and her body disengaged from her mind. Mared caught a sob in her throat and brought her hands to her face, mortified by what had just happened and utterly astounded by the pleasure of it.

Payton was still near enough that she could feel his body stiffen, could feel his head lift away from her, his hand fall away from her body. And even though he was standing very near, she suddenly felt alone and very cold.

She opened her eyes. Payton was rubbing his forehead, his jaw clenched. When he realized she was watching him, he stooped down, picked up her gown and pushed it into her hands. "Ye've chores to attend," he said gruffly.

She couldn't bear the look in his eyes, that mix of disappointment and resignation, and perhaps even a wee bit of disgust. The light had gone out of them, that burning, deep light that had made her feel woozy and desperate to be near him.

He turned to leave, and as he walked up the hill to Murdoch, Mared panicked again. "Payton!" she called out to him. Her cry clearly startled him; he jerked around to her. But Mared couldn't find words to explain the vicious conflict of emotion battling inside her. She was so stunned, so mortified, so alarmed by her actions that she just couldn't find any words at all.

He waited, but when she could not speak—or would not, as it must have seemed to him—he mounted Murdoch in one long stride and took him by the reins, sending him on through the brush toward Eilean Ros.

He did not look back.

Thirteen

❖ᗷ

*D*ays passed after that hot afternoon without Mared's catching even a glimpse of Payton. She recognized that it was her doing, and though she wanted to see him, she had no real cause to see him. Her feelings for Payton had changed somewhat—but she still wanted her chance to live life on her own terms.

One Sunday, Mared donned her green walking gown and her boots and marched off to church to meet her family. After services, the Lockharts returned to Talla Dileas, where her family insisted on hearing every detail of her servitude to Douglas. Mared assured them she was being treated well. She did not tell them that she had refused to take on the role of housekeeper completely and had, in fact, managed to bypass, for the most part, the hard work that housekeeping entailed. Frankly, her family seemed much more interested in the way Douglas lived than in her housekeeping responsibilities.

Later that afternoon, when Mared accompanied Ellie and Anna to the gazebo, Ellie asked her how she truly fared.

"Quite well," Mared said with a halfhearted shrug. "He leaves me well enough alone." He left her completely alone. For all she knew, he'd up and moved to Edinburgh to avoid her.

"Oh?" Ellie asked, exchanging a look with Anna.

"Aye. I think he scarcely cares if I should live or die," Mared said with a sniff of indignation.

"That seems odd," Anna said thoughtfully. "He was so very caring before . . . now."

Mared shrugged and drummed her fingers against the railing.

"What of the supper party?" Ellie asked.

Mared stopped drumming her fingers. "Supper party?"

"The supper party he is hosting in a few days."

Her stomach clenched. "What supper party is this?" she asked, her voice noticeably less sure.

"Oh," Ellie said, turning a wide-eyed look to Anna. "We assumed you knew. W-we declined, of course," she said quickly. "We didn't think it was proper, with . . . you know . . . " Ellie put her hand to her nape. "The situation," she muttered.

"What sort of supper party?" Mared asked suspiciously.

Ellie rubbed her nape harder. "A rather large one. More than a dozen guests, I should think."

"Who?"

"Who?"

"Who is invited to attend?" Mared demanded impatiently, turning fully to face her sisters-in-law. The two of them glanced at each other from the corners of their eyes. "*Who?*" Mared asked, a little louder.

"Miss Crowley," Ellie said. "And her family, I believe."

The knot in Mared's belly tightened a little more.

That Monday, Rodina and Una were practically bubbling with the news that there was to be a supper party and that Miss Crowley would be in attendance. They were of the firm opinion that Miss Crowley would soon be their new mistress. Mared feigned indifference, much to the girls' chagrin.

As the week wore on, Mared grew weary of hearing about the blasted event. On the day the happy affair would occur, Beckwith found her reading a newspaper from Edinburgh while Una dusted in the green salon. He glowered at her.

"Aye?" Mared asked politely.

"The stores, Miss Lockhart. There hasn't been the least bit of work done on the stores since Mrs. Craig's passing, and therefore, they are pitifully low on a variety of household goods."

"Oh," she said, and turned back to her paper. "Must I really, Mr. Beckwith? I don't care for it down there. It's dark and cold and it smells."

"*Aye*, Miss Lockhart, ye *must*."

"Oh all right!" she said curtly and stood up. "Carry on, Una!" she said brightly, and with a smile for Beckwith, she headed for the dungeon.

The task seemed to take forever. But it wasn't the tedium of the inventory that kept her so long—it was that she could think of little else besides Beitris and Payton and the horrid affair that was to be held here tonight.

It didn't help that as she worked, she could hear Beckwith and the footmen preparing for the arrival of guests. At one point, she was called upon to open the china closet, and the expensive blue Wedgwood china was removed to be used for the supper, along with the Storr silver serving pieces. Mared knew from her family's plunder of their own silver and china that the contents of the two closets could bring enough for the upkeep of Talla Dileas for an entire year.

Charlie also took two trays of crystal stemware, and Mared saw Beckwith come up from the wine cellar more than once with several dusty bottles. So Douglas thought to make a show of it, did he? She wasn't surprised. Douglases, by their very nature, were a bunch of preening peacocks. One need only look at Miss Douglas to know it was true—the woman was absolutely obsessed with her appearance.

Mared was still laboring over the inventory, trying to remember what she'd just counted instead of thinking about Douglas, when Beckwith came for her again. "The laird would see ye in his chambers, Miss Lockhart," he said stoically. "There is something to do with his clothing and having it repaired."

A rush of fire flared up in her chest. She couldn't see him now, not after all these days had passed, not when he was on the verge of offering for Beitris. "His clothing! Do ye no' have someone to see after it, Mr. Beckwith?"

He frowned at her and glanced at his pocket watch. "As ye surely must have noticed, we've no valet here at Eilean Ros. Now I'll thank ye to hurry along, Miss Lockhart, for 'tis nigh on six o'clock and guests are expected within the hour."

"Perhaps ye might *suggest* a valet, sir," Mared said impertinently, but Beckwith had already walked smartly away. "He's extraordinarily fond of his clothing, aye?" she called after him. "Perhaps in addition to suggesting a valet, ye might suggest he employ another housekeeper!"

Beckwith responded by disappearing up the stairs.

Mared slammed the accounts book shut. "Repair his clothing, indeed, as if I am expected to be the bloody house seamstress as well!"

Nevertheless, she put the inventory away, snuffed out the candle, locked the dry provisions room, and marched on to see after the emperor. She walked past the main dining room on her way up and clucked at the large bouquets of white hydrangea on the table.

She rolled her eyes at the extravagance and continued on, pausing only briefly in the foyer to check her appearance in a mirror. With a little pinch of her cheeks and the smoothing of a thick strand of hair that had fallen from her braid, she continued up.

The door to the master suite of rooms was slightly ajar, and when Mared knocked, she heard a muffled reply from somewhere deep within. She hesitated briefly, for she'd not clearly heard him bid her enter, but then again, he'd sent for her, and surely he'd find fault if she didn't enter promptly. So she pushed the door open a little farther, poked her head around the door, and almost shrieked.

He was just walking from his dressing room, looking curiously at the door. He was wearing formal black trousers that were precariously unbuttoned and riding low on his hips. And nary a stitch more.

The rest of him was completely and deliciously bare.

Mared felt the heat rise up in her face as she glanced at the thin line of hair snaking up out of his trousers, over the flat plane of his stomach, and to a very muscular chest. His golden brown hair was wet and brushed back and touched broad shoulders that looked as if they were capable of holding up the entire world. His square jaw was cleanly shaven. He folded his arms across his chest, muscles protruding beneath his skin as he watched her staring at him.

She gulped down the unwelcome lump of longing and tried to think what to do instead of imagining what he might look like completely naked. Unfortunately, her thoughts were rather jumbled and her entire body seemed intent on looking at him.

He was, judging by his glacial expression, quite aware that she was ogling him, and while she knew it was unseemly and really quite rude, she could not, no matter how she tried, turn her gaze away. He was just so . . . breathtakingly handsome. Desirable. *Delectable*. She would, she thought baldly, were she a harlot and he not a Douglas, very much like to swim with him in the loch.

Payton cleared his throat; she jerked her gaze from the obvious outline of his male parts to his eyes. "Are ye quite finished with yer inspection, then?"

Her blush deepened and she looked away. "I, ah . . ." She looked at the ceiling. The bed. The floor. Anywhere but at him. "I beg yer pardon, milord, but ye did indeed startle me," she reminded him.

"That is why, Miss Lockhart, I bid ye to wait a moment."

She risked a peek at him from the corner of her eye. He was still staring at her, half-naked, as if he expected her to speak. How could she possibly speak to him when he looked so magnificent? Damn him, but it rendered her completely incapable of reasoned thought. "I didna hear ye well," she said.

"Obviously."

Was it her imagination, or was there the barest hint of a smile in his gray eyes?

He put his hand to his waist. "What is this, Miss

Lockhart? Why are ye blushing like a maid? Surely ye've seen a man before now."

"Of course I have," she said hastily and cleared her throat. "I mean to say, I've two brothers, ye'll recall."

"How could I possibly forget them?" he drawled.

She put her hand to her nape and looked at the floor. "Ah . . . beg yer pardon, but Mr. Beckwith said ye had clothing that needed repair."

He snorted. "Repair is putting it kindly. Replacement is more likely. I warned ye to have a care with the laundering."

"I donna know what ye mean," she lied.

"I mean," he said, walking to the bed and picking up a shirt from it, "that when I saw the purple neck-cloths, I foolishly gave ye the benefit of the doubt. I know ye donna want to be here, but I'll no' abide such carelessness with the clothing."

"I'm no' careless," she protested.

"Then explain this, if ye will," he said, and with one hand still on that trim waist, he held up a shirt with one finger. A blue shirt. A blue shirt that had once been very white. "'Tis abominable."

Abominable. What *he'd* done was abominable, enslaving her and then making her come out of the pool when she wasn't decent. She was so offended by his attitude, she frowned at him. *"I've* done what ye've commanded, sir! I told yer Mr. Beckwith I had no notion how to launder, and he wouldna help me in the least!"

"And why would ye assume Beckwith would know a whit about laundering, lass? He's a man, a butler, and men and butlers are no' in the business of laundering clothes!"

"That, sir, is *yer* fault."

"That, miss, is the way of the world. Now come closer, will ye, and look what ye've done."

"There's no need. I saw it plainly the day I laundered it," she said, folding her arms tightly.

"Aye, but I'd like for us to look at it together. Come *here*," he said sternly.

Mared sniffed and reluctantly walked forward. He held the blue shirt out on his finger. She gave him a look of impatience, tried to ignore the pleasing scent of his cologne, his freshly washed skin, and stared down at the garment. It was indeed awfully blue—it had not looked *quite* so blue in the moonlight when she gathered it from the drying bench. And he'd kindly not even mentioned the wrinkles.

"I suppose this is yer idea of revenge, aye? To ruin my clothing when I have fourteen guests arriving within the hour?"

"Fourteen!" she exclaimed.

"Aye. Fourteen. Now what shall I wear, Miss Lockhart?"

"*Ach*, ye've plenty ye might wear," she said with an impertinent flick of her wrist. "Ye'd know it if ye looked in yer wardrobe instead of leaving that to others."

"Thank ye for the advice. Now if ye would, fetch me a *white* shirt."

Mared tossed the shirt onto the bed and whirled around, marching for the dressing room.

"And donna think for a moment I've no' noticed the gaping hole in the bed linens!" he called after her. "That hole is the size of a dinner plate! How could one *possibly* create a hole so large?"

By working very hard at it, Mared thought, and bit

back a triumphant laugh as she threw open the doors to his wardrobe. "If ye donna care for my laundering and ye are incapable of dressing yerself, then perhaps ye might hire a valet, milord!" she shouted at him from the dressing room.

"I am perfectly capable of dressing myself, provided the clothing is laundered and properly pressed!"

"Bloody hell ye are," she muttered beneath her breath and dug through the various coats and waist-coats and shirts and finally found a pristine white linen shirt. She removed it from the wardrobe and returned to the master chamber, and paused, curtsied deep, then held the shirt up for his inspection.

He snatched it from her hand and pulled it over his head, then shoved one arm into it. "Ye are fortunate that ye found this shirt, ye are."

"Oh, aye, I am so *very* fortunate!" she said with a roll of her eyes. "And what might ye have done had I no' found it, pray tell?"

He laughed darkly and slipped the other arm into his shirt. "No' what ye'd hope, ye wee *banshee.* I'd have turned ye over me knee, bared yer bottom, and spanked ye like a child since ye insist on behaving like one."

That certainly brought a provocative image to mind. "Honestly!" she scoffed. "Ye may have kid-napped me, but ye'll no'—"

"*Kidnapped* ye? Rubbish!"

"Aye, ye did!" Mared insisted, unable to keep her gaze from his hands as they disappeared into his trousers to tuck in his shirttail. "Ye hold me ransom from my family, and *that* is kidnapping!"

"I hold ye as collateral on a *debt.* That is no' kidnap-ping, that is mercy on yer family."

"Say whatever will allow ye to sleep at night," she answered primly.

"I sleep quite well, never fear."

"Do ye indeed? And who makes yer bed in the morning? Ye donna sleep—ye struggle."

He scowled at her as he buttoned his trousers, unnoticing as her gaze followed his hands. "If I donna sleep at night it is because a madwoman closes the rooms of my house and ruins my clothing and hides the silver to avoid polishing it and lies about as the housemaids perform her work! Fetch me a neckcloth. A *white* neckcloth."

"Fetch this and fetch that," Mared mimicked him and walked to the bureau, opened the drawer, and stared down at a row of neatly folded neckcloths. Only three were suspiciously blue. "I never claimed to be a housekeeper or a laundress," she reminded him. "If ye seek yer laundering from the likes of me, ye shouldna expect it to be done properly."

"I expect ye to learn it!"

Mared snorted. "Aye, that's a man, expecting so much," she said. "And it's just like a Douglas to expect a Lockhart to do his bidding!"

"It should be the pleasure of the Lockharts to do my bidding when the Lockharts owe me three thousand pounds with interest!"

He walked to where she stood, pushed her hand aside and reached in, gathering the three bluish neckcloths in his big hand, and held them up to her. *"Mo chreach,* what have I done to deserve such torture?"

"I beg yer pardon, but what have *I* done?" Mared responded and handed him a perfectly white neckcloth.

Payton shoved the three blue neckcloths at her. "Ye've added another day to yer employment, that's what ye've done, for I shall need to replace these. Are ye pleased, then?" He pushed them against her chest.

With an indignant sniff, Mared took the blue neckcloths from his hand and dropped them carelessly in the drawer.

Payton's gaze locked on hers . . . long enough for it to resonate throughout her entire body. But then he abruptly looked away, stalked to the bed, and tossed the white neckcloth down with his coat and waistcoat.

Diah, but he looked so regal and masculine, and his courtly appearance was stirring something inside her. She foolishly thought of the day on the bank of the pool and imagined him touching her like that again . . . and touching him.

As he pulled the cuffs of his shirt to straighten them, Payton glanced up and nodded at a lacquered box on the bureau. "Ye've had no reason to destroy my gold crest, I should hope."

Mared shook her head to clear it. "No' as yet," she said and turned around before Payton could see the heat he generated in her.

She lifted the lid of the box; within were several jeweled pieces. She picked up the Douglas crest pin. "There ye are," she said cheerfully. "Unscathed and unimaginative."

"Hardly surprising ye'd take issue with the Douglas crest after ye've taken issue with all that I am."

She detected a slight note of bitterness and wasn't entirely certain how to take that. "No' *all* that ye are," she muttered, laying the pin on his neckcloth.

He looked at her again, but this time, she saw the old, familiar twinkle of amusement in his gray eyes.

He picked up his neckcloth. "I must insist that ye no' destroy my clothing, Mared. Furthermore, donna tie neckcloths on cows and dogs. Conduct yerself as a housekeeper. Launder properly, clean properly, and donna lie about and watch others do yer work, aye? If ye do so, we'll pass this year quickly enough."

Mared sighed.

"Mared?" he asked, glancing at her from the corner of his eye as he attempted to tie his neckcloth.

"Aye, I understand that ye would have me do yer woman's work. I understand that ye want me to clean and tend any bairns that might crop up and weed the gardens and feed the sick and prepare food and clothing and beds."

"Aha," he said, smiling a little. "I believe ye've got it." He stood back, frowned at the tails of the neckcloth in his mirror, then unwound it again.

"And while I, the woman who is enslaved in this household, toil away at all the important tasks, pray tell what will be left to the mighty laird to do?"

He actually laughed a little as he began to wind the neckcloth again. "It is my solemn task to provide and protect our hearth and home," he said, peering closely at his reflection in the mirror and his neckcloth, as the ends had come out uneven once more. He untied it.

"Ah, of course," Mared said politely. "A man must be at liberty to sit about in his study, surrounded by servants and whiskey, and think of nothing but protecting his hearth and home!"

"Bravo, lass. Ye seem to grasp the basic tenets of how a man shall occupy his time."

"Frankly, I'm a wee bit surprised that ye've managed to define the fairer sex as completely as ye have, seeing as how ye live without one."

"Oh, I've no' defined the fairer sex in her entirety," he said with a hint of a smile. "There is at least one more function for which a woman is infinitely handy to have about. Lend a hand, will ye?" he asked, turning to her.

Mared sighed impatiently.

"This falls well within the bounds of tending to my clothing," he said, sauntering toward her.

"Perhaps, but I should think a man of yer considerable stature would be capable of tying his own neckcloth. If ye learn to do it, we might count ye as handy to have about, too."

He stopped before her, smiled down at her, and said quietly, seductively, "Go on, then, lass . . . lend a hand."

She reluctantly took the neckcloth he held out to her and stood on her tiptoes, draped it around his neck, then measured the ends against one another, blatantly ignoring his dark smile and the way his gaze roamed her face, or the surge of energy that seemed to flow between them, much as it had that day at the pool.

"By the by, lest ye doubt it," he said quietly as she began to wrap the cloth, "I assure ye that I am handy to have about for more than one task."

She knew very well that was true, and the memory made heat rise rapidly to her face. "Aye. Someone must do the ordering about," she quipped, her eyes steady on his neckcloth.

"No," he said, his gaze on hers. "That's no' what I meant at all, and ye know it. Frankly, I think it rather a pity that ye shall never know how handy I am."

She wanted desperately to press a cool cloth to her face. She squinted at his neckcloth. "Ye must think me naïve," she said flatly, pleased that she was able to speak at all with her heart fluttering so helplessly in her chest.

"Naïve? Absolutely," he said with a lopsided grin. "Clever? Even more so."

She couldn't help her smile in return. "I am indeed clever, for at least I know how to tie a neckcloth," she said and gave it a firm yank.

"*Ow*," he choked, and with a slight grimace, he reached up, wrapped his thick fingers around her wrist. "It need no' be so bloody *tight*—"

"No?"

"No!"

She loosened it. "There now," she said, smiling happily.

He grinned at her impudence, provoking flutters of her heart and little waves of pleasurable anticipation. His hand was still on her wrist, and he casually slid his fingers around, caressing her skin. "If only ye were as tender with the laundry as ye are with the tying of my neckcloth," he murmured.

"If only," she said, matching his smile with a coy one of her own. "Will ye have me pin the cloth, milord? Or do ye intend to hold my wrist all night?"

He chuckled and casually caressed her wrist. "Killjoy."

Her gaze fell to his lips. "Scoundrel," she murmured, one brow rising above the other.

"Impertinent," he uttered, leaning down, so close that she had only to move slightly to kiss him. An inch, maybe less, and her lips would touch his. He was challenging her, she realized, forcing her to take the initiative if she wanted a kiss.

She wanted to kiss him. She honestly, desperately wanted to, but she'd learned a very valuable lesson at the pool. She was here because he had forced her to be here. Not at Talla Dileas. Not in Edinburgh, where she so wanted to be. *"Enslaved,"* she whispered and pulled her hand free before she did anything as foolish as kiss him. But she couldn't help smiling as she picked up the crest and pinned it expertly on the knot of his neckcloth.

Payton felt the neckcloth. "Aye," he said, nodding his approval. "Well done." He gave her a smile that absolutely curled her toes as he picked up his waistcoat and slipped into it, buttoning it quickly. Then he donned the evening coat.

He looked splendid. He'd make Beitris delirious with joy, she thought morosely. But the image of him with Beitris did not mix with the warmth he had created in her, and she felt suddenly out of sorts. Inexplicably angry. She didn't want to feel this warmth for him.

"Is there more ye want from me, then?" she asked impatiently.

Payton turned and looked at her with surprise, and Mared felt something slither between them, a thought, perhaps, a hope . . . something so hot and hard that it intimidated her, and she unthinkingly stepped back.

His gaze went from warm to confused. "No," he said quietly, shifting his gaze away. "Ye may leave."

She quickly walked to the door and exited his room before that thing between them could slither around her conscience and squeeze all good sense from her.

Fourteen

✦

*M*rs. Mackerell had outdone herself—turtle soup, sweetbread au jus, cullen skink, a stew make of haddock, and asparagus in a lemon cream sauce were served to Payton's supper companions, which included the lively Glaswegian guests of Payton's neighbor, Mr. Sorley, and Miss Crowley and her parents. The former, Payton had invited because he needed Sorley's agreement to siphon water from a particular stream running down Ben Cluaran for his distillery.

Miss Crowley and her parents had been invited, truthfully, to annoy Mared, for he harbored no desire to court Miss Crowley, and she had no desire to be courted. She'd confessed to him, on one of their walkabouts of Aberfoyle, that her heart was rather firmly set on the smithy's son. She indicated there was some resistance to the match from her father, who, Payton surmised, preferred his educated daughter marry someone with greater fortune than a blacksmith's apprentice—him, to be precise.

The Sorley party, surprisingly, was made up of several young unmarried women—Sorley's sister and her husband and their daughter had come, as well as Sorley's niece, whose four dearest and closest friends had tagged along. Undoubtedly because Sorley's two nephews were also present.

The young women were absolutely giddy to be at Eilean Ros, but the nephews seemed bored. They were young yet—Payton rather imagined that they'd find nothing less agreeable to them than a supper in the country. Alas, none of the attractions of town life were to be had as far away as Eilean Ros.

The young Sorley party was rather unruly, and Payton wondered if the loud and lively conversation was the way of society in Glasgow and Edinburgh these days. When he was a young man, he'd spent quite a lot of time in Edinburgh. But when his father died, he'd been needed here, and now his trips were infrequent—only once or twice a year, it seemed, to call on bankers and to procure provisions they could not obtain in Aberfoyle.

The Sorley party reminded him of many people he'd met among the so-called high society of Edinburgh. For all their finery, they could be as shallow and loud as the eight young people here tonight, convinced of their own self-worth and piteously lacking in regard for others less fortunate than they.

As if to prove it, the Glaswegians argued about the increasing industrialization of Glasgow, which the two young gentlemen insisted was necessary for progress, and the women insisted was turning Glasgow into a town of tenements. From what Payton could make of the conversation, the young ladies' objection to the tenement buildings that were springing up across Glasgow was that they were not aesthetically pleasing.

"Ye can't mean ye dislike the poor, Miss Alyshire,"

one of the nephews teased one of the lassies. "Have ye forgotten yer charity, then?"

"Not in the least," she said imperiously. "But with all the poor flocking in, they shall turn our Glasgow into a Londontown."

"Then where," Payton asked quietly, "would ye suggest they go, those who canna make a living off the land any longer?"

"However should I know?" Miss Alyshire had asked, wide-eyed. "I suppose other towns and villages in Scotland."

Payton smiled thinly and turned his attention to the haddock on his plate, which, he mused, might be capable of more intelligent conversation than Miss Alyshire.

After supper, Payton invited the ladies to enjoy wine in the green salon while he and the men partook of the American cigars Payton had ordered from Miss Alyshire's overly poor town of Glasgow. And while the two young nephews smoked the American cigars, they boasted to their uncle and their host that they had indulged in cigars of higher quality when recently in France.

The boasting continued when the gentlemen rejoined the ladies—the nephews were keen to impart that they had sampled the best of all dessert wines while in Paris, too, and implied, of course, that Payton's French offering was not the best.

Payton was appalled by their rudeness, but more by their apparent oblivion to it.

One look at Miss Crowley and he could see that she was not enjoying the evening, either. The young ladies from Glasgow had made no attempts to include her, and had, he thought irritably, rebuffed Miss

Crowley's polite efforts to engage them in conversation. They were much more interested in arguing uselessly with the two pompous, arrogant young men.

In the middle of one young man's tale of how many francs he'd won at a French gaming hall, Payton abruptly stood and walked across the room to sit with Miss Crowley.

She smiled gratefully as he took a seat next to her. "How do ye fare this evening, Miss Crowley?"

"Very well, milord. Please accept my compliments on the supper. It was excellent."

"I'm glad ye enjoyed it," he said with a tight smile. "But I must beg yer pardon for the company. 'Tis rather boorish."

"Oh no, no' at all!" she politely disagreed, but it was clear by the look in her eye that she did indeed agree with him.

Payton smiled, and so did Miss Crowley, and he thought the smithy's son was a lucky lad. "And do ye bring any news of Mr. Abernathy?" he asked in a whisper.

Miss Crowley instantly blushed and stole a sideways glimpse of her parents.

"I take it he's no' as yet spoken to yer father?"

Miss Crowley's smile instantly faded. "No. And I daresay he never shall."

"No? He'd be a fool no' to do so."

Miss Crowley suddenly twisted in her seat and looked earnestly at Payton. "Because he doesna believe he has the proper pedigree or occupation! He swears he esteems me, but that he shall no' offer until he has a venue of his own at the very least. But he'll no' have that for several more years, no' until Mr. Abernathy is prepared to put away his anvil!"

"Ah," Payton said, uncertain what to say to her sudden entreaty.

She groaned and shifted forward again, her hands clasped tightly on her lap. "Oh, I do so beg yer pardon, milord! I shouldna burden ye with such silly affairs of the heart!"

"Affairs of the heart are never silly, Miss Crowley. True happiness is important to one's physical health and should no' be treated lightly."

"Do ye really believe so?" she asked hopefully.

More than he could ever hope to convey. He nodded.

"My very thoughts, milord," she said weakly, sobering again. "At least I try to believe it. I shall never understand why my troublesome heart should attach itself so intractably to the one person who canna seem to find his way to me!"

Her sentiments struck a chord; Payton looked to the windows for a moment, swallowing hard before turning back to her. Miss Crowley's head was bowed; she was looking at her clasped hands, and a single tear was sliding helplessly down her cheek.

Payton instantly reached for a kerchief in his pocket. "There now, Miss Crowley," he whispered, pressing it into her hand. "We canna have this, aye? I'll fetch ye a wee tot of whiskey—that shall make ye feel better."

She nodded and daintily dabbed the kerchief to her eye.

Payton stood up, looked around for Beckwith, but he was busily attending the Glaswegian women, who demanded quite a lot of attention. That was just as well—he'd fetch the whiskey. He could use the fresh air.

Payton slipped out the opposite end of the salon,

walked to his study and helped himself to a healthy tot of the Eilean Ros barley-bree he hoped to manufacture. He then picked up the decanter and two clean tots in one hand and retraced his steps. As he neared the dining room, he noticed the door was open, and he heard two voices—one male, one female—and the female sounded quite familiar.

His step slowed as he neared the open door. He could hear Mared's labored breathing, which he thought odd, and realized that she was standing just inside.

"*Ach*, lass!"

Payton instantly recognized Jamie MacGrudy's voice and stopped cold. "I want only a kiss, just a simple wee kiss from yer accursed lips."

"Do ye no' fear for yer life?" Mared asked breathlessly. "Have ye no' heard the tales, then? I shall curse ye as well!"

"What shall ye do, make me into a toad?"

"That would be the kindest thing I might do! Be gone with ye now, Jamie!"

"*Ach*, Mared . . . surely ye know by now I donna fear *a' diabhal*, and I donna fear ye. Stop resisting, lass! Stop, now! I mean only to kiss ye!"

Payton abruptly strode through the open door. Jamie had Mared penned against the wall, one hand on the side of her slender neck. Mared's hands were between them; she was struggling to push him away.

Payton grabbed Jamie by the collar before the man saw him and shoved him up against the wall. Jamie stumbled, then quickly straightened, and glanced guiltily at Mared, then at Payton. "Beg yer pardon, milord. Miss Lockhart and I were just having a wee spot of fun."

Payton looked at Mared; she was staring at her feet, her hands clasped so tightly before her that her knuckles were white, her chest rising with her breath. But it was the red mark on the side of her neck that caused Payton's pulse to spike.

He shifted a cold gaze to Jamie. "Gather yer belongings," he said quietly. "Ye have a quarter of an hour to collect them and be gone from Eilean Ros."

The color bled from Jamie's face. "Beg yer pardon, milord—be gone?" He laughed nervously. "Milord, it was just a bit of fun, aye? Tell him, Miss Lockhart. Tell him it was a wee bit of fun!"

"Shut yer bloody gob," Payton said sharply. "Go on with ye now—gather yer things and get out!"

"Milord, please donna do this," Jamie begged. "I've been in yer employ for eight years. Where shall I go?"

"I shouldna care if ye go to hell, McGrudy. But ye will leave this estate at once and never set foot on it again, and if ye donna go now, I shall cart yer dead carcass out myself."

The man looked wild with shock, his eyes darting to Mared, then Payton, then to Mared again. But as the realization that he was dismissed set in, something ugly passed over his face and he suddenly laughed. "Aye, I see what it is," he said coldly. "Ye will protect yer whore and send away yer best footman."

Mared gasped, but Jamie was already moving. He shoved past the dining furniture, knocking into one chair in his haste to quit the room. As he passed Payton, he paused. "Eight years of me life, and this is the gratitude ye show me?" He spat at Payton's feet.

Payton stoically watched him until he had disappeared in the corridor, then turned around to Mared.

She was standing against the wall, her eyes wide with consternation, her arms folded tightly across her. She withered beneath his scrutiny and drew her lower lip between her teeth as pink patches of shame rose on her cheeks.

Payton strode to her, laid his palm gently against her cheek and brushed her lip with his thumb. "Are ye harmed?"

"No, no. I'm quite all right," she assured him and glanced up through her lashes, smiling tremulously. "But ye might have allowed the curse to take him."

He said nothing, but carefully moved her head to one side to have a look at the mark on her neck. It was a small bruise, one that would fade quickly, but it hardly mattered—it made his blood boil with anger, and he thought that if Jamie had the misfortune to still be standing here, he might have killed him with a single mark such as this to the man's throat.

He moved to touch the bruise, but Mared quickly lifted her hand and covered it. He put his hand to hers, intent on moving it to have a better look, but she leaned away from him. "'Tis trifling," she said, and slipped to one side, out of his reach, and moved to the dining table.

"Mared . . . I'm sorry, lass," he said genuinely and marveled at the burden she bore under the mantel of that curse. "There is much ignorance in this world."

"*Ach*, ye need no' apologize!" She glanced at him over her shoulder and smiled weakly. "I am quite accustomed to it. The disdain, I mean to say. Yet others are no' usually so bold in their disdain as he." She turned back to the table. "I'm really quite all right."

He could only guess how it was to spend her entire life under the veil of that miserable curse; to have every aspect of her life touched by it. But Mared resumed clearing the table, and the sound of laughter from the green salon reminded Payton of his duties as host. "If ye will excuse me, then." He wanted to say more to her. He wanted to tell her that were she his, she'd never fear that curse again. But he'd said it all before, and more. So Payton walked out of the dining room, his fist clenched with rage.

He did not see Mared again that night, for another argument had erupted among the Glaswegians, and it took the combined efforts of him and the footmen that remained to see them to their carriages for the ride home.

Payton did not see Mared, but when he retired that night, exhausted and out of sorts, he smelled the lilac, her scent. She'd been here. She'd touched his things, had touched his bed. He'd grown used to detecting that scent every night and found he could hardly sleep without it.

Yet he slept badly, for his dreams were familiar—of longing or searching for Mared, of big oaken kegs of Eilean Ros whiskey, of his late father. But mostly, he dreamed of Mared, and when he dreamed about her, they were dreams of frustration, and he thrashed about, until the linens and pillows of his bed were strewn haphazardly about.

He arose early the next morning with the trouble-some task of replacing Jamie on his mind. In spite of Jamie's atrocious lack of judgment, he'd been a good footman, and he would not be easy to replace.

After some discussion, Payton left it in the capable hands of Beckwith for the time being and rode to Aberfoyle, where he was to meet with two men who were interested in investing in his distillery. That was followed by a discreet, but informative call to the smithy's son.

When Payton returned to Eilean Ros, it was well after dark, and it wasn't until he'd retired to his suite of rooms and emptied his pockets that he realized he'd forgotten to call on the late Mrs. Craig's husband.

"Damnation," he muttered. He hadn't missed a week since Mrs. Craig had died. He was faithful in his vow to see after the welfare of the elderly Mr. Craig, and his grandson, chubby-cheeked Graham, a lad who'd had the misfortune of losing his mother in childbirth and his grandmother soon after that. His father had long since departed to some foreign port. Payton had promised Mrs. Craig on her deathbed to look after the two of them.

He'd intended to call with a pouch of gold crowns so that Mr. Craig might purchase what dry goods he and young Graham might need before the weather turned to autumn and the rains set in, but his thoughts had been otherwise occupied today. And as he had promised Miss Crowley to attend kirk services with her and her family on the morrow, he'd be riding in the opposite direction of the Craig house.

He'd ask Beckwith to deliver it, then.

But Sunday morning, he could not find Beckwith—he'd left to call on his elderly mother, Charlie said. Payton walked outside to have a look, hoping to catch Beckwith before he departed.

While Beckwith was nowhere to be seen, Mared was there.

Aye, Mared, wearing her old purple gown, her *ari-saidh* wrapped around her shoulders. She was speaking with the two maids, who, Payton noticed, were wearing gowns that had once belonged to his cousin

Sarah. Rodina was twirling this way and that, and Una was inspecting the hem of her sleeve.

It was Una who saw him first and dipped a quick curtsey, which prompted Rodina and Mared to turn and have a look.

Rodina curtsied, too, but when Mared turned, she smiled and waved.

"Good morning, ladies."

"Good morning, milord," Rodina and Una muttered.

"Good morning, Douglas!" Mared chirped, and the two young women looked at her as if she'd lost her mind. "What is it, then? Oh! Ye must think me impertinent," she said, and with an easy laugh, she shook her head. "I beg yer pardon, but on Sundays I'm no' in his masterful employ."

Rodina's eyes grew wide, and she looked anxiously at Payton. Una was too shocked to peel her gaze from Mared.

"Sundays ye are free to come and go as ye please," he politely corrected her. "But ye are still very much in my employ, Miss Lockhart."

"Am I?" she asked cheerfully, and put a hand over her eyes to shield them from the sun as she looked up at him. "Then I do beg yer pardon, milord, for I misunderstood completely."

"I'm scarcely surprised, as ye seem prone to misunderstanding."

"I prefer to say I am open to differing interpretations," she cheerfully retorted and bobbed a curtsey at him, all the while looking at him with a devilish spark in her eye.

Rodina and Una gaped at both of them.

Payton shifted his smile to them. "Yer gowns are quite lovely," he said.

"Thank ye, milord," Una said. "Miss Lockhart gave them to us."

"Well . . . no' *me*," Mared clarified. "The gowns were a gift from Miss Douglas."

Payton knew better than that. Sarah lumped servants and dogs together in her thinking, and she would not make a gift of her gowns to two lowly housemaids.

"She was very pleased with Rodina and Una's service. She told me so more than once," Mared added, looking at him pointedly.

It took him a moment, but when he realized that as it was customary for a lady to pass her gowns to a housekeeper when she had grown tired of them, he assumed Sarah must have given them to Mared. Mared, in turn, had given them to Rodina and Una, extending the thanks that would never come from Sarah.

He glanced at Mared. She cocked her head.

She'd have no argument from him. Rodina and Una were good chambermaids, and they'd both worked hard to keep Eilean Ros in order after Mrs. Craig's death. He greatly appreciated Mared's act of kindness, and he smiled at Rodina and Una. "Aye, she said as much to me, as well. In fact, it was the last thing that she said upon her departure."

"Oh!" Una said, obviously surprised, and looked at Rodina.

"She *did?*" Rodina asked with a bit of a squeal.

"She did indeed." The two women grinned at one another. "If ye ladies would be so kind as to pardon me, I'd have a word with Miss Lockhart."

"Oh, indeed, milord!" Una said, linking arms with Rodina, and the two housemaids walked away and up the drive, whispering and laughing as they stole a glimpse over their shoulder at Payton.

Mared watched them walk, and when they were out of hearing distance, she smiled slyly at Payton. "Thank ye."

"It is I who should be thanking ye," he said. "How very kind of ye to give them those gowns when ye are obviously in need of them yerself."

She laughed fully. "Honestly, sir, surely ye deduced by now that I'd die before I'd accept charity from a Douglas."

"On that I may depend as fiercely as the sunrise."

Mared laughed again and glanced at Rodina and Una walking up the drive. "Will ye attend kirk services today?"

"Aye. In Aberfoyle."

"Ooh, I *see*," she said, giving him a sidelong look.

"*Ach*, ye donna see at all," he said with a grin. "And before ye attempt to convince me that ye do, I'd request a favor of ye."

"A favor of me? I suppose ye wish me to speak with Miss Crowley, then? Attempt to convince her that ye're no' as obstinate or hardheaded as she might fear?"

He chuckled. "No, no' that. I'd ask that ye call on Mr. Craig," he said, withdrawing the pouch of gold coins from his pocket. "I had meant to come round yesterday, but I was detained in Aberfoyle, and regrettably, I must be to Aberfoyle again today. Might I impose on ye to take this to him on yer way to Talla Dileas?"

"Of course," she said, and looked curiously at the bag. He took her hand, turned it palm up, and deposited the bag in it. "'Tis coin," she said uncertainly, feeling the weight of it, and squinted up at him, assessing him with a lopsided smile. "Gambling debt, I'd wager. I've always heard a Douglas canna hold as much as a shilling when he gambles."

"Interesting. I'd always heard the same of the Lockharts."

"Wicked lies and mean conjecture." She winked as she slipped the pouch into her pocket.

"Thank ye kindly. Now ye best run along and catch them," he said, nodding to Rodina and Una. "Ye'd no' want to startle the poor vicar by stepping into the kirk alone and risk bringing the whole of the heavens down on yer heathen head and his congregation."

Mared laughed, a gloriously warm laugh. "And ye'd not want to keep Miss Crowley waiting for yer odious company. But before I go," she said, "I'll thank ye for coming to my aid last night."

He considered that progress of a sort, for there had been a time Mared Lockhart would not thank him for anything but perhaps his own death. Impulsively, he touched her hand. "'Twas trifling," he said, repeating her words. He nodded in the direction of the two chambermaids. "Ye best go, then."

"I'm going." And she stepped away, walked down the drive, her step light, her braid bobbing behind her. Payton watched her, ignoring the peculiar ache in his chest, smiling when she paused at the end of the drive and turned around to see him once more.

"Aye, go on, then," he muttered quietly. "Go now before I fetch ye back to me."

Fifteen

❦

*L*iam was waiting for her where the kirk road joined the main one, as he had every Sunday since her enslavement. Mared's heart filled with joy at the sight of him, and she ran. Liam caught her up in his big arms, holding her tightly to him. "What has kept ye? We expected ye a half hour ago!"

"I stopped to pay a call to Mr. Craig. He's alone with his grandson now."

Liam grunted and set her down, held her at arm's length to peer closely at her. "Has he harmed ye, lass? Has he laid as much as a finger on ye?"

He asked the same questions each week. "No!" At Liam's skeptical look, she laughed. "I've hardly seen him at all, Liam."

It was a slight alteration of the truth, and still, Liam frowned. "Aye, then what is this mark on yer neck?" he growled.

"A rather unfortunate accident with an apparatus in the washroom," she said lightly, and reached up on her toes and kissed him on the cheek. "Where is Duncan?" she asked. "I've so longed to hold him!"

Liam grinned irrepressibly at the mention of his young son, wrapped his arm around Mared's shoulder, and together, they walked to where the rest of the Lockharts awaited her in the kirk yard.

It was later that afternoon, at Talla Dileas, that Grif announced they had a new plan to free her. "'Tis rather brilliant, in our estimation," he said, and the six of them nodded in almost perfect unison.

"Brilliant?" Mared asked, perking up. "What is it, then?"

"We sell acreage to Sorley," Grif said. "I donna know why we didna think of it before now! Douglas may have refused land in exchange for ye, but Sorley? Aye, he'll want it, he will. We'll sell enough to buy ye back."

"How much?" Mared asked.

Grif blinked. "How much?"

"How much land will ye sell?"

"Ach," he said, flicking his wrist, "'No' so very much."

"How *much?*" Mared insisted.

"Thirty acres," Grif said, his smile fading.

"Thirty!" Mared cried. "Ye'd sell thirty acres of Lockhart land? Ye must no' do so, Grif! No, no, I'd rather give a year of my life to Douglas than sell as much as an inch of this land!"

Grif exchanged a perplexed look with Carson, who asked, "But ye'd agreed we'd trade the same amount of land for ye to Douglas, did ye no'? 'Tis the same, lass. Sorley or Douglas, it makes no difference."

Mared tossed her head and looked at a painting of a Lockhart ancestor. "Aye, perhaps I did agree then. But upon further reflection I now believe that one year can be borne with the proper fortitude. And I seem to possess the proper fortitude."

That opinion was met with perplexed looks all around.

"Tell her of Hugh!" Anna said excitedly.

"'Tis rubbish, Anna, I've told ye as much," Liam said gruffly.

"It may very well be rubbish, but it also may very well be true, Liam. If you won't tell her, I will," she said firmly and struggled to her feet—it seemed to Mared that Anna had ballooned overnight. "We've heard a rumor that Hugh is in Scotland," she said, her brown eyes glowing with excitement.

"In Scotland?" Mared echoed skeptically. "What have ye heard?"

"That he has returned from a rather *long* journey."

"Aye? And from where has he returned?"

"Oh, we've not the slightest idea," Anna cheerfully responded.

"Aha. And from whom have we heard this?"

"Ben MacCracken," Anna said, and both Liam and Grif rolled their eyes.

"All right, *yes*, we heard it from Ben MacCracken, but that does not mean it isn't true!" she insisted.

Mared smiled at her sister-in-law, but she agreed with her brothers' skepticism. Ben MacCracken tended to suffer from illusions brought on by far too much barley-bree consumed in the man's lifetime. He'd most recently vowed he'd supped with bonny Prince Charlie, in spite of that man's death at least thirty years ago. If old Ben knew anything of Hugh, it was what he'd dreamed after a few drams of his beloved barley-bree.

"Then I'm hopeful," Mared said to spare Anna's feelings and took Duncan from Ellie. "But I'll not allow my hopes to be raised to such heights that they would be dashed to pieces in a fall."

With a sigh, Anna nodded and fidgeted with her

sash. "I know Mr. MacCracken is a bit addled . . . but it is entirely possible that he heard something about Hugh in a public house," she muttered.

"Of course it is," Ellie said soothingly. "And the fact that he offered to share what he'd heard in exchange for coin should not sway your opinion in the least."

"Oh please," Mared said, pausing to kiss Duncan's chubby cheek. "I donna want to spend our day speaking of Hugh MacAlister! I should much prefer to hear wee Duncan speak. Can ye speak, lad?" she asked, tweaking his cheek.

The baby gurgled and shook his chubby hands in the air, and the Lockharts were suddenly encircling Mared and Duncan, urging him to speak.

Later, during a very lean supper of fish—creamed finnan haddie—the conversation turned to how they might convert an old maid's chamber adjacent to Anna and Grif's chambers into a nursery.

Mared smiled and nodded at the conversation, but her thoughts were elsewhere. She thought about the fury she had seen on Payton's face when Jamie had touched her, the set of his jaw, the murderous look in his eye. She thought about Mr. Craig, who had told her how Payton had devoted himself to Mrs. Craig's grandson, ensuring that the two of them should never want, and how he called personally at least once a week to see to their welfare.

Mared wasn't certain any of it was a surprise, but it had cast him in a different light. A light that was less Douglas . . . and more that of a man.

When supper was over, and the port was drunk, Mared glanced at the clock on the mantel. "*Ach*, I suppose I should be getting back," she said.

"'Tis late, lass. I'll take ye on the morrow," Liam said.

"No, I best go tonight, Liam."

Her family stopped talking all at once and looked closely at her.

Mared colored slightly. "He'll, ah . . . he'll add another day to my enslavement if I'm late," she quickly explained. "He's added three as it is."

"That was no' our agreement!" Carson said sternly. "What right has he?"

"Ah, well . . . *ahem* . . . there was the broken ewer, I suppose. And the ruined neckcloths," she said, smiling weakly. "And I think, perhaps, the silver."

Her mother's eyes narrowed.

"I'll endeavor to be more careful," she quickly assured them. "But I best go back now and no' brook his displeasure."

The family exchanged another look; Ellie hid a smile behind a dainty cough.

"I'll get the cart," Liam said and left the table. Mared could feel her mother's eyes on her and glanced at her from the corner of her eye. Aye, her mother was smiling in that way she had that made Mared feel completely exposed. This time was different only in that she wasn't certain of what, exactly, she was exposing. So she abruptly downed her port, stood up, and began her good-byes.

They all saw her out, and her mother, the last to hug her, tightened Mared's *arisaidh* at her throat and smiled. "Mind ye have a care, daughter," she said and hugged Mared once more, whispering, "Be kind to him, lass. He'll return it tenfold." And she let go, smiled knowingly at Mared's look of surprise, and gestured to the carriage. "There is yer brother now."

Thank the saints! Mared gave her mother a tight smile and hurried to Liam.

The night was still and beautiful, a full late summer moon lighting their way, no sound but the creaking of their old, battered cart and the occasional braying of one of their two donkeys.

When they came over Ben Cluaran, and Eilean Ros could be seen clearly below them in the moonlight, Liam brought the donkeys to a halt and gazed down on it. "He's done well," he said simply. "No one can deny he's made a pearl of it."

Mared looked down at the massive estate. "Do ye think I chose the proper course, Liam?" she blurted.

Her question obviously surprised her brother. He blinked, then cleared his throat. Then once more. "The proper course?" he repeated after a long moment.

"Aye . . . refusing to accept his offer, that is."

Liam frowned thoughtfully. "I canna rightly say, Mared. I suppose there was a time we might have sent ye to Edinburra to escape yer fate, but as we canna do even that for ye . . . ."

"Escape my fate?"

"Aye, aye, the curse. 'Tis absurd, but the fact remains that there are many around the lochs who put some stock in it. Ye'd never have a proper offer of marriage here, and we might have sent ye to Edinburra, where yer chances of a good match would have been a far sight better, I should think. But we couldna do so. Therefore, I suppose Douglas's offer seemed rather generous."

"But he's a Douglas," she reminded him.

"Aye, a Douglas," Liam said and sighed. "Much has gone on between Douglas and Lockhart for nigh on four hundred years—enough to hate the Douglases for all eternity. But if we are to live by principle and measure a man by his actions, then this man, in spite of his bloody name, can only be said to be a good man."

His answer surprised Mared. She expected him to be the first to say she'd done the only thing she could do. "Ye think I should have accepted his offer?"

Liam sighed and shrugged uneasily. "I donna know, Mared. 'Tis hard to ignore what has gone on between Lockhart and Douglas. But when I look at ye, and I see the beauty and the spirit in ye, I could rest easy knowing a good man held ye fast to his heart and protected ye from harm . . . even if he were a Douglas."

Held her fast to his heart. . . . Mared looked down at Eilean Ros again.

"There, then, that's enough of my prattling," Liam said and flicked the reins against the backs of the donkeys and started them trotting down the winding road to Eilean Ros.

Sixteen

❧❦

An hour or so before Liam deposited Mared at the front door of Eilean Ros, Payton had ridden Murdoch into the drive and handed him over to wee William for stabling.

As he walked inside, he recalled that Sarah had once accused him of being just like his late mother in that he was plagued with the Celtic curse, what with his dark moods. His mother had indeed been plagued with dark moods, but he'd only had the one in Sarah's presence, an evening after one too many barley-brees. His mood had been black because of Sarah's carping. He'd told her, in no uncertain terms, that he was master of Eilean Ros, and if it pleased him to drink too many barley-brees, then by God, he'd drink them.

At the moment, he wished he'd not been so pleased to have quite as many tots of the barley-bree this afternoon, for his legs felt entirely too heavy to lift, and his belly was protesting so loudly that he was beginning to fear he had partaken of a particularly green batch. It was certainly possible—the barley wash had been made using water from the Ben Cluaran stream a few weeks ago, and the distilling of one small keg had been accelerated so that he and the master brewer might sample it.

In fact, Payton had insisted on testing it, even knowing that it had not been fully distilled.

Whatever the cause, he was feeling so poorly that he went straight to his chambers, and a wee bit unsteadily at that. Inside his master suite of rooms, he made his way to the bed, stared blurry eyed at it with the vague thought that perhaps he ought to remove his clothing first, but fell onto his back on the soft goose-down mattress, looked up at the embroidering of the canopy, and made a mental note to speak with his master brewer about the water.

He closed his eyes, and the image of oak barrels of whiskey danced around his mind's eye. Yet he felt as if he'd not even closed them for a moment when he heard her voice.

"Ye'll no' rouse him like that," he thought she said, which he thought rather odd, since he did not need to be roused at all. Someone grabbed his boot and roughly twisted his foot until he yelped. Incensed, Payton came up quickly, and dizzily noted that the room was spinning. When his vision cleared, he was vaguely surprised to see before him a worried Beckwith—in his nightshirt, no less—and Mared, who was still wearing the purple gown she'd been wearing this morning.

He thought it all very strange and meant to ask the time, but he couldn't speak because of a sudden and blinding rush of pain to his head.

"There, do ye see?" Mared asked, apparently of Beckwith, as Payton rubbed his forehead. "It takes a wee bit of force to arouse a man from a drunken stupor."

"Miss Lockhart!" Beckwith gasped.

With what little strength he had, Payton lifted his

head and bestowed a frown on her. Mared was clearly amused, so Payton shifted his frown to Beckwith. "I closed my eyes for only a moment," he said thickly.

Beckwith and Mared exchanged a look. "Beggin' yer pardon, milord, but ye've been lying here for more than an hour," Beckwith said carefully.

Payton blinked up at his butler and shook his head, wincing at the pain it caused him. "No, no, only a moment. I closed my eyes, that's all . . . there's something no' quite right with the barley-bree," he tried to explain.

Mared snorted; Beckwith leaned over him. "Shall I help ye to undress, milord?"

"*Diah*, no!" Payton wearily exclaimed and put his hand over his eyes. "No, thank ye, Beckwith. Just . . . just turn down the bed, will ye?"

"Aye, of course. The man canna sleep without his bed turned down," Mared said blithely. "I'll do it, Mr. Beckwith. I'm sorry that I roused ye from yer bed."

"Are ye certain?" Beckwith asked, but whatever Mared might have returned was lost on Payton, for the lightheaded feeling suddenly dipped to his belly, and he felt as if he would be ill and bowed his head again, forcing the illness down.

He heard whispering and the sound of a door opening and closing, and when the feeling finally passed, he opened his achy eyes and looked up.

Mared was bent over him, peering closely. She slowly straightened, folded her arms, and frowned down at him. "Aye, ye've that look, ye do."

"What look?"

"The look of a man who canna hold his barley-bree."

"*Ach*," he said gruffly, falling back onto the bed

and closing his eyes. "I can drink barley-bree as well as any man in these hills. But no' green barley-bree."

She made a clucking sound, and he heard her move around to the other side of the bed, felt her turn down the linens there. In a moment, she had come back around to where he was half lying, half hanging off his bed.

"Do ye intend to sleep in such a manner?"

"What difference will it make?" he asked and rolled over onto his stomach, clawed his way to the top of the bed, so that his head was resting on a pillow, and closed his eyes at another lurch of his belly. "It was green whiskey," he said again.

"*Mo chreach*," she said softly and put her hands on his foot.

"What are ye doing?" he protested weakly.

"Removing yer boots, lad, what do ye think? Ye canna sleep like a rapscallion." She tugged at his boot. It finally slipped off with a bit of grunting on her part, and she repeated the process on the other leg. He heard the boots drop, one by one, onto the floor, then could sense her moving closer to him, could smell the faint scent of lilacs as she leaned over him and put her hand on his shoulder.

He wanted to move, but he couldn't; the pain in his head was making him ill.

She shoved a little, and when he did not respond, she leaned over; her braid dropped from her shoulder to tickle his cheek. "*Payton*," she whispered, "ye must roll over now."

He smiled inwardly at the sound of her gentled voice and managed to roll over, onto his back. He felt her hands at his neck, the fluttering of her fingers as she deftly untied the knot and unwound it from his neck. When he felt the last of it pull free, he opened his eyes, caught her hand. *"Mared,"* he whispered earnestly. "I think I'm dying."

She laughed and gave him a charmingly dimpled smile. "That's impossible, for if ye were to die, who would torment me? Ye've been felled by drink, sir, nothing more."

"Are ye certain?" he asked, hearing the tinge of desperation in his voice.

"I am quite certain. *Ach,* and to think all this time I believed ye to be quite invincible," she said softly. "Had I known ye might be brought down with a mere tot of yer own barley-bree, I would have brought round a full dram long ago."

She thought him invincible. His eyes closed again and he smiled dreamily.

He had no idea how long he slept. It might have been a moment, perhaps hours. His stomach was rumbling fiercely, and his bowels cramping painfully. But he was awakened by a hand on his face and the soothing scent of lilacs.

"Diah, Payton, what is wrong with ye?" Mared exclaimed in a whisper. *"Mo chreach,* ye are burning with fever!"

"I'm a wee bit under the weather, that's all," he said and slowly realized Mared had already left him. "Wait!" he cried weakly. "Where do ye go?"

"To fetch Beckwith," Mared said. "I'll have him send for a physician straightaway."

Mared hurried down the ground-floor corridor, frantically looking in one room after another for Beckwith. When she'd arrived to clean Payton's chamber that morning, she'd been surprised to see him still atop the coverlet, still fully clothed, the cold cloth she'd pressed to his head flung to one side of the massive bed. She'd even chuckled to herself as she thought of the rather disagreeable day he'd have after that sort of drinking. But then he'd not roused when she drew the drapes, or when she shook him.

It wasn't until she was sitting beside him and felt his fever that he opened his eyes, and a deep shiver of fear ran through her. The man was quite desperately ill.

Mared found Beckwith in the study. "He's terribly ill," she said. "He's possessed of a raging fever."

Beckwith's eyes went round, and he quickly stepped back from Mared. "Fever?"

"Aye, fever!" she said impatiently. "Ye must send someone for a physician at once, Mr. Beckwith!"

"Aye," he said, nodding. "Aye, straightaway."

"And ye must help me undress him and put him to bed. He still wears the clothing from yesterday."

"I'll send Charlie—"

"No, Mr. Beckwith! We donna know what sort of fever possesses him! What if it bears contagion? We canna risk the health of the others."

"Contagion?" Beckwith uttered, and the blood drained from his narrow face. Mared knew what he was thinking, for she was thinking the same thing: Killiebattan. It was a village on the northern edge of Loch Chon. All seventy some odd residents had died from a mysterious fever that emanated from their bowels and spread from house to house, taking inno-cents to their deaths. Locals said the wild dog that allegedly lived at the bottom of Loch Chon had bitten a fisherman. Whatever the true cause, it had been devastating.

Beckwith cleared his throat, straightened his waist-coat, and nodded. "Aye. I'll send the gamekeeper's lad to fetch the physician. Meet me in his chambers, then."

Mared found Rodina and Una and bade them stay away from her and the master's chambers.

"Is he very ill?" Rodina asked, wringing her hands.

"We willna know until the physician comes," Mared said, fetching clean linens from the linen closet.

"A bad fever took all of them at Killiebattan," Una whispered.

"No!" Mared said sharply, startling the two girls. "I'll no' allow ye to spread fear! This is nothing more than an ague, so go on about yer work!"

They dipped curtseys at her dark frown and scur-ried off. She hadn't meant to be so sharp with them, but the mention of Killiebattan sent another shiver of fear through her heart. She'd known more than one soul in her life who'd been consumed by a mysterious wasting sickness and perished, but the devastation of Killiebattan had happened so quickly.

The thought sent her running.

When she reached Payton's room, she was over-whelmed by the stench. A grim Beckwith appeared from the dressing room with a nightshirt draped over his arm. He nodded at Mared and walked to the bed and lightly shoved a sleeping Payton.

"*Ach*, what are ye doing?" Payton groused from the bed.

"We must change yer clothing, milord," he said smartly and snatched up Payton's boots and handed them to Mared.

"Why? It's the bloody crack of dawn!" he complained, and she heard the creak of the bed as he sat up, looking very green.

"'Tis no' the crack of dawn, milord. 'Tis nigh on eleven o'clock in the morning."

He blinked up at Beckwith. "Is it?"

Beckwith nodded.

"Bloody hell," Payton muttered and suddenly stood, but swayed, and grabbed onto one of the four posts of his bed for support. "I'm to be sick again," he said and lurched toward the privy.

Mared quickly stripped the bed and laid fresh linens. When Payton emerged from the privy, he looked as green as the lichen moss that grew on one side of Ben Cluaran and unsteadily wiped his mouth with the back of his hand.

"Are ye quite all right, milord?" Beckwith asked and got a hooded look in response. Honestly, Payton didn't seem capable of answering and made his way to the basin, put both hands in the ice cold water, and splashed it on his face.

Mared and Beckwith watched him warily as he did it again, then grasped the edge of the bureau and held on tightly. "Is he here, then?" he asked.

"Who, milord?" Beckwith asked.

"Who! *Padraig.*"

Beckwith and Mared looked at one another— Padraig was Payton's brother who'd gone off to seek his fortune in America. When neither of them answered, Payton jerked a bloodshot gaze to Mared. "Is he?" he demanded.

"Padraig is in America, milord."

He blinked; her answer seemed to confuse him. Mared cautiously moved toward him. "Might we have yer waistcoat?" she asked gently.

He glanced down, swaying a little, and fumbled with the buttons, but lost his balance and lurched toward Mared. She caught him by the arm and righted him, then quickly undid the buttons of his waistcoat, and lifting his arms, one by one, managed to slide it off his body.

"Mared," Payton said, grasping weakly at her hand. *"Mared!* Ye'll no' launder it, aye?" he asked desperately.

Mared reared back. *"No,* milord!" She gestured for Beckwith to help her, and between the two of them, they managed to remove his shirt, too. But as they did so, Mared noted with some alarm that Payton stopped protesting and seemed far too weak to care what they did to him. He spoke only once, and that was to inquire if it was true that Padraig was in America.

They had him on the bed again, on his back, but still in his trousers. Beckwith insisted she leave the room. "I'll no' have ye ogling his lordship's privates," he whispered hotly. "Go and wait for the physician, aye?"

Mared reluctantly agreed and hurried downstairs to wait. A cold rain had begun to fall, however, and it seemed that the physician took his sweet time in coming. It was almost three o'clock in the afternoon when he arrived at last.

"I thought ye'd no' come, Dr. Thomson," Mared said impatiently as she helped him in the door and took his hat and gloves.

"I beg yer pardon, but Mrs. Walker's bairn was determined to make his arrival this soggy morning." He shook off his coat and handed it to Charlie, who had come running at the sound of Mared's bell.

"Where is Beckwith?" he asked.

"With the laird in his chambers."

The physician looked curiously at Mared. "And what brings ye here, Miss Lockhart? Surely ye did no' come across Ben Cluaran on such a wet morn?"

With Charlie's curious gaze on her, Mared said simply, "He sent for me. This way, please."

Dr. Thomson picked up his bag and followed her up. When they walked into the room, Mared was relieved to see Beckwith had successfully undressed then dressed Peyton again—he was lying in bed, his face remarkably gray. Dr. Thomson frowned. "I'll have a moment alone with him," he said, and Beckwith hurried to shut the door before Mared could come in.

She stood staring at the door for a moment, struggling to hear what was being said. When it became apparent that she'd not hear anything, she sighed with frustration and went downstairs, determined to do something useful with herself while they waited.

She thought to finish her inventory of the stores, but her work was careless, and she finally shoved it aside, distracted by a singularly ugly and desperate thought—what if he died?

She could not imagine the lochs without Payton Douglas. He seemed as much a part of these hills as the trees and birds and cattle, and all right, the sheep as well. And how strange, she thought, but he seemed as much a part of *her* life as the glens and the lochs and the people around Aberfoyle. She'd never known a time when he was not nearby.

How could such a strong and virile man be struck down by a mere fever? *What if he died?*

"Miss Lockhart!"

Rodina's urgent whisper startled Mared, and she jerked her gaze up. "Beckwith says ye are to come at once!"

It was, unfortunately, as bad as she feared. Dr. Thomson wasn't entirely certain, but he believed it was possible, given Payton's sampling of newly made barley-bree, that he had contracted the sort of wasting fever that had obliterated Killiebattan.

The news sent a shiver through them all. Dr. Thomson was quite clear—none of them were to leave the premises until he'd given his approval, and none of them, save Beckwith and Mared, were to see to the laird. The illness was highly contagious, he warned them, and the more they isolated themselves from it, the better their chances of avoiding contagion.

Beckwith took it all in, standing by the hearth, his arms folded, looking very pale and drawn.

"But . . . but what about the laird?" Mared asked, her heart pounding with fear.

"Ye'll tend him," Beckwith snapped. "I've the house and everyone else to think of."

He had his own skin to think of, but Mared could certainly understand his fear. She felt it rather keenly herself. "That's quite all right, Mr. Beckwith. I'll tend him."

"I'll return on the morrow," Dr. Thomson said. "If he's no' improved, we'll leach him." He picked up his bag and walked to the door. "He's no' to have any food or liquid. It will feed the fever. Let his body expel it naturally."

He walked out of the room, Beckwith on his heels. Mared bowed her head, tried to get her thoughts together, and finally turned around, to face the others.

They were all standing near the window, as far away from her as they could possibly be in the confines of the room. Only Alan was standing a little apart from them. "Maybe Jamie was right," he said low. "Maybe this is the work of yer curse."

"W-what?"

"Maybe this is yer curse, Miss Lockhart."

"Alan!" she said sternly. "That is nothing more than an old wives' tale!"

"'Tis true," Alan said. "I've had it from MacFarland in Aberfoyle."

Rodina and Una exchanged a wide-eyed look at that. Iain MacFarland was an old and revered man, widely regarded as the historian of the lochs.

"Then surely he told ye the curse threatens whomever I am *betrothed* to, and by any account, I am most certainly no' betrothed to any of ye."

"Aye, but 'tis commonly known the laird thought to marry ye, he did."

Mrs. Mackerell sucked in a sharp breath.

Mared sighed wearily and pinched the bridge of her nose to stave off a headache that was suddenly upon her. "Such fear and superstition is too ridiculous to even warrant a response," she said quietly. "I am no' betrothed to the laird. He doesna have any particular esteem for me. And any talk of a blasted curse is fantasy," she said and dropped her hand, giving Alan a heated look. "*Fantasy!*" she exclaimed loudly. "And now is no' the time to engage in bloody fantasy!"

She quit the room and hurried to Payton's chamber, and carefully opened the door. He was lying on his side, his back to her. She started to back out, to let him rest, but he suddenly moaned, and Mared forgot Alan and the others.

She went to his bedside and sat gingerly on the edge.

He rolled over onto his back and his eyes fluttered open for a moment. "What's that smell?" he asked hoarsely. "A sweet smell, it is."

"The lilac of my soap," she said and thought to bring some oils to his room to mask the smell of his illness.

"Ah," he muttered, his eyes sliding shut again. "I thought it was flowers for my grave."

"No. Of course no'," she murmured, alarmed he'd say such a thing, and laid her palm to his forehead, wincing at the heat in him.

"If it comes to that, Mared, I should like lilacs on my grave, aye? They will remind me of ye."

She caught her breath in her throat; Payton opened his eyes again and squinted painfully at her. "Ye should go from here," he said. "Save yerself."

"Go? No. It would take more than the likes of ye to harm me, Douglas."

He managed a weak smile, and his eyes fluttered shut again. "*Ach*, I could never harm ye, Mared—I could never harm the one I love," he murmured, and his head drifted to the right, away from her.

He had slipped into unconsciousness.

Seventeen

❖

*P*ayton did not know that they leached him—the illness ravaging his body kept him in a dreamlike state, alternating between moments of lucidity and delusion.

After the physician had gone, Mared brought some fragrant oils to Payton's room and burned them, hoping they would mask the smell. She also brought the soap she and Natalie had made at Talla Dileas. They had used lilac to cover the smell of ashes and lye. He apparently found the scent soothing, so she washed her hands in it before she mopped his brow. She opened the windows to bring fresh air into the room. When he shivered with fever, she laid blankets atop him. When the fever would break, as it did from time to time, she would wash his face with a cloth soaked in the ice cold water of the loch she had lugged to his room.

When the hearth went cold, Mared discovered most of the servants had left, save Moreen the scullery maid, who had no place to go. And Beckwith, who was fiercely loyal, but terrified of entering Payton's room. Mared convinced him to at least bring wood or peat—whatever she might burn—and lay it outside Payton's door so that she might build a fire.

And she gave Moreen two pence to go and fetch Donalda, whose healing powers were rumored to be superior to that of modern medicine.

When Payton's nightshirt clung to him with the grit and stench of his illness, she knew she had to bathe him. She struggled to remove the garment from him, for he slipped in and out of consciousness, but at last she managed to do so.

He lay before her bare as the day he was born, an imposing and resplendent figure of a man, long and lean and hard, even in the grip of death.

As she bathed his body in lilac water, she could not help but look at him. His body conjured up a number of lurid images that had Mared blushing—even on what she feared was his deathbed, he had the power to stoke the flames inside her.

She tended him around the clock and prayed fervently she'd not fall ill, that she'd see him through. But the rain was relentless, soaking the world around them, dragging her hopes to the depths of despair.

She was heartened when Donalda came at her request on the third morning of Payton's illness, smelling a bit like a wet dog. The old woman did not bother with pleasantries, but walked straight to Payton's bedside and stared down at him. She put her gnarled hand to his brow, then to his throat.

"Putrid air, it is," she said. "I'll build a smoke to clear it." She took something from the pocket of her old gown, went to the fire, and squatted down. Whatever she held, she tossed into the fire. It flared and hissed, and a rather pungent smoke filled the room.

Mared coughed, waved her hand before her face to dissipate the thick smoke. "What is it?" she asked, her eyes watering.

"Open the windows. The smoke will take away the putrid air," Donalda said. Mared was more than happy to oblige. When they had opened all the windows, they stood together, Mared shivering, watching Payton as the smoke cleared the room.

After several moments passed, Mared said softly, "The potion didna work, Donalda."

"Aye, what?" the woman asked, peering up at Mared.

"The potion ye gave me to keep me from him," Mared said, nodding at Payton.

Donalda gave her a grin lacking several teeth. "Did it no'?"

Mared shook her head. "I'm here, am I no'?"

The old woman cackled and hit her hand on her thigh. "Of course it didna work, silly lass! Do ye believe ye need a potion to see what is truly in yer heart?" She laughed harshly again.

"I beg yer pardon?" Mared asked, feeling suddenly a bit miffed. "I came to ye in an hour of need, Donalda!"

"And I gave ye a bit of sweet wine!"

Mared blinked at the hag. "No' a potion to make him see the truth in my heart?" she demanded, incensed.

Donalda laughed until she was overcome with a fit of coughing. "No, lass," she wheezed. "I'm no' a witch!"

That was debatable, but nevertheless, Mared asked "Then why—"

"*Ach,*" she said, flicking her wrist, interrupting Mared's question. "I only told ye what ye wanted to hear. I'm an old woman. I know things," she said, tapping her skull. "I *see* things," she added, pointing to her eye. "And I know that ye will eventually set free the truth in yer heart, ye will."

Now she was speaking nonsense. Mared frowned down at her. "I donna understand."

"Aye," Donalda sighed, nodding. "They never do. All right, then, the smoke has cleared. Give him water," she said, nodding at Payton.

Mared looked at his sallow face. "The physician said I must no'. He said it might kill him."

"Rubbish!" Donalda croaked. "Man canna live without water. He must have it to replace the body's water he's lost. Give him water when he asks." She tightened her threadbare *arisaidh* around her bony shoulders and turned toward the door.

"Wait!" Mared cried.

"I'm done here. There's naught more I can do for him."

Mared fished two crowns from her pocket and hurried to give them to Donalda. The old woman took the money, then smiled up at Mared, her old eyes glittering. "Set it free, lass," she said, and with a loud bark of laughter, she hobbled out of the room.

"Bloody old bat," Mared muttered and shut the door behind her.

Payton did not improve with Donalda's smoke, and his moaning frightened Mared; she was afraid to leave him, afraid he would perish in the night, so she slept on the small settee in his room, curled into a ball, her neck and back aching from it.

During the night, after his body had nothing left to expel, he began to ask for water. "I canna give it to ye, Payton," she said soothingly. "It will kill ye."

"Water," he said again, grasping her arm and holding it with amazing strength for one so weak. "*Water.*"

"No," she said firmly. "It will kill ye, do ye understand me? Ye canna have it!"

But he continued to beg for it, and on the fourth morning, when the day dawned a steel gray with cold rain, he begged her for water like a madman, his eyes glazed over, his hands wringing her gown, her arm. She noticed that his hands and feet had turned blue, and when she at last freed herself from his maniacal struggle, she found Beckwith and begged him to send for Dr. Thomson.

"The end is near," Beckwith said ominously.

Mared glared at him. "His hands and feet have turned blue and he begs for water as if he were thirsting in the desert, and I donna know what to do! Ye *must* send for Thomson!"

"I'll send for him," Beckwith said, and in an uncharacteristic act of gentleness, he put a hand on Mared's shoulder. "But the end is near, lass."

She angrily shrugged his hand off and stepped back. "He willna die," she said sharply and turned away, unable to look at Beckwith and his certainty. Exhausted and afraid, she returned to Payton's room and found him hanging halfway off his bed.

"Payton!" she cried, running to him, and tried to help him up.

"Give me water," he said thickly and looked at her with red-rimmed eyes. The skin beneath his eyes looked bruised, his lips were cracked, and his cheeks sunken. He was, she realized, truly nearing his end. Tears filled her eyes, and somehow, she managed to help him up to his bed.

The man was dying and his dying wish was to drink water. He grabbed her skirt with surprising strength and beseeched her. *"Give me water!"*

She prayed Donalda was right, for this was more than she could endure. She went to the basin, poured a glass of water from the ewer, and brought it to Payton. He grabbed for it, spilling some of it in his haste, and drank it like a dog. "More," he said, handing the empty glass to her.

She gave him more. And when he finally had his fill, he fell against the pillows, his eyes closed, exhausted. But the wild look had left him.

Exhausted, Mared went to the kitchen and ate some bread, then returned with more water and wood, and built the fire up in his room. It seemed as if days had passed since she'd last slept. She eyed the settee . . . then his bed. It was huge. Too tired to care what she did, Mared crawled in beside him, fully clothed, and drifted into a deep sleep.

Sometime during the night, she was awakened by a hand on her shoulder. When she opened her eyes, Payton was looming over her, his hair wildly mussed, his dark eyes squinting. With a bit of a squeal, she came up.

His hand fell away and he blinked. "Did . . . did we marry, then?" he asked.

Mared bit her lip, quickly weighed her answer. "Aye," she whispered, wincing inwardly at her lie.

"Ah," he said and lay down. Mared stared down at him. Was it possible that he'd turned a corner? Was he mending? After a moment, she lay down, too, on her side, her back to him. But Payton moved until he was at her back, his breath on her neck and his arm securely around her waist, holding her to him.

She held her breath, did not move . . . and when she heard his shallow breathing, she sighed and

closed her eyes. She was hopeful that he was improv-
ing and hopeful that if he did, he'd never remember
her in his bed.

Aye, but she rather liked it. She felt safe. And warm.

Payton heard the physician talking above him, could
feel him holding his hand. "I've read accounts from
India in which the patient was given water and broth
and brought round," the doctor said and turned
Payton's hand over, traced a path down his palm with
his finger. "'Tis no' in keeping with what we know
here in Scotland, but it doesna seem to have harmed
him."

His hand was laid at his side.

"Aye, it was the bloodletting that did it. The fever
had left his body by the time ye gave him water, so it
didna have an adverse effect." Someone shook
Payton; he opened his eyes. "Give him water when he
asks." The physician was peering down at him, holding a glass of water, which he helped Payton to drink.
And then another. And then Payton closed his eyes,
feeling incredibly weak.

"Aye."

Mared. He knew her lilting voice, could detect the
scent of lilac around him, the scent from his dreams.
Or had he perhaps walked through a stand of lilacs?
Everything in his mind was so faint and indistinct—
he could only remember lilac.

"And a bit of broth, I suppose. He'll come round, I
should think, but he'll be quite weak. I'd advise him
to stay abed the next three days. I'll be round then to
have a look."

That was followed by a clinking sound and a
rustling of clothes or linens. Payton could feel them

moving away from him, leaving a draft in their wake. He rolled over onto his side and slipped into a dream of lilac again.

When he next awoke, the room was dark. There was a flicker of light from the hearth, and he slowly turned his head in that direction, blinking several times to clear his blurred vision; everything around him seemed to swim in soft waves of weak light. His head throbbed, his throat was dry, but he felt truly awake.

As his eyes focused to the dimly lit surroundings, he saw her, seated in one of the winged-back chairs, her feet curled under her, her head bowed over a book. The thick braid of her hair lay over her left shoulder, and the sleeves of her housekeeper's gown were rolled to her elbows.

"Mared," he croaked.

The sound of his voice startled her; her head jerked up and the book went flying off her lap. "Payton!" she cried and clambered to her feet, rushed to his bedside, and knelt beside it, her hands clasped on the edge of the bed, her eyes nervously roaming his face. "Ye're awake! Thank heavens, ye are awake!"

"Aye," he said, wincing a little as he pushed himself up. She quickly stood and reached for the pillows behind him, propping them up so that he might lean back. It took every ounce of strength he had. "I've been quite ill, it would seem," he said, uncertain as to what, exactly, had happened to him.

"Aye, ye have." She sat carefully on the edge of the bed. "A wasting fever . . . like the one in Killiebattan."

That startled him—he closed his eyes.

"But ye have survived it," she said and reassuringly touched his hand. "Ye're out of danger, thank the Lord."

"Are there others?"

She bit her lower lip and dropped her gaze. "The master brewer," she all but whispered. "They found him dead. Dr. Thomson believes ye did indeed partake of a green batch of barley-bree. He believes the water was tainted with sheep dung."

"*Mi Diah*," he whispered and thought of the brewer, an old man who had made whiskey his entire life. "There was a cask of it—"

"Properly disposed of, I am given to understand," she said.

Payton forced his eyes open and looked at her. "I thought I was dying."

She nodded. "Ye . . . ye actually came quite close to doing just that."

"I remember that ye gave me water."

Mared smiled a little. "I did." Her smile deepened into dimples. "Are ye surprised? Did ye think I'd deny yer last wish?"

In spite of how awful he felt, Payton felt a hint of a smile on his lips. Mared rose from the bed. He heard her move to the bureau, heard her pour water into a glass. In a moment, she returned and handed him the glass, and he gratefully accepted it, drank it in one long swallow.

She took the glass from his hand. "Ye should rest now, Payton," she said and caressed his brow. "Ye must regain yer strength."

Payton did not argue. His lids were sliding shut and he felt as if he could not lift his limbs.

When Payton awoke again, the sun was streaming in through the windows, and he was in desperate need of a privy. It took great effort for him to push the bedclothes off him, but he managed, and swung his legs over the side and tested his weight. He felt dizzy, and his legs felt as if they would collapse beneath him, so he grabbed the post of his bed and lurched forward.

The sudden movement of a head popping up at the foot of the bed startled him badly, and he lurched sideways, banging up against the bed and rattling the posts.

"Milord!" He didn't recognize her at first as she pushed herself up to her knees. Her hair was unbound, flowing wildly around her, and her housekeeper's gown was loose at the collar, unbuttoned to her bosom. She scrambled off the bed so quickly that Payton could not gather his thoughts.

"What are ye doing there?" he demanded, eyeing the bed suspiciously.

"What are ye doing *there?*" she returned, ignoring his question as she hurried to slip an arm around his waist. "Ye're no' to be up and about. Bed rest is what the physician said." She draped his arm around her shoulders.

"I'm in need of the privy, but I donna need ye to escort me there."

"Of course ye do! Ye've been abed five days now—do ye think ye will just stand and walk about as ye please? Here then, put yer weight on me—"

"Mared . . . I am grateful for yer care and concern, but I canna abide ye escorting me to the privy."

"Fine, then," she said and suddenly stepped away from him. Payton's knees began to buckle, and he grabbed onto the bedpost again. She folded her arms and watched him through narrowed eyes. "Go on, then. To the privy with ye."

He glanced at the privy door—he could no more reach it unassisted than he could stand. With a sigh, he gestured for Mared to help him. Wearing a pert little smile, she stepped up, put her arm around his waist, and helped him to the door of the privy. At least he was able to convince her he'd find something to hold onto within and shooed her away.

He managed to return to his bed by himself but she shadowed his every step, her arms out wide, as if she meant to catch him if he fell. When he was safely in his bed again, the bedclothes tucked neatly around him, he drank more water and asked for food.

"Ye may have a bowl of broth."

"Broth?" he groused. "I donna want broth! I want a wee bit of food. Have Cook prepare something."

"Ye'll have broth," she said, rolling down her sleeves. "I'll go prepare it."

"Ring for it. There is no need to trouble yerself." Mared calmly finished buttoning her gown, then turned to face him, her hands firmly planted on her hips. "Ye will have broth until the physician says ye may have food, milord. And ye are no' to leave this bed, aye? I must go and prepare the broth for ye, as everyone else has fled."

"Donna jest now, Mared," he said weakly.

"It is no' a jest. They've all gone, for they feared another Killiebattan."

Payton blinked and tried to absorb that. "They've *gone?*"

"All save Beckwith."

"How long?"

"This is the sixth day."

"Who . . . who tended me?" he asked, fearing her answer. "Beckwith, then?"

She smiled broadly. "Beckwith has no' stepped foot in this room."

"Then who?"

"Who do ye think, lad?"

Who . . . he had a sudden rush of memory—the scent of lilac, a soft pair of hands cooling his brow, the shadowy figure of a woman standing before the windows and looking out. It seemed impossible—of all the people on this earth to tend to him in his darkest hour of need, it seemed impossible that it might be Mared.

He blinked again, and Mared's smile grew brighter. Another memory came back to him—Mared, on the edge of his bed, the end of her braid tickling his chin as she leaned over him, wiping his brow. Then his arms . . . *and his torso.*

The memory spawned a rush of gratitude and overwhelming dismay—he panicked at the thought of being in such a vulnerable state, but at the same time, his heart swelled with thanks for the care she must have given him.

"Ye put yerself at risk," he said quietly. "Ye might have contracted it."

"Aye. But I've no', apparently," she said as she quickly braided her hair.

"It took courage to stay."

She smiled softly and glanced at him from the corner of her eye. "There was never any question of it. I'll fetch yer broth," she said and glided out of the room.

He tried to imagine what had happened, but he

was still far too weak, and closed his eyes until he was aroused by a rap at the door.

Beckwith entered cautiously. "I'm right thankful to see ye well, milord. We all feared for yer life."

"Thank ye, Beckwith," he said, wondering why his loyal butler hadn't been the one to stay by his side. "The staff? . . ."

"Gone, milord. But I am confident we can round them up."

They'd all deserted him. Even Beckwith. Only Mared, fearless Mared, had stayed by his side. He pondered it until she returned with the broth, but by that point, he was too exhausted and ravenous to think. Mared watched him warily as he ate, as if she thought he might expire yet. When he had finished the bowl of broth, she took it away. When she returned she gazed down at him, her eyes roaming his face and his upper body.

"Aye," she said, nodding. "Ye've a wee bit of color. I donna believe ye will expire . . . at least no' from this fever. So if ye will excuse me, milord, I shall take my leave of ye for a time."

For some reason, that alarmed him. "Leave? Go where?"

"To my room, to have a bath and sleep."

"But I've only awakened," he protested.

"Here ye are," she said, walking to the bureau and picking up a silver tray. "Ye may amuse yerself with the post. These letters have come during yer illness." She put them by his side, turned around, and walked to the door.

"Mared!"

She paused, turned halfway toward him.

"Thank ye," he said sincerely. "From the bottom of my heart, thank ye for saving my life."

With a laugh, she tossed the braid over her shoulder. "Donna thank me. My motives were entirely selfish—who would be left to enslave me if ye were gone, then? Beckwith?" With a wink, she went out, her braid bouncing above her hips.

Eighteen

❦

$\mathcal{M}$ared's patient went from helpless and dying to demanding and pouty.

She returned to his room several hours later after bathing in ice cold water, because she was too exhausted to heat the water for her bath, and choking down a few bites of stale bread and broth, because she had no time to prepare anything. She was beyond fatigue.

When she rapped lightly on his door, he bade her to enter. He was sitting up in his bed, his hair wild and sticking out in every direction. His six-day growth of beard obviously bothered him, for he scratched it mindlessly, and his wrinkled bed shirt was gaping open so that she could see his naked chest.

"I should like to know how long I am expected to be abed," he demanded as Mared entered carrying fresh bed linens and a clean nightshirt.

"Three days at least."

That earned her a glower. Then, "When will Dr. Thomson come round again?"

"Day after the morrow."

"But I canna wait as long as that!" he complained loudly. "Surely he has something that will put me on my feet!"

"What? A magic potion?" she scoffed. "Really, ye've been quite ill and ye must regain yer strength."

"But I donna care to simply lie here," he groaned and leaned his head back, thrust his hands through his hair, and made it stick up even more.

Mared sighed, walked to the bed, and held out the nightshirt. "If ye feel well enough to be abroad, then perhaps ye feel well enough to change yer nightshirt."

His mood suddenly lightened, and he smiled slyly, looking up at her from beneath hooded eyes. "I'm a sick man, lass, ye've said so yerself. Ye must change it for me, aye?"

"I think," she said, carelessly tossing the shirt on his lap, "that ye can manage."

"But I should be bathed," he quickly countered. "The remnants of fever washed away, that sort of thing."

The very mention of his naked body stirred her, and Mared gave him an exasperated smile. *Mary Queen of Scots*, even though the man had lain close to dying when she'd bathed him, his body had taken her breath away. She had not imagined a man could be so powerful in his build—his strapping torso atop even stronger hips, legs that looked as strong as Ben Cluaran.

And there was *that* part of him, too, fascinating in and of itself. She had tried not to ogle a dying man, had tried not to imagine that part of him engorged and moving inside her, and had been piteously unsuccessful, for it seemed that since that afternoon, every time she closed her eyes she saw him holding himself above her, sliding into her.

"Then who will wash me?" Payton insisted, unaware of the desire pooling within her. "By yer own admission, I am too weak to do it myself." And the roué was smiling suggestively.

"So it is at last borne out . . . ye are indeed a madman."

"Me? No, no, I'm a sick man in need of yer assistance."

"Ye've scarcely escaped the grip of death and now ye would entertain lascivious thoughts?"

"Lascivious? *Ach*, lass, ye make it sound so vile. I merely seek a wee bit of pleasure after facing death . . . *mutual* pleasure, I should say."

She smiled, drumming her fingers on her arm. "I suggest ye seek yer good health instead."

His frown returned and he groaned impatiently. "What bloody else shall I think of, locked away like an invalid such as I am?"

"How very grateful ye are to be alive?" she suggested lightly and picked up the bed linens and started for the dressing room.

"Wait! Where are ye going?" he called after her. "Come back, Mared! I swear I'll no' make improper suggestions, aye? No, donna go, come and keep me company! I canna bear the solitude!"

She glanced at him over her shoulder, and with a little smile of triumph, she turned into his dressing room, where she put the linens away. When she returned to his master suite, she strolled to the middle of the room and gave him a stern look, hands on hips.

"I thought ye meant to leave again," he said, reading her look and seeming a wee bit abashed by his outburst.

"No, milord," she said sternly. "I *canna* leave. There is no one to see after ye until Dr. Thomson comes on the morrow. We are, for better or worse, compelled to remain in one another's company. So will ye change yer nightshirt?"

He sighed and reached for the thing. "If it is to be only the two of us, then perhaps ye will assist me in answering the post. There are several that must be answered straightaway, and I donna feel up to writing."

"I'd be delighted. I'll just fetch pen and paper."

When she returned, Payton had managed to change his nightshirt and had combed his fingers through his hair, making it seem less wild. She handed him the post, and he sighed, closed his eyes for a moment, then read the first one. "Aha. Direct this one to Mr. Farquart, Esquire, if ye will." He glanced up. "If ye would, please use the perfect penmanship ye employ when writing me?"

Mared smiled.

"Mr. Farquart," he said and proceeded to dictate a letter that impressed Mared with its eloquence and off-the-cuff thinking, particularly considering the man was still recovering from his near death bout of fever.

And so they went—Mared remarking on the vast sphere of his influence, Payton reminding her that the influence might have been the Lockharts' as well, had it not been for their stubborn loyalty to cows. At the end of their session, when Mared's hand was aching and Payton was obviously tiring, he held up one more letter.

"This is from my cousin Neacel," he said. "He's to be wed in a traditional Highland wedding next month."

"Felicitations to yer cousin, then," she said.

"There is to be a three-day wedding *ceilidh*."

"It will be a joyous time for all," she said blithely, and put a sheet of vellum before her on the dining table. "Might I suggest that ye begin, 'To my cousin Neacel Douglas, greetings and felicitations on yer happy news from one important Douglas laird and master of all he surveys, to another Douglas laird who is likewise impressed by himself?'"

Payton chuckled weakly at her beaming smile. "Quite poetic. But I suggest we start with this: 'Cousin, greetings and felicitations,'" he dictated. "'Please accept my heartfelt congratulations on the happy news of yer betrothal. I quite look forward to meeting yer intended bride, for I fondly recall from our childhood that Miss Braxton was indeed a bonny lass, and I trust she will make ye a good and dutiful wife. . . .'"

He paused there and slanted Mared a look. "Ye are writing this down, are ye, word for word?"

"Do ye doubt it?"

"Of course I do. Ye're writing it down as I say, aye?"

"Of *course.*"

He looked skeptical, but leaned his head back and continued. "'I am right pleased to inform ye that ye may count me among the number who will attend and witness the celebration of yer betrothal. I shall require lodging for myself and three servants. Until the time I may congratulate you personally, I remain, as ever, yer loyal and faithful cousin.'" He thought for a moment, then nodded. "Aye, then, ye may put my name to it."

"Where shall I direct it?" she asked as she signed his name.

"Kinlochmore, near Fort William."

"Diah," she said absently. "That's quite a journey, aye?"

"Two days. Longer if there is rain. Ye best pack warmly."

That garnered her immediate attention. "Beg yer pardon?"

"Ye might bring the purple gown ye are so fond of—ye'll need a heavy fabric in a month's time, I'd wager."

He confused her, and for a moment, she thought perhaps his fever was returning. "Are ye quite all right, milord?" she asked, putting the letter aside.

"Quite." And he flashed a weak, but devilish smile.

Oh no. No, no. "But as I'll no' be traveling to Kinlochmore, I'll have no need of anything but this plain black gown," she said sweetly.

"Ah, but ye will be traveling there," he said calmly.

"I donna see how ye can possibly say I will," she said patiently, thinking how she would very much like to stuff the letter down his throat at present. "Ye will go in the company of yer footmen. I will remain here and do what it is I've been enslaved to do."

"But I donna keep a valet, and I'll need ye along to tend to my clothing."

"Yer *clothing?"* she cried, coming up out of her chair. "Can ye no' impress on one of yer footmen the importance of keeping yer bloody clothing neat and tidy and at the ready, then?" she demanded. "I shall go to my grave wondering how a man so fully convinced of his own glory might have managed this long without a valet!"

"But I have. And I need ye to accompany me."

"How can ye ask it of me? Can ye imagine what will be said? Have ye thought of how I'll be persecuted in the midst of so many blasted Douglases?"

"Hmm," he said thoughtfully. "That is a rather appealing thought, a Lockhart surrounded by Douglases. But ye needn't fret, Mared. There was no talk of Mrs. Craig when she accompanied me. Most saw it for what it was—a laird with his housekeeper along to tend to his clothing and his suite. Neacel's household will be taxed enough as it is, what with Douglases coming from far and wide. I canna impose on him for my own needs."

"Yer needs!" she exploded helplessly. "I willna go along as yer lackey!" she insisted, striding angrily to the bed. "Ye can humiliate me into what ye will within the walls of this house, but I shall no' go abroad and be presented to all the bloody Douglases of the world as yer servant."

"Of course ye will," he said, sinking low into the pillows, his brow creased in a frown. "For ye are my servant. A wee bit of broth, aye, Mared? I'm feeling rather weak."

"*Augh!*" she cried, and whirled away from the bed, marched to the door, and flung it open. Then she just as suddenly slammed it shut and whirled about to argue her point again. Only Payton had rolled over onto his side and was already sleeping.

Mared's fingers dug into her palms as she struggled to maintain her calm. She snatched up the post and left his room to make his damned broth.

Had she walked over to the bed and leaned over to have a look, she might have seen his smile.

As the days unfurled, Payton grew stronger quickly and chafed at the confines of his illness. The servants who had fled in terror of wasting fever had slowly returned as news of his rather miraculous recovery spread through the lochs.

The house returned to its natural rhythm, and Payton saw less and less of Mared.

He took to walking the long corridors to regain his strength, and from time to time he'd pass by one room or another and see her, usually in the company of Rodina and Una, usually completely idle, or occupied in some worthless task, as the two chambermaids worked around her. It was inevitable that he would stop to gaze at her, that he could not seem to make his body move forward. And it was inevitable that Mared would sense him and turn around, her gaze meeting his.

He supposed, in the quiet of the night when he sat before his hearth, that it was possible the fever had left him partially addled, for he believed on those occasions their eyes met, her deep green eyes would soften with what he thought was affection, and something would pass between them, something he felt deep inside him.

He was desperate to know if Mared felt it, too . . . yet he could not bring himself to inquire, primarily because there never seemed to be an opportunity. She was always surrounded by servants. But perhaps more to the heart of it, Payton did not want to know if he had misjudged the look between them. He rather preferred to go on privately believing that she felt it, too, rather than be summarily disabused of that notion.

He preferred to let his tiny glimmer of hope rise up like a bird and begin to beat its wings soundly within him.

Nineteen

❖

As summer slid into early autumn, and the days grew cooler and shorter, Mared had become accustomed to living at Eilean Ros. She'd found a happy balance with Rodina and Una, helping out where she could without compromising her promise to never serve the laird Douglas. She'd even managed to befriend Beckwith somewhat, who had, since Payton's illness, seemed to have developed a newfound respect for her.

She took long walks about the estate, usually accompanied by Cailean, Payton's sheepdog. Sometimes she'd see Payton ride out on Murdoch, bent over the horse's neck, pushing hard, as if he sought to escape. Other times she'd see his grand coach roll by, bound for God knew where. But he was, she noted, always alone.

When Cailean gave birth to pups that looked suspiciously like her dog at Talla Dileas, Mared delighted in the puppies and with the neckcloths she'd removed from the milk cows, she made little collars for them.

One day, when she was playing with the litter of pups, Payton walked out to the stables accompanied by the coachman. He paused when he saw her at the kennel with the puppies and strode over to have a look. She smiled as one of the puppies climbed over the toe of his boot.

Payton smiled, too, but as he looked down, the smile slowly faded, and he leaned down, squinting at them. "What . . . are those my neckcloths?" he asked incredulously.

Mared smiled pertly and picked up one of the fattest puppies, holding him to her neck to coo in his ear. "They are indeed. Ye said the cows were no' to wear them. Ye said nothing of puppies." She gave him a sly smile and turned and walked deeper into the kennel, leaving Payton to stare at eight puppies with purple collars.

While Payton grew noticeably stronger and more robust with each day, Mared worked to convince herself that she was merely biding her time until her year was up and refused to acknowledge that she did, in fact, long to see him each day. She likewise refused to acknowledge that during that late stretch of day that struggled into evening, she caught herself looking for him everywhere—in his study, the salon, the stables. The drawing room, the billiard room, the gardens.

She told herself the circuitous path she took through the long corridors of Eilean Ros was to check the rooms under her charge.

On the occasions she did see him—in the corridor, perhaps, or standing in the door of a room she was tending—she could feel the strength of his gray gaze, could feel it sink into her, its talons gripping her heart and lungs, then stretching down to the deepest part of her to drag up a jumbled heap of emotions. She could never hold his gaze for very long, for the depth of it oddly frightened her, made her feel more vulnerable than she'd ever felt in her life.

Yet she continued to seek him.

The one place she saw him routinely was the dining room. Night after night she'd walk quietly by that open door, and night after night she'd see him there, sitting alone in the vast room with no company but Alan against the wall, his supper laid on expensive china and silver, his wineglass full. The light of six candles flickering in the cavernous room.

He seemed to Mared to be the loneliest man in all of Scotland.

Almost a month had passed since Payton had survived the fever—which, thankfully, had not spread beyond the master brewer's cottage. Life had returned to normal.

One night, Mared was in her room, seated on the edge of her lumpy bed, darning her old stockings and idly wondering how many more months she might make use of them, when there was a knock at her door.

Rodina or Una, she gathered. The two were constantly seeking advice on one thing or another. "Come, then," she called cheerfully, without looking up, and continued to darn her stockings.

The door opened slowly; she barely spared it a glance. "What is it now?" she asked airily. "Mr. Beckwith has made you sullen, aye? Or another lad has turned yer head."

"I should hope neither."

He startled her so badly that Mared stuck herself with the needle. She awkwardly gained her feet and forgot the bloody stockings, forgot everything, and nervously tried to straighten her old green gown as she quickly surveyed her tiny room.

"I beg yer pardon, I didna mean to disturb ye—"

"No, no," she said hastily. "I was . . . was repairing . . ." Repairing her stockings? She thought she'd keep that to herself and let her voice trail off as she forced herself to look at him.

Diah, but he looked fully recovered—strong and vital and terribly, terribly alluring. He was dressed to go out. His hair was neatly combed over his collar. His navy coat was superfine—she knew because Grif had come home from London with something similar, a coat made of an exquisite cloth. He wore gray trousers and a gray silk waistcoat heavily embroidered with dark blue thread, and his neckcloth, naturally, was perfectly pressed, thanks to Rodina.

He quite literally made her pulse leap to her throat, made the blood rush to her temples and pound like a drum, for she'd not seen him look so . . . *healthy* . . . in weeks.

She cleared her throat and smoothed her damp palms on the side of her gown as Payton just stood there, gazing at her, his eyes dark and unfathomable. She felt ridiculously apprehensive—since when could this man make her feel like a blushing maiden? "Was there something ye required?" she asked, privately cursing herself for sounding so breathless.

"No," he said softly and stepped into the room, slowly closing the door at his back. He leaned against it as his gaze traveled down the length of her and up again. His gaze felt blistering, scorching. She'd seen this look before, recognized the desire in it, and suddenly believed he'd come to tell her he would have her in his bed. Unthinkingly, Mared stepped backward.

Her movement seemed to shake him from his thoughts; he glanced at the threadbare rug, then lifted his eyes again. "Ye should have a warm rug."

"It is warm enough."

But he was shaking his head. "No. A *warm* rug." He looked at her again. "I've come to remind ye about Kinlochmore, and I will require ye to attend with me."

Mared's heart dipped. She thought he'd forgotten or reconsidered his decree that she would accompany him to his cousin's wedding *ceilidh*. Certainly he hadn't mentioned it since she'd written his reply to his cousin more than a month ago. She had a sudden image of herself surrounded by dozens of Douglases, the whispers of her curse spreading like fire, the looks of censure, the disdain for her name. "No," she said with a firm shake of her head. *"No."*

A lock of dark sandy hair had fallen over his eye, and he looked so very different now, as if it pained him to tell her this. "I need ye with me, Mared," he said quietly. "I'll consent to bringing one of the maids along so that ye may rest assured of yer virtue. But I need ye with me."

"Please donna ask this of me. Please, Payton," she begged him. "I'll be humiliated—"

"No! I'll no' allow that to happen, on my life. But I . . ." He tore his gaze from her, looked at the ceiling, ran a hand over his hair, then abruptly pushed away from the door, walked to her bureau. "I must have ye there. That is my decision."

"But I—"

"'Tis no' open to debate," he said evenly.

Mared gaped at him, her mind whirling, and Payton turned from the bureau. "We will depart Monday morning at dawn, then. Choose one of the maids to travel with ye, aye?"

"Mi Diah, ye are a bastard," she whispered.

The muscle in his jaw flexed, but Payton said nothing; it seemed to Mared that he did not know what to do or say. He sighed and lowered his head, looked at her from beneath his lashes, his lips pursed.

"What?" she asked angrily. "What is it ye would say?"

"I need ye in Kinlochmore, and that is final."

Mared glared at him.

"Good night." He walked to the door of her room and opened it. With one last look at her, he stepped out and shut the door.

"Bloody hell," Mared whispered and sank onto her lumpy bed, staring at the wall, her mind racing ahead to the horror of a Douglas wedding *ceilidh* deep in the Highlands.

That Sunday, at Talla Dileas, Mared, Ellie, Natalie, and Anna, who in her pregnancy had grown as big as a walrus, stared at the gowns spread on Anna's bed. "They're all lovely," Mared said. "Where did ye get them, then?"

"My sister Bette sent them after last Season."

"They are a wee bit fancy for the likes of the Douglases," Mared muttered as she sorted through them.

"Will you tell us all what he said once more?" Natalie asked, looking wistfully at the gowns.

Ellie smiled at her daughter. "Natalie's head is full of romance, thanks to several books she found in the library and Anna's penchant for telling stories."

"Well, it is rather romantic," Anna said dreamily. "A handsome lord takes a lowly wench to a mountain castle."

"The opinion of this wench is that it is no' the least bit romantic. 'Tis servitude," Mared said morosely.

"Not even a little romantic?" Natalie asked hopefully.

"No' even a wee bit, lass. 'Tis no' romance when one is ordered about like a dog."

Anna laughed, but stopped at once when Mared turned a pointed gaze on her.

"What precisely did he say?" Ellie asked, her brow wrinkled thoughtfully.

Mared sighed impatiently. "He said that he needed me to be with him. That I should take one of the maids to guard my virtue, but that he needed me there."

"*Ooh,*" Anna and Natalie sighed at once.

"*Ach,* ye'd find romance in nothing more than the morning mist!" she scoffed at the two of them.

"But he loves you, Auntie Mared," Natalie insisted.

"He doesna love me, Nattie, or he'd no' ask this of me."

"He does, Mared," Anna said. "You can't possibly deny it."

With a shrug, Mared picked up the blue silk and held it up to her as she stood before the old mirror.

"Oh, that's lovely, isn't it, Ellie?" Anna said, and to Mared, "Try it on."

Mared, who was already in her chemise having tried on a coral-colored dress that they all agreed made her look sickly, stepped into the pale blue silk and struggled to pull it up. "It's rather *tight,*" she said.

"Natalie, be a love and fetch a needle and thread," Anna said. "*Blue* thread."

"Yes, mu'um," Natalie said politely and skipped to the door and out as Anna came to stand behind Mared, admiring Mared's reflection. "Oh, Mared. You look beautiful. He won't believe his eyes when he sees you in this."

"You should carry a kerchief so that you might mop up his drool," Ellie added, and the two of them giggled.

"I'm happy that ye can laugh," Mared said petulantly as Ellie tried to button the back of the gown.

"Don't be silly," Anna said, pushing the cap sleeves off her shoulders. "We adore you, Mared. We want you to be happy. We just think that you are perhaps denying what is in your heart."

Had they been speaking to Donalda? "What is in my heart is that I shouldna march into the midst of so many Douglases."

In the mirror's reflection, she saw Ellie and Anna exchange a glance with one another. Then Ellie stepped forward, put her hands on Mared's shoulders. "Mared. He's a fine man. It doesn't matter in the least that his last name is Douglas. What matters is that he adores you completely. Do you know how many women there are in this world who would give all that they had for a husband who adores them?"

"*Husband!*" Mared cried, shocked.

"Here's a piece of advice, darling," Anna added, her head popping into view over Mared's right shoulder. "Allow him to make love to you before you commit to marrying him."

"*What?*" Mared cried, whirling around. "Have the two of ye gone completely daft, then? Marry him? Make love with him? What madness!"

"Don't be so prudish," Ellie said cavalierly. "It's just that . . . compatibility in the marital bed is very important, and as you have nothing to lose—stop looking at me like that will you? You've nothing to lose! From your very own lips hath come a vow to never marry!" Ellie insisted, touching Mared's lips with her fingertip. "Do you truly intend to go to your grave a virgin?"

Mared could feel the heat rising rapidly in her neck and face and looked down at her gown. "I *intend* to go to Edinburgh and live my life. I deserve that chance."

"Of course you do," Anna said soothingly. "But in the absence of that opportunity, you'll be here, and you've very few chances for remedy, isn't that so?"

It was so. Mared groaned and looked at the gorgeous blue silk. "But what of my virtue? Would ye have me throw it away?"

"Of course not," Ellie said sternly and grabbed Mared by the shoulders and turned her around to face the mirror again. "You must *always* guard your virtue, for it is all a young woman has. Just don't guard it *too* closely, or you will become quite miserable and spinsterly and lose any hope of ever experiencing a man's physical desire for you."

"And *that*, Mared, is one of the most sublime pleasures on this earth," Anna added. "Don't allow it to pass you by."

"Ye're both as mad as hens," Mared said, but she was looking at herself in the blue silk, thinking.

They managed to fasten it, and while she could scarcely breathe, she realized that she looked pretty, as pretty as she'd ever been. And while she might deny it to the entire world, she could not deny to herself her curiosity about men and their love and, well, how Payton would react when he saw her in this gown, and how . . . how he might go about making love to her. . . .

When Natalie returned with the needle and thread, they made a few hasty adjustments that would allow

Mared to breathe, then fussed over her undergarments until they were quite certain she had everything she needed for a night of bliss. Only then did the three of them descend to the main salon where the rest of the family was gathered.

Duncan lay on a blanket near the hearth with the puppy Mared had brought him. Natalie attempted to play the pianoforte, but it was terribly out of tune, and since leaving London, her lessons had fallen by the wayside. But they endured her determined efforts all the same, nodding and smiling politely.

They were just about to retire to the dining room when Dudley walked into the room carrying a tarnished tray, on which there was a letter. "A messenger, sir, from Laird Munroe."

"Munroe?" Carson muttered, and took the letter, broke the seal, and scanned the page. "*Ach,*" he said after a moment and flicked his wrist dismissively.

"What is it, Father?" Grif asked.

Carson frowned darkly and looked at Mared. "A wee bit of rubbish. Munroe claims to have seen MacAlister. Says he's about in the lowlands."

Grif quickly strode to where his father was sitting and took the missive.

"But this is wonderful news!" Aila cried.

"No!" Carson said sharply. "We've gone down more rabbit holes than a bloody rabbit! The bastard is no' in Scotland, and he'll never return to Scotland. No, *mo ghraidh,* he's living quite high on the hog at our expense in some foreign land."

"Aye," Grif said, nodding as he folded the letter, having read it. "That is undoubtedly true, Father. But we canna ignore any rumor that he's returned."

Carson shrugged. "I'll no' raise our Mared's hopes

again. He's no' come back to Scotland, and he never will."

He looked at Mared. She smiled reassuringly at her father, for she had resigned herself to that truth several weeks ago.

Twenty

The weather held for the journey deeper into the Highlands, and the Douglas party from Eilean Ros arrived at the tiny village of Kinlochmore in two days' time. Another mile and they reached the old castle on the banks of Loch Leven, surrounded by the Mamore Forest.

The castle was typical of highland fortresses, built high against a hill. About half of the old castle wall was still intact, along which carriages and carts were parked and servants were carrying in the luggage of guests. There were two towers anchoring the structure at the west and east ends, and between them stretched a massive stone structure that housed the great room, the dining hall, and various old chambers turned into sitting rooms and parlors.

Entrance to the main living area was made across a narrow bridge which led into an even narrower and dark corridor that had once served to keep invading enemies from entering in droves. It was the same sort of entrance as the one at Talla Dileas, and in fact, the only difference between this old castle and Talla Dileas was that Talla Dileas had been expanded over the centuries, so that now it was a peculiar mix of architectural styles and different kinds of stone.

It was along those narrow corridors that Mared and Una were led by a very congenial footman, who had, apparently, caught Una's eye, judging by the way she giggled and hurried to stay beside him.

Mared followed stoically behind, carrying her own luggage, watching carefully where she stepped, for she knew from her own home that years of foot traffic had worn down some of the stones and made them treacherous.

They walked along, Una chattering like a magpie, the friendly footman pointing out various features of the old castle, including the dungeon, which he found particularly amusing, until they reached a narrow curl of stairway that rose up. Mared struggled to fit herself and the luggage within that narrow space, until they reached a small landing. There was a door to their right and another corridor stretching out to their left.

"Here ye are, lassies," the footman said, and opened the door, gesturing for them to precede him through. Una and Mared walked into the small, circular tower room. The ceiling was low and beamed with thick slabs of wood; the walls were made of stone. There was a single bed, big enough for two. A worn Aubusson carpet covered the flagstone floor, a vanity and bureau were near the hearth, and a pair of narrow windows looked out over the Mamore Forest.

"'Tis lovely," Una said, her fingers trailing across an old tapestry that covered a wall.

"This room belonged to the first Lady Douglas. She died in childbirth in that very bed," he said. "Naturally, the mattress has been replaced."

Una giggled.

"And the laird Douglas of Eilean Ros? Where are his rooms?" Mared asked.

"The west tower. The rooms are larger and more comfortably appointed, befitting a laird. Yer footmen and coachmen will be housed in the old stables. They've been made into servants' quarters." He smiled at Una. "Shall I recite the agenda for ye, then?"

"Do, please," Una said.

"This evening, when the ladies and gents are served their supper in the formal dining room, the remainder of us shall be fed in the old stables. On the morrow, there will be traditional Highland gaming. Friday morning, the wedding ceremony will be held at the kirk in Kinlochmore, and Friday evening, the wedding *ceilidh* will be held on the south lawn by the loch to honor the bridal couple."

"Ooh," Una said. "It's all so lovely."

"Very well then, lassies," he said with a click of his heels and a bow. "Supper for the downstairs staff is served promptly at eight o'clock. I shall hope to see you there."

He and Una smiled at each other before he quit the room. The moment the door closed, Una whirled about, her hands at her breast. "'Tis bonny here is it no'?" she asked dreamily and walked to the window and looked out at the forest. "I hope that one day I shall marry in a fine celebration such as this, in a castle in the forest. Do ye, Miss Lockhart?"

The question took Mared aback; she'd never really thought what sort of wedding she might have—it seemed such an improbable, unlikely event. She glanced uncertainly at Una.

The poor girl instantly realized what she had said and clapped a hand over her mouth. "I do beg yer pardon, Miss Lockhart!" she whispered and frantically looked about the room for something to attend.

"Calm yerself, Una," Mared said with a thin smile. "I've lived with the curse all my life and scarcely give it a single thought." *Never a single thought . . . but maybe a million.*

They unpacked their things and put them away, made two trips to the well in the courtyard for water, and when they were satisfied that they were refreshed, they made their way down the spiraling narrow staircase to the main floor of the castle in search of Alan and Charlie.

They encountered dozens of people, so many that it was difficult to say who were servants and who were masters. Some of the men were dressed in fashion typical of the Quality—trousers and coats and waistcoats. But several wore coats and waistcoats and the *féileadh beag,* their clan plaid, as well as the *ghillie brogues* and *sporrans* and all that went with it. The women wore the *arisaidh* wrapped around their shoulders or like a sash across one shoulder and fastened with the *luckenbooth* at their waist. Everyone was laughing; the mood was festive.

In the old bailey, Mared and Una found their way to the stables where the male servants had been housed. The renovations had consisted of changing stalls into small rooms and not much else. But the mood within, like that outside, was decidedly festive; men shouted back and forth to one another, and one man played a lively tune on a bagpipe.

They found Alan and Charlie quickly, and both men were in fine spirits—Charlie instantly grabbed up Una in a dance and whirled her around the small space. "There she is, me bonny lass," Charlie sang happily. "Come to give this lad a kiss."

"Donna be silly, Charlie!" Una cried laughingly, playfully pushing him away.

"Come on then, ladies," Alan said, offering his arm to Mared. "We'll dine together, we lowly servants."

What had once been the tack room had been made a dining hall, and two long tables, filled with what seemed dozens of servants, swallowed the entire space. The close proximity of so many people from so many different houses, and most of them Douglas, made for a raucous affair. There was a lot of friendly ribbing back and forth both in English and Gaelic; several challenges were issued for the games that would be held on the morrow.

Ale was served along with mutton chops, and the laughter grew louder and more boisterous as the meal went on. When the wooden plates were cleared away, the man with the bagpipe appeared, and another man joined him, carrying a flute. An old pot was made into a drum, and the little trio began to play Highland *ceilidh* tunes.

It was only a matter of time before several of the men moved the tables and benches aside, and Charlie grabbed Una to dance.

Mared's feet were moving, too—she'd not danced often in her life, but when Alan looked at her, she smiled, and he eagerly grabbed her hand and led her onto the makeshift dance floor, into the thick of laughing men and women. Round and round they went, kicking up their heels to the gay Scots music, laughing and pausing only to gulp their ale before they went again.

It was a night of magic for Mared—she'd never danced with such abandon. She felt as if she was free of the curse somehow, as if she had found a place

where it had not followed her, and for the first time
that she could remember, she could breathe.

But fate had never been kind to Mared, and that
night proved to be a Judas kiss, for as she broke
away from Alan to drink some ale and wipe her
brow, she saw him. He was in the back of the dining
hall, his back against the wall, a tankard of ale in his
hand.

Jamie McGrudy was standing there, calmly watching Mared dance.

Payton had escaped the stiflingly formal dinner
inside the castle and had walked out onto a flagstone
terrace to enjoy the crisp night air and a cheroot. The
sound of gay music and laughter drifted across the
terrace on a breeze; he walked to the far edge and
looked down at the old stable block below. The dancing had spilled into the paddock; the servants were
clearly enjoying themselves.

Of course he wondered if she was down there. If
she danced. If she graced the lads with her devastating smile and if they desired her as much as he . . .

But he'd not had the simple pleasure of her smile
in days.

On the journey from Eilean Ros, he'd been too
mindful of her position and reputation and had kept a
respectable distance, lest he cause any indelicate talk
among the others. And since they'd arrived at Castle
Leven, he'd been engaged with his many cousins and
the bridal couple. As a result, he had no idea where
Mared was or what she did.

Aye, but he missed her and dreadfully so. He
missed her laughter, her smile, the wicked light in her
green eyes when she had no intention of doing what

he bade her. He missed her disdain, her delight, her pensiveness, and her grit.

Why had he brought her here?

It was a question he'd asked himself a thousand times over since departing Eilean Ros. He'd had nothing but endless moments to ponder it—at the time, it had seemed the only way—he'd been fearful she would leave Eilean Ros if he left her there, and he'd selfishly wanted her with him. He couldn't have her, but at least he might see her, feel her nearby.

His folly was in not thinking clearly. Of course she'd be separated from him, stowed away in some outbuilding with all the servants so that people like him would not be bothered with the sight or sound of her, or any other servant. The only opportunity he'd have to see her and speak with her at all would be in the morning, when she'd come to take his clothing and do God knew what with it.

He had no one to blame for his misery but himself—he'd created this perplexing situation when he'd demanded her servitude. Mared had not been born to a servant's station, and she'd be blissfully unacquainted with it now had it not been for his anger at her rejection. He wished that he could change it—a thousand times he'd regretted his rash decision. And now, he felt as if he was stuck between a rock and a stone, unable to go back, and quite unable to see his way clear.

The only thing he knew with any certainty was that he was destined to feel a hole in the middle of his heart, for he likely would never have her, and she would, eventually, leave him.

With a weary sigh, Payton tossed his cheroot aside and ground it out with the heel of his boot. He forced himself to walk away from the sound of the laughter below and return to his host's tedious supper party.

The next morning, however, Payton was dressed and waiting for her, anxious to have his single moment with her out of the thousands of moments that would pile up to form the day. He had guessed she would come at dawn when there would be no one afoot to see her enter and exit his chambers. And in fact, the sun had scarcely touched the morning sky when his door opened slowly and quietly, and her dark head slipped through the opening.

She did indeed seem surprised to see him sitting there, but quickly slipped inside and peered out into the corridor. Only when she was assured she had not been seen did she close the door and turn to face him, her hands behind her back, her smile bemused. "What are ye about so blessed early in the morning, then?" she asked him.

He gave her a wry smile, watched her walk into the room and pick up the coat he had left draped over a chair. She glanced around the tower room. "Ah, this is very grand, is it no'? The lad was right—it is befitting of a laird."

He hadn't given the room the slightest thought. It had a bed, a basin. "How are yer accommodations?" he asked, curious.

"A wee bit medieval," she said. "And a single bed, which would do perfectly well, but then, I didna realize I would sleep with Una."

"I should think Una would be no trouble."

"Oh, aye, she's no trouble," Mared said, smiling a little. "But she snores."

He smiled. "Loudly?"

"A *banshee* couldna be as loud."

Payton chuckled, and Mared cocked her head to one side, looked at him closely. "'Tis no' like ye to be so quiet, milord. I am accustomed to yer ordering or complaining."

He glanced away. "I suppose I've nothing to order or complain about," he said, and casually rose to his feet. "My cousins are determined to make me comfortable."

She took in his hunting attire. "Ye donna look dressed for the wedding games. Ye look as if ye intend to ride. Will ye no' participate?"

"The gentlemen are to hunt," he said. "The wedding games are for those who willna hunt today," he added carefully.

"*Ah*," she said and gave him a knowing nod. "The *servants*, ye mean, are to enjoy the games."

He said nothing. She laughed at his unwillingness to say it and walked to his bed to make it. "*Ach*, tossing and turning again, are ye?"

Like a madman. Her remark made him feel uncomfortably exposed, and he walked to the windows overlooking Loch Leven. "Did ye enjoy the festivities last night?" he forced himself to ask.

"Aye," she said. "Yer cousin is to be commended, for he treats his servants well."

Payton closed his eyes and imagined the many men gathered around her last night. He opened his eyes, clasped his hands behind his back, and asked, "Did ye dance, then?"

"For a time. No' as much as ye did, I'd wager."

"Ye danced for a time . . . and then what?"

She laughed at the question, and Payton turned to look at her. She was carelessly fluffing a pillow. "Then I retired. Did ye fear I would run off to be another man's housekeeper?" She laughed again.

But Payton's conscience was pricked, and he did not respond.

Mared tossed the pillow onto the bed and walked around the end of it. She picked up his coat, laid it on the bed, and folded it rather haphazardly. "Hmm," she said, frowning down at it. "It always seems better when Una does it." With a sigh, she picked up the coat and put it away in the bureau, gracefully avoiding Payton as he moved to the hearth. She turned around, rubbed her palms together. "All seems in order—"

"My shoes," he said hastily, spying his shoes on the floor near the hearth.

She looked at his feet.

"Have Charlie shine them, aye?" He stooped down, picked the shoes up, and held them out to her.

Mared gave him a dubious look. "They seem to have been polished."

"No."

With a shrug, she walked forward and reached for them, and as he handed them to her, Payton impulsively, foolishly, put his other hand to her face, touching the soft flesh beneath her ear lobe. Mared gazed up at him. There was no fear there, no consternation . . . just a soft curiosity as his fingers traced the line of her jaw, then trailed to her nose, and to her lips.

"What is it?" she asked quietly.

You. Us. Everything. He shook his head, let his hand drop to his side. "Enjoy yerself, Mared. Enjoy the wedding festivities. Ye deserve to do so. I'll no require yer services any longer this weekend. All of ye are to enjoy the wedding as a holiday."

She lifted one curious brow, but smiled sweetly. "*Mo chreach,* ye must have a care, milord. Ye've a reputation as a mean and black-hearted laird to uphold, aye?"

"Aye," he said, and turned away from her green eyes, to stare at the fire in the hearth. "Good day, Mared," he said quietly.

She stood there a moment longer; he could feel her gaze on him, and he silently begged her to go, to leave him. At last, at long last, she turned away and walked to the door. "Good day, Payton," she said evenly. He heard the door shut and glanced at it over his shoulder, then stared again at the fire.

Twenty-one

❧◦❧

Outside Payton's room, Mared lingered a moment, wondering what any of that meant. She put her fingers to her skin, where his touch still lingered, and then to her lips.

But she hurried from that door, lest she suffer a weak moment and throw it open and beg him to keep her safe from Jamie.

The curse had risen up from its black crypt almost the moment she saw Jamie's cruel smile and the ugly look in his eyes. Then came the whispers and looks she'd feared, the murmur snaking through the crowd like a poisonous asp. Eyes were suddenly on her, watching her closely.

She'd not imagined it, she knew she hadn't, for she'd felt it too many times in her life.

But as practiced as she was in dealing with the fears of suspicious Highlanders, she would guard herself closely, keep her distance. The same as she'd always done, keeping to herself to avoid speculation and talk.

She made her way to the old stables and handed Payton's shoes to Charlie.

"Clean and shine them again!" he complained. "I've only just done it, then!" But he took them nevertheless and turned around, walking into the room he shared with Alan. "Will he compete in the games?" he asked over his shoulder. When he received no response, he turned to look . . . but Mared had already slipped away.

She returned to her tower chamber. Una had long since disappeared—undoubtedly in the company of the smiling footman. But in the afternoon, when the games began, Mared could not endure the stuffy old chamber, and with her *arisaidh* covering her head, she walked outside into the crowd of visiting servants and villagers and some highborn guests. She moved about, keeping her head down, her face obscured by her *arisaidh*, admiring the crafts of the artisans who had come from the village, watching with other enthusiastic onlookers the hammer and rock throw that pitted two enormous men against one another.

The Douglases of Castle Leven had left no detail undone—the ale flowed freely all afternoon, and the longer the games went on, the more unruly the crowd became and the louder they cheered their favorite competitor.

She was relieved that she did not see Jamie, but the boisterous behavior made her nervous, for one never knew what an ale-soaked Douglas crowd might find offensive. Or amusing. So Mared had slipped away, into the forest, content to walk alone.

Diah, but she missed her long walks around Talla Dileas and Loch Chon! And as it was a glorious autumn day, she determined there was no time like the present to avail herself of the beauty surrounding Loch Leven.

It was a blissful, peaceful walk, and she had gone on for two hours, she guessed, judging by the movement of the sun. When it seemed that the sun was beginning to sink behind the trees, Mared made her way back to the castle. But as she neared the property, she was a bit disoriented. She could not see the castle for the trees and wasn't certain which of the two paths before her led back to the castle and the old stable block and which led to the new stables and wash-house.

She picked the path to the right and strolled on, admiring the flora. When she heard the laughter of men, she was certain she had reached the castle grounds and walked out of the forest . . . and arrived at the west end of the new stables.

"Mary Queen of Scots," she muttered beneath her breath. At least she knew where she was. As she rounded the stables, she saw the source of the laughter, and her heart dropped to her toes. She instantly backed away, but it was too late, for Jamie McGrudy had seen her.

He and three men were on their haunches, rolling dice on the dirt next to the stables. The moment he saw her, he instantly rose up, glaring at her.

One of his friends turned to look, and he came to his feet, too, with a surly smile on his lips. "Ho there, *co tha seo?*"

"I'll tell ye who it is, lad—none other than the witch of Loch Chon, the accursed Miss Lockhart."

"Accursed?"

"Aye," Jamie said, walking out of their circle toward Mared. "'Tis said that she has the eye of *a' dia-bhal.*"

He would not, apparently, ever announce her curse correctly, Mared thought and took an uneasy step backward. Correct or not, what he'd said had caused a ripple of exclamation to rise up from his companions, and the remaining two came to their feet, one of them looking at her curiously, the other looking at her with fear.

"Donna be foolish, Jamie," she said, the lightness in her voice belying the terror she felt. "I told ye—'tis an old wives' tale."

"Is it?" he drawled, casually moving toward her. "Then why have yer own blood forsaken ye and given ye over as whore to the laird of Eilean Ros?"

"A whore, is she?" One of the men asked, so drunk he could scarcely stand on his own two feet.

"Aye, a bloody whore," Jamie said, and his brown gaze went terribly dark as it hungrily swept her body.

Mared's terror was quickly turning into a choking panic. She was an inexperienced woman in some respects, but she instinctively understood the look in his eye, understood all too well his intent.

"What do ye think of it, lads? Shall I kiss *a' diabhal*, then?"

Frantic, Mared thought of what to do and glanced over her shoulder.

"*Ach*, ye donna think to run from us, do ye lass?" Jamie asked with a cold chuckle. "I'd fetch ye back in a moment, I would, and I'd no' be pleased."

One of the men laughed. "Let her run, Jamie! I'll wager ye canna catch her, but if ye do, I'll pay ye a bloody crown, I will."

Mared took several steps backward; her plaid slipped off her head.

"Oh, she's bonny, lad," one of the men said. "If *a' diabhal* doesna take ye, perhaps I'll have a go."

The men laughed, and Mared's heart climbed to her throat. In her panic, she turned to run, twisting about so quickly that she tripped, but she quickly regained her footing and ran as fast as she might.

She scarcely made it to the edge of the paddock before she was knocked to the ground and the breath knocked from her lungs.

The men were suddenly shouting, but she could not make out what they said, she could not make out anything other than the hate in Jamie MacGrudy's eyes when he roughly rolled her onto her back and glared down at her. "Ye bloody accursed little *whore*, ye cost me a position in a fine house!" he spat. "Do ye think I willna take what is—"

He never finished his sentence, for he was suddenly flying. Someone leapt over Mared and fell upon him, beating him mercilessly. Mared scrambled to her feet and struggled to catch her breath. It was a moment or two before she could focus and realized that it was Payton beating Jamie senseless, and that two gentlemen were pulling him off Jamie, forcing him back. Payton lashed out with his boot, kicking Jamie in the small of his back.

"Leave him, laird!" one of the men bellowed.

Two more gentlemen appeared and crouched down to examine Jamie, who was moaning and gripping his stomach.

Payton shook off the men who held him as if they were gnats and leaned over, grabbed Jamie by the collar, and hauled him up to his feet. "If ye ever so much as *look* in her direction, I will kill ye, aye?"

"Aye, aye," Jamie whimpered. One of the men pushed Payton aside and two more put their arms around Jamie to help him walk.

"Lock him away!" Payton roared.

"Aye, laird, aye," one of the men assured him, patting him on the shoulder. That man glanced at Mared, then at Jamie's back, and walked on, the other men falling behind him and the two that led Jamie away.

When they disappeared around the corner, Payton pivoted around to Mared. He had blood on his waist-coat and his shirt. His jaw was clenched tightly shut, but he suddenly strode forward and in three long strides, he caught her, yanked her into his arms, and cradled her head against his shoulder.

"I'm sorry, Mared, so very sorry," he said and suddenly released her, set her back from him so he could study her closely. There was still fire in his eyes, and his jaw was implacably set. His nostrils flared with each furious breath, but he carefully laid his palm against her cheek, his eyes searching her face.

She couldn't help herself—her hands were trembling, her nerves had made a mess of her belly, and there was something so fiercely protective in the set of his jaw and the hard glint of his eye that she crumpled. Tears slipped from the corners of her eyes; she could feel twenty-seven years of defense melting away, and without thought, Mared flung her arms around his neck and buried her face against his shoulder.

Payton caught her around the waist and held her tightly to him as she sobbed onto his shoulder. She felt such relief and safety in the circle of his arms, felt connected to this man by some thick and indestructible bond. Her heart was falling, slipping out from beneath the stone wall she had erected, sliding and tumbling out from its armor. She could hear Donalda whisper, *The truth is in yer heart, lass. . . .*

She believed.

Mared turned her face from his shoulder to his

neck, her lips landing on the curve of his jaw. She heard his quick draw of breath, felt him hold it. "Ye saved me," she muttered helplessly against his cheek. "How will I ever thank ye?"

"*Diah*, Mared, do ye no' know it well by now? I'd lay down my very life for ye."

She did know it. She'd always known it, but this was the first time she'd been willing to acknowledge it deep within herself. She opened her eyes and looked up at him, this man, this powerful laird, who was looking at her in astonishment and with hope in his eyes. She thought it odd that he could appear so strong and vulnerable all at once. Her gaze swept his handsome face—the thick brows over slate gray eyes, the aquiline nose, the proud cheekbones, the square jaw . . . the dark flesh of his lips. How had she resisted him for so long? How had she let something like a name keep her from him?

Now her heart tilted, knocked her off her bearings, and she caught Payton by surprise with a sudden kiss to his mouth. A hard, unyielding, determined kiss. Payton took her chin in his hand, turned her head slightly, and opened his mouth to hers, stroking her with his tongue. His other hand swept down her back, to her hip, and clutched her, pressing her into him, then sweeping up, to the swell of her breast, cupping it reverently, squeezing against the fabric that confined her, his fingers brushing the bare skin above the bodice.

He kissed her deeply, so deeply that she felt as if she were falling away into an abyss with nothing surrounding her but the warmth of his body, the pressure of his soft lips, the strength of his hands and arms that held her. She could feel his desire in the hard ridge that he pressed against her, could feel his esteem for her in the way he laid his hands so tenderly on her skin.

Her tears stopped flowing and she began her own search of him, her hands running up his arms, down his back, around the trim waist, and up the hard plane of his chest. Her body felt on fire, and she wanted nothing more than to pull the seams of her gown apart so that his breath might cool her skin.

But a sound in the distance, the steady rise of voices nearing them, filtered into her consciousness. Payton's, too, apparently, for he gripped her arms tightly and slowly pushed her away from him.

"Bloody hell," he muttered and quickly kissed her again, nipping at her lip, and then, breathing quick and hard, he stepped away from her and looked at her with a depth of emotion that made her shiver. It was devotion in those gray eyes—and at the very least, a raging desire that stoked her own.

Payton touched her cheek once more, then turned and strode forward to greet the men who had come around to see what had happened.

Twenty-two

❖

*N*eacel Douglas was, understandably, horrified by what had happened by the stables on the occasion of his wedding and handled the matter expeditiously. Jamie and his companions were hauled off to the nearest constable, and from there, Jamie was to be taken to a gaol at Fort William, where his fate would be determined by a judge whose surname happened to be Douglas.

In the aftermath, Payton wasn't entirely certain what had become of Mared, but when their hosts had come rushing to the stables to see after them, she had retrieved her *arisaidh* from the ground and wrapped it around her and was surrounded by his aunt Catrine and cousin Edme, Neacel's sister, who had hurried Mared away with their arms securely around her.

He assumed they had taken her to her chamber and that she was, at the very least, physically well—but he could not vouch for her emotional state.

His thoughts quickly turned fearful—fear that she regretted her passionate, soul-searing kiss, fear that he had laid his heart bare again, and would, therefore, feel its demise once again.

When Charlie brought him the polished shoes, he

feigned ignorance and asked after his household staff. "All is well with us, aye?"

"Aye, laird," Charlie said, his young face glowing. "We've been right entertained, we have. Alan participated in the caber toss."

That surprised and pleased Payton. "Oh? How did he fare?"

"Dead last, milord," Charlie said with a laugh. "But the lad was game about it and gave it his best toss for Eilean Ros."

"I must thank him," Payton said, smiling. "And the women?" he asked, turning slightly. "How do they do?"

For some reason, Charlie laughed a little. "Quite well, laird, quite well indeed. Aye, they are a bonny pair—there was a bit of a queue to dance with them last evening."

That only gave him a stab of unexpected jealousy.

"If there is naugh' else, milord . . ."

"No," Payton said, smiling thinly. "Go, then, and enjoy the wedding. I'll no' have need of any of ye on the morrow. Ye are free to join in the festivities."

Charlie's face brightened considerably. "Thank ye, laird! I shall give word to the others."

Payton waited until Charlie had quit the room before he dragged both hands through his hair and, like a green lad, wondered how he might endure the night without her. He needed her. And he'd let his damn hopes wing free again.

But he was a grown man and he managed. He dressed for the evening and muddled his way through a rather raucous supper, where tall tales of hunting were told. After supper, the women took the bride up to her chambers to perform the traditional foot washing and to play the bridal games that were likewise traditional on the eve of a wedding. The men departed with Neacel to parade him about the village with a lot of fanfare and noisemaking and then drink as much ale as they could collectively consume.

When they returned to the castle, it was well past midnight, and they were well into their cups. Most of the women had retired, but there were still a few hearty souls up and about. Payton's Aunt Catrine made her way to his side with a young woman in tow.

"Ye willna recall yer distant cousin Dora," she said as she introduced them.

She was the third unmarried woman Catrine had brought around to him since his arrival, but Payton was a seasoned veteran of matchmaking attempts, and he smiled, came to his feet, and bent over Dora's hand.

"Dora is me husband's nephew's daughter," Catrine explained. "Ye met her when she was a wee lass."

"I canna believe so, Aunt, for I would no' have forgotten such a bonny lass," he said gallantly, and the young woman blushed.

Catrine smiled happily, put her hand on the small of the bashful Dora's back, and gave her a nudge toward Payton.

He sat with the lass, making polite conversation. But when he looked at her lips, he thought of Mared's lips. When he looked at her brown eyes, he saw green. And when he glanced at her hair, so artfully arranged, he saw Mared's long black braid.

When Dora waxed dreamily about the wedding and spoke of her interest in art, he thought of Mared tromping about the Highlands in her boots, pilfering berries and penning his sheep.

The night was interminable.

Because of her brush with disaster, Mared spent the evening in her chamber, afraid to go out and join the other servants, who were wild with joy and helped along by a significant amount of ale. When a giddy Una asked where she'd been, Mared lied. "In the bailey. Did ye no' see me there?"

Una swore that she had not, but then, she had seen only the handsome footman.

Mared didn't emerge from her chamber until the next morning, in time for the wedding.

The Douglases were ecstatically happy that the day had dawned so crystal clear and cool. It augured a good beginning for the bridal couple.

Mared donned her purple gown and with Una, stayed at the fringes of the crowd for the traditional processional to the kirk. There were three hundred souls attending the processional, and another hundred or more already waiting in the kirk yard. As the old stone kirk was so small, the servants and villagers were to stand outside while Douglases filled the pews and lined the walls within.

Mared and Una stood together under an elm tree, Una watching for Harold, the footman whom she had come to love desperately in the space of forty-eight hours, and Mared no longer pretending not to look for Payton.

But how could she miss him? He was part of the family processional, looking quite resplendent in his black coat, a white, frilled lawn shirt, a green waistcoat, and the *féileadh beag,* the plaid tartan of Eilean

Ros, belted at his waist. He'd also donned the traditional *sporran* and *ghillie brogues*.

Behind him and his cousins, two young girls
skipped along, tossing rose petals on the path the
bride would take. *"Diah*, but she's bloody beautiful!"
Una sighed as the bride appeared.

She was resplendent in her cream-colored gown.
She wore a garland of heather around her fair head
and carried a bouquet of Scottish roses and thistle. As
she neared the kirk, a piper began to play the bagpipe,
welcoming her in traditional fashion.

The bagpiper stood aside as the Douglases filed
into the kirk, followed at last by the bride and her
father.

Those standing in the kirk yard could not hear the
ceremony as it was performed, so Mared made her
way through the throng to get as close to the door as
possible. And while she could not see the couple—
there were too many men standing along the back
wall of the kirk—she could hear the priest conduct the
ceremony in Gaelic, could hear the couple recite their
vows.

At the conclusion of the ceremony, the happy couple kissed to the wild approval of those congregated
inside the kirk, and Mared drifted to the fringe of the
crowd once more as the couple burst forth, their
hands clasped, their faces beaming. The groom threw
coins to the children as they hurried to the carriage
parked nearby, and they were whisked away to Castle
Leven, while the hundreds of guests walked, accompanied by the bagpiper and joyful wedding songs.

Mared did not see Payton in that crowd—there
were too many people, too much movement and
jostling about.

The wedding breakfast had been split—the servants would dine in the old stables, and the family and guests of the Douglases in the castle. Following breakfast, there would be a rest period, and the common celebration, at which servants and their betters would mingle, would begin late in the afternoon with singing and speeches in advance of feasting and dancing that would carry on well after the newlyweds were shown to their bridal chamber.

After the breakfast, Mared and Una returned to their room to rest and dress for the big celebration that evening.

Except that they did very little resting, as Una was too enamored of Harold to keep quiet for more than a moment. She chattered endlessly as to how kind he was, and how very thoughtful, and when he kissed her, Una felt as if she'd contracted a tropical fever and felt close to fainting.

Mared wished she would go on and faint, then, for it was impossible to hear so much joy and anticipation of love without wanting to feel that all for herself. Accustomed as she was to pushing those sorts of feelings down, it was difficult to let them out, if only for an evening.

But as Una arranged her hair in a most artful style on the back of her head, chatting all the while about Harold, Mared managed to let a small ray of joy beam inside herself. And she allowed herself the tiniest sliver of hope that she, too, might marry one day and hold her own baby in her arms, as fat and happy as wee Duncan. A hope that she might be loved and not feared, that no one would die in the course of loving her.

That hope buoyed her, and when she donned the blue silk with Una's assistance, her appearance steeled her. She couldn't help but stare at her reflection in the mirror, for she'd never looked so elegant as this, had never possessed the aristocratic bearing necessary to carry it. By some miracle, she did this evening. Something about the way Payton had looked at her there by the stable had made her feel beautiful and entirely immortal.

"Oh, Miss Lockhart!" Una exclaimed behind her, blinking at her reflection. "Ye're even bonnier than the poor bride!"

Mared laughed. "Bring the roses there, aye?" she said, nodding at a vase on the windowsill. "What do ye think? We shall put them in our hair."

Una was delighted, and so it was with Scottish roses entwined in her hair and jewelry borrowed from Ellie that Mared joined the common wedding feast at dusk.

She was instantly aware of the many eyes on her. Some looked at her in fear, but some—men, really—looked at her with a sort of admiration. And lust, if she were quite honest about it. From the women, there was perhaps a bit of coveting of her gown.

That put a smile on Mared's face.

With her hands clasped behind her back, she found a small Scotch pine and she and Una stood with their backs to the tree so they could watch the enormous crowd as the wedding speeches were made. The setting sun looked as if it was straight out of a painting, glistening on the surface of Loch Leven. Butterflies swooped in and above the crowd as several shouted their gay and bawdy words of encouragement to the bridal couple, demanding kisses and cheering the couple when they playfully touched their lips together.

As the speeches wound down, and the sun had slipped into the hills, five large fires were lit about the large parklike lawn, signaling that the feast and dancing were soon to begin. A pair of bagpipers and flautists made their way onto the platform that had been vacated by the bridal couple and began to play lively tunes.

Una spied Harold, and with a shriek of glee, and after Mared assured her she'd be perfectly fine without her, off the girl went, leaving Mared to stand alone under the limbs of the pine tree. Only a few moments passed before she sensed someone watching her and very deliberately turned and looked over her shoulder.

He was standing a good distance from her, but Mared saw him instantly and her heart stopped beating at the sight of him. He was still dressed in the traditional plaid with his legs braced apart, his hands clasped behind his back, and gazing at her with the sort of smile that suggested he very much liked what he was seeing.

Mared tilted her head in acknowledgment of that and smiled.

Payton returned the nod.

Her smile broadened; she gestured to her gown, how it gathered tightly beneath her bosom then flowed into silky layers of embroidered panels over an underskirt. He cocked a brow. She turned a little to her right so that he might see the train, then to her left, and then laughingly dipped a tiny little curtsey.

Payton smiled fully and bowed low. And then he began to move, his stride unhurried, his gaze never leaving her as he made his way through the lively crowd, the hem of his plaid kicking up with his gait.

Mared turned fully toward him, her heart pounding harder and harder with his every step.

She was practically levitating out of her blue silk slippers when he finally reached her and paused to let his ravenous gaze take her in. "Good evening, Miss Lockhart," he said, a roguish smile of delight on his lips.

"Good evening, Laird Douglas."

"Ye are a vision of beauty, lass. Ye've surprised me."

"Thank ye," she said, bowing her head with pleasure. "And how pleasing to see ye so nattily turned out in yer Highland dress. Many was the time I thought ye a Highland imposter."

"I should be offended, I am sure, for I am as true a Highlander as ye are a beauty," he said, casually bracing his arm against the tree on which she was leaning.

She laughed and glanced around at the crowd, several of whom had already begun to dance. "Ye flatter me, and yet ye know I'll no' be the least bit enticed by it."

"Donna be so certain," he said with a low chuckle, "for I have no' yet begun to flatter ye."

"Ye shouldna waste yer breath."

"But I canna be deterred. I shall continue shamelessly, for a gorgeous woman deserves every flattery a man can offer."

"Mmm."

He laughed. "I've naugh' seen this gown, for I am quite certain I would remember it very well. Very well, indeed," he said and grinned roguishly at her décolletage. "There is no' a more admired woman here this evening, ye may rest assured." His gaze drifted down the entire length of her, then languidly lifted his gaze again, skimming over the curve of her hip, lingering on her bosom, and rising to her lips and then smiling in her eyes again.

His gaze was beginning to burn through her silk dress, and Mared unthinkingly lifted her hand to her neck and asked, "How have ye found the wedding?"

"'Tis bonny," he said absently, still admiring her hair. "Weddings always are."

"I feel rather sorry for the poor bride," Mared sighed, fanning herself with the tip of her shawl. "Poor dear, marrying a Douglas. She'll know nothing but vexation and stubborn pride all her days."

"Oh, I rather think better a Douglas than a Lockhart, for a Lockhart would undermine her fortune at every opportunity with his inordinate fondness for hairy *coos*," he said, and with the back of his hand, he traced a line across her collarbone.

Mared drew a steadying breath. "She must descend from shepherds, then."

"Of course. Do ye think a Douglas would marry ought else?" he muttered as his caress drifted down her arm to her hand.

She would melt, she was certain of it, and glanced anxiously at the crowd. "No' unless he was assured that he might dictate the very course of her life, no."

He laughed, turned her hand over, and held it in his, palm up. "Ye obviously didna hear the priest then, or ye would be reminded that when a woman gives herself in marriage, 'tis her duty to faithfully obey her husband."

Mared laughed gaily at that and watched him bring her hand to his lips to kiss her palm. A hot rush of fire spread rapidly through her arm to her heart. "Rubbish," she managed to say. "'Tis a man's duty to honor his wife, and I should think that would imply all her customs and manners as well. But alas, I didna hear any of the ceremony, save the last wee bit, and I didna care for even that, for it was quite wrong."

"What part? Tell me, and I shall disabuse ye of yer obvious misunderstanding," he said with a lopsided smile and carelessly kissed the inside of her wrist.

"Very well," she murmured, quietly sucking in her breath as his lips moved on her wrist. *"Gus an dèan Diah leis a' bhàs ar dealachadh."*

Payton smiled. "'Until death shall separate us'? Pray tell, what fault could ye possibly find with that?" He paused to kiss the inside of her elbow. "Unless, of course, ye donna believe in vowing yer fidelity and devotion to yer husband for all yer days?"

"I believe in vowing fidelity and devotion, ye may rest assured. But I'd no' like it to end with death. I should think the vow would swear devotion for an eternity."

That prompted him to look up from her arm with surprise. "How very romantic of ye." His gaze dipped to her lips. "And to think that all this time, I've believed ye possessed no' even an ounce of romantic thought in that . . . heart," he said, his gaze dipping to the swell of her bosom.

"Ye might very well be surprised, sir."

"Oh? Pray, tell—I am dying of curiosity."

"And I am dying of hunger," she said in a moment of cowardice and pushed away from the pine. She began to walk toward the tables where the feast had been laid, pausing only briefly to glance over her shoulder to see if Payton followed.

He followed all right. Much like a lion calmly stalking his evening meal.

She smiled when he caught up to her and tucked

her hand securely in the crook of his arm to escort her across the grassy lawn.

Tables had been set with enough food to feed an army, while two pigs were roasted over open pits. Payton grabbed a plate and piled game, sweetmeats, and cake onto it. Mared managed to find an entire flagon of wine—handed to her by a smiling footman who could not seem to take his eyes off her—but Payton was quickly at her side, scaring the footman away with a single look, and led Mared to a grassy spot where they could see the dancing and the wedding games.

They sat together as if they had long been lovers, watching as the bride prepared to jump over the besom broom for good luck, laughing together when a dog caught the broom in his mouth and gleefully ran with it dragging from the side of his mouth and darting just ahead of the three footmen who tried desperately to catch him.

They ate roasted fowl and bannock cakes with their fingers, nibbled on sweetmeats, and made a game of which couples would be married next. Their conversation was light, Mared's heart even lighter. She felt, for the first time in her memory, that she was part of something and not simply standing on the outside looking in. Payton put her completely at ease, and even as a number of cousins and relatives approached the two of them sitting there, and some of them were clearly surprised to be introduced to a Lockhart, she felt oddly content to be a Lockhart in the midst of so many Douglases.

She felt something else she could not quite as yet name . . . but it left her feeling warm and golden.

When the sun had gone down and enough ale and

whiskey had been drunk to float a galleon, the dancing was begun in earnest. Alan found them on the
hillside and asked Mared to dance a Scottish reel.
Laughing, the two of them went around the ring of
eight, turning left, then right. When the dance was
ended, Alan handed her to a friend, and they danced
a jig, and then she danced with Harold at Una's urging, then a rather stodgy Douglas cousin who eyed
her bosom the entire set of another reel.

When another country dance was begun, she was
handed back to Alan, and she twirled away from him,
stepped to her left, then to her right, and back again.
But it was not Alan's hand that landed on her waist, it
was Payton's.

"Ye're even bonnier when ye dance, Mared," he
said in her ear, and she stepped forward, to the right,
to the left, and back again. "I shall dream of this dance
in far more intimate circumstances," he added, and
Mared laughed as he twirled her around. Her twirl
was stopped by the hard wall of his chest. He grinned
down at her with smoldering eyes—she could feel the
force of his gaze rifle through her like a shooting star,
landing squarely in the middle of her chest.

They continued the dance, Payton expertly
twirling her this way and that, catching her close to
his body, then letting her go. They were spinning and
twirling and going around again in the light of five
campfires, grabbing hands and pulling into one
another, then letting go and drifting on to the next
dancer, until they were united again, their eyes never
leaving one another.

They danced until their breath was labored and
they finally stopped for ale, at which point they
noticed a boisterous crowd had begun to take up the

call to send the bride and groom to their bridal chamber.

In the golden glow of the firelight, Mared watched the happy couple and the friends who would attempt to assist them.

Payton touched the small of her back. Impulsive, foolish thoughts, born out of Anna and Ellie's speech to her, were suddenly rattling around in her head like a caged animal, desperate to be out, and Mared put aside her ale and turned to face Payton, eyeing him quizzically. "How would it be, do ye think, if the bride were a Lockhart, and he a Douglas?"

He seemed surprised by the question. "No consequence."

Mared smiled a little and lifted a skeptical brow. *"No?"*

"No. There is no Douglas or Lockhart where they go tonight."

"How is that possible, assuming he was a Douglas and she a Lockhart? How could they possibly forget it?"

"Very easily, lass," he said with a grin, and at her look, he took her hand in his. "Rather plainly put, when a man loves a woman, his heart calls to hers. And if the woman loves the man, her heart responds. The two hearts, then, they begin to beat as one. Names cease to exist—nothing exists but the rhythm of those two hearts, beating in time with one another . . . until one is practically indistinguishable from the next." He lifted her hand to his lips and kissed her knuckles.

The roar of the crowd caught their attention, and they both turned to look. The crowd was moving with the bridal couple down the path to the front entrance of the castle where they would be wildly serenaded as they were escorted inside.

Mared twisted her hand so that her palm was against Payton's and laced her fingers through his. She stared at their hands for a long moment, then asked, "Does a lass know if a lad's heart is calling to her?"

"Aye," he said quietly. "She knows."

"Do ye suppose," she whispered, stepping closer to him, "that his heart knows when hers has tilted in his direction?"

"He doesna know . . . but he hopes," he murmured, his gaze falling to her mouth again. He leaned down and touched his lips reverently to hers.

When he lifted his head, Mared smiled softly and stepped backward, tugging at him, silently asking him to come with her.

Payton's brow wrinkled—but Mared tugged at his hand again and stepped back, still tugging, until they were slowly but surely moving.

"Mared—"

She quickly pushed a finger to his lips, and with a low laugh, she tugged once more.

A wickedly seductive smile suddenly spread across his lips, and he caught her chin in his fingers and kissed her soundly before catching her around the waist and making her run with him into the dark.

Twenty-three

❧•❧

ecause the crowd followed the bridal couple to fete them on the way to their marriage bed, Payton and Mared slipped in through the servants' entrance unnoticed, and made their way in complete darkness to his chamber, where he slid the bolt in place and locked them away from the world.

He turned around to Mared. She'd lit two candles and was standing in the middle of the room, looking, all of a sudden, rather small. The willful and playful smile she'd used when tugging him along, the bravado with which she'd laughed and rushed headlong into this bliss, was gone.

This was not right, his conscience told him. Mared was so much more than a tryst. He'd been captivated by the exhilaration of her wanting him and his overwhelming desire to make love to her that he'd not really considered what she was suggesting.

Like him, she'd been caught up in the thrill of the wedding celebration, for she was a passionate woman—but she was not usually a foolish woman. And he thought, as he stood there gazing at her by the light of two single candles, his hands on his hips, that she regretted her impetuosity now.

"Ye need no' fear," he said quietly, prepared to be a gentleman, no matter how much it pained him.

Mared blinked; her silk shawl slid, unnoticed by her, to the ground. "Take off yer clothes, then," she murmured.

Payton started, and then he laughed. "Never one to mince words, are ye, *leannan?*"

"I donna pretend to know . . . *how*, precisely," she said, her voice a little stronger, and she swallowed as her gaze flicked over him. "But I am rather certain that ye must remove yer clothing."

Aye, the grit of the gods she had in her. Payton strolled toward her, shrugging out of his coat and tossing it aside. "It can be achieved with clothing, but it is much more satisfying without," he agreed.

She gave him a small, self-satisfied smile. "What of the waistcoat?" she asked, gesturing to him.

He untied his neckcloth and threw it over his shoulder, and then divested himself of his waistcoat and tossed it aside, too. And then he reached her, straddled her skirts and put his hands on her arms, ran up them lightly, feeling her satin skin. "'Tis customary for a man to direct the proceedings, if ye donna mind."

"Why?"

"Why? Because that is the way of it, particularly when a woman has no experience and a man has quite enough."

"Is that a rule?" she asked, frowning up at him.

"No' a rule, Mared. But men prefer to be the one in pursuit, not the one to be pursued."

"That scarcely makes any sense at—"

He silenced her with a kiss. Mared sighed into his mouth and curved into him, tilting her head up, opening her mouth to him.

But Payton lifted his head and gave her a gentle shake to make her open her eyes. "Tell me why," he softly demanded.

"Why?" she asked dreamily, looking at his lips. "Why what?"

"Why this. Why now?"

The question sobered her; she straightened, fixed her gaze on the open collar of his shirt. Shrugged a little. Bit her lower lip. And winced. "Because . . ."

"Because?" he prompted.

"Because . . . I have determined that ye are no' as . . . repugnant . . . as I once believed."

He snorted. "How ye flatter me," he said and leaned his head down, took in the scent of her hair— lilac and roses.

She caught the fabric of his shirt and held on as if she feared she might fall. "I only mean to say," she tried again, her grip of his shirt tightening as his mouth grazed her temple, "that ye are—"

As he touched his lips to her eye, she gasped softly.

"Ye were saying?" he murmured, feathering her skin with light kisses to her neck.

"Th-that perhaps I have feelings for ye I didna . . . concede," she said shakily, and twisted the fabric of his shirt as he moved, dipping down, to kiss the curve of her neck into her collarbone.

"Mmm," he said. "Go on, then."

She drew a shaky breath and slowly released it as he moved to the other side of her neck. "I have come to understand that the . . . the Douglas in ye doesna matter."

Whoa. Didn't matter? Payton stopped his attentions to look at her, to see if she teased him.

"It seems rather unimportant now," she admitted, blushing.

He refrained from shouting *victory* and tossing her on the bed in triumph and thought, as he resumed his feast of her neck, that those were possibly the sweetest words he'd ever heard.

"Ye seem to be less Douglas and more . . . *man*," she murmured breathlessly.

"I assure ye, I am both Douglas and man." He dipped to kiss the hollow of her throat.

"My heart has tilted, Payton," she whispered. "It heard yer heart call and it has tilted toward ye, and I donna even know when it happened."

Her admission galvanized his adoration of her. He'd longed to hear her say she esteemed him in some small measure, and her words squeezed hard around his heart, lifted it up, and gave him a joy he'd never felt in his life. He raised his head, cupped her face in his hands, and kissed her lips, her nose, her forehead, then wrapped his arms around her, holding her tightly to him. "*Criosd*, Mared, ye donna know how I've desired to hear ye say it," he said, and then reluctantly let go of her. And made himself step back.

She looked at him with confusion. "What are ye doing, then?"

"Something I never thought I'd do. But I'll no' take ye like some tavern wench. I hold ye in too high regard for that."

Mared closed her mouth. Her brows knit together, and she slowly folded her arms across her middle and shifted her weight to one hip. She glared at him. *Gaped* at him. He seduced her confession of feeling for him, and now he would walk away? "Have ye any idea how much courage it took to ask this of ye?" she demanded.

"Aye, but I am a gentleman, and one who cares very much for yer virtue."

He had to be jesting. "Of all the bloody times to fret over my virtue!"

"Mared," he said laughingly, and put his hands on his waist and regarded her with a smile. "Ye are a bonny lass, but ye are impetuous as hell, aye? I canna allow ye to make a mistake as grand as this."

The corner of Mared's mouth tipped up, and she reached for the belt that held his plaid. "Just like a Douglas, is it no', to determine how grand my mistakes are. And would a gentleman really force a lady to ask *thrice?*" she asked, wrapping her fingers around the thick edge of his belt.

Payton glanced down at her hand. "Do ye truly know what ye do?"

She rose to her toes and kissed him on the corner of his mouth. "No. I was rather hoping ye might show me."

The expression in his eyes changed then, and he leaned down, caught her bottom lip between his teeth as his arms went around her. "God save me, for I'll show ye, then. I want ye, Mared, I've always wanted ye. I want the taste of yer lips, the touch of yer tongue to mine. I want to feel yer breath on my skin, feel ye surround me when I am inside ye. I want to fill ye with hope and love and babies, I swear to the heavens I do."

Mared sighed longingly and dropped her head back as he held her tightly to him, his lips on her neck.

"I just pray ye think twice before taking me to yer bed, *mo ghraidh*, for I will have yer virtue," he growled.

"I believe ye will take me to *yer* bed," she whispered, bending her head so that he might have better access to her neck.

Payton groaned. He let go his grip of her and pushed the small cap sleeves of her gown from her shoulders. His hands were at her back then, expertly working the row of tiny buttons there. "There will be a wee bit of pain, aye?" he whispered.

"I know."

"And I will always be a part of ye—have ye considered it?"

"*Diah*, Payton, do ye always speak as much as this?"

He paused in his work on her gown to grin down at her. "Heaven help us both," he said and grabbed her up and kissed her with all the emotion she was feeling.

He unfastened her gown with the deftness of a man who'd known many such gowns, and she felt it slip away from her body. His hands were everywhere then, flitting over her arms, caressing her breasts, her hips, her legs, and back. His touch made her lightheaded; she felt ethereal. And she wanted more.

Mared threw all caution aside and grabbed her chemise in hand and lifted it over her head, letting it fall from the tip of her fingers, exposing her breasts. Payton drew a deep breath and reverently cupped them both, feeling the weight of them. He dipped his head to take one nipple in his mouth, flicking his tongue against it, nibbling it with his teeth.

A gasp of pleasure escaped her, and Mared seized his shoulders to keep from falling as he moved his attention to the other breast. She'd never felt such exquisite sensations in her life; desire pooled quickly in her groin.

Desire was so heavy in her that her knees felt wobbly, so Mared lifted her head, peeled his hand from her waist, and stepped back. Payton's hooded gaze, made dark by his own desire, provoked Mared, and she giggled wantonly. She felt impossibly free and capable of seduction, of enticing a man as strong and handsome as Payton to her. She'd not understood the power a woman might wield over a man until that very moment, and she would bask in it.

He seemed intent on allowing her that. He suddenly grabbed her and pushed her against a bedpost, trapping Mared against it so that he might ravage her breast with his mouth again. But this time, his hands slipped down her waist, over the flare of her hip, and around, between her legs. The sensation of his mouth on her breast and his hand between her legs was breathtaking; Mared arched into him, pressing against him, urging his hands to feel all of her.

She was floating, buoyed by his strength and his determination to have her, the wildly pleasurable sensations overtaking all conscious thought. With his mouth and his hands, he slid down her body, to his haunches, his mouth leaving a hot, wet trail on her belly. Her drawers followed his mouth, sliding down her legs until she was completely bare.

With his hands, he pushed her thighs apart, then kissed them. Mared moaned and held onto his head for support. But then Payton moved slightly, and his mouth was on her sex.

She gasped at the raw sensation. "What are ye doing?" she cried. "Ye're no' to do that!"

"The hell I'm no'," he said with a low laugh and slipped his tongue between the folds of her sex.

Her protests died on her lips with a gasp for air, and Mared's head fell back against the post. He held her firmly with his hands and casually tended her, his tongue dipping in and out languidly at first, carefully tasting her, exploring each crevice, moving up to the core of her desire, then down again, to where her body throbbed for him.

Mared groaned, lost on a sea of pure physical sensation. The lap of his tongue took on new urgency. The stroke of his tongue was coming harder, his mouth covering her.

She couldn't help the way she moved against him; she had no conscious thought. She gripped the post above her head—it was as if her body wanted to escape him and press into him all at once, and she writhed shamelessly against his mouth. Payton was undaunted; he gripped her legs, holding her firmly as he stroked and licked, suckled and nibbled her into a frenzy of delicious torment, until Mared was gasping for breath. When the world around her erupted into brilliant light, she felt as if she were falling and soaring all at once, aloft on a cloud of pure pleasure, sailing away from everything and everyone except Payton.

Payton. She loved him. She knew it in that moment, knew it completely and unequivocally—it was love that had been burning in her heart these long months, love that exploded within her now.

As the aftermath of that eruption whispered through her, he drew up to his full height and lifted her; she heard a groan of wood as Payton lowered them onto the bed. His hand skimmed her breast and her belly; his fingers skated up her legs to the spring of curls at their apex.

Free of all her clothing, gloriously naked and fantastically sated, Mared smiled as he pressed his lips against the hollow of her throat and pulled the pins from her hair, setting her tresses free. She reached for him as he moved lower, pushing her hands into his hair as he laved her nipples.

She reveled in the feel of him against her body, the power and reverence in his hands, the tender pressure of his mouth. All the many times she had imagined what lovemaking would be like, she could not have imagined such pleasure.

"Ye're beautiful, Mared," he said. *"Bòidheach."*

Hearing the ragged edge of his voice made her feel beautiful. And she felt not a glimmer of self-consciousness when he lifted up from her; she felt gloriously wicked and desirable.

She came up on her elbows, her legs stretched out in front of her, to watch him disrobe, to watch the linen slide over corded muscles. His health had definitely returned, and gloriously so—his was a magnificently robust body, utterly virile, from the breadth of his muscled shoulders to the taper of his lean waist, and as he unbound the plaid at his waist, to his muscular thighs and hips.

And of course there was the most masculine part of him, standing erect in a thatch of darkly golden hair, long and thick and sleek.

Standing naked before her, Payton openly admired her as she admired him. She coyly put her hand to her breast and smiled up at him. "It would seem ye have recovered yer good health, milord."

Payton laughed low, and with a wolfish smile, he came over her, settling lightly atop her as he stroked her hair. "Do ye know, then, that I love ye?"

"I've suspected it, aye," she said, smiling.

"Aye, I love ye," he said earnestly. "I've loved ye since we were bairns, and I've never stopped loving ye."

Those words enchanted her, made her glow. When he playfully bit her neck, she laughed. When he kissed her throat, she sighed. And when he whispered *"Bòidheach"* again, her eyes fluttered shut, and she felt the burgeoning of her heart, felt it beating in time to his.

Payton slipped his hand around her waist and moved her fully onto the bed. "I've longed to hold ye, Mared, to love ye," he said, as he moved between her legs and spread them wider, so that the tip of his hard cock was touching her, moving lightly against her. "Ye've made me a happy man this night . . . but we can end it now if ye choose."

With a throaty giggle, she abruptly rose up, grabbed his jaw with one hand, and kissed him with as much passion as he'd just shown her. Instinctively, she lifted her knees. *"Donna stop."*

"Mi Diah." His voice was raging with emotion, and he held himself above her, his arms taut with his restraint. Slowly, respectfully, he moved so that he was pressed against her, and Mared gasped with gleeful exhilaration.

"There will be pain," he said, wincing.

She stroked his face, his brow. "Do it, then."

He sighed, lowered his head, and eased the tip of him inside her, stretching her, moving his hips in small circles to help her body open to him. And then he pressed a little farther, and Mared gasped again, this time at the discomfort.

"Hold me," he said roughly. "Hold me tight and put yer mouth against my shoulder," he said, easing himself down to his elbows. "And know that I love ye, aye?"

Mared wrapped her arms tightly around him,

closed her eyes, and put her face to his shoulder. Payton held her tightly to him, but she had the impression that his efforts to restrain himself, to move slowly with her, were taking every bit of his strength. He stroked her hair, whispered in her ear that he loved her once more, and thrust powerfully into her.

Her cry of pain was muffled by his shoulder, and he stroked her hair, her shoulder, her face. "Easy," he murmured, "rest easy, *leannan*," kissing her eyes and her lips. "The pain will be gone soon, *m'annsachd*, beloved."

The pain did begin to ease as her body adjusted to him, and she thought it a miracle that a man and woman could fit like a hand and glove, and when he began to move so seductively inside her, tantalizing her with the breadth and the depths to which he smoothly stroked, Mared was amazed at how bottomlessly intimate this single act was.

Now she understood.

Now she knew what he'd meant when he said he'd always be a part of her. At that magical moment, she could not imagine ever being apart from him at all.

His strokes lengthened, and her body seemed to know inherently how to respond, for she was starting to move with him, her hips lifting to meet his thrusts, her knees squeezing around him. Payton groaned; his breath was coming in gasps, his strokes had deepened within her, and he suddenly came up on his elbows, his eyes wildly roaming her face, stroking her brow and her cheeks, kissing her passionately as he drove into her, over and over again until he closed his eyes and found his release with a powerful thrust and a strangled cry.

His release was hot and potent; she felt him fill her

completely, felt the fluid slide deeply inside her as he murmured her name. With one last shudder, he collapsed beside her, gathered her tenderly in his arms and kissed the top of her head. *"Mared,"* he whispered into her hair. *"Tha gaol agam ort."*

She loved him, too.

Twenty-four

❧·❧

They lay in the bed as the candles melted away, holding the world and their past at bay for a time, engaged in a gentle exploration of one another, both physically and mentally. It was a slice of peace and contentment neither had ever known, a feeling of being one with another person that, in the light of day, they both might have sworn was impossible.

While Mared giggled, Payton helped her dress before dawn and, with a kiss, sent her hurrying back to her room at the other end of the castle before anyone was about.

He dressed, too, and packed his things. They were leaving for Eilean Ros that very morning, and he bade Alan and Charlie to hurry things along, for he wanted to be home, where he believed that his dreams would finally come true.

On that bright, sunlit morning at Castle Leven, Payton truly believed that Eilean Ros would finally be filled with laughter and love and wee bairns underfoot. What had happened between him and Mared last night had the might of a sea change, and while he had not had an opportunity to fully absorb it, he believed in its power.

He even thought the sun was an omen. The early

autumn was usually quite rainy, but the weather had held for his cousin's wedding and had dawned clear and bright for their journey home. He believed that the sun was an indication that God was smiling on him. Personally.

He said his farewells to his family, caught Mared's eye and winked as she dutifully boarded the smaller coach, and told the coachman to make haste, for he wanted to be home as soon as possible. He and Mared had agreed that they would ride separately in their departure from Castle Leven, for it would not do to have any of the servants or relatives believe something had occurred between them during the journey. As they set out, Payton anticipated paying a call to her family to tell them the happy news, then perhaps rounding up the staff for a bit of a chat before making a public and formal announcement.

When their little caravan stopped for the night, Payton tried to linger at the coach to speak to Mared, but his good and loyal staff would not hear of his helping, and he felt compelled to go inside the inn and make the arrangements, lest they begin to suspect something was amiss.

And even later, when he had a dram of ale in the common room, he could not seem to catch Mared without the ever present Una. He resigned himself to the idea that he would have to wait until they reached Eilean Ros the next evening before he might touch her again.

So therefore, when the second coach threw an axle pin the next morning, Payton was not as agitated as he otherwise might have been, for he saw a golden opportunity when Mr. Haig, the coachman, announced that he could not mend the axle without a new pin.

"Then take Charlie and Alan with ye into the next village," Payton responded easily, withdrawing his purse and a few shillings. "I'll remain with the women."

"Aye, milord."

He even helped Mr. Haig and the two footmen saddle the mounts and eagerly sent them on their way. That left Una. As he turned around to the two women, he saw Mared's sly smile as she pulled her *arisaidh* tightly around her and Una's look of boredom as she glanced at the trees about them.

"I rather wonder how long they'll be," Mared said.

"Two hours at least, perhaps more," Payton responded.

Mared stole a glimpse of Una from the corner of her eye. "Then if ye will give me leave, milord, I'll have a bit of shut-eye."

"Take my coach," he said, quickly catching on to her idea. "Ye may both rest within."

Una's eyes widened. "In yer coach, milord? Oh no, we'll do just as well to wait under a tree."

"I insist, Una," he said, opening the door for her. "I wouldna feel right about ye sleeping out in the open where any number of wild and hungry animals roam."

That was all that was required—Una's eyes widened for a moment, and she hastily stepped forward, toward the door that he held open. As Mared climbed up behind her, she flashed him a tiny smile of approval.

His wait was a short one, as it turned out. A quarter of an hour later, as he sat beneath the boughs of a pine tree, the door of his coach opened, and Mared very slowly and carefully climbed out, and quietly shut the door behind her. She gathered the tail of her *arisaidh* and ran to where he was sitting, collapsing to her knees before him with a laugh.

"Is she sleeping?" he whispered.

"Like a bairn!"

Payton grinned and leapt to his feet, caught Mared by the hand, and pulled her easily into the forest.

"Where are we going?" she asked him.

"Somewhere I might kiss ye properly," he said low, "for I have missed ye terribly." Mared laughed; he gathered her inside his cloak. They walked along until they reached a stream tumbling down the side of the hill. Payton stopped there, grabbed her up in his arms, and kissed her with abandon, with all the pent-up longing he had held in check for the thirty-six hours that had passed since she had left his room.

Mared pressed against him, kissing him with as much zeal as he was showing her. He twirled her about, backed her up until she was against a tree, and then gentled his kiss, taking his time to taste her mouth and feel her lips against his.

When he lifted his head, Mared smiled seductively and traced his bottom lip with the tip of her finger. "Do ye love me, then?"

"I do. I always have," he answered sincerely.

She made a sound of delight deep in her throat, caught his head between her hands, and kissed him passionately. It was enough to unravel Payton completely. Since their extraordinary night together, he'd thought of nothing but her. He'd felt no hunger, no thirst, nothing but the need to be with her. He grabbed her skirt with both hands, groping for the hem as she kissed him.

"What do ye think to be doing, lad?" she whispered when his hands found the tops of her stockings and the bare skin of her thighs.

Payton grinned and nipped at her lower lip. "I want to be with ye, lass."

Her eyes darted to the trees behind them. "But there is Una—"

"Sleeping," he reminded her as his hand found the warm, soft patch between her legs. Mared's green eyes shifted to him, and she smiled provocatively as his fingers slipped deeper.

"Ye're a wicked laird, to seduce yer housekeeper," she whispered huskily.

"Ye're a wicked housekeeper, then, to seduce me so completely with a mere smile."

Mared's smile deepened, but her eyes slid shut and she leaned her head against the tree. One long, shapely leg rode up his leg, to his waist. "Una might wake," she muttered.

"Then ye must be very quiet," he responded, kissing the column of her neck.

"And the others? What if they return?" she whispered as she dipped her hand in between them and stroked him over the fabric of his trousers.

"Then we best be quick," he mumbled against the smooth flesh of her breast. His hand moved over her leg, caressing it, holding it in place, while with his other hand, he unbuttoned his trousers and bared himself. He began to stroke her, stoking a fire inside of her that would rage as it did inside of him, stroking and tweaking until her head began to loll against the tree.

"Ye make me feel so weak when ye do that," she mumbled.

"Weak?" He chuckled. "Ye make me feel on fire."

He slipped inside her then, sliding into her depths, and let out a long breath of relief as he slid deep to the hilt.

She sighed with pleasure and pressed against him. "Make me feel fire, lad," she muttered.

Payton did not need any encouragement, for he was feeling the burn of his own desire rather acutely. He began to move inside her, watching her eyes as he did, watching the frown of concentration as he stroked her to climax, and watching her seductive smile as he reached his climax just after her.

Her leg slowly slid down his body, and she tenderly kissed his mouth.

They remained against that tree, Payton's cloak wrapped around them, in one another's arms, kissing one another indolently, relishing the sensation of being so close again, whispering intimate endearments to one another.

But a distant sound brought Payton back to his senses, and he kissed Mared fully once more, then helped her shake her skirts out. Taking her hand, he led her back. They laughed together, conspirators in love, and walked languidly through the forest, pausing now and again to examine a flower or a tree, or a peculiarly shaped pine cone, laughing quietly at their private jests.

It seemed to Payton that the world was suddenly brimming with color—everywhere he looked there were various shades of the reds and golds of autumn and the greens and blues of the forest. His world, he realized, was suddenly bursting with color.

His future, he thought later, when the men returned and the axle was repaired, was only a few short hours away, bright with color and brimming with possibility.

They did indeed reach Eilean Ros late that afternoon, and as the baggage was unloaded and the coaches and teams put away, Payton divested himself of his cloak and hat and retired to his study to have a look through the post. He'd scarcely begun to do so when Beckwith announced the Lockharts had come calling.

He foolishly believed they had come to welcome Mared home again, for it was his sun that was shining—not theirs.

He found them in the green salon. Mared was already among them, holding Liam's wee son on her hip, coaxing her long braid from the lad's grip.

"Good tidings, good tidings!" Carson Lockhart bellowed the moment he entered the room.

"Good afternoon, laird," he said and smiled at the child in Mared's arms. Did she know how beautiful she looked holding a wee one? That she'd be a mother one day? That conceivably, she might already be a mother? Did she yearn for one of her own as much as he? "How good of ye to come and welcome yer daughter home again."

"For good, it would seem," Grif said from his position near the hearth. He was smiling, Payton noticed, his gray-green eyes as brilliant as Mared's when she smiled. "We bear wonderful news for all involved."

"What is it, then?" Mared laughingly insisted. "Ye canna keep me in suspense another moment!"

"Hugh MacAlister has returned," Grif said, and Payton felt the air rush out of his lungs.

"What?" Mared exclaimed, clearly shocked by the

news, forgetting the baby she held for a moment. "What did ye say? He's here? In Scotland?"

"No' only is he in Scotland, but at Talla Dileas," Grif said proudly. "Old Ben was right for a change. He's come home, he has, and he's even come with the beastie."

For a moment, Payton heard no sound, saw nothing. He was only aware of the laboring of his heart as it struggled to pound its way out of his chest, calling to Mared.

But Mared seemed lost in the news. She stared at Payton as Liam's wife took the bairn from her arms. "Hugh MacAlister is at Talla Dileas?" she repeated, clearly disbelieving.

"Locked in the old dungeon, aye," Liam said. "We'll no' risk losing him again."

"There's more," Lady Lockhart said and came forward, took Mared's hands in hers, her smile joyous. "Oh Mared . . . we've solved the curse!"

Her eyes as big as moons, Mared blinked. "I donna understand. What is there to solve?"

"When Hugh returned with the beastie, we took it to the smithy in Aberfoyle to have it cut into smaller pieces. But there was a surprise—there, in the belly of the beastie, in a bed of straw, was an *emerald*."

"An emerald the size of a bloody goose egg, it is," Liam chimed in.

"An emerald?" Mared echoed weakly, her eyes still wide with shock.

"Aye, *leannan,* do ye no' see?" her mother said excitedly, squeezing her hands. "Think of it—the curse is that no daughter born to a Lockhart will marry until she looks in the belly of the beast. No' *a' diabhal*. The *beastie*. The first Lady Lockhart gave the beastie to her daughter, aye? It must have been a dowry, cast in that hideous thing for safekeeping. But it would seem that over the years, the promise of the dowry was separated from the beastie, and it became a curse."

"But . . . but no daughter of a Lockhart has ever married!"

"Aye, but no' because of some ridiculous curse," Grif explained. "Mother read our grandfather's accounting, and the daughter of the first Lady Lockhart, for whom the emerald was undoubtedly intended, killed herself when her lover was slain by her own father for having aligned himself with the Stuarts. The second daughter drowned in the firth with her lover when they tried to elope. And there were several ugly daughters, too—ye need only look at the family portraits to see that is true."

"Grif!" his comely wife cried.

"What?" he asked innocently. "'Tis true!"

"Do ye mean to say then, that all this time I was to look in that creature's belly, and not the belly of *a' dia-bhal?*" Mared demanded, looking very confused.

"That's it precisely, lass," Carson said happily.

It seemed to Payton that Mared did not know what to make of the news. She sank into a chair and looked at him—but then she looked away, and her gaze seemed to be on something far away. Something far from this room, if not this world. Certainly not on him.

He awkwardly started toward her, his mind racing ahead of his body, intent on going to her, but then Grif was there before him. "Do ye see what this means, *leannan?*" he asked her. "Ye are *free.*"

"Aye, Mared, quite free," her mother echoed joyously.

But still, Mared could only look at them, tears brimming in her eyes, thunderstruck.

"Ah, the poor lass!" Carson laughed. "She's overcome!" He grabbed his daughter up and hugged her, then passed her to Liam, who hugged her fiercely.

When he let her go, Mared looked at her father. "I'm free?" she asked, seemingly unable to absorb it.

Grif turned a beaming smile to Payton as Carson laughed and assured his daughter she was free. "There ye are, then, Douglas. We're able to pay our debts now, aye? Ye can release our sister to us."

Payton was dumbfounded. He tried to find his tongue, but he couldn't seem to think, not with Mared, who was clinging to her mother now, looking oddly relieved and saddened at the same time. The rest of the Lockharts seemed not to notice—they were smiling and laughing and chattering wildly about traveling to Edinburgh.

"When will ye pay it, then?" he asked of Grif in a desperate bid for more time.

"Ah!" Grif said, holding up a finger. "We've a plan to pay before our year is through," he said happily. "We are to Edinburra this week—all of us. We shall have the gold sold in a matter of days and pay ye our debt, with interest. Will that meet with yer satisfaction?"

No, no, it would never meet with his satisfaction! He'd only just found happiness, and now the goddamn Lockharts would *take* it from him? He turned an icy gaze to Grif. "And what of our other agreement?" he snapped. "What of Mared?"

"*Ach*, now, Douglas," Grif said, his smile fading. "Surely ye willna keep her in servitude when we've a way to repay our debt."

"And ye would take her now and leave me with-out a housekeeper?"

Grif's smile faded to a glower. "I donna give a bloody damn about yer lack of a housekeeper," he said quietly. "Ye willna keep our sister in servitude another moment."

No, of course he wouldn't. Mared did not deserve servitude, and he tried frantically in those few wild moments to convince himself that if she was no longer his housekeeper, they might proceed with the original plan to marry. Quickly. As soon as this week, perhaps.

He tried desperately to believe that, but something inside him warned him that it could not be. Something inside him had died a little when she whispered the words, *I'm free.*

"Look, now, Douglas, we all know that ye hold her in high esteem, and we donna mean to disregard it, no' in the least," Grif said, his voice a bit softer. "But we canna allow her to spend even as much as one night more in the service of anyone. We'll take her today, aye?"

Payton glared at Grif, hating him as he had never hated anyone in his life. "I urge ye to pay yer debt as quickly as possible, for I will seek the harshest of remedies if ye donna."

With a cold smile, Grif nodded his assent.

"I'll have one of the maids gather her things," Payton said and strode from that happy family reunion into an empty corridor, where the echo of his boots was deafening to his ears.

Everything had happened so fast that Mared could hardly grasp she was leaving Eilean Ros, much less leaving the enormous burden of her curse. *Much less leaving Payton.* God help her but she couldn't seem to *think.* Her mind was racing wildly around the news, and her exuberant family surrounded her, all speaking excitedly and at once of Edinburgh and the things they would buy. It was hard not to be swept up in the exhilaration of their mutual good fortune.

But she could not share their elation completely because of Payton.

"Think of the balls and gatherings you will attend," Ellie said, having accompanied Mared to her room to finish packing her things. "You'll be highly sought after, I predict. It will be such fun for a time."

Yes, life in Edinburgh would be a far cry from the bucolic life of the lochs. Far from the accusing eyes of a superstitious people. And far, far from Payton.

"And the gowns, Mared, think of the gowns you will have!" Ellie exclaimed, holding up Mared's old purple gown. "You'll never have cause to wear this old thing again." She turned around to Mared, her fair face beaming. "Aren't you thrilled?"

"I am thrilled to be free of the curse," Mared readily agreed. "And I have long wanted to be gone from these hills," she added as she folded a pair of stockings.

"Yes, you've long wanted to be in Edinburgh, where life will be full of exciting new people!" Ellie exclaimed, prompting her.

"Aye, to Edinburgh," Mared said with much less enthusiasm than Ellie. *Edinburgh. Full of new people. Not Payton.*

"Then what has you so downcast, darling?" Ellie asked laughingly. "One would think you'd be dancing on air!"

"I am, truly, I am," Mared tried to assure her in a less than convincing manner.

"But?" Ellie prompted.

Mared looked at Ellie. "But . . . but I canna seem to fathom how everything has changed so suddenly," she said quietly, and she felt her heart tilt a little.

"Is it Laird Douglas?" a smiling Ellie asked as she put the purple gown in Mared's portmanteau.

Mared shrugged, uncertain as to what she was feeling.

"You will still see him, darling. But first you must have your turn in Edinburgh, just as you've always wanted."

Yes, her turn. It was her turn now.

"Douglas will still be here, waiting for you, I'd daresay. But you deserve a bit of happy freedom for a time. He'll understand, I am certain of it. You've been denied life too long."

A lifetime. She'd been denied a lifetime.

With her family at her side, Mared said good-bye to the servants, feeling as sad in leaving them as they apparently felt about her leaving. Rodina and Una seemed especially disturbed by it. But when Mared took them aside, all she could think of was Payton. "Donna forget the laird's laundry, Rodina," she urged her. "He's very particular about it, aye? And Una—ye must make his bed and clean his chambers every morning while he's abroad."

Una exchanged a look with Rodina. "Aye, miss," she said, trying to smile.

Even Mr. Beckwith seemed a little downcast by Mared's departure as he wished her good luck.

After Alan and Charlie had carried her things down to the cart, Mared gave her little room one final look, then walked out, her head and heart reeling so badly she could scarcely see. Her world had altered so quickly and so dramatically that she felt almost as if she was another person entirely, her familiar self noticeably absent and replaced by painful confusion.

And there was Payton, the man to whom she'd given her virtue. *Payton.* What was she to do?

He was waiting there by the cart, next to her father and mother. He looked very grim, and she frantically racked her mind for what to say to him. But how could she possibly know *what* to say to him? She scarcely knew what to think herself, much less what this must seem to him. Even worse, she hadn't reached a firm conclusion about what had really happened between them at Loch Leven and afterward. What it really *meant.* The only thing she knew in all certainty was that she did love him.

But in the midst of her desperate confusion, there was something else that she knew with all certainty— her curse was lifted. She felt it, almost as if it had been physically lifted from her shoulders, and she had never felt more light in bearing than she did at that very moment. For the first time in her life, it seemed as if the whole world was open to her. All of it. The whole fat globe and everything and everyone on it.

That was, perhaps, why she smiled at Payton when her mother patted his arm and said, "Ye must no' be maudlin, laird. This is quite good news for ye, for ye donna want Mared as yer servant, aye?"

Payton did not respond.

Her mother's smile was emphatic, and she squeezed his forearm. "Just give her a wee bit of time, Douglas, please? Just a wee bit of time to taste her freedom at long last."

He nodded and looked at Mared, and she smiled instead of showing him the sorrow, the ache in her heart.

She just needed a moment of peace in which she could *think*.

Payton did not return her smile, but looked at her with his heart in his eyes. He said nothing as he took her hand in his to help her up on the cart—but he squeezed it meaningfully and looked directly into her eyes, obviously searching for her, obviously wanting a word, some signal. He deserved one, he did . . . but she didn't have the right word to say as yet.

Instead, she squeezed his hand back and blurted helplessly, "I . . . I must think."

"I understand."

What? What did he understand? What could he possibly understand when she couldn't understand anything at all? She slowly disengaged her hand from his. "Good-bye, milord."

With jaw clenched, Payton nodded and stepped away from the cart as Liam sent the donkeys trotting, telling everyone with his booming voice that the first thing they'd purchase was a team of four grays. "And I'll no' brook any argument!" he loudly insisted. Her family laughed; Mared laughed, too, but her eyes were on Eilean Ros and Payton, who stood in the drive, his chin high, his hands clasped behind his back. His expression frighteningly unreadable.

Twenty-five

❖

hey argued over their sherry—the one bottle they had saved for this very occasion—as to whether or not they would allow Hugh to join them for dinner. The men were firmly of the opinion that the bounder could rot below. The women were less convinced.

"He did return the beastie," Anna said to no one in particular. "I can't see how we might possibly hold him prisoner."

"He's right fortunate he is no' twisting in the wind from the highest tree," Grif said as he laid his hand on Anna's belly to feel the baby kick.

"But it's awfully dark and cold down there," Natalie said to Carson. "He might be very afraid."

"There, there, *leannan*," Liam said soothingly. "Let the lad rot."

"Well I, for one, should like the courtesy of an explanation," Mared said.

Liam sighed and looked at Grif. Grif groaned. "Very well then," he groused and reached in his pocket to produce a key. "Will ye no' fetch him, then, Mared, and escort him up? He may give ye his ridiculous version of events, but I canna possibly hear it again."

"Natalie, darling, please find Dudley and have him add another setting for supper," Aila said.

Hugh wasn't *really* in a dungeon—certainly it had been one long ago, but now it was just a room, below ground, devoid of light and heat. Mared and her brothers had played there as children; for a time, the family had stored dry goods there. Holding a candle high, she walked down the worn narrow steps and paused at the edge of the darkened corridor.

There was a flicker of light from the cell where they kept Hugh. "Ho there, who comes to tend me body?" he called.

She stepped off the last step and into the corridor. Hugh MacAlister, as devilishly handsome as ever, was standing at the bars that went across the door, his arms hanging uselessly through them, his weight cocked on one hip.

"I canna see ye—come closer, then. Who is it? Mrs. Griffin Lockhart? Ah, Anna, bless ye, lass! I knew ye'd rescue me. I always believed it was me ye loved above that bloody scoundrel!"

"'Tis no' Anna, Hugh," Mared said and walked closer so that he could see her. "'Tis me . . . the reason ye doth exist. Remember?"

"Mared!" he cried joyously. "On me honor, I hoped ye would come. Can ye imagine how I've yearned for ye, then? I've wasted away in grief for having lost ye, I have."

"Ye donna look wasted away to me," she said, holding the candle above her head to see him clearly. "Ye look as well as a fatted calf. *Tsk-tsk*, Hugh MacAlister. After all ye've done and still a rogue."

"I'm no' a rogue!" he gamely insisted. "I've kept ye in me heart, Mared! Why do ye think I came back, then?"

"Grif said ye tried to steal the beastie and run away with an Irish lass."

"Ah, how he seeks to hurt me!" Hugh cried, clapping a hand dramatically over his heart. "Why should he spread such vicious lies? No, no, *leannan*. Miss Brody stole yer beloved beastie, and I, being the true friend of Lockhart that I am, went after her to retrieve it. I almost lost me life in Ireland, mind—all so that I wouldna return to ye, *m'annsachd*, empty-handed."

"How very gallant of ye," she said. "And if I am truly yer beloved, did ye no' think to write and tell me ye'd gone to Ireland?"

Hugh blinked. And then he smiled beatifically. "Mared, lass . . . I had no' even a coin to me name. How might I have purchased paper and pen? No, *leannan*, I believed ye would trust me."

She laughed roundly at that. "I wouldna trust ye if ye were the last man on God's green earth, MacAlister," she said, but fit the key in the lock and turned it, opening the door.

Hugh was instantly through it, his arms going around Mared without a care for the candle she held. "*Diah*, how is it that ye've grown even bonnier since I last laid eyes on ye?" he asked, attempting to nuzzle her neck. "I didna dream ye'd be so beautiful. Ah, lass, yell no' regret rescuing me from this bloody pit," he whispered wickedly in her ear.

Mared slapped his arm from her waist and stuck the candle between them. "I didna come here to rescue a bloody fool. I came to hear for myself why ye put me in such jeopardy. And if ye tell me true, to bring ye to supper."

"Supper!" Hugh said eagerly, then sighed at her stoic look, and put his hands on his waist. "Ye donna look any worse for it, on my word—ye are indeed a beautiful woman, Mared. I do think ye are bonnier than whence I last laid eyes on ye, aye. Ye seem different somehow."

She was different, all right, and in so many ways. She gestured toward the stairs. Hugh caught her hand and with a charming smile, put it on his arm. "If I'm to escort ye, allow me to do so properly," he said and gazed at her lustfully.

They exited the dark underground corridor, and as they made their way up to the main floor, Hugh tried to convince her that it was she he had thought of, her image that had kept him on course when it seemed there was no hope. Aye, it was Mared who had brought him back to Talla Dileas instead of London, where, he reminded her, he might have sold the beastie and kept it all to himself.

By the time they reached the dining room, Mared was laughing at his fervent whispers of utter devotion, for which one could not help but laugh at Hugh.

Grif mistook her laugh for something altogether different, and clapped Hugh on the shoulder the moment they entered the room, and hauled him to a seat between himself and Liam. "Ye'll keep yer distance from my sister, aye?" he warned him.

"Aye," Hugh said, boldly winking at Mared across the table.

Over supper—which, Mared couldn't help noticing, was rather poor fare compared to what even the servants ate at Eilean Ros—the family discussed their plans. It was agreed they'd all go to Edinburgh—including Hugh—save Anna and Grif, due to Anna's pregnancy. Natalie would remain behind to help Anna.

They would sell the gold and rubies at once and pay their debts, then have the emerald cut into pieces to be sold as they needed. The emerald lay in the middle of the supper table. Mared couldn't keep her eyes from it. *That* was the thing she was to have found. Not *a' diabhal.* Not death. An emerald. A bloody dowry! How could a reference to that magnificent jewel have been so terribly misinterpreted as a curse?

"How much shall the gold and rubies bring?" Aila asked.

"Tens of thousands," Grif assured her.

"Less five percent," Hugh hastily reminded him, for which he received a rather harsh glare from the Lockhart men.

"And the emerald?" Aila asked.

Grif glanced at it. "I canna be certain, but I would think tens of thousands more."

They all stared at the emerald, their thoughts on how close they had come to losing it.

Later, they determined it was safe to leave Hugh unlocked, for as he pointed out, he had no money or means of transportation, and therefore, was entirely dependent on them to take him to Edinburgh and give him his due. Carson, still rather miffed, agreed that Hugh could have use of one of the old servants' rooms at the far end of the house until they left for Edinburgh.

All of the Lockharts were eager to put their poverty behind them, and they decided they would do so at once. They would leave two days hence.

That night, safely ensconced in her old tower chamber, Mared paced before her warm hearth, her braid swinging above her hip as she turned, again and again.

At last she took up pen and paper.

To the Right Honorable Laird Douglas, Master of
Sheep and Other Dubious Livestock, Greetings from
Talla Dileas.
    I hope this letter finds you well.

She glanced up, looked out the narrow window to
the star-filled night. *How are you?* she wanted to ask.
Will you sleep at night? Who will turn down your bed and
straighten the linens the next morn once you've thrashed
about? Who will launder your clothing?

The shock of her abrupt change in fortune had
begun to wear down, and now all Mared could seem
to think of was Payton . . . and where this reversal in
her family's fortune left them. They had enjoyed a
magical weekend—she had thought it marked a
change in their mutual history. She supposed she had
thought she would marry him. But now, she wasn't so
very certain of that. Didn't she owe it to herself to
experience the life that had been denied her because
of that curse?

    I am pleased to inform you that we are to
Edinburgh on Thursday so that we may reclaim our
fortune and our destiny and pay our many debts.
Naturally, we will pay our debt to you first and
foremost.

She paused and gazed out at the stars again. *How*
can I leave you behind? How can I not? I am free now,
Payton. I am free to travel and to dance and to walk among
citizens of the world without fear of censure.

    We shall reside in Edinburgh for at least a
fortnight while we tidy our affairs. I hope in that time

*you will keep your sheep from grazing our land, for
we may bring home more cattle. Father has spoken of
it with great enthusiasm, in spite of Griffin's assertion
that the market for Highland cattle is dwindling.*

She stopped writing. *I don't know what to do. I don't
know where to turn. I don't know if I can even breathe if
you are not near. I only know that I must reclaim the life
I've lost in the course of suffering the curse. I've never
tasted true freedom, not like you, and not a day in my life. I
must know what it is.*

*Anna and Griffin will stay on at Talla Dileas, as
Anna cannot travel, and someone must look after the
property and my dogs. I have asked Mr. Dudley to
keep a vigilant eye on them, for I know you do not care
to have them herd your sheep.*

She paused again. *I can't say when I shall return to
Talla Dileas. I feel an overwhelming and necessary obliga-
tion to go into the world and live. Do you want me to
stay? Now that your debt is repaid, do you still have the
same feelings for me? You didn't say anything, you said
only that you understood.*

*Please give my regards to Una and Rodina. I shall
keep my eyes and ears open for a housekeeper to suit
you; one with fine laundering skills, of course.*
　　　　　　　　　　　　　　　　　Yours always,
　　　　　　　　　　　　　　　　　　　　M

*My heart will always be tilted toward you. You are for-
ever a part of me.*

She put down the pen, took a bit of wax and sealed it, and then, for at least the tenth time that day since hearing the news of her freedom, she put down her head and cried.

A steady, cold rain had begun to fall, and Payton stared out through the rivulets on the window at the bleak countryside. He'd read her letter a third time, trying to read something—anything—between the lines, but he could find nothing. No hint of her feelings, nothing but the giddiness she felt at her imminent departure for Edinburgh.

He had, with the help of copious amounts of whiskey, resolved himself to the inevitable end once again. He had made himself face the fact that the feelings she might have developed for him while in his service had not held up under the mantle of freedom.

He understood how that might be so . . . yet he could not, in his heart of hearts, conceive of how she could ignore the magic that had happened between them. She had given him her virginity. She might very well be carrying his child. Could she leave without at least a *bit* of conversation?

He glanced at the mantel clock. She'd been away from him for thirty-six hours. In twenty-four hours more, she'd be beyond his reach. Payton glanced at the letter, and gritting his teeth, he crumpled it in his hand and tossed it in the fire. He'd not accept this. She would not leave Talla Dileas without at least giving him a proper farewell.

He arrived at Talla Dileas just after luncheon the following day. Dudley took his cloak and hat, showed him to the small drawing room where he might warm himself and dry his boots. He was standing before the fire doing precisely that when Mared entered the room.

He felt her before he saw her—he had come to sense her presence and miss it as much as the air he breathed. He turned, and his heart sank at the sight of her—she was wearing an old green gown he'd seen her in a dozen times before, but it hardy mattered. In his eyes, she was achingly beautiful. Her hair hung freely down her back in long waves, pinned back from her face with green ribbons. She wore her boots, and he noticed a bit of mud on them, as if she'd just come back from a walk in the rain. Indeed, she must have done so, for her cheeks were flushed and her eyes sparkling.

She glanced at the open door when she saw him and very carefully pushed it to—not completely shut, but enough to afford them a bit of privacy—then turned around, clasped her hands before her, and smiled uncertainly.

This was not the same eager woman he'd last held against that tree. This one seemed nervous. Out of sorts.

"How are ye?" he asked quietly.

"Well," she said unconvincingly. "And ye?"

He shrugged. Looking at her now, he was struck by a vivid reminder of her naked body, how she had felt in his arms. How their coupling had been so very right.

There was no reason to prolong his agony. "Ye are to Edinburra, then," he said shortly.

She dipped her gaze to the hearth and nodded. "We will reclaim our fortune."

"So ye've written," he said, feeling suddenly at sixes and sevens. He didn't know what to say. It seemed as if he'd already spent too much time begging Mared to requite his love for her. He had only the ravages of his pride left, and he did not believe that he could give that up, too, to beg her to stay now. With a frown of frustration, he shoved a hand through his hair and looked at the fire.

"It is the social season," Mared said behind him. "There will be balls and soirees and such."

Yes, yes, he knew all about the social season. He'd been through enough of them that he didn't give a damn about it. The people who comprised "society" were leeches, and they would suck the uniqueness from her, seek to mold her in their image.

"I've no' been through a social season," she said with a bit of a nervous laugh. "I've no' had the liberty until now. . . ."

She didn't need to say more. It was clear to Payton that she would choose the chance to attend endless soirees over him.

His head was suddenly aching and he put his hands to his temples, rubbing them. "Have ye considered that ye might be with child?" he asked hoarsely.

The lass blanched. Then blushed furiously and glanced at the door. "I am no'—"

"How can ye be sure?"

"I can be sure and I am *very* sure," she said, looking pointedly at him.

He sighed and dropped his hands, fighting the urge to take her into his arms, hold her captive. He made an effort to gather up the last bit of his courage, for he would need every bit of it to say good-bye.

Mared was looking at him with concern and, he hoped, a wee bit of affection. She took a few halting steps toward him. "Are ye . . . are ye all right?" she asked softly.

His pride now completely shattered, Payton felt the blood drain from his face, and he grimaced. "How could I possibly be all right?" he bit out.

Mared's eyes softened, and she stepped closer. "Payton . . ." She put her hand on his arm.

One touch was all it took. He looked up at those green eyes and moved before he could think, roughly embracing her, holding her tightly to him.

"Oh, Payton!" she cried softly in his ear. "I'm so sorry, I am! But I donna know what to do! I feel I must go, for it is something I have needed all my life. I have needed to be free. I have needed to be normal!"

"Why can ye no' be normal here? What about *us?*" he demanded, grabbing her by the shoulders and setting her back a bit. "After what has gone between us, what about us?"

"I donna know, I donna *know,*" she cried and closed her eyes, pressed her forehead to his shoulder. "I am so confused!"

Damn her, but he could feel her confusion acutely and with a weary sigh, he let go of her and put his arms around her, his hand to the back of her head. "How long, then? How long will ye be away?"

"I canna say."

He closed his eyes, pressed her head to his shoulder. "Mared . . . I love ye, lass," he managed to say.

She reared back, took his face between her hands, her green eyes shining. "I know, I know, and I . . . I love ye, too, Payton. I do. Ye canna believe otherwise. But I have lived with the curse all my life, and the one thing I have wanted was the chance to be like everyone else. I want to feel what that is like. I want to meet people who have no notion of that wretched curse. I want to see the world outside of these lochs where that wretched curse has existed. I was once in Edinburra and I *know* I will be completely free there. I will never be completely free here, no matter that the curse is solved. There will always be those who believe it. Can ye understand?"

He could understand it clearly—she wanted the one thing he could never give her. She wanted to be away from the lochs, where he was bound to remain by duty and honor and history.

With a sad smile, he covered her hands at his face and pulled them down, kissed the backs of them, then kissed her tenderly. "That's it, then, lass," he said quietly.

"'Tis no' the end, Payton—"

"Let's no' fool ourselves, aye?" He dropped her hands and stepped back. Mared looked down, away from his gaze. She knew it, too, and his heart wrenched so badly that he grimaced with the pain of it.

He pushed a thick lock of her hair over her shoulder. "I've a good-bye gift for ye," he said and reached into his pocket.

She reluctantly lifted her head as he withdrew it and opened his palm. He held the *luckenbooth* he'd commissioned on the occasion of their long forgotten betrothal.

Mared gasped softly and looked up at him with dark green eyes for a moment, then at the *luckenbooth* again. Carefully, she took it from his palm, held it up, admiring the twinkle of the gems in the firelight.

"Donna throw it at me, aye?" he asked wryly.

"*Payton* . . . it is even more beautiful than the first time I held it. I canna take it. I donna deserve it."

"Aye, ye donna deserve it in the least," he agreed. "But I want ye to have it, Mared. I had it made for ye, and . . . and I hope that ye will wear it in Edinburra."

She turned it over, smiling as she examined the fine craftsmanship. "How did ye ever find it again?"

"A lot of kicking about," he said, ashamed that his voice had gone rough with emotion.

She closed her hand around it and glanced up at him. "Thank ye, Payton. I'll treasure it always." She rose up on her toes and kissed him lightly as her hand trailed lithely down his arm, until she slipped her hand into his.

There seemed nothing left to say. They stood staring at one another until Payton could endure it no longer. With his lips pressed firmly together, he touched her chin with two fingers, and with the pad of his thumb, he wiped away the single tear that had fallen from her eye. "Godspeed," he said and stepped away from her.

He felt the draft of her leaving him even though she hadn't moved, and made himself walk out of Talla Dileas before his grief consumed him.

Twenty-six

❧❦

EDINBURGH, SCOTLAND
TWO MONTHS LATER

The gowns were still arriving several weeks after the Lockharts had landed in Edinburgh, in all the colors of a silken rainbow, as well as slippers and hats and gloves and jewelry.

Ellie worked to keep Duncan's chubby hands from the parade of clothing as Mared displayed her latest purchases. "Heavens, Mared!" she exclaimed. "Will you give your new fortune to the modiste?"

Mared laughed and held up a celery green and plum silk dress. "Can ye blame me, then?"

"No," Ellie said, her smile fading. "In truth, I cannot. You deserve these things after what you've endured. But there are so *many*."

"Father gave me funds to do with as I please," Mared reminded her.

"Yes, but . . . but I wonder if perhaps he thought you might put some of it aside for your future?" she asked and caught Duncan's hand and led him away from the slippers he'd found.

"I am putting it into my future," she said airily. "I

may very well receive an offer of marriage. Can ye imagine, Ellie? Someone to offer marriage for me?"

"Someone has offered," Ellie quietly reminded her.

Mared stilled and glanced at Ellie from the corner of her eye. "'Tis no' the same. Besides, *ye* were the one who urged me to come here, aye?"

"Yes I did, didn't I?" Ellie asked. She sighed wearily and sat in an embroidered armchair with Duncan on her lap.

"Why do ye sigh so?" Mared asked, putting aside the celery green silk and picking up a red one to hold before her.

"Because I only meant that you should come for a time and enjoy yourself. But now I fear I encouraged you wrongly and you will be hurt."

Mared laughed and looked over her shoulder at Ellie. "Why on earth would I be hurt? Have ye no' heard, Ellie? I am the season's shining star."

"I've heard from Miss Douglas that you are quite the favorite among gentlemen of the season."

"Oh?" Mared asked, smiling over her shoulder.

"Mmm," Ellie said. "You are the talk of all the drawing rooms on Charlotte Square, apparently."

With a laugh, Mared turned around again to admire the red gown. "There, ye see?"

"Mared, listen to me. Aristocratic gentlemen will say anything when they dance with you, but an offer of marriage would only come after they had ascertained your worth. And even then, there are family lines to consider, pedigrees . . ."

"Ellie!" Mared cried. "Ye sound as if ye donna believe the Lockharts are a proud and true Scottish family."

"Of course I do, Mared. I am one, after all," Ellie

said politely. "What I am trying to impart is that these men are not particularly interested in the Lockhart name. They are interested in how far they might . . . well, *know* you . . . without offering for you."

"Is that what has ye fretting?" Mared asked laughingly. "I'm no' a blushing young maid, Ellie. And I've no' seen one that I'd consider marrying, in truth."

"Then what is all this talk of offers?"

"Only talk. Because I've never been in a position to be admired. And because it is great jolly *fun*."

"Mared, *please* be careful. There are many insincere people around you and your good reputation could be irrevocably tarnished with as little as one wrong word!"

"Honestly, Ellie!" Mared scoffed. "This is no' London, and I'm no' so naïve as that," she said blithely, missing Ellie's dubious look as she picked up another gown.

It was true that Mared had spread her wings in earnest since arriving in Edinburgh with her family. After a couple of outings with her brothers, it wasn't long before she was on the guest list of every soiree, ball, and supper party held in aristocratic circles, for she was thought to be exotically pretty and heretofore unknown. She'd danced more in the last month than she had in her entire life. It seemed that her dance card was always quite full and gentlemen—married, unmarried, and those quite undecided—would whisper naughty, wicked little things in her ear.

Talla Dileas seemed so far away from the glittering life in and around Charlotte Square.

And Mared reveled in the attention she was receiving. She coveted each and every invitation that came her way. She bought gowns and shoes and hats and coats, and cared not a whit for the cost, for the beastie, and especially that enormous emerald, had made her family wealthy once again.

For two months, she had lived life fully in the shadow of Edinburgh Castle. So fully that she rarely had time to think of Payton other than at night, in that quiet moment between consciousness and sleep.

He never failed to visit her there. Every blessed night.

Mared would lie with her arms wrapped around her pillow, wondering what he did with his days, picturing him dining alone and riding along the base of Ben Cluaran.

She heard of him from time to time. Her mother—who had returned with Father as soon as their affairs were handled to settle all their debts—wrote often, as did Anna, and they would mention Payton now and again. Mother reported that he had accepted the payment of their debt and had given them written confirmation that they were cleared of owing him as much as a pence. She did not say if he'd asked about her.

Anna wrote that he regularly accompanied Miss Crowley to Sunday services at the kirk, and that everyone speculated there would be a wedding very soon. Even Grif wrote once, saying that Douglas had persuaded him to lend a hand in building a new barn for Mr. Craig, and that he had been quite surprised that Douglas was as skilled with a hammer and nails as he was.

Mared wasn't surprised. She rather thought he could do anything, for he was that sort of man—powerful and immensely capable, as comfortable building a barn as he was hosting an important social affair.

Grif also reported that Payton had secured the funding necessary to complete his distillery, and that

construction was already under way. Mared rather guessed he spent his time overseeing that—he was quite proud of his whiskey, despite its having almost killed him.

She'd written him twice since coming to Edinburgh, both times to tell him all the things she'd seen and the places she'd gone. He'd only responded to her letters once, and it had been a terse reply.

She kept the letter in a jeweled box on her dressing table and reread it often. Almost every night, in fact, because she would take the *luckenbooth* from the silk wrapper and wear it to whatever affair she was attending that night. The letter read:

> My dear Miss Lockhart,
> I am pleased to hear that Edinburgh suits you well. I never doubted it. We are all quite well, but the dogs rather miss you.
> You will be delighted to know that Una has consented to marry Mr. Harold Fuquay from Loch Leven. She leaves our employ at the end of this month and will serve as a maid to my cousin Neacel and his bride. We begin shearing soon, which should please you, as the sheep will not be grazing on your land. I can assure you that they have not "ruined" the landscape for your cows as you feared. Do have a care for the residents of Edinburgh and try not to startle them out of their wits.
>
> Douglas

Aye, Mared thought of Payton often and held him dear in a quiet corner of her heart. But she rather supposed he had carried on without her. How very lost that made her feel.

But every morning, she rose eager to know what the day might bring and pushed him and the sadness from her mind.

There was so much she wanted to see and do, so much she had missed! She scoured Edinburgh Castle, roamed the grounds of Holyroodhouse Palace, and walked along the castle grounds to Charlotte Square where she resided. At night she attended one fete after another and enjoyed herself immensely.

From time to time, Mared would see Hugh at a soiree or ball. Like her, he'd opted to stay in Edinburgh after he'd collected his due for returning the beastie. When she saw the scoundrel, sometimes he'd scarcely acknowledge her presence before disappearing into one of the rooms where the gentlemen gambled— she'd heard that he'd parlayed his share of the fortune into a greater fortune at the gaming tables. Other times, he'd be the first to ask her to stand up with him and would make her laugh by whispering his devotion in her ear. He was something of an enigma.

She rather supposed she'd see him tonight, too, for tonight was the Aitkin ball, an event that would purportedly draw at least two hundred. Mared could scarcely wait. As Ellie had declined the invitation in favor of staying with Duncan, Liam was to escort her.

She donned the celery green and plum gown with the matching slippers and Ellie wound her hair into an elaborate coif, wrapped her head with ribbons in the Grecian style, and clasped a generous piece of the emerald around her neck. Her family had given her the necklace, along with a pair of earbobs.

"Oh my, Mared," Ellie said, standing back to gaze at her, shaking her head. "I've never seen anyone as beautiful as you, I swear it."

"Ellie, ye flatter me!" Mared laughed.

"No," Ellie insisted, shaking her head in wonder. "Sometimes I can scarcely believe it is you. You're like a different person entirely in all your finery."

Ellie had no idea how different Mared truly was. She smiled warmly and kissed Ellie's cheek fondly. "I'm the same person, Ellie, but I suppose a bit of silk and an emerald or two might make me appear a wee bit different."

"Perhaps." Ellie took in Mared's gown and her jewels, and she smiled as Mared pinned the *luckenbooth* to her shoulder. "My guess is that there will be a rather long queue of men, and all of them inquiring as to the availability of space on Mared Lockhart's dance card."

Mared laughed gaily and picked up her wrap. "It's all quite a dramatic turn of fate, is it no'?"

Liam and Mared arrived at the mansion overlooking the Firth of Forth in a gilded carriage pulled by a team of four grays, which Liam had recently purchased for Talla Dileas. Liam cared not a whit for balls, so he left Mared to be the center of attention and headed for the gaming room where he said he intended to double his military pension, preferably by taking it from Hugh MacAlister.

Mared entered the ballroom and snapped open her hand-painted fan, as she'd seen many of the women do, and was immediately set upon by several gentlemen.

But David Anderson, son of Viscount Aitkin, the host of this affair, was the first one to draw her away. With his gloved hand on her elbow, he murmured, "A vision has descended into my father's home."

Mared glanced at him from the corner of her eye and smiled coyly. "Sounds rather like a buzzard."

He laughed gently and pulled her to one side. "The vision is indeed a bird," he murmured, "and one that I should very much like to capture and keep in a gilded cage so that I might gaze upon her at my leisure."

"Keep her in a cage?" Mared laughed. "Rather barbaric, sir."

"There is something to be said for a wee bit of barbarism, aye?" he suggested with a wink. "Shall we dance?" he asked and escorted a smiling Mared onto the dance floor for a minuet.

She loved dancing, and stepped and turned and flirted with Mr. Anderson while smiling at other men who endeavored to catch her eye. Her behavior had the desired effect on Mr. Anderson. "You're bloody gorgeous," Mr. Anderson said as he took her hand and stepped forward to meet her, then back. "There's not a lovelier lass in this town."

Mared smiled playfully.

And so it went, her dancing and flirting and smiling, her delight immeasurable, the lighthearted and gay feeling absolutely divine.

When Mr. Anderson reluctantly gave her up, she danced on, with one gentleman after another, smiling and flirting. She left Lord Brimley after the eighth or ninth dance and made her way to the ladies' retiring room on the second floor. And having availed herself, she stepped out onto the second floor balcony and walked around the railing, her fingers absently trailing along the mahogany balustrade as she stared down at the dancers below her.

They were playing a reel, and she watched as the

women twirled, their colorful skirts flaring out. Men in their black evening clothes, so handsome and debonair, gracefully led the women through the dance steps.

Mared reached the staircase and began her descent, absently surveying the crowded ballroom. But as her gaze swept the crowd, her heart suddenly stopped beating. She instantly looked back, to the person she thought she had seen, and her heart plummeted to her knees.

It was him. *Payton*. Her heart began to beat again, only quickly, so quickly that she could not seem to catch her breath. *Diah*, but he looked impossibly majestic, far more dashing than her mind's eye had recalled him these last two months. He was dressed in black trousers and coat, a white silk waistcoat and neckcloth, his hair unfashionably long, yet sleek and rather becoming. His was an imposing figure and certainly the most agreeable of the many men in the room.

Judging by the many admiring looks he was getting, she was not the only female who thought so.

He stood on the edge of the dance floor, a glass of champagne in his hand, and he watched her calmly, almost expressionless . . . save the twinkle in his bonny gray eyes that she could see from even this distance. She recalled, with no small shiver of delight, how those eyes had shone when he thrust into her.

That delicious memory made her smile spread wider.

Payton smiled, too, and she wondered with a small laugh if he, too, was recalling that very moment. Below her, he cocked a brow at her. She smiled and gestured to her gown just as she had that night at Loch Leven, turning first one way, then the other.

And just as he had done that night, he bowed his head in acknowledgment of her gown and lifted his flute in silent toast to it. With a flick of her wrist, Mared opened her fan, and slowly fanning herself, she floated down the stairs. He began to walk in her direction, his eyes never leaving her.

He met her at the bottom of the stairs and held out his hand to her. With a laugh of pleasure, Mared put her hand atop his, allowed him to guide her down the last step, at which point, she curtsied deeply. A smile of amusement tipped the corner of his mouth, and he bowed politely over her hand, pressing his lips to her gloved knuckles. When he rose up, she looked up into his gray eyes, felt them tug at something deep and familiar within her. *"Feasgar math,"* she murmured.

"Feasgar math," he replied to her greeting as he casually perused her gown.

She blushed a little at his perusal and asked, "How do ye do, then? Ye seem well . . . very well indeed."

"I am much improved now that I've seen ye. Aye, as bonny as ever ye were, Mared. A Highland beauty."

"Do you like it?" she asked, gesturing to her gown, then leaned forward and whispered, "I paid one hundred pounds for it. Can ye imagine!"

"Diah," he said and looked her over again, his gaze landing on the *luckenbooth* she wore. "I like it very much," he said and lifted his gaze to hers. "Ye are undeniably the most beautiful woman here."

Her heart, she noticed, gave her a bit of a bump at that—she'd been told she was beautiful by more than one man this evening, but when Payton said it, she could feel the compliment radiate throughout her body and beam back at him through her smile.

"Will ye dance with me?" he asked, and when she nodded, he led her out onto the dance floor.

When the music began, he opened his arms and Mared stepped into them, slipping her hand into his. With his hand securely around her waist, he calmly and smoothly drew her toward his chest as he expertly led her into a waltz.

She smiled up at him. "It's good to see ye." She meant it. It was damn good to see him.

He smiled warmly.

"What news have ye brought of Eilean Ros?"

He shrugged a little. "All is the same."

"And the staff?"

"Happy in the service of the new housekeeper," he said. "Mrs. Rawlins."

"Aha, a new housekeeper," she said with approval. "That would account for the perfection of yer clothing, then."

"It would indeed," Payton said with a lopsided smile.

"And the distillery? Grif says it will proceed, aye?"

"Eilean Ros whiskey will be bottled by the end of the coming year."

"Congratulations," Mared said, nodding her head in a mock bow. "I know how ye've wanted it."

"Thank ye," he said, nodding back. There was a glimmer in his eyes, that ever-present hint of amusement that she realized she missed.

"Ye seem to have settled into . . . this," he said, glancing around at the grandeur of the Aitkin mansion.

"Oh, 'tis bonny, the soirees and the balls."

He pulled her a little closer; his gaze fell to her décolletage. "I am overcome," he said quietly, "at how beautiful ye are, Mared. I always thought it, but to see ye like this . . . ye astonish me."

Mared felt that peculiar tug again, as if some invisible rope had circled her heart and was pulling it from her chest. "Ye should come to Edinburra more often," she suggested lightly and smiled. "I've more gowns."

That earned her a sad smile, and Payton shook his head. "I've Eilean Ros to care for. And the distillery. And God help me if I should leave the sheep unattended—yer dogs might herd them all the way to the sea, aye?"

"Aye," she laughed. "I trained them well, I did."

He chuckled and pulled her closer. "It's damn good to hold ye in my arms again."

A palpable heat was unfurling in her, a heat that only Payton seemed capable of arousing in her. "It's damn good to be in them," she admitted in a whisper.

That pleased him, for he smiled deeply and pulled her even closer, his gaze, deep and intimate. They danced on that way, their gazes locked, Mared's smile bright and her awareness of anyone or anything else rapidly fading away.

When the waltz ended, Mared curtsied, but Payton did not let go her hand. "Walk with me."

She laughed. "Where shall we walk? 'Tis terribly cold out, and the house is filled to the rafters."

He smiled confidently. "*Walk* with me." He gave her a subtle wink, firmly placing her hand on his arm, and led her out of the ballroom. They walked into the corridor, which was equally crowded, but Payton led her purposefully toward the entrance.

But just as they might have stepped into the foyer, Payton ushered Mared into a room on their right and shut the door behind him. It was the room where the footmen had laid the coats and wraps. A pair of rush torches on the drive provided a soft amber light by which they could see. Payton walked to the windows and peered out for a moment.

"What if someone thinks to leave?" Mared asked. "They shall want to fetch their wrap."

"No one is leaving this ball for some time." He turned around and looked at her. "I've missed ye, lass."

"I've missed ye as well."

"The house is so empty without ye."

For a moment, neither of them moved, just stood staring at one another. Mared felt as if someone had turned everything upside down, but then Payton was striding toward her. She met him halfway, launching herself into his arms, her mouth eagerly seeking his. His tongue swept hungrily into her mouth, his hands sought her face, her shoulders, her ribs. *"Mared . . ."*

She was just as hungry for him; it was a mad moment, one without conscious thought or breath. Mared ran her hands up his chest and arms, recalling every living inch of him, the feel of his body on her and in her, the strength of his passion as he drove into her.

Payton seemed to recall it, too, for he suddenly picked her up and carried her to a small settee. He came over her, his mouth on her neck, her bosom, his hand somehow beneath her skirts, caressing her leg, rising higher. In the amber light, Mared could see the longing in his eyes. Her hands swept inside his coat, feeling the hardened wall of his chest, then sliding down, to his waist, and then the evidence of his hard desire. She pushed seductively against it as desire pooled between her legs. She ached to be with him, ached to feel him inside her.

Payton groaned and kissed her deeper and madly,

his lips full of mutual longing and anticipation. His hands swept every inch of her, his mouth sought every bit of bare skin. *"Diah,* how I've missed ye. How I've wanted ye, to be inside ye, to put my mouth to yer skin," he breathed.

"Oh, Payton," she whispered, arching up and pressing her bosom against his mouth.

"Say ye want me, Mared. Say ye want me to love ye—"

"Aye, I want ye, Payton," she whispered against the top of his head.

He suddenly pulled away from her, his breathing ragged, and caught her face between his hands, gazing at her. He kissed her once more, then dropped his hands and stood up. His neckcloth was askew, his hair mussed, but he seemed not to notice, just kept gazing at her.

Mared pushed herself up to a sitting position, curious. Payton reached into his coat pocket, and went down on his knee before her.

Mared suddenly panicked. "Payton!" she cried, scrambling to her feet, grabbing his arm, trying to make him stand. "What are ye about? Stand, then!"

"It occurred to me that our betrothal had been arranged under less than romantic circumstances. I never asked for yer hand properly, lass—I should have thought to do so long ago," he said and withdrew a ring.

"No!" Mared cried out, and panicking, she fell to her knees before him. "No, no," she said, grabbing his hands in hers and closing his fingers over the ring, squeezing them tightly. "Donna do this, Payton, I beg of ye!" she cried and pressed her forehead to the knuckles of his hands which she was holding.

"What . . ." He did not finish his question.

Mared looked up—his mouth gaped open and raw emotion shone in his eyes. Tears welled in her eyes as he glanced down at their hands, as if he did not know whose hands they were.

But his humiliation swiftly turned to anger, and the emotion in his eyes turned to steel. He jerked his hands away from hers and quickly gained his feet, then reached down and grabbed Mared by the arm, bringing her roughly to her feet.

"Mared," he said, obviously working to keep his emotions in check, "I am asking ye to come home with me. I've missed ye, and I . . ." He paused to groan with frustration. "Bloody hell, I love ye, Mared! I still *love* ye! Come home with me, aye? Ye donna belong in Edinburra. Ye are a Highlander, and ye belong in the Highlands—no' among snakes and wolves as ye are now."

"Oh, Payton," she said, and reached for his face, but he shoved her hand away.

"I donna want yer bloody pity!" he spat acidly. "I want ye to be the woman I made love to, the woman who loved me back with such great passion!"

Mared swiped unsteadily at the tears on her face. "I do love ye, Payton. More than ye know." It was true—she did love him. But she loved her freedom, too, and she was only now discovering who she was without the curse. Her distress and confusion came out in a groan. "But I canna come with ye."

Payton's hands fisted at his sides. He abruptly whirled around and struck out at an unlit lamp, toppling it over, unmindful of Mared's cry of alarm. "Is it so bloody wonderful here, then?" he demanded angrily. "Ye find this a bonnier place than the Highlands ye love?"

"I am finally living!" she insisted. "Can ye no' understand? I've no' had a life 'til now!"

"That is where ye are wrong," he said, and suddenly whirled around, catching her face between his big hands. "If it is life that ye want, I'll give it to ye, Mared," he argued heatedly. "I'll give ye whatever yer heart desires. Do ye want to see the world? We'll see it all. Do ye want gowns and jewels and fancy trappings? I'll give ye whatever ye might imagine. Just . . . just *be* with me."

His plea was heartfelt. She knew, because her heart had tilted dangerously toward him again, even deeper this time, and it pained her to say no. She did love this man, with all her heart, she did love him. But she was afraid of going back, of being what she'd been before. "Will ye no' come to Edinburra, then?" she asked weakly.

He groaned painfully, pressed his forehead to hers. "I canna leave Eilean Ros."

Mared swallowed a lump of despair. "But I . . . I canna go back," she whispered tearfully. "I canna be who I was then."

Payton sucked in a breath as if he'd been physically hit. He dropped his hands from her face and with a weary sigh, he pocketed the ring he had intended to give her. The bewilderment in his eyes was devastating.

"Very well then," he said, sounding completely dejected. He glanced up at her, and she could see how deep his hurt ran. "This is the last time I will impose on ye, *leannan*," he said quietly. "I have loved ye, aye, I've loved ye all my life. But it seems I've been a bloody fool. . . ." He sighed again, and turned partially toward the window. "Aye, but I'll no' be a fool again, for I donna believe," he said, his voice getting hoarse with emotion, "that I can love ye any longer."

He might as well have kicked her in the gut, and in fact, Mared felt her knees begin to buckle. She grabbed on to his arm, but he shook her off and moved out of her reach. Payton, the man who had been the constant in her life, the man who had adored her, wooed her, courted her, enslaved her, seduced her . . . he wouldn't love her any longer? The very notion shook her to her core. "Please donna say that," she pleaded.

"'Tis too late, Mared," he said wearily. "Whatever I have felt for ye all these years has died with yer refusal. Go then. Live yer life. Leave no stone unturned." He started to walk past her.

Mared tried to catch his arm, to make him turn around, to make him take it back, but he shrugged out of her grip, opened the door, and strode into the brightly lit corridor.

She did not see him again.

Twenty-seven

✦✦

$\mathscr{I}$t was Ellie who informed Mared that Payton had left Edinburgh. When she and Duncan came in from their afternoon stroll around Charlotte Square, Ellie handed her bonnet to the footman and said excitedly, "You did not tell me that Laird Douglas had come to town!"

Mared froze at the writing desk where she was reading the post. "Douglas?" she echoed weakly. "In Edinburra?"

"Yes, of course! I encountered Miss Douglas, and she told me that he'd come and gone in two days' time. But he attended the Aitkin ball last evening—surely you saw him there."

"No," Mared said, looking up. "No, I didna see him."

Ellie looked quite surprised. And even more skeptical.

"It was horribly crowded," Mared quickly added.

"Hmm," Ellie said, looking at her curiously. "I would think that the laird would seek you out, what with his regard for you."

"Oh," Mared said airily, turning back to the morning post, "he's not had any regard for me in months. No' since I ruined his neckcloths."

"*Really,*" Ellie said.

"No' the slightest," Mared insisted and nonchalantly picked up an invitation and stared blindly at it as the heat of her lie crept up her neck.

"Well then, I suppose I shall inquire *why* he didn't call when I see him next," Ellie said pertly.

Mared jerked her gaze up. "When you see him next?"

"At Loch Chon. We're to go home soon, you know."

"No, I didna know."

"Anna's time is near, and the winter weather will be setting in soon. Didn't Liam tell you?"

"No," Mared said, frowning. "He didna, for I would have told him that I canna go back to Talla Dileas."

Ellie's gasp of surprise was nothing compared to Liam's roar of disapproval over supper. They argued well into the night, Liam insisting that she could not remain behind, unchaperoned, without at *least* a companion, for it would not do for an unmarried lass to cavort about Edinburgh without escort.

Mared argued just as vehemently that she was a grown woman, and she'd lived her entire life at Talla Dileas wasting away under that curse, and now she was determined to live life fully and become the person she was meant to be. Not a spinster. Not a woman stuffed away in some dreary rotting castle in the Highlands.

Liam took great offense at that comment and he reminded her rather loudly—so loudly that Ellie ran from window to window, ensuring they were all soundly shut—that she was a Highlander born and bred, and he'd never let her forget it. Mared swore she'd never forget it, how could she? But that did not mean she was destined to be tucked away in the Highlands all her life. She reminded Liam that he and Grif had had their share of travel and adventure before the family fortune had turned, and now it was only fair that she had hers.

"No' without a companion or escort, no' over my bloody body!" Liam shouted.

Mared shrugged. "I donna care for a companion. But if that means ye'll leave me in peace, then I shall have one. But I am no' going back!" *Especially not now that Payton hates me.*

The next morning, as a light snow dusted the streets of Edinburgh, Liam stormed out of their apartments. He returned several hours later accompanied by a plump gray-haired woman who was dressed in black bombazine. "Mared, *leannan*," Liam said politely, "please meet yer chaperone, Mrs. MacGillicutty."

"Pleased to make yer acquaintance, Miss Lockhart," the woman said brightly. "Won't we have a bonny time of it until yer brother can return for ye, aye?"

"Oh, *aye*," Mared said, and shooting a look at Liam, she took the woman in hand and showed her about their apartments.

Liam, Ellie, and baby Duncan left a week after Mrs. MacGillicutty's arrival, once Liam was satisfied that the old woman knew her business and would keep a watchful eye on Mared. As they loaded the ornate traveling chaise, Liam reviewed Mrs. MacGillicutty's duties, which were, concisely, to ensure that Mared was never left alone in the company of a man of any sort. Gentleman or pauper, Liam cared not.

"She's rather popular at the moment," he said. "She'll be even more popular when the gentlemen learn I've gone, aye?"

"Oh, indeed," Mrs. MacGillicutty said, her lips pursed disapprovingly.

"I canna be plainer than this, Mrs. MacGillicutty," Liam said and put his arm around Mared, yanking her to his side and pointing his finger at her. "Ye canna trust this one, aye? Our Mared is right charming when she's of a mind and wants ye to behave in a certain manner, but ye *canna* allow yerself to be fooled, woman. Do ye quite understand?" he asked as Mared groaned and huffed toward the gray sky.

"Quite, Captain Lockhart."

He let Mared go. "I'll expect ye to write at least weekly if no' more frequently."

"It will be me pleasure!" the old bat swore and smiled sweetly at Mared.

And with a lot of farewells and Godspeeds, Liam and his family departed for Talla Dileas as Mrs. MacGillicutty waved good-bye with one hand and snaked the other around Mared's elbow, holding it in an ironclad grip as if she expected Mared to bolt then and there.

Mared did not bolt then and there. She fancied herself more clever than that . . . but Mrs. MacGillicutty proved to be a worthy opponent. If a gentleman called—and several did—Mrs. MacGillicutty sat on the settee with Mared and read a book while the gentleman tried to make polite conversation with his mouth and love with his eyes and steal a touch of Mared's hand when he could.

When the gentleman left, Mrs. MacGillicutty would invariably make a comment or two about him.

"Rather surprising Lord Tavish has time to make so many social calls, what with his wife and six children needing him at home, aye?" Or "Mr. Anderson seems to be a frequent caller all around the square, does he no'? He seems to have placed ye right between Miss Williams there," she said, pointing to one side of the square, "and Miss Bristol just there," she'd say, pointing to the opposite side of the square.

Mared ignored the old woman, for she didn't know what was really happening between Mared and her gentleman callers. She did not attend Mared at night, when she was afforded a modicum of freedom to attend all the fashionable supper parties and routs.

At these events, she flirted with abandon with all the gentlemen who paid her heed and chatted and gossiped with all the women who were kind to her. She avoided Miss Douglas, for that one rarely acknowledged Mared when they chanced to meet.

There were two gentlemen among several who seemed to be uncommonly interested in her. Mr. David Anderson, the son of Viscount Aitkin, had made it perfectly clear in both word and deed—whispered desires in her ear, stolen kisses under the cloak of darkness—that he would like their friendship to expand beyond its current boundaries, which, of course, she took to mean an offer of marriage. And Lord Tavish, the married earl, had also made it abundantly clear that he enjoyed Mared's witty repartee. And her bosom.

Mared did not care for Lord Tavish in the least, really, and she'd never consider any sort of relationship with him beyond the innocent banter at supper parties, as he was quite married and quite old. And frankly, Mr. Anderson did not suit her entirely, either, in that he wasn't Payton. He seemed neither as strong nor as intelligent nor even as witty as Payton. But he was the son of a viscount, the sort of match her family had always wanted for her, but believed she'd never have.

Shouldn't she want it for herself? She had recently begun to think that perhaps she should be happy to marry a man of Anderson's stature, and the fact that he wasn't Payton—couldn't hold a candle to Payton, really—she just ignored, pushing it down inside her, where all her feelings for Payton resided. Very deep. Dead and buried, as it were. He didn't love her anymore—it seemed she *should* look to marriage elsewhere.

While she found him pleasant enough, Mared knew she'd never feel love for Mr. Anderson. She simply thought him a proper match. Love rarely entered into these arrangements, she'd learned. It was a matter of properly aligning fortunes and mutual expectations.

Having thus convinced herself, it wasn't until the wedding of Miss Clara Ellis to Mr. Fabian MacBride that the thought of Payton dug its way out of its grave and rose up from the dead to torment her like a bloody nightmare.

On that occasion, Mared arrived at the kirk, all smiles in the ice blue gown Anna had given her. She walked down the aisle to take her place among the other guests, smiling and greeting—*Good afternoon, Mr. MacBain. How lovely yer bonnet, Miss Caraway.*

The wedding ceremony was rather boring, Mared thought. There was no lively crowd, not like in the Highlands. This was a very stilted affair, in which people nodded approvingly, but no one sang out their heartfelt congratulations to the couple.

Afterward, at the wedding breakfast, which was served in a hall on Princes Street, Mared sat alone. The gentlemen she knew were in the company of their families or wives and were not free to flirt with her. As the breakfast ended and a celebration of sorts began, Mared spied Mr. Anderson, who had been quite solicitous and charming the night before. She made her way to him, but he seemed oddly shocked that she was in attendance when she met him. "Good morning, Mr. Anderson," she said.

"Miss Lockhart?" He looked around, smiling nervously.

"Wasn't the wedding bonny?" Mared asked. "I thought the bride particularly so."

"Aye, she was indeed." He licked his lips, his gaze scanning the crowd around them.

Mared smiled, cocked her head to one side, and tapped him on the arm with her fan. "Are ye quite all right, Mr. Anderson?"

"Ah . . . very well," he said, seeming startled she would even ask. "Grand to see ye, Miss Lockhart, but if ye will excuse me, I must attend my grandmother."

"Oh. Of course." How odd, she thought. Mr. Anderson was always so hotly in pursuit of her, but now he nodded curtly and walked away.

Mared's smile faded completely when he did not attend his grandmother, but a young woman Mared had seen a few times before. She suddenly had the very old and familiarly uncomfortable feeling that people were whispering about her. The hair stood up on the back of her neck as it used to do in the lochs when people would close their doors as she walked by.

So it was with great relief that she spied a familiar

and friendly, albeit roguish, face in Hugh MacAlister, standing near the entrance in the company of two men. Mared walked across the room to him and tapped him on the shoulder. "Here I am, sir, the object of yer desire," she teased him.

"What?" Hugh said sharply, turning around. His frown instantly turned to a smile when he saw Mared before him. "Ah then, look at ye, Miss Lockhart! How bonny ye are! I'd wager ye are the object of more than one man's desire, aye?"

Mared laughed. "I'm very happy to see ye, Hugh. I could use a friend just now."

"Ah," he said, clasping his hands behind his back. "I would that I might stay behind and lend an ear, *leannan,* but I've another engagement and several ah . . . *persons* awaiting me there."

"Ye are a scoundrel, sir!"

"That, lass, is quite well established," he said with a wink. "Very well, then, good—"

"Wait!" she cried, realizing that he was indeed leaving her. "Ye donna truly intend to walk away just now? Please stay, Hugh. I am alone and feeling rather strangely reviled by a man I thought rather keen on me."

"A pity," he said, his smile gone. "But I canna stay. I am wanted elsewhere."

She frowned petulantly at him. "I thought ye adored me. I thought ye came all the way back from Ireland just for me."

Hugh surprised her by laughing. "*Ach,* lass, how naïve ye are! Ye believed that?"

Mared blinked. Of course she didn't believe Hugh had come back from Ireland for her, but she *did* believe he held her in some regard. Why else would he say all the things he'd said? Of course she didn't believe he loved her, but certainly he held her in *some* esteem, for he'd said so, many times.

When Hugh saw in her expression that she did believe he esteemed her, he leaned forward and said bluntly, "Donna be a fool, Mared. That is what men and women do, aye? They flatter and they flirt, and they dance around the point of it all until one or the other is successful in taking the other to their bed."

She blushed and snapped open her fan. "Perhaps that is *yer* manner of operation, but it's no' the way of a gentleman. I've had several gentleman callers in Edinburra, and no' one of them has suggested such a thing!"

"Indeed?" Hugh asked and looked across the room to where Mr. Anderson was still speaking with the young woman. "And do ye think, then, that Mr. Anderson's attentions to ye were in the course of building to an offer of marriage?"

"How would ye know of that!" she demanded.

"Poor lass," Hugh said and laughed roundly. "Everyone knows of his interest in ye. Everyone knows that Anderson would have ye as his mistress. Really, then, did ye think he'd marry ye? A woman of yer age and situation?" He laughed again and patted her on the arm. "Ye really are a lamb, *leannan*. Run back to the Highlands, aye? Ye're too good for the likes of Edinburra, and ye are far too naïve to play the games that amuse people here."

Mared bristled at the condescension in his tone. How dare he speak to her as if she were an ignorant child! She glared at him icily. "I beg yer pardon, Mr. MacAlister, but I should have thought twice before renewing my acquaintance with a *roué!*"

Hugh chuckled, grabbed her hand and lifted it to

his mouth, kissing her knuckles fondly. "That, *mo ghraidh*, is me point precisely," he said, and let go her hand. "Go home, then. Ye'll be happier there, I assure ye. Ye'll be eaten up here," he said, and with a wink, he clasped his hands behind his back and walked away to join his companions.

Would that Mared had taken his advice and left at that moment, too, for she would have been spared the humiliation that occurred a scant quarter of an hour later, when the father of the happy bride gained the attention of the room by tapping a spoon to his champagne glass. "Ladies and gentlemen, if ye would be so kind," he called loudly.

The room quieted. Mared stepped back, leaned against the wall, apart from the rest of the crowd. More from habit than need, really, but she'd spent a lifetime standing apart.

"On this occasion, I've another happy announcement to make," he said, and a murmur instantly ran through the crowd. "I am pleased to say that another fine young couple has made known their plans to wed."

Now the crowd tittered with delight and pushed forward to see which couple. "May I present to you the future Mr. and Mrs. David Anderson!" he exclaimed, and Mr. Anderson, the very man who'd whispered such decadent and witty remarks in her ear, and the young woman to whom he'd been speaking, stepped forward to receive hearty good wishes from the crowd.

The floor seemed to dip at Mared's feet. What of all the flirting? The many calls to her apartments? She was shocked, completely shocked, to learn what Hugh had said was true. And she realized with a sickening feeling, glancing around at the people in the hall, that she was the woman who had come down from the Highlands to reclaim her happiness, only to be made the fool.

It was all so suddenly clear to her now! Ellie's warning, Liam's concern, Mrs. MacGillicutty's remarks. And it was likewise crystal clear to her now that in all the years she had thought her happiness had been robbed from her by some silly curse, it had been hers to have and to hold. With *Payton*. But no, she'd let fear and stubborn clan pride drain that from her. She'd allowed the dream of being someone other than herself to cloud her judgment. She'd destroyed the one chance at true happiness she might have had with her embrace of her so-called freedom.

All because she thought she had not yet lived.

But she *had* lived! She'd lived freely and she'd had the love of a man who had adored her. And she had tossed it away to seek something that had been in her heart all along, exactly where Donalda had said. Oh, what a bloody, silly, fool she was!

She wanted out of that stuffy room, away from Edinburgh. She wanted Payton. But first, she had something to say to Mr. Anderson. She lifted her chin and marched across the room to him. He could not help but acknowledge her.

"Congratulations, Mr. Anderson," she said with a smile.

"Ah . . . thank you, Miss Lockhart. May I introduce my fiancée, Miss Linley."

Mared turned a blindingly bright smile to her. "Miss Linley! May I offer my heartfelt condolences!"

"Wh-what?" the poor lass stammered, looking

helplessly to Mr. Anderson, who was turning a rather unbecoming shade of red.

"Oh, I am certain ye shall have all that yer heart desires—a fine house. Children. His father's fortune. But ye seem like a very nice lass, and I hate to see ye married to a liar and a blackguard all yer days," she said pleasantly.

Miss Linley was too stunned to speak, but she gasped.

"Miss Lockhart!" Mr. Anderson protested.

"Mr. Anderson!" Mared replied pleasantly. "Ye seem rather surprised that someone might call ye on it! I assure ye I donna do it for myself, but on behalf of Miss Bristol and Miss Williams, who have likewise suffered yer perfidy."

"Miss Bristol?" Miss Linley said weakly, looking at Mr. Anderson.

"And donna forget Miss Williams," Mared said brightly. "He had quite a full plate at Charlotte Square, aye?"

Miss Linley again looked at Mr. Anderson, who now looked as if he wanted to crawl in a hole. "Very well, then! Good day," Mared said and twirled about, intending to make a quick exit.

But she was stopped at the door by Miss Sarah Douglas. She folded her arms across her middle and looked Mared up and down. Mared expected a tongue lashing and was prepared to do battle, but Miss Douglas suddenly smiled. "Well done, Miss Lockhart."

Mared blinked. "Praise? From ye, Miss Douglas?"

Miss Douglas shrugged and looked over Mared's shoulder. "He's a despicable man and I am rather fond of Miss Linley. So thank ye for having the courage to say what no one else would."

Impossibly pleased, Mared beamed at her. "Ye are quite welcome." She stepped around Miss Douglas and walked on. But then she suddenly paused, turned around, and walked back to Miss Douglas. "And by the by, Miss Douglas, I love Payton. I may no' be what ye imagined for him, but I love him."

Now it was Miss Douglas's turn to blink. Mared smiled. "Good day, Miss Douglas," she chirped and sailed through the doors of the hall and out into the bright sunlight and bitter cold. Mared reached up and swept the bonnet off her head. She never cared for the damnable things anyway. She blinked up at the sun. Funny, but it always seemed colder here than at home. She longed for her boots, for the rocky sheep trails that crisscrossed Ben Cluaran through heather so thick you could lie on it. She longed for the smell of spring, the fields of thistle, and the streams that gurgled down into the lochs. She longed for the mists that would come down from the top of the hills and swallow her whole, so that she walked in a dreamy fog with nothing but years of walking the same trails and her dogs to guide her.

She missed the Highlands. She missed her family.

And she missed Payton desperately.

She was going home, where she belonged.

Mrs. MacGillicutty was not the least bit surprised that Mared wanted to go home and happily set about helping her pack her things into two new trunks. She laughed as Mared related what had happened to her. How she had thought Mr. Anderson's attention sincere, and how terribly naïve she'd been to believe it could be true affection, given that the talk never progressed beyond banter. How she had been loved very deeply by a man and had tossed him aside like so much rubbish.

"If he loved ye as much as that, lass, he will love ye still," Mrs. MacGillicutty assured her.

"No," Mared said morosely. "He said he didna love me any longer."

"Men say such things when they are angry and wounded," Mrs. MacGillicutty said. "But they rarely mean what they say. A man's pride is quite fragile, like fine crystal, but it is easily rebuilt, what with a bit of kowtowing. So go home, lass. Ye will find that his heart is still calling to ye."

Mared caught a breath in her throat and whirled around to the woman. "What did ye say?" she whispered.

"That ye will find his heart still calls to yers," she said with a smile.

Tears suddenly welled in her eyes, and Mared quickly turned away.

She hadn't felt his heart call to her in weeks.

Twenty-eight

❦

The snow began falling when the public coach reached Callander. A merchant agreed to take Mared a few more miles to Aberfoyle, but the journey was excruciatingly slow, given the snowfall.

It was dusk when they reached Aberfoyle, and Mared had no choice but to take refuge at the public inn. She was given a room that overlooked a meadow, and beyond it, Ben Cluaran stood majestically in the distance. She stood at the window and stared at the mountain in the waning light of day, longing for Payton, traveling the hill in her mind's eye, cresting it, and seeing Eilean Ros below her.

How ironic, she thought as the sun finally slipped behind Ben Cluaran, that she'd spent so many years despising him for the sake of his name, and now, she couldn't possibly care if his name was Douglas or Lockhart or Diabhal. Just as long as he forgave her, that was all that mattered. Just as long as he looked at her with those warm gray eyes, the glitter in them the evidence of his adoration for her.

The very next morning, she washed and dressed and had her luggage carried to the confectioner's shop, where she knew she might stow it until she could send someone back for it.

"Ah, Miss Lockhart!" the confectioner called as she walked in the door. "I had thought ye were in Edinburra!"

"Aye, I've been away for a time, but I've come home now," she said. "Might I keep my luggage here until I can send my brother for it?"

"Of course, lass. Come here, come here, then . . . on the occasion of yer homecoming, I've a new sweet-meat ye must try."

"Oh, I shouldna—"

"Ye best come now, lass, for Laird Douglas takes them all. He has a sweet tooth, he does, and he bought them all up yesterday to give to Miss Crowley."

That remark dealt her a blow. "Did he?" Mared asked weakly and glanced down at her gloves and blindly fumbled to remove them.

"Aye," he said with a chuckle. "Constantly together, the two of them. I wager they'll marry at Christmas."

Another blow, and a much stronger one. "Marry, ye say?" she asked as she pretended to look at the hard candies.

"Aye." He looked over his shoulder at her as he lifted the lid from the glass case. "I suppose ye've no' heard then, having come from Edinburra. Aye, there is an announcement to be made this Sunday, after services. Laird Douglas and Miss Crowley are to be wed."

So that was it, then. It was over. She'd had her chance—no, she'd had dozens of them—and had squandered them all.

"Are ye all right, Miss Lockhart?"

She jerked her head up. "Just anxious to be home, I think."

"'Tis too cold to walk. I'll have me son drive ye up, then, aye?"

"Aye, please, Mr. Wallace, that is awfully kind."

He smiled, put several sweetmeats in a plain wrapper, and handed them to her. "Enjoy these on yer way home. Consider it a welcome-home gift."

"Thank ye," she said and tucked them in her reticule. Small consolation in light of what she'd lost, but Mared smiled.

The Lockharts were, predictably, quite happy and surprised to see Mared, and showered her with hugs and kisses and dozens upon dozens of questions.

She weathered the inquisition well enough without giving anything terribly personal away. She smiled, she laughed, she talked with great animation about Edinburgh and all the parties, and all the while her heart was breaking, crumbling into tiny pieces, scattering with the wind that suddenly seemed to be blowing through her. She felt so empty.

She begged off supper that night, citing a headache from her traveling, and retired early. In truth, she was exhausted. She tossed and turned in her bed, and when she grew weary of that, she got up and paced before the hearth, her mind racing and spinning and her heart twisting and twisting until she felt absolutely ill.

She had lost him, that much was obvious. Yet she was compelled to see him, to confess that she'd wronged him, that she was terribly sorry for it, that she'd been a frighteningly naïve lass with cotton in her head. And that her heart, which had tilted to him long ago, had tilted and tilted until it had fallen over and shattered completely without him there to catch it.

But how could she tell him? It would not do to march up to his front door and announce to him and his staff that she was a bloody idiot. And besides, she hardly had the nerve to face him after all that had gone on between them. Or on the eve of his betrothal to Beitris.

The next day dawned bright and full of sun, and the snow quickly melted from the roads and sheep trails. Mared tried to settle into her life at Talla Dileas again. She romped with her dogs, played with Duncan, plaited Natalie's hair and told her of Edinburgh, then helped her mother inventory the repairs that needed to be made to Talla Dileas. Everyone, it seemed, was more relaxed now that they were free of the worry over money. Everyone seemed to be happily and patiently waiting for Anna's baby to come, and for Christmas, which was little more than a fortnight away.

As she helped inventory the list of repairs that afternoon, her mother remarked that she could now afford to hire the help they needed to maintain Talla Dileas. "I am in need of a good housekeeper. Perhaps I should inquire after Mrs. Rawlins."

Mrs. Rawlins . . . that was Payton's housekeeper; Mared remembered the name quite clearly. "Who?" she asked.

"Mrs. Rawlins. She was hired as Douglas's housekeeper, but apparently it was no' a very successful engagement."

"No? Why is that, then?"

"Oh, I donna know, really. Other than he's been a wee bit of a bear of late. I hear he's been rather demanding. I suppose building a distillery and arranging a wedding are rather trying."

Mared's heart did a funny little lurch. "He's always been demanding," she muttered, but all she could think was that Payton was without a housekeeper. There was no one there to turn down his bed and launder his clothes and open his drapes in the morning.

For the first time in two days, she smiled from within.

In the midst of a dream of oak barrels and enormous vats, Payton was moved to consciousness by the scent of lilac. It startled him out of sleep, really, for he'd not smelled that heavenly scent in what seemed an eternity now.

He opened his eyes, rolled onto his back, and glanced around the room. It was dark; the drapes were drawn and he could see nothing but the red embers at his hearth. He rubbed his eyes, heard the rustle of cloth, and quickly dropped his hands, pushed himself up, and looked around the room.

The sound of drapes being pulled garnered his attention, and as he looked to the windows, he felt his body go cold with shock.

She pushed the drapes aside and shook her head. "A rather dreary day by the look of it."

Mared. She was in his room, opening his drapes and wearing the black gown and white apron of a housekeeper. Still shaking off the fog of a deep sleep, he tried to make sense of it. Was he dreaming? How could he be? Yet what else might explain it? It was so startlingly real that as she moved to the next set of drapes, he caught the scent of lilacs again.

"Snow again, I'd wager." She clucked her tongue. "I donna suppose ye can build a distillery in weather such as this, aye?"

It was no dream—she was real. She'd walked out of his dreams and she was here, before him, in the flesh. "What are ye doing here?" he asked roughly, anger and wounded pride filling him instantly.

She turned around and flashed that brilliant, green-eyed smile that had, for so many years, accompanied him to sleep. "I've brought ye a treat, milord," she said sweetly. "Sweetmeats. I know how much ye like them."

He didn't want her bloody sweetmeats, he didn't want anything but for her to be gone from him. He'd spent the last month purging her from his heart and mind, and he'd not allow her back in. Not ever, and notwithstanding what Sarah had written him about the brave Miss Lockhart. He didn't care if she claimed to love him—he didn't love her anymore.

When he didn't respond, Mared walked to the small dining table, unwrapped several delicacies and put them on a plate.

"How did ye get in here?" he demanded.

"Mrs. Mackerell," she said and turned toward him, the plate in hand. "She gave me the plate as well."

"I donna want yer damn treats." He threw aside the bedcovers and stood, hardly caring that he was completely naked. He grabbed up his dressing gown and put it on. "I donna know what ye want or what game ye play, Mared, but I will kindly ask ye to leave."

"I'll leave them here," she said and put them on the bedside table. She turned away, and Payton thought she would leave . . . but she walked to the hearth, put aside the fire screen, and got down on her knees to stoke the fire.

"God blind me!" he exploded. "Go, Mared! I donna

want ye here, I donna want to lay eyes on ye!" he said angrily and walked into the privy, slamming the door behind him.

But when he returned a moment later, she was still there, calmly cleaning the riding boots he'd left to dry at the hearth. "Dammit, donna touch them!" he roared and grabbed her by the arm, jerking her up to her feet and shoving her away from his boots. "What the hell are ye doing?"

Looking chagrined, she fidgeted with the ill-fitting housekeeper's gown, and Payton realized how wrong he'd been to ever put her in it. "What I am doing," she said softly, "is apologizing."

"By shining my *boots?*"

"I asked that a hot bath be brought up. That, too."

That stopped him; he gaped at her.

She nodded.

Payton groaned heavenward. "What are ye doing to me, lass? Do ye mean to torture me unto death? Ye have rejected and dismissed every overture I've ever made, ye've told me quite plainly that ye were going on with yer life, away from the lochs, away from me. It is done, Mared. And now ye appear out of nowhere to draw me a bath?"

She nodded again. "I donna know what else to do," she admitted quietly. "I donna know how to make ye understand other than to open yer drapes and turn down yer bed . . . and to give ye sweetmeats and stoke yer fire and draw yer bath, and anything else I might do to humble myself before ye and beg forgiveness for the horrible, wretched mistake I've made."

She said it so sincerely that Payton felt a small fissure develop in his impenetrable resolve. Love, he was discovering, was a stubborn bedfellow, unwilling to leave him just because he'd demanded it. The hell if he didn't still love her, and while part of him wanted to rejoice in her return, another part of him was still hurting. That part didn't trust her and wanted to turn her out before she could hurt him anymore.

There was a knock on the door that Mared quickly answered. Charlie entered, wishing Payton a cheery good day and carrying two pails of hot water. He was followed by Alan and the new footman, Angus, who eyed Mared curiously. She directed them to the adjoining bath. They poured their buckets, but Mared was not satisfied. She sent them for more.

Payton fell into a chair. What would he do with her? He couldn't let her back into his heart so easily, not after she had wounded him so. Aye, but she had come crawling back to him, in a housekeeper's gown, no less. A very difficult thing for a proud Lockhart to do.

He sighed and shook his head. "It willna work," he said quietly.

Mared bit the inside of her mouth, but she said nothing.

"Ye might serve me all day long and it won't change my feelings for ye," he said, meaning it sincerely.

"Will ye no' allow me to explain, then?" she asked.

He shrugged.

"I love ye, Payton," she said. "More than life, I love ye."

He did not speak. He did not dare speak. Those were exactly the words he'd longed to hear.

She glanced at her feet. "I canna rightly say why I believed I had to leave. I donna know why I couldna understand that the happiness I sought was here for the taking, if I'd only allowed myself to believe it. *Diah,* look what I've done. I've turned away the one man who would love me all me days—"

He gazed at her impassively.

"And I've lost the only man I shall ever love. *I am so sorry, Payton,*" she whispered plaintively. "I'm so sorry that I hurt ye. I would give ye the heavens would it convey how very sorry I am. To the depths of my soul, I am sorry—"

There was a knock at the door. Mared glanced at it, then at him. He looked away. With a sigh, she walked to the door and opened it to the footmen, returning with more pails of hot water. They trooped into the bathing room and emptied them.

"That will be all," he said as they emerged from the bathing room. Charlie nodded, and the three of them went out, Mared shutting the door behind them.

Payton stood up, hardly sparing her a glance. "I'll have that bath now," he said. "If ye are determined, ye might do whatever it is ye do," he said, gesturing to the room, and walked into the bathing room.

He divested himself of the robe, climbed into the tub and lowered himself into the hot water. And there he remained a few moments, listening to her move about his room. Making his bed, he thought. She was serious, it seemed. She meant to humble herself. Another very large step for a Lockhart.

"Mared," he called out, absently toying with a sponge.

He heard her move to the open door behind him. "Aye?"

"Ye said ye were sorry for what ye'd done, then, aye?"

"Payton . . ." She suddenly appeared at his side, her eyes meeting his, beseeching him. "I am *very* sorry."

He nodded, pressed the sponge to his shoulder and squeezed. Rivulets of hot water sluiced down his chest. "And are ye sorry for the neckcloths and shirts and linens ye ruined?"

That caught her off guard. "The . . . pardon, the neckcloths?" she asked uncertainly.

"Aye. Are ye sorry for them?"

"Ah . . ." She glanced heavenward, bit her lip, then muttered, *"No."*

That was the Mared he loved. Unfailingly honest and too stubborn by half. "What of the tales ye told the chambermaids?" he asked. "The tales of ghosts and wicked Douglases? Are ye sorry for that?"

Mared pressed her lips firmly together and shook her head.

The crack in his resolve burst, and a chuckle escaped him. Mared instantly jerked a wide-eyed gaze to him, and Payton laughed. Before she could speak, he reached up and caught her wrist and pulled her down to the side of the tub. "Ye are no' sorry for any of it, then?"

"No, not the poor housekeeping. How could I possibly be?"

"Then I suppose I will take what I can get," he said and yanked her into the tub.

She landed with a shriek and a splash on his lap. He silenced any protests about her gown or propriety by putting his arms around her and kissing her with all the anger and hurt and grief and love he'd held for her these many long years. Love he'd not been able to purge from his veins, love that seemed to be hemorrhaging from his heart now.

He at last lifted his head, pulled the tie from her braid of hair and began to unravel it into long, wavy tresses of black.

"I love ye, Payton. More than life, I love ye."

"*Diah,* Mared, I've waited an eternity to hear ye say it."

"I know," she said, and her smile faded as she snaked her arms around his neck. "But now that I have found me way to yer heart, it is too late! I'll never forgive myself for being such a bloody fool!"

"Too late? It's no' too late, lass."

"It is!" she insisted. "I know about Beitris!"

"Beitris Crowley?" he asked, momentarily confused.

"Aye! Ye're to marry her!" she cried and with a moan from deep inside her, she closed her eyes, let her head drop back in agony.

"No, no, *m'annsachd,* no," he said, caressing her neck. "Miss Crowley is to marry the smithy's son. She's to marry Mr. Abernathy."

Mared's head snapped up and she opened her eyes. "That handsome lad?"

"Aye," he said, a smile returning to his face. "*That* handsome lad."

"But Mr. Wallace said *ye* were to marry her! That ye were often in her presence! Ye took her sweetmeats, ye did!"

Payton laughed. "I brokered the offer for the lad. I took sweetmeats to present the offer to her father. They will announce it at services this Sunday."

Mared blinked. "Then . . . ye donna love Miss Crowley?"

"*Criosd,* Mared! No, I donna love Miss Crowley! And Miss Crowley doesna love me. In spite of yer attempts, we determined long ago that we were no' suited for marriage, and she confided in me then her love for Mr. Abernathy. I merely helped her."

"Then . . . then I'm no' too late," she uttered, and something sparked in her green eyes.

He looked into those forest green eyes, so full of life, the ruby lips, the dimples in her cheeks that deepened with her pleasure. There was nothing that could keep him from loving this stubborn, impetuous, vibrant woman. "On my honor," he said with a sigh, "ye could never be too late." He enveloped her in his arms and kissed her deeply, like a man who had thirsted for love and who would never let her go, not again, not ever.

Her hands slipped to his body, her warmth radiating through the water into his skin, and he felt himself rise up, his cock hard and eager to make love to her, to the woman he thought he'd lost.

"Love me, Payton," she murmured, reading his thoughts. "Please show me ye still love me, aye? And please donna make me ask thrice."

He grinned, but he was already unfastening that awful housekeeper's gown and helping her to pull it over her head. Mared smiled, her cheeks dimpling as she lifted her chemise over her head, too, then splashing carelessly about to straddle him.

With a sigh of contentment, Payton lay back in the tub and let his hands glide over her wet skin—her arms, her ribs into her waist, and the flare of her hips above the black thatch of hair. Mared's eyes darkened; her gaze dipped to his body. And then she closed her eyes and sighed with what he thought was relief.

He sat up, his arms around her, his face pressed against the swell of her bosom, tasting her flesh.

She wrapped her arms around his neck as his lips grazed the curve of her throat. His hands had started a slow ascent up her rib cage, and he drew her breast into his mouth, flicking his tongue over the nipple.

Her body shivered at his touch, making his desire burn. He slid his hands down to her bottom, kneading it, holding her tightly against his rigid shaft while his tongue dueled wildly with hers. His mind, his eyes, his every fiber was filled with the scent and the feel of Mared, returned to him at last.

There was no need for words between them; he was dangerously aroused and desperate for her body, and he moved from her lips to her breast, taking her fully into his mouth, hungry for the taste of her. Mared whimpered with pleasure as he devoured her like a madman, without care of anything but the need to feel her, to touch her, to be deep inside her.

"Take me," she said, her voice rough with passion. "I belong to ye now. Freely. With all my heart, I belong to ye."

Something primal and deep stirred in Payton's groin; blood was raging through him like a swollen river. He had never desired anyone or anything so completely in his life. He pressed his mouth against hers, thrust his tongue inside as he grabbed her hips, lifting her up, lifting her onto him. Her chest was heaving; she looked down at him with a wickedly lustful look in her eye, and he smiled.

He slowly lowered her, anchoring her to his lap with one arm, slipping his free hand between them. Mared sighed when his fingers slipped deeper, and let her head fall back, moving her hips in such a way that sent the blood pounding through Payton, engorging him.

Mared's response to his touch was explosive; she was moving harder against him, gasping for breath, the little cries of pleasure coming quicker and quicker in anticipation of release. He was quick to oblige her and began to move harder inside her—she was hot and wet and so bloody *tight*. Her body wrapped firmly around him, she met his rhythm, moving in time with him to help find her release. He helped her, too, rubbing and stroking as she rode him, higher and higher.

They were both panting; Mared had fallen over, bracing herself against his chest, her eyes closed, her brow furrowed as he stroked her to the same oblivion he felt weighing down on him. When he thought he could not deny himself another moment, Mared sobbed; her body contracted tightly around him and he felt the shudder of her release.

He was right behind her, his own release coming in quick, hot spurts at the end of savage thrusts.

She collapsed onto him, her wet hair covering them. As he drew deep breaths, Payton gently leaned back against the tub, taking her with him, stroking her back, and kissing her neck.

Neither of them spoke.

He was, in that moment of the purest love, unable to take his eyes from her, unable to believe that she had come back to him. She lay with her head on his shoulder, her eyes closed and her lips slightly parted, her hair a mass of wet and riotous waves, her breasts lifting with each ragged breath. Mared Lockhart made love like a woman who had been cursed for a thousand years.

And he had never been so completely, so wholly satisfied as he was at that very moment.

She opened her eyes and smiled at him. Then she put her hand on his heart, pressing lightly against it, then took his hand and pressed it against her heart. "Listen," she whispered. "Our hearts, they are beating as one."

Epilogue

❖

*L*iam and Ellie Lockhart had no more children after the birth of Duncan, but Anna Lockhart was delivered of a baby girl on February 2, 1819. The following year, she and Grif had another girl, and Talla Dileas was thriving with children and wealth again.

In 1820, having completed their grand tour of Europe and America while Grif looked after Eilean Ros, Mared Douglas gave birth to twin boys. Her husband could not have been more delighted. In 1822, she bore Payton a stillborn daughter, but in 1824, she bore him a healthy boy. In 1825 and 1826, respectively, she bore him two more children, another son and a daughter, who became the apple of her father's eye.

Eilean Ros, the big rambling Georgian mansion on the banks of Loch Ard, was, at long last, filled with laughter and love and the sound of many children.

In 1828, the Douglas and Lockhart lands were at last united, and the region surrounding Loch Ard and Loch Chon did indeed became renowned for its sheep *and* its Highland cattle. In 1830, the first batch of Eilean Ros Whiskey, aged ten years, was distributed to America and Europe with great success. That was the same year that Natalie Lockhart returned to London and made her successful debut there. She became a renowned artist, her work desperately sought after among the highest echelons of London society.

On Christmas Eve 1831, the green salon of Eilean Ros was decorated with mistletoe and a dozen stockings hung by children awaiting Father Christmas. On the sideboard, a large, half-eaten platter of plum pudding was next to an even larger—and emptier—bowl of wassail. The sound of children laughing and shrieking with pleasure echoed up and down the long corridors of Eilean Ros.

All the Lockharts and Douglases were in attendance; even Natalie had come home. Anna was at the pianoforte, leading a rousing chorus of all their favorite Christmas hymns. Mared sat on the divan with their daughter, Lilias, who, having foregone the benefit of a nap earlier, was becoming quite cross and weary at the long day's end.

Payton stood at the mantel, watching the raucous family gathering, his heart filled to the brim with happiness. This was precisely what he'd always wanted for Eilean Ros—laughter, warmth, and love. So much love. He was a fortunate man. He had four healthy, robust sons, a beautiful daughter, and the most beautiful wife God ever divined.

He looked at Mared, singing to her daughter. She was a little rounder now, and there was a bit of gray in her long black hair, but nevertheless, in his eyes, she was perfect. It seemed to him that her beauty deepened with age, gave it a rich character. And it was precisely that beauty that he'd endeavored to capture for all eternity. Which was why he held up his hand and called for Anna to stop playing the pianoforte, so that he might share his gift to Mared with her entire clan.

"If I might have a moment, I have something I would show ye," he said and motioning for Natalie to join him, walked to the corner of the room, where his gift was draped. The children scampered after him, anxious to see the gift.

"Really, Payton," Mared said laughingly, "ye've made quite a production of hiding whatever the thing is. Would ye end it all now?"

"Hush, now, woman, and come here," he said with a grin, holding his hand out to her. Mared rolled her eyes, but nevertheless handed Lilias to her grand-mamma, and joined Payton as she exchanged looks and bits of laughter with her brothers.

When she reached him, she slipped her arm around his waist and kissed his cheek. "All right, then, sir, here I am. Whatever do ye have behind there?"

"Do ye recall the day I made ye sit for a pocket portrait?" he asked her, touching her nose with his knuckle.

"Aye."

"And do ye recall that I insisted I meet Natalie in Glasgow when she returned from London?"

"Of course!" Mared said, and winked at a beaming Natalie.

Payton grabbed the drape and yanked it. Mared and her family gasped as the drape fell away, for behind it was a six-foot portrait of Mared, intended for the family gallery.

"It's Mummy!" one of their twins exclaimed. "And us, too!"

Mared looked up at Payton, wonder in her eyes.

He grinned. "Our Natalie is a gifted artist," he said, as Liam, practically blubbering with pride, grabbed his daughter up and hugged her tightly.

It was, Payton thought, a most regal picture. He'd been very pleased with the result; Natalie had done a remarkable job.

In the portrait, Mared was sitting on a lawn, surrounded by her children and her dogs. She wore the dress she'd been married in more than ten years ago. The emerald her family had given her was around her neck, and the *luckenbooth* he'd had made for a betrothal gift pinned her *arisaidh* to her breast. Her black hair was braided and falling over her shoulder. Her expression was beautiful and serene and with just a hint of a smile on her lips, one lone dimple in her cheek.

But there was no mistaking the glint in those green eyes. Mischievous, through and through. Natalie had indeed captured Mared's essence.

"Definitely an improvement to the Douglas line," Grif said, nodding approvingly.

Mared leaned forward to read the gold engraved label. "'The Tenth Lady Douglas,'" she read aloud . . . and then paused, moved closer and squinted. "And beneath that, it says, *'a Douglas in name, but a Lockhart at heart.'*" She straightened and beamed at Payton. "Ye remembered, *mo ghraidh!*"

"*M'annsachd*, have ye let me forget it as much as a day?" Payton asked with a laugh, and indeed, she had not. Since they had married that Christmas so long ago, not a day had passed that he had not laughed and loved and been thoroughly exasperated at one point or another.

"It's breathtaking," Mared said, and looked at Natalie. "I canna imagine how ye did it, Nattie, what with nothing more than the little pocket portrait."

Natalie shrugged shyly. "It was easy."

"It's absolutely gorgeous," Mared continued. "It's the most beautiful gift I might have hoped to receive. It's . . ." Her voice trailed off, and she suddenly squinted, then moved forward, through her four sons, peering hard at the portrait. "I beg yer pardon, but are those *sheep* in my meadow?"

Payton laughed and grabbed her up before she could protest, for in the portrait, his lovely wife was indeed surrounded by sheep.

Some things never changed.